THE LANGUAGE OF LOVE

Colby's strong arms released her. But when she did not move, he lifted her bodily out of the tub without rising.

"You'd better get out of here," Colby growled softly.

Amy was shocked by her reflection in the mirror. The sodden, transparent wrapper revealed every curve of the body. Water from her hair and body pooled on the floor at her bare feet. She looked like a drowned rat.

Amy snatched a towel from the dresser and gathered up her clothing. "You are the most despicable man I have ever met. You—you are a thief, a liar, and probably a cheat. And—and you should be ashamed of that rag you call a newspaper. Ha! You can't even spell!" With her free hand, she turned the knob on the door.

"P-r-o-v-o-c-a-t-i-v-e," she heard behind her.

She whirled to face Colby and hissed through the open doorway. "And you are i-n-s-u-f-f-e-r-a-b-l-e!"

PRAIRIE FLOWER

PAT MUCHMORE

LEISURE BOOKS **NEW YORK CITY**

To the brave and courageous men and women numbering in the tens of thousands who flooded to the Cherokee Outlet on September 16, 1893. And to the man who nurtured me in a love of the history of the Indian Territory, my late husband, Gareth B. Muchmore, co-publisher and editor of *The Ponca City News*.

A LEISURE BOOK®

January 1995

Published by

Dorchester Publishing Co., Inc.
276 Fifth Avenue
New York, NY 10001

The name "Leisure Books" and the stylized "L" with design are trademarks of Dorchester Publishing Co., Inc.

Printed in the United States of America.

PRAIRIE FLOWER

Chapter One

September 16, 1893

Amy Elizabeth White gripped the reins of her father's nervous team of grays as she held her place in the unruly line of humanity that snaked along the southern border of Kansas to the west as far as the eye could see—for 150 miles, someone had said. All waited for the rifle shot that would signal the opening of the Run into Oklahoma Territory for the Cherokee Outlet lands.

Black roiling ashes from the prairie, fired the week before by the cavalry to discourage Sooners, swept over the parched and anxious thousands.

Amy sweltered in her heavy riding suit as the sun beat down on the waiting throng. Salty perspiration blurred her vision, and her nostrils constricted against the stench of sweat and excrement from man and beast.

"Mon Dieu! Quil fait chaud!" She glanced around to see if anyone had overheard the French expletive. She squinted through the swirling, malodorous dust that

sifted itself in the air, and looked over the teeming crowd of humanity.

Riders on horseback far outnumbered ranchers and sodbusters who waited in covered wagons and open carts overflowing with household goods and farm implements. Caged chickens, geese and rabbits were tied alongside. Milk cows, goats and an occasional bull calf were tethered behind. Here and there, family dogs of the cur variety scrounged for scraps or napped in the shade of a wagon.

Sandwiched into the line a few yards west of Amy, the Santa Fe special belched acrid smoke and cinders. The train waited between barbed-wire fences that ran parallel on either side of the tracks and disappeared into the southern horizon.

From every car of the train, arms, legs, hats, bundles and rifles poked through windows. Those unable to squeeze inside had climbed to precarious positions on top of the engine tender or the coal car. Others hung with deadly determination from platforms, fighting to keep their places in the midday sun that blistered their lips and swelled their tongues.

Waiting also were a number of desperate souls on foot with small bundles on their backs and hatchets in their hands to drive a stake into the virgin soil.

Amy felt the tension in her own body increase, and knew that at any moment pent-up emotions in the crowd could explode and turn the roiling mass into an angry mob. Late arrivals on horseback continued to throng to the scene, jockeying for front-line positions. Their maneuvers forced the line south inch by inch until the front runners were now positioned on the southern boundary of the Chilocco Indian School, where curious dark-skinned youngsters with shaved heads stood along the tree-lined lane to watch history unfold.

On Amy's immediate right, a sun-bonneted woman held the reins of a mule-drawn wagon that had pulled into the line at midmorning. A sandy-haired boy of ten or twelve bounced impatiently on the hardboard seat beside her. His small bony knees protruded through faded and threadbare britches.

On Amy's left, Horace Carrington watered the sleek bay that pulled his stripped-down rig. Horace caught her eye and nodded. Yesterday, he had introduced himself to her and Papa by offering a can of beans to go with their sparse meal of boiled eggs and hardtack. He had talked of his plans to open a hardware store in the Territory and of sending for his wife and daughters. Amy envied his confidence and the funds in his pocket that would make his dreams come true.

Holding the reins of her father's team of grays, Amy went over the plan in her mind again. Like many others here, she would make the run on horseback, carrying no more than a canteen and a bedroll. She had dismissed the idea of stripping away her saddle to lighten the load and ride bareback, as a number of other riders had done. She smiled confidently when she thought of her own mount, Sultan, a beautiful black gelding that her father had given her before hard times had struck. Her Arabian breed, known for its speed and endurance, was in top form.

On their arrival in Arkansas City, Amy had limited Sultan's diet of corn and increased his oats. Daily she had raced the black horse, gradually extending the distance until she was satisfied with his ability to withstand the rigors of the race.

She was confident that on the back of her beautiful Sultan she could race ahead and stake her homestead. The 160 acres she hoped to claim lay directly east of the new government-designated town of Cross. Once she found the flag and noted the corner markers, she would make camp and wait for Papa. He would bring the wagon with the bulky Washington hand press, the boxes of type and the meager belongings they had brought with them from their home in Milford, Nebraska. Later, they would ride to the townsite of New Ponca, where they would establish a newspaper for the newly opened territory.

Amy stood up in the wagon and scanned the throng behind her and sighed impatiently when she found no sign of Sultan or her father. The nervous team of grays danced sideways and jolted Amy back into the wagon seat. She scowled. There wasn't room for the strawberry roan forcing itself through the crowd. The tall, lean-muscled man in brown denims wedged his horse into the waiting line anyway. A dusty Stetson shadowed his eyes.

Snorting at the four-legged stranger, Amy's team jerked at their traces and threatened to bolt.

"Whoa! Whoa, there!" Amy shouted, gloved hands tight on the reins, boot-shod feet braced against the footboard of the canvas-covered wagon.

"Whoa! Whoa, I said!" She yanked again on the leather reins as tendrils of her once properly coiffured chignon slipped free of the pins and fell about her face. A few more jerks on the reins and the team settled down with one last quiver in their hind quarters.

"*Espèce d'imbécile!* Of all the inconsiderate . . ." Amy muttered and turned to glare at the horse and rider.

Flecks of gold danced off the intruder's light brown mustache in the hot September sun. Muscles tensed in man and beast as the horse reared.

"Easy, ol' girl," he soothed in a baritone drawl. The ugly roan immediately calmed under the man's big, soothing hands.

"My apologies, ma'am." The man doffed his big-brimmed hat. Eyes squinted against the swirling dust and a broad, confident smile spread beneath his mustache.

"What nerve! Why don't you watch where you're going, *jacques!*" Amy stormed.

The man kept his left eye shut, but the right eye was

brazenly blue and wandered impudently from the top of her dark head to her boots on the footboard peeking out from under the hem of her green riding skirt.

Colby Grant saw the color rise in the woman's face, but he couldn't turn away. What in hell was a woman like her doing out here? Woman? Her tawny skin was flawless as a young girl's. The waist maidenly tiny beneath a nicely shaped bosom. And yet, she was smartly dressed as if she were going fox hunting in a wool jacket and riding skirt that had to be merciless in this heat. She wore gloves as dark as the raven hair that fought against the pins in the updo so properly pinned in place, and her eyes—her eyes were smoldering gray, and angry. On second thought, maybe the little missy wasn't that proper if she could curse in French.

His appraisal caused a flush to spread over Amy. The collar of her Victorian blouse constricted at her throat. The primly buttoned jacket that hugged her narrow waist and flared over her hips suddenly felt too tight. Every stave of her tightly cinched undergarments burned into her skin.

"My—my team almost bolted." She bit her full lips to still the trembling. With one hand she brushed back the fallen wisps of hair and checked the carefully positioned curls on her forehead that hid what Amy considered to be the one flaw in her high-cheekboned face, a small blue birthmark near the widow's peak.

With his hat pushed back, Amy could see the man's eyes crinkle at his sun-bronzed temples. Muscles in his lean body tightened and rippled as he stretched his tall frame out of the saddle and extended his large hand toward her.

"Colby Grant," he said.

Amy ignored the offered hand, involuntarily sucking in her breath as a tremor shook her body. The tiny silk hairs on her arms bristled. She clutched the reins for support. Papa had warned her you couldn't tell a renegade from a preacher out here, and this man was definitely not a man of the cloth, not when he looked at her with one eye shut as if he were zeroing in on a target. Amy raised her trembling chin ever so slightly and turned away.

Colby chuckled. Scared as a rabbit, he thought.

Amy shivered again as the man continued his brazen appraisal. The threat of a runaway had shaken her more than she thought. She could have been hurt. A lot Colby Grant cared. Or anyone else in this teeming, tumultuous crowd salivating for free land.

But nothing could frighten her away. Not a runaway. Not the heat, dust, noise, the long wait or any other discomfort. And certainly not the impudent stranger. She would ignore it all. She would ignore Mr. Grant most of all. She and Papa had staked their last dime and their last hopes on this new land, and on their dream of a new beginning.

A tremor of panic rose in Amy's breast. *Where are you, Papa?*

As time ticked by in the broiling sun, traders made last-minute brags on prime horseflesh and demanded exaggerated prices from those desperate to make the run. Drummers hawked their wares with "last chance" warnings. Gamblers licked their lips in anticipation of the new saloons to come and played one last hand of poker among themselves.

As Amy surveyed the scene, she concluded that the crowd was primarily one of ordinary men and women who waited as anxiously and with as much trepidation as she for the sun to reach high noon. She suspected that many were victims of the depression now in full swing in this fall of 1893. Downtrodden souls who had staked their health and their fortunes, however meager, on a chance for free land. She wondered if their hearts beat with the same hope and anticipation as hers, and if her eyes mirrored the same desperation as they scanned the horizon.

The well-known frontier photographer William S. Prettyman climbed up the scaffold to a platform towering over the train. He adjusted his camera and checked the scene once more through his lenses. He added powder to his flash, checked his pocket watch and picked up the triggering bulb with its long tube.

As time neared for The Run to start, Amy fought the irritation rising in her breast. *Where are you, Papa?* She sighed. He was most likely listening to one more story as he slaked his thirst in one of the saloons back in Arkansas City.

Alfred White was a born newspaperman, of that Amy had no doubt. He loved people of all walks of life and he loved to listen to them talk. He relished putting their stories in print. Only since his wife's death had his naturally garrulous nature been supported by too much liquor.

The depression hadn't helped, either. Bankrupt store-keepers and farmers with unsold wheat didn't buy advertising or newspapers. But here in this new land, Amy was confident her father would once again be the respected publisher of a thriving newspaper.

Amy harbored hopes of teaching in the newly opened territory. Perhaps there would be less prejudice than in Milford, Nebraska, where her Eastern education and dress, her awareness of the world in general, seemed to threaten the Quaker women who led quiet, God-fearing lives. Men were still the preferred choice for schoolmasters. And she suspected that her French heritage and her occasional slip into the language posed a threat to the plain-speaking people. Even if she couldn't teach in the new land, she could help her father with the newspaper. It didn't matter as long as she staked her homestead and began putting down roots in this new country.

With a resolute sigh, Amy relaxed her grip on the reins as a little self-satisfied laugh escaped her lips.

No one in Miss Stevens's finishing school in Boston would believe that she, Amy Elizabeth White, would deign to be where she was at this moment.

That she had stood in line for three days to register to make The Run they would put down to Amy's well-known streak of stubbornness.

But the proper Miss Amy White would never, ever endure a week of camping in a wagon at the edge of an Indian school reservation with only a flimsy canvas for privacy and protection from the elements.

Nor would they believe her tolerance of the dismal diet of fatback and corn pone washed down with muddy river water.

Nor three days, for heaven's sake, in the same hunter green riding suit that would never be clean again.

But then the young ladies at Miss Stevens's school had never been as desperate as she.

Amy shrugged her shoulders. "*C'est la vie.* Or life on the frontier, anyway. But a bath would be nice."

"Ma'am?" queried Colby in a baritone drawl.

She felt a flush rise in her face. "I—I was talking to the horses—calming them down."

The mouth broadened into a grin beneath the golden mustache.

Flustered, Amy turned away from the impertinent Colby Grant and stood up in the wagon to scan the waiting crowd for some sign of Papa and her horse, Sultan. But it was impossible to find anyone in the beehive of activity around her. How could the U.S. marshals and the smartly officious blue-coated soldiers hope to control the mob once the race had begun?

Amy's gaze fell once again on the man and his ugly roan. He was a hard man to ignore. Grant, who appeared to be about thirty, yanked on leather ties to secure a large bundle wrapped in manila paper strapped behind his saddlebags.

She raised her gloved hand to hide a smirk. Mr. Grant would no doubt regret the extra weight of that odd package when the race got under way. She looked up into the sky. The sun, filtering through the dust, neared its peak. She furrowed her brow. If Papa didn't hurry, she'd not have time to check the cinches on her English saddle or refill the canteen.

"Oh, Papa," she whispered, "we've gambled everything."

Colby's keen ears picked up her words. He was relieved to know she was not alone. Maybe, just maybe, she and her Papa would be among the lucky ones. Too many had already gambled and lost.

An old veteran in a faded blue uniform with tarnished badges had been found dead in his blanket as he waited for the No. 9 registration booth to open. Heat exhaustion and dust-aggravated consumption had claimed scores. And at least a half dozen heart-attack victims had been carted off to the hospital or burial plots in Arkansas City.

Death had even claimed some who had no plans to make the race. A cook working around the clock to feed the people gathered in Arkansas City for The Run died when a can of coal oil exploded. And a young deputy sheriff came out second best in a gunfight with an unruly drunk.

One young mother had given birth in the registration line and promptly named her infant Ruth after President Grover Cleveland's new daughter. Cleveland had signed the law opening up the Oklahoma Territory to settlement. Several women waiting to register without food or water for days were taken from the line so ill they were unable to stand.

And more than one would-be settler had been victimized by thieves who robbed them of their horses, water kegs and food supplies with unusual daring.

Colby dusted his hat on his denims and looked over at Amy. There was a harshness to this land, a harshness that would turn soft, young French girls into dried-up and wrinkled matrons long before their time. It was too bad, but he'd probably never see her again. Well, she hadn't been very friendly, anyway.

Amy tried to ignore the man and turned her thoughts to her father. At first, Alfred had adamantly refused to consider Amy making The Run. But when he had started to argue with her, she knew she had won even though he continued his protestations.

"Give up this hare-brained idea of making the race, Amy," he had pleaded. "Barnes has promised us lots in New Ponca."

Amy strained her neck and sought out the span of black horses and hired riders who would secure the townsite of New Ponca for Mr. Barnes. The former Michigan furniture maker had convinced her father and many others that his planned community with its natural spring and the only safe crossing of the Arkansas River would be far better than the federally sanctioned townsite of Cross. With officious-looking drawings of a town that did not exist and might not ever exist, the fast-talking Mr. Barnes had sold lots at two dollars each.

"I want more than a town lot, Papa."

"I know, lass. But making The Run is crazy. You're just a slip of a girl. And I don't want to lose you, too. Staking a homestead is a life-and-death matter for these folks, and anybody who gets in their way is a goner. Life out here's nothing like boarding school life. You're not jumping hurdles at the Rothchilds' in New Haven."

"That's just the point, Papa. I will always be grateful to you for sending me back East to school, but I never truly belonged. I was never really one of them. As accommodating as they were, I always felt like a charity case."

"Hannah and I did the best we could."

"Oh, Papa, I know you did. But—but it wasn't the material things I lacked. It—it was not belonging—not having roots or a history like the other girls. They came from estates in New England or plantations from the South that had been handed down from generation to generation. Lands their fathers, grandfathers and great-grandfathers had toiled over and passed down through the ages. I want that for my children, for my grandchildren, for myself . . ."

"Amy, gal, I'm sorry."

"It's not your fault, Papa. But if my parents . . ."

Amy had always known she was the adopted daughter of Hannah and Alfred White. She suspected that much of her upbringing had been dictated by deathbed promises made almost sixteen years ago to her biological parents lest Amy forget her French heritage. But her parents' identity would forever remain a mystery. All she had ever known about them was that they were French immigrants and had succumbed to consumption on their way west in a wagon train when Amy was less than two years old.

Alfred and Hannah had taken her in and were the only parents of her memory, and she loved them dearly. Amy had grieved deeply at Hannah's death shortly after her return from Boston. An impossible year had followed, with her father turning to drink in his grief, and then the depression hit, depleting Alfred's failing fortunes. In his despondency, it had not taken much to convince her father that they could start a new life in Indian Territory. But she had no intentions of settling for less than her own homestead. She wanted to put down her own roots and lay the groundwork for a new generation, a new beginning. A town lot in New Ponca was not enough.

Noting the powerful steeds around her, Amy began to

feel less confident. If Mr. Barnes's hired hands failed to reach the site first, her father's two dollars would have been wasted, and they would no doubt have to pay an inflated price for a town lot in Cross. Amy straightened her back and raised her chin. New Ponca or Cross, the first issue of the *Democrat* would most definitely be off the press next Thursday! Even if they had to print it from her homestead.

Amy fought against the tiny shred of doubt growing ever larger in her breast. A quick calculation of the numbers who jostled and crowded her wagon made it clear there weren't enough 160-acre parcels to go around. Over 100,000 had registered, someone said, and only a little over 35,000 quarter sections were available. Papa had tried to impress upon her that disputes would be inevitable and claim jumpers rampant. But she had dismissed his suggestion that she take along a rifle. It would be a nuisance and add unnecessary weight. Besides, she didn't like firearms.

She glanced to her right. Colby Grant certainly seemed to be familiar with his gun. The cylinders of the heavy Colt spun smoothly under his thumb. Apparently satisfied, he slid the revolver into the oiled holster tied with a thong on his bulging right thigh.

Colby Grant caught her watching him. Heat mounted in her cheeks and she quickly averted her eyes. He's probably a renegade of some sort, maybe a killer, she thought. She shuddered. His striking good looks were no doubt deceiving.

She shook off the moment of fear that tingled her spine. There was really no cause for concern. Really! She didn't need a nasty, smelly old gun! Astride Sultan, her swift black beauty, she would be able to escape any danger she faced. And if she and Sultan couldn't outrun them all, surely she could best most of the people lined up here today. With her loyal gelding's speed, what chance did the people on foot have? Or that raw-boned woman in the faded bonnet with the plodding mules and overloaded spring wagon wedged in on the other side of Mr. Grant?

According to the surveyor's map, the homestead Amy sought lay some four miles east of the Cross townsite. Half of the 160 acres appeared to be grassland. The rest was wooded, with blackjack and cottonwood, becoming fairly dense along a spring-fed creek that meandered through the quarter section of land before it entered the Arkansas River. Trees would supply firewood, fence posts and maybe even a cabin. The creek would provide relief from the heat, quenching the thirst of man and beast during the long summer months on the plains. And one day—one day there would be a big white house, a two-story house, with large round pillars, an entry with double doors, and rooms and rooms filled with fine furniture and children, lots of children.

"But first," Amy laughed to herself, "you have to find *un homme*." And Mr. Grant was most certainly not the kind of man she was looking for. Oh, no! Her husband would be a refined gentleman, a man of distinction with superior intelligence and, of course, handsome features.

Colby Grant raked a hand across his mustache to hide the grin. So she was looking for a man, was she? A husband, no doubt. Miss Proper wouldn't settle for anything else. She was the marrying kind—the dangerous kind. Well, don't cast your eye my way, little missy. I'm just not cut out for that kind of responsibility. Crissy could attest to that if she were alive. Crissy—

"Water! Git yer water here!" The water wagon, with a grizzled old man at the reins, moved across the front of the restless line and waved a water dipper in query to the waiting crowd.

Amy shook her dark head. It was ludicrous to pay more than twice as much for a cup of water as her father had for two lots in the town of New Ponca. But the people couldn't live without water, especially in the heat that bore down on them. Thankfully, her father had placed a large keg in back of the wagon. It was warm, but wet. She wished the Arkansas City townsfolk who had supplied sandwiches and cool water for those waiting in line to register had extended their humanitarian efforts to the line where the race would begin.

"Water! Last chance for water!"

The water wagon pulled by two white mares halted at the approach of the freckle-faced boy from the wagon with the tired woman. The boy, his bare ankles showing beneath frayed britches, scuffed his shoes as he walked. His soles flopped in the sandy earth, and a thin oversized shirt hung limply on his frail body.

Amy's throat knotted. The boy reminded her of the sweatshop children back East.

"Please, mister, jist a cup. Fer my ma." He raised a small, thin hand toward the man.

The water peddler squinted down at the boy and sneered. "Ya got five dollahs?"

The boy shook his head.

"Water ain't free, boy. Less'n ya wanna go back t' Ark City and lose your place in line." He guffawed, baring tobacco-stained snags before moving on down the line. "Water, five dollahs a barrel. Last chance for water!"

The shoulders of the young boy sagged. He tried to still a quivering lip and walked back to the spring wagon.

With an agility that surprised Amy, Colby Grant swung his tall frame from the saddle of his mare and stepped into the boy's path, extending a canteen.

"Here, son." The deep voice was barely audible.

The boy's eyes fell on the canteen. "I ain't got no money."

"It's free."

The boy hesitated before taking the flask. His eyes

never left the man. Still unsure, the boy hugged the canteen to his chest with both hands and backed away in measured steps until he had reached the mule-drawn wagon with his mother perched on top.

"Here, Ma."

The raw-boned woman took a couple of swigs and handed the canteen back to her son. She smiled over at Colby. "Thank ya, Mister—?"

"The name's Grant, ma'am."

The firm jawline relaxed. White teeth flashed from under his mustache. The steel blue eyes softened. Amy shivered. She must be having a sunstroke. With effort, she focused on the woman's sun-leathered face.

"Much obliged, Mr. Grant. We're the Rhodie family from Tennessee. That's m'boy, Danny. We ain't had no water since yest'day."

The boy brought the canteen back to Colby.

"Don't you want a drink, son?"

Danny shook his tousled head and scuffed the dirt. "Not thirsty."

"Well, I was hoping you could take that canteen off my hands. My horse is carrying too big of a load."

Amy knew one more canteen couldn't possibly make a difference to Colby Grant's ugly mare. Not with that manila-wrapped package tied behind the roan's saddle.

The boy squinted upward. "Yuh sure, Mister?"

"I'm sure," he said. "Where's your pa?"

"Ain't got none, Mister. But I'm growed up. So it don't make no matter. I can take care of Ma." The boy marched back to his wagon and climbed up, carefully protecting the canteen.

Amy averted her eyes from the old woman and her boy, embarrassed at being privy to their misfortunes, and found herself looking at Colby Grant. He blinked his eyes several times.

"Confounded dust!" His eyes met Amy's, a small, guilty smile on his face as he beat his Stetson on his

21

sleeve, dust exploding into the air.

Amy acknowledged his compassionate lie with a conspiratorial smile. The lump in her throat wouldn't go away. Her eyes stung, her body felt feverish, and her insides quivered under his steady gaze.

She forced her eyes away from the man and fingered the neckline of her bodice. It was far too hot out here! Her clothes were smothering her. Drenched in perspiration, Amy silently conceded that her father had been right. Dressing properly just wasn't sensible out here on the prairie. She could very well be near to succumbing to a sunstroke.

With the Stetson still in his hand, Colby squinted his blue eyes up at her. She looked a little faint.

"Are you all right, ma'am?"

Amy nodded, swallowing hard. "I'm—I'm a little warm," she said. After all, when you're close enough to smell the sweet aroma of a fine cigar on a person, or perhaps just camp smoke, you couldn't totally ignore him.

"Don't wonder."

"I beg your pardon?"

"I said it's no wonder you're warm, wrapped up in that getup. May be stylish, but kinda hot for wool, isn't it?"

Amy blushed. What did that wrangler know about fashion?

"Be cooler if you took off the jacket."

Amy's fingers went nervously to her bodice, and she tried to still her breathing. "I'm told the prairie can get cold when the sun goes down."

He nodded. "Yep, it can. But you're not making The Run?"

"Oh, yes!" Amy proudly raised her chin and gave Colby a smug smile. "I am most certainly making the run! And on horseback, Mr. Grant."

"Well, ma'am, it's not something a lone woman

ought to be doing." The right blue eye zeroed in on her again.

Her cheeks flamed and she hated her body. "We aren't living in the dark ages, Mr. Grant. Some women even have the right to vote. Though it would be no surprise to me to learn you've never heard of Wyoming."

The mustache twitched, glints of gold flickered over at her. The dusty air crackled with static.

"I reckon you're joshing me. You're waiting for your papa, and maybe a husband?"

"My *father* will follow in the wagon. And you, Mr. Grant, don't make the rules. Single women have as much right as anyone to homestead in the new territory! And kindly step away from my wagon."

Colby took off his Stetson and, with a swagger, bowed deeply.

Amy turned a straight, rigid back to Colby. "Oh, Mr. Carrington," she called, "any sign of my father?"

The man in the rig to her left looked up, startled at being addressed, and shook his head.

Where is Papa, anyway? She had hoped he would return in time to spell her a few minutes. She needed to stretch her cramped legs, cleanse her face, tidy her hair, and get away from that piercing blue eye. Obviously, her own sorry disarray had given Mr. Grant the impression that he could take the liberty of ridiculing her.

Amy clinched her eyes to shut out the man. Anyone, man or woman, was eligible to make the race as long as they were American citizens and could prove they were eighteen years or older. And Amy had six months to spare.

Yes, Mr. Grant, she would run and stake her own land. She would put down strong, solid roots for the first time in her life. She would build a future for herself, for Papa and for the family she would have one day.

An involuntary sigh escaped her. The Mr. Grants of this world would never understand. Not that it mattered.

After the race started, she'd never see him or his ugly strawberry roan again.

Out of the corner of her eye, Amy watched Colby cinch up his saddle and secure once again the manila package fastened behind his bedroll. What in the world could he be carrying into The Strip?

Colby swung his muscle-hardened body back into the saddle as Amy brushed at her damp, unkempt tresses and prayed for patience. Papa had promised to be back in time.

"Papa, where are you?" she mumbled through clenched teeth.

"Right here."

Both relief and love swept over Amy as she turned at the voice to find her portly father alighting from Sultan. Rivulets of sweat ran from the bushy head of white hair down his ruddy face and neck into the stiff celluloid collar. Dust covered his dark cheviot suit.

"Just cinching up your saddle. Damned unmanly to ride sidesaddle," he puffed.

Amy laughed. "You took your time, Papa," she scolded mildly.

"Sorry, lass," he said as he tied on her knapsack. "I was hoping you had changed your mind. It couldn't have been pleasant waiting out here."

"I'm fine, Papa. Really!"

"Aren't you burning up in that outfit? Seems to me if you're going to act like a man, you ought to dress like one."

"Papa!" She heard Colby's low laugh and looked over to see him rake a hand across his mouth. His eyes, even the left one, opened wide with mock innocence. She glared at the arrogant man.

Trembling, Amy wrapped the reins around the wagon brake and accepted her father's help in getting down. She smelled the pungent odor of whiskey on his breath. *Oh, Papa, if I could only take away your pain.*

Amy went to the back of the wagon and dipped out a ladle of water from the keg. She took a sip and poured the rest on her handkerchief and dabbed delicately at her face. She arched her back and shook out her shoulders to ease the tension in her body before walking over to Sultan.

Alfred wrested the watch fob from his vest pocket and snapped open the gold case. "Just a couple more minutes, lass, but you can still change your mind."

Amy shook her head and gave him a determined smile.

"Then let me take your place," he pleaded. "I only slid out of that dang saddle once on the way to Ark City."

Amy laughed. "Let's not argue, Papa. We haven't much time." She looked up at the sun.

Alfred kissed the dark spot at her hairline. "Be careful, lass." He lifted her into the English saddle on Sultan. "I don't want to lose you, too."

Amy bent down to kiss her father's cheek. "I'll be fine, Papa."

Alfred stepped away. "If I had any sense, I'd tie you in back of the wagon."

"You wouldn't dare!" She tempered her reproof with love for her aging and bewhiskered parent. She knew he would never admit that he was secretly proud of her determination to make the race. "As soon as the crowd thins out, you'll follow?"

"I'll be right behind you." He handed Amy a fresh canteen and smiled up at her.

"Good luck," Colby said as he tied the buckskin thongs of his hat beneath his chin. The little missy with smoldering gray eyes was going to need it.

Amy's hand tightened on her quirt. Fear raised a giant, hideous head in her breast, but she said, "I don't need—"

"And good luck to you, young fellow," Alfred's booming voice interrupted, making Amy seethe that

25

her father had acknowledged Colby Grant.

"And good luck to you, ma'am." Colby doffed his hat to the thin woman and her son in the mule-drawn wagon. God knows they would need it.

"Thank ye, kindly," Mrs. Rhodie said. "With the good Lord's help, we'll make it." The young boy, Danny, grinned and waved excitedly.

Alfred shook hands with Mr. Carrington and climbed into his wagon with a wave. "Good luck, Horace. I'll see you in New Ponca."

Amy shifted her skirted body in the saddle and trembled with anticipation. She licked her dry lips and turned her eyes southward.

Mounted blue-coated soldiers and deputy marshals planted every 200 yards in front of the line of hopeful settlers raised their rifles skyward.

Abruptly, the once belligerent and raucous crowd grew quiet. The photographer high above the crowd ducked under the black shroud of his camera. Conversations hushed, and in an almost painful silence, all ears strained for the rifle shot that would start the run.

When it came, it was not one loud crack at high noon, but an unsynchronized echoing of rifle shots along the snaking black line. The crowd roared. The train whistle blew. And the multitude lunged forward as the photographer ignited his flash from his high scaffold.

Amy snapped the quirt above the rear flanks of her Arabian horse and spurred him boldly south as Colby Grant's lean and hardened body thrust forward in the saddle on his ugly mare. Together, but separately, they joined the thousands racing into the blackened and desolate prairies of Indian Territory for their share of tomorrow.

Chapter Two

The crack of rifle fire ricocheted down the line of mounted soldiers and faded into silent puffs of smoke. The crowd exploded across the blackened prairie of Oklahoma Territory.

The earth trembled from the thundering hooves. Cinders sparked and smoke billowed from the Santa Fe special as it shrieked and rumbled slowly southward on its narrow-gauge rails. A deafening roar filled the skies. Horsemen yelled at their mounts and fired guns in the air as they took the lead, raising dust and ashes in a roiling wake. Traces rattled. Whips cracked across rumps. Wood and iron-forged wheels creaked and careened as the buckboards, buggies, wagons and carts hurtled at breakneck speed over unsuspected washes and prairie-dog holes of the virgin soil. Desperate men and foolhardy youths on foot dodged horseflesh and veering vehicles. Debris from unsecured wagons cluttered the prairie as the land claimers raced daringly forward. Left behind them, on the Kansas line, were the very young who cheered them on, and the very old who stared vacantly toward the horizon of Oklahoma Territory with unfulfilled dreams.

Amy White, one hand clutching the reins of her black gelding and the other grasping quirt and saddle horn, rode neck and neck with the strawberry roan and Colby Grant.

His lean, taut body stretched forward and low across the mare's red mane as his spurs lightly grazed its flanks. And behind his saddle, the manila-wrapped package stayed snugly in place.

Colby looked over at Amy. His eyes squinted through the dust as he motioned and yelled for her to move to the left, to get away from the compacted throng, but through the roar she did not hear him.

Amy ignored Colby's attempt to wave her over and gave her Arabian free rein, feeling no need for the quirt. With a thoroughbred's instinct for winning, Sultan lowered his powerful neck and stretched his ebony flanks. With giant strides, he fled across the uneven ground ahead of the avalanche of horses and wagons that threatened to overtake and run him down.

Wisps of dark hair whipped across Amy's face as the Kansas border fell miles behind and Colby Grant on his ugly roan spurted far ahead. The searing winds burned her eyes and caught in her throat. Rivulets of perspiration streaked her cheeks and ran down her narrow back to the tight waistband of her green riding skirt.

In the west, horses raced alongside the Santa Fe special as it labored forward. Smoke trailed back into Kansas as the engine churned southward, falling behind the crowd. At intervals, the impatient jumped from the train, scattered like quail, and raced on foot for the coveted flags that marked the homesteads in the Cherokee Outlet of Oklahoma Territory.

Amy glanced back at the stampeding crowd just in time to see a cart tip over. The man and his belongings were strewn across the prairie. The frightened plow horse walled its eyes and plunged on ahead. The cart's broken shaft bounced menacingly behind.

Sultan broke his speed and shied, drawing Amy's attention forward again as a dislocated rider rolled dangerously close to the gelding's flying heels. Amy instinctively reined her mount around the dun-colored bronco that was becoming more hysterical with each flap of the empty stirrups in its flanks.

Amy could still see Colby Grant atop his distinctive roan, but the few yards that had separated them earlier had grown to a quarter mile. Even farther ahead, silhouetted on the bleak horizon, sped a rider grasping the reins of fresh, unridden mounts. They crested the rise and dropped out of sight. To the west, where fires set by the soldiers still licked at the prairie grass, Amy saw a phaeton bouncing across the countryside.

Amy wanted to laugh, and cry. Are we all mad? Deranged or not, she had badly underestimated the competition. She had not believed there were other steeds as strong and fast as Sultan.

Giving way to her frustration, Amy flicked Sultan in the left flank with her quirt, forcing the gelding too near another rider. The angry man struck at Sultan's head with his boot. Momentarily frightened, the horse whirled from the offense into the path of another animal, which added to his confusion until Amy could rein him clear and they could both get their bearings.

She would not give up! She would force her mind to remain optimistic, and with renewed determination spurred Sultan south again. Time became meaningless as she rode on and on, numbing her body and mind to the bone-jarring ride. She ignored the scorching sun, the taste of ashes and prairie dust in her throat. Her nostrils compressed against the stench of laboring horses. Her ears roared with the sound of hooves trampling hardened ground and saddles slapping against horseflesh.

But soon, far too soon, Sultan began to lather, and an inner sob shook Amy. "I'm so sorry, Sultan." Only her love for the proud gelding overrode her desire to force him on. She pulled back on the reins and allowed her black mount to slow to an easy trot. Within seconds the desperate and frenzied multitude rushed past in a choking dust.

Angry shouts filled the air as riders overtook her. Horace Carrington raced by in his rig and waved his bowler. A cow pony shot past, the rider's legs wrapped Indian fashion around the unsaddled ribs.

"Git out of th' way," the man yelled.

A trotter, its measured pace never slackening, pulled past the disheartened Amy. The driver of the sulky wore goggles and a morning coat, and except for his speed, looked like a Sunday-afternoon pleasure seeker in his first heat.

A woman in men's trousers toppled off a buckboard tailgate and immediately drove her hatchet into the sun-baked ground, staking her claim where she landed. Her burly spouse in a red plaid shirt turned out his mules and circled back to join her.

Amy thought of doing the same and at the next section marker reined up Sultan and dismounted. The land looked sterile, the soil cracked from drought. Fighting off her inner panic, she gritted her teeth in determination. No! She wanted land near the river or nothing at all. She swallowed a gulp of water from her canteen and moistened her handkerchief to wipe the froth and dust from Sultan's nose. She caressed his wet flanks, no longer black but gray with lather.

As the dust settled, Amy saw desolate faces among scattered wrecks of wagons and carts. Riders weary with lost hope led lame mounts northward back to the starting line at Arkansas City.

Within minutes, the roar of thundering hooves and creaking wagon axles faded into the horizon as the crowd fanned out across the land. And the churning wheels of the Santa Fe Special grew louder as it gained on her.

With rising frustration, and satisfied that Sultan had regained his wind, Amy remounted and reined the gelding back into the race, deciding to veer southeast and avoid the melee ahead. The blackened prairie began to sport a scrubby bush here and there. Before long, cottonwoods sprouted sparingly on the barren horizon, and blackjack thickets could be seen in the distance.

Within minutes the details of the surveyor's map became clear to Amy. The bend of the Arkansas River came into view; she neared the spot she sought. Amy topped each new rise with anticipation, but as the miles passed, so did her hopes. In valley after valley, Amy found horsemen unsaddling their mounts and wahooing their success. At one homestead, a man raised an American flag in the center of his claim. She had to go on, and the jubilant settlers waved their hats as she swept past.

The terrain became ugly with high bluffs and deep ravines, the ground savaged by washes, topsoil so poor the grasses of the prairie had given up. She seemed to be alone, though to her west, the dust of other riders could be seen.

She reined Sultan to the left and headed due east into the scraggly and hilly terrain. Her heart ached and her spirits sagged, but she went on. Sultan jumped gullies and raced through brush that raked Amy's clothing and hair as she dodged limbs and briars.

Exhausted, Amy slowed her blowing horse, her eyes no longer squinting at each rise for the elusive red flags that marked each homestead. But when she and Sultan topped the next knoll she found herself looking down on the Arkansas River. Amy wiped a hand across her eyes and blinked several times, afraid to breathe lest the mirage fade away. Down below, a stream flowed southeast through a green valley, land fertile with blue-stem grass. Near the riverbanks and on the southern crest were forests of hardwood, oak, walnut, pecan and cottonwood trees.

As Amy moved Sultan down the slopes toward the valley, she caught a slight flicker of red out of the corner of her eye. Her heartbeat quickened and she spurred Sultan forward, her eyes focused on the red flag waving lightly in the calm valley.

Amy reined Sultan up short and withdrew her cramped right leg from around the saddle horn and let her stiffened body slide to the ground. She crawled to reach the flag and seized it, and in its place she drove her stake. She started to laugh, to cry as she surveyed the land. Sultan whinnied and nosed her face as she lay in a heap, exhausted, jubilant and grateful. Assured by an affectionate rub on the nose, Sultan stalked around, blew and began to graze on the sweet blue-stem grass.

Hoofbeats broke into Amy's reverie and she looked up to see a couple of riders silhouetted in the west and heading in her direction. She struggled to her feet, and when the horsemen saw her they slowed their mounts and reined them to the south.

With relief, Amy untied the canteen on Sultan's saddle. Her knees wobbled and she collapsed on the ground, the red flag still clutched in her hand. She poured the last of the water on her swollen tongue and let it trickle down her chin to cool her throat. She took the hem of her petticoat and dabbed at her face and neck, smudging her white undergarment beyond redemption. She unbuttoned the green riding jacket and fanned her coat lapels across her bodice soaked with sweat. Less than two hours in the saddle and she ached all over. But a feeling of accomplishment swelled her breasts, and she shivered with unbridled pride.

Amy couldn't rest. She had to get water for Sultan. Wearily and stiffly, she rose again and unsaddled her mount. She left the bridle in place and dropped the rigging and her knapsack in a pile on the ground. Clutching the red flag and her empty canteen, Amy led Sultan toward the river.

Sultan reared his head and whinnied as a horse broke through the trees, its rider in brown denims and wearing a Stetson.

Colby Grant and his strawberry roan!

Amy halted, let the reins drop and watched as Sultan trotted down to the Arkansas River and waded in. Smugly, Amy stood her ground until the rider was near enough so she didn't have to shout.

"I believe you're trespassing, Mr. Grant." She waved the red flag.

"Ma'am," he tipped his hat. Golden hair shimmered in the sun, and his lower lip reached up to chew on his mustache as he stared at her with that bold blue eye. "Hate to dispute a lady—"

"Then don't!" she snapped.

Colby grinned and held up three corner markers. He dismounted, saddle leather creaking and spurs jangling. He walked toward her in long strides, but his eyes were on the ground behind her.

Amy turned to follow his gaze and realized with a panic that he was looking at the fourth corner marker. Amy raised the hem of her dusty riding skirt and nimbly sped ahead of him to claim it. She struggled to pull the stake from the ground, hair falling about her face, boots dug into the ground. Colby leaned down to the stake.

"It's mine!" she hissed, flailing her boots to keep him away.

A grin broke across Colby's face. She was a scrapper, he'd give her that.

When the ground yielded, the propulsion knocked Amy flat on her back, the marker clutched tightly in her hands. "It's mine!" she exclaimed breathlessly. "And I'm not leaving this property, Mr. Grant." She shuffled to her feet, placed one hand on her hip and squared her shoulders.

Colby grinned. He couldn't believe he was standing here arguing with the little missy, but he couldn't keep his eyes off her bodice. Perspiration had soaked her blouse, leaving it transparent. Her breasts jutted forward, nipples hard and dark through the damp chemise. Her face was smudged with grime and perspiration.

Amy walked over to Sultan's rigging to retrieve her quirt, but not before Colby saw the heat rise in her face.

He wedged the three corner markers between the saddle and the manila package on the roan and turned back to Amy. He pushed the Stetson back from his sun-bronzed face, his left eye closed and his mustache bristling.

"I could take it away from you." He reached into his shirt pocket and withdrew a small, thin cigar. "But I'll be nice about it. I'll give you—let's say—forty dollars for that last marker."

"That's a lot of money, Mr. Grant. If it's that valuable, I'll keep it, thank you."

"You're wasting your time, Miss White." He struck a match against the heel of one boot and lit his smoke. The sweet aroma drifted toward Amy. "I've got three of the four corner markers," he said. "We'll just end up in a trial that you haven't got a chance of winning." Stubborn little cuss.

"We'll see about that! Besides, we're not supposed to remove the markers, Mr. Grant, only the flags. And you have to have a witness."

"Seeing as how I didn't have a witness, I took the markers." The blue eyes narrowed and he took a step toward her.

Amy's quirt sliced through the air.

Grant winced and fingered the tiny droplet of blood on his right earlobe. Damn she-cat. Was she that accurate with that quirt, or had it been just luck that she missed his right eye, his one good eye?

"For a proper lady, albeit one with black soot on her face, you sure are stubborn and mule-headed," Grant said.

"Well, you certainly are no gentleman." Amy wiped her face on the sleeve of her jacket.

Colby folded his arms across his chest and stood there, his boots wide apart, like a steel giant looking down on her. A muscle hardened and pulsed in his jawline and he stared at her as if he were trying to check his anger. The ends of his mustache marched up and down. Cigar smoke wafted into the air.

Amy held her breath, her gray eyes unflinching, her body tense and ready for flight.

She didn't scare easy, he'd give her that. Colby relaxed his stance and took a deep draw on his cigar, exhaling a large puff of smoke. Give her a day or two out here alone on the prairie and she'd be tired of playing homesteader. If she didn't, he'd let the courts settle it. He was through fighting by force, be it fists or guns.

"Let's hope you don't meet up with any more gentlemen," he said as he mounted up and headed his ugly mare southwest.

Amy slowly let out her breath. A shiver went through her as she watched Colby Grant ride off at an easy gallop without a look backward. She resisted the impulse to call him back.

"Good riddance," she yelled triumphantly after him.

Assured that Colby was leaving, Amy went to the river and retrieved Sultan who stood belly-deep in the Arkansas River. After she had freshened her face and re-pinned her hair, Amy walked her faithful horse to dry him off and explored the river boundary of her new homestead. She ran across an arbor, a shady room in a grove of blackjack and cottonwood trees. A covey of quail scattered at her approach, a jackrabbit bounded through a thicket, and a white-tailed deer darted through the trees. Amy found thorn bushes with a handful of late blackberries shriveled on the vine. She sat down on an outcropping of sandstone rock and ate them, savoring their sweet taste. In the cool arbor, Amy gave way to her physical weariness. She cradled herself at the base of a tree, closed her eyes and yielded to her exhaustion.

Amy awakened to a whinny from Sultan, stretched her sore limbs and walked to the edge of the arbor. She looked into the sky. Four, maybe five o'clock. The sun would set in a few hours, but her father would no doubt find her before dark. But not if she stayed hidden in this canopy of trees.

Amy walked the Arabian back to the pile of their belongings and fed him an apple from her knapsack. She leaned against her saddle and stretched out her legs as she chewed on a piece of hardtack and dried jerky.

Sultan neighed softly. Silhouetted on the horizon were two riders. Their horses kicked up dust as they approached. Amy rose to her feet and waved them away, but they did not turn as had the previous men. She slipped on her riding jacket as they came on. They rode straight toward her, not slowing their gait until they reined up in front of her.

Apprehensively, Amy lifted her hand to her brow to see through the glare of the sun into the faces of a barrel-shaped man and his Indian sidekick.

The heavy man on the big bay heaved himself out of the saddle. His bulging stomach strained at the buttons on his brown shirt. Bowed legs were encased in grimy denims that were tucked inside well-worn boots. The rowels on his spurs gleamed sharply. A gun hung low beneath his big belly. Under the brim of his weathered hat was an ugly red scar on his left cheek. His red mustache failed to hide a leering mouthful of broken and rotten teeth.

Amy fought against the apprehension building inside.

The Indian alighting from the pinto wore a flannel shirt of broad red and blue horizontal stripes. He was smaller in stature and of wiry build, but no less menacing. A narrow band of rawhide on his brow held back long, dark hair that hung to his shoulders. At his waist, he wore a knife instead of a gun.

Instinctively, Amy knew she dared not show fear. With her feet planted firmly, she smiled broadly and waved her red flag and the fourth corner marker.

"I'm afraid you're too late, gentlemen," she said with bravado. "Mr. White and I have already staked this property." She looked toward the Arkansas River, hoping to imply she was not alone.

The dark man grasped the hilt of his knife, eyes on the river and the trees behind Amy. With thumbs in his belt loops, the big-bellied man stepped forward. "I'll take that flag, gal."

She backed away. "This is my land, get off while you can! Mr. White has a gun—"

"Now, you're not being very sociable, ma'am. We asked you polite like."

Amy's stomach churned. This was no Colby Grant she was dealing with. And they certainly weren't going to be scared off easily. *Oh, Papa, where are you?*

"No! You'll not jump my claim!" She plunged the flag and marker under her jacket and into her waistband.

The large man guffawed. Ugly, stained teeth leered at Amy. "I think she wants us to find 'em, Charlie. Ain't that right, purty lady? Who'd of thought it? Her lookin' so prim and proper." He grabbed her arm and pulled her roughly to his body, his rancid breath in her face.

Amy jerked free of his grasp. Her arms flailed at the scarred face and knocked off his hat to reveal a bald pate, white above a sunburned brim line. "Get away from me, you filthy—"

The man bared his rotten teeth in a sneer. "Looks

like this snooty little squaw needs to be taught some manners, Charlie. Maybe what she needs with that sour disposition is a little lovin'.' "

Rough hands held Amy. One hand wrenched her arm painfully behind her, the other seized her head, displacing hairpins and letting her hair fall in disarray about her face.

"Well, lookey here, Charlie. She's already been branded."

Amy struggled against the man, feeling naked as he gawked at the birthmark.

The Indian came closer and stared at Amy's small blue stain on her forehead and then into her eyes. "Maybe better leave her alone, Bat," he said quietly.

"And leave this little prairie chicken for the coyotes? Not on your life, Charlie."

Amy kicked at the man called Bat, but he entwined her legs with his, holding her steadfast.

With one huge paw, the man ripped off Amy's riding jacket and tossed it on the ground. He yanked the marker and flag out of her waistband and threw them at Charlie. "Be nice, you whoring squaw, and we won't have to shoot your horse."

"How dare you call me filthy names—" A huge, rough hand went around her throat and strangled her protest. Sultan snorted and pawed the ground, dangerously close to the sinister monster who held her captive, but Amy knew that Sultan was helpless to rescue her.

Bat yelled at Charlie, "Give me some help, ya damned half-breed. Tie that nag out o' th' way or I'll shoot 'em both. One pair of flying heels is all I wanna worry 'bout at one time."

"Not Sultan, please," Amy whispered and ceased her struggle. She called to her horse, and the gelding seemed to calm. He no longer kicked at the Indian, but continued to shy as Charlie maneuvered cautiously to catch the Arabian's reins.

"That's more like it." Bat breathed heavily and raked his dirty hand through Amy's fallen hair. "It can be kinda fun if you fight a little." He seized Amy's hair again and licked his lips, his foul breath suffocating. Amy struggled to turn aside as slobbering lips landed on her ear. Her stomach revolted at the filthy body touching hers.

"I'll—I'll give you money," she pleaded.

"Where's it at, little lady? Any more fancy hiding places?" Bat guffawed.

Bat's hands violated Amy's breasts. Nausea rose in her throat. She swallowed and shut her eyes, hoping to blot out the nightmare, but she refused to cry. She would not give him the satisfaction.

"I—I don't have it with me, but when—when Mr. White arrives . . ."

He laughed. "Take me fer a fool, do ye? I'll take my pay now."

Bat knocked Amy's feet out from under her, and her body slammed to the ground. She gasped for breath as his malodorous body weighted her down. His knee pushed between her legs. One hand held her head in a grip, the other yanked at her riding skirt as he forced his mouth on hers.

Amy kicked, clawed and spit like a hissing cat as she fought Bat's weight and the horridness of what was to come. Even when the roughened hand slapped her face, Amy refused to surrender, but she knew that all she could do was delay the inevitable.

"Hold it right there, you two!"

The heavy weight of the man lifted from Amy, and she scrambled to her feet, gasping for breath. The setting sun formed a halo around Colby Grant astride his strawberry roan. His Colt was drawn and the barrel moved back and forth from Amy's attacker to the half-breed who had attempted to tie up Sultan.

Amy cradled her face in her hands. "Thank God!"

Colby motioned to the Indian. "Get over here with your partner." When he had complied, Colby slowly dismounted, the hammer cocked on his revolver, the barrel pointed at Bat's bloated midsection.

"Drop your guns and get your hands up, slow like. The knife, too." Colby's steel blue eyes were narrowed and unflinching, his jaw firm, his hand steady.

Amy picked up the dropped marker and flag and rushed to Colby's side. He put a protective arm around her, his gun never wavering from the two renegades.

"We didn't mean no offense," the half-breed whined.

"You oughtn't to leave your Mizzus out here all alone," growled Bat.

"Get off my property," Colby interrupted. "Take your horses and get out of here before I change my mind." He emptied Bat's gun of its bullets and threw it on the ground at Bat's feet. He slid the Indian's knife into his belt.

Amy remained tense until the pair had mounted up and gone. Only then did she allow herself to collapse against Colby.

"They said such aw—awful things to me." Amy buried her head in his chest and breathed in the sweet aroma of tobacco. She trembled at the steady beating of his heart and accepted the comfort of his strong arms as tears welled up in her eyes.

"It's okay, ma'am," he whispered. "I heard your horse, so I thought I'd better come take a look. I slipped in around by that arbor over there." He could feel the warmth of her breasts against his chest, the rapid thumping of her heart. This was one scared little girl he held in his arms.

"Thank goodness you came in time," she said between soft sniffles. "How will I ever thank you?"

"Well now, I couldn't very well let them get my hundred-and-sixty-acre homestead, could I?"

Amy jerked away from the strong, comforting arms.

"Your homestead?" she stormed. "My homestead, Mr. Grant! And you—you had the audacity to let them think I was your—your wife!"

"I could have stayed in the cottonwoods," he said, glaring.

"Well, I guess I do owe you my appreciation for getting rid of those horrid, despicable men," she shuddered, "but I don't need your help anymore, Mr. Grant, so I'll thank you to leave my property right now!"

Another small laugh rolled out from under the mustache. He pulled another little cigar out of his pocket and took an infuriatingly long time to light up. When he left, maybe she could stop trembling.

"It'll be dark soon," he said, exhaling slowly, his eyes squinted toward the western horizon. "Your father should have been here by now. Maybe he ran into trouble. You ought to go back to Ark City or ride into New Ponca with me and rent a tent or something." Perfect smoke rings drifted lazily above his head.

Amy faked a grimace and waved away the cigar smoke. She didn't want him to know how intoxicating the aroma was. "I don't need your help anymore, thank you. And I'm not going anywhere. I'll not leave this property and let you steal my claim. Oh, no, Mr. Grant," she said through pursed lips. "I'm sure Papa will be along soon."

"Of all the fool, stubborn, ornery women I've ever met in my life—and I've met my share—you take the cake."

"I'll just bet you have, Mr. Grant, but spare me the details of your lurid love life."

She glared at him, defying the clenched jaw and the eyes narrowing in the sun. Determination challenged disbelief, until the corners of his mouth below that infuriating mustache turned up ever so slightly. He chuckled.

"Those men have left, Mr. Grant. I wouldn't like to detain you any longer."

Pat Muchmore

He shrugged his shoulders and mounted up. "Better build you a campfire pretty soon. It'll be dark before long, so gather some wood while you can still see. You *can* build a fire, can't you?"

"Of course I can!" It couldn't be that hard, could it?

He looked down at her. Yep, she was lying. He threw a box of store-bought matches down to her.

"Just in case," he said and laughed at the relief mirrored in her face.

The last rays of sun danced off his mustache as he turned to ride away, and Amy noticed for the first time that the manila package he had carried all through the race was no longer tied behind his saddle.

Amy quickly gathered fallen tree limbs, placing a small boot on the longer ones to break them apart. In the fading light she began her first attempts at making a campfire. The winds of the prairie snuffed out each match as she struck it. In desperation, Amy built a tent with her torn and soiled jacket to protect the small limbs and dried grass until a blaze caught.

She retrieved the singed and smoked jacket and moved the saddle near the comforting fire. Another piece of jerky satisfied her hunger. By the time she fed Sultan his small ration of oats, twilight had been cloaked with darkness.

In the east, a harvest moon rose in the sky, blotting out most of the stars. Coyotes howled. Each yip echoed across the valley and seemed to mock her and unnerve Sultan, who stomped the earth and whinnied. The blue-stem rustled with bedding doves, fireflies flickered in courtship, and the night air cooled.

Where was Papa? Had there been trouble? Perhaps he had camped for the night. Certainly, he had no chance of finding her in the dark. Especially since she was miles away from her original choice for a homestead.

Amy shivered. She wasn't really cold, or frightened, but pulled the saddle blanket around her shoulders, and kept the reins of Sultan's bridle wrapped loosely around her hand—just in case.

Weary and in need of sleep, Amy rested her arms on her bent knees and laid her head down, the flag and marker safe in the folds of her skirt. Exhaustion crept over her limbs, and sand closed her eyes.

A hoot owl startled the dozing Amy, who recognized a second hoot for what it was. Mentally chiding herself, Amy started to relax again when she spotted two shining red eyes across from her. A little yelp erupted from Amy and the red eyes were gone—but then they were back.

Holding her breath, fighting to control her fears, Amy slowly inched back away from the blinding glare of the campfire. The animal was black, with a tail curved over his back, a white stripe—a skunk!

Amy abandoned the campfire for the safety of her snorting but loyal mount, Sultan. Still clutching the flag and marker in one hand and holding the blanket about her shoulders, Amy sat on her horse for some time staring at the fire and the red eyes that blinked off and on. But when she began to nod from weariness, she knew she had to find another sanctuary. She couldn't sleep on Sultan all night. It wasn't fair to the gelding, and she would probably fall off. But she could rest safely in a tree. And with the light from the fire and the golden moon, Amy reined Sultan toward a likely candidate on the outer edges of the campfire light. Fighting the clumsiness of her long riding skirt, Amy pulled herself up into the limbs of a cottonwood.

Satisfied that the tree would suffice, Amy dropped Sultan's reins so he could seek his own resting place. He would not go far. With her last ounce of energy, Amy made herself somewhat comfortable in the narrow fork of the small cottonwood. She took the coveted flag and marker and wedged them between two small limbs for safekeeping. Opening her blouse, she loosened the ties of her corset. Extending the sleeves of her tattered jacket, she had enough material to tie herself to the tree. Finally, she draped the blanket over her torso as best she could.

The long day had taken its toll. She'd never been so tired. Or so filthy. If only her father would arrive with the wagon. Clean clothes and a good night's sleep would do her wonders. But the sun had surrendered to darkness, and only by sheer luck would Papa find her now. What else could happen to her after this long and terrible day? That despicable man and the half-breed . . .

She shuddered. It was more pleasant to think of Colby Grant's strong, comforting arms around her, his mustache that glinted gold in the sun, the piercing blue eye so tender and warm for a thirsty young boy and so cold when facing those terrible renegades.

"Amy Elizabeth White," she scolded aloud. "Colby Grant is trying to steal your homestead. If he's not a renegade, just who is?"

But when she thought of how he had saved her from those awful men, how he had soothed her in strong, comforting arms, a smile played upon her lips.

With her thoughts battling each other, Amy White drew the blanket close and let her head drop back on the cradling tree limbs. Under the moon's nightshade, courting crickets and singing cicadas serenaded her to sleep.

She did not see the fire or smell the smoke of a small camp in the next draw some three hundred yards away, or hear Colby Grant say to the stars, "She looks nothing like Crissy. And she sure as hell doesn't act like Crissy." His left eye began to throb.

Chapter Three

In the early morning light, a red-tailed hawk spread his marbled wings and launched an unsuccessful dive at an alert field mouse. His thin, shrill scream over the cotton-wood awakened Amy from her deep sleep. Her long, dark lashes fluttered and gray eyes opened to a canopy of leaves. Fear welled up in her throat at the thought the claim jumpers had returned and somehow caught her unawares. Disoriented, Amy instinctively fought the bonds restricting her body until full consciousness caused her to remember that she had tied herself in the cottonwood tree the night before.

She groaned and untied the jacket sleeves that secured her. She became aware of a weariness deep in the marrow of her bones. Every muscle was bruised and swollen from yesterday's grueling ride. Even the small tendons in her hands were painfully sore from the hours of gripping the reins and the saddle horn. The staves of her corset and the rough bark of the tree were imprinted on her body. Her neck ached and her temples throbbed.

Her lips were cracked and the taste of dust was in her throat. Her dark hair was a mass of tangles.

But in spite of her languor and the awareness of her disheveled appearance, pride stirred in the breast of Amy Elizabeth White. She had done it! Nothing had stopped her. Not the sun and wind, the hardships of the race, or those despicable claim jumpers. She had her homestead in the Cherokee Outlet of Oklahoma Territory, and not even Colby Grant would take it away from her.

Amy sought out the corner marker and flag still safely wedged in the overhead limbs of the cottonwood and sighed with reassurance.

Sultan whinnied.

"Good morning, *mon chéri*," she called to the black Arabian steed.

With the reins dragging on the ground, Sultan snorted and walked over to the tree.

Amy tossed the blanket and embattled jacket to the ground and began extracting herself. Her long, full skirt was cumbersome and restricted her movements. She grappled clumsily for support to pull herself upright. Her arms hugged the tree, her nails raked over the bark as she sought sure footing.

If she could just swing her body around slightly and stand up on that branch, she could clear her feet and drop to the ground. Amy pulled herself cautiously around the limb. Her boots were disentangled, and she could see a clear opening to the ground. All she had to do was step off the sturdy branch on which she stood. Amy took a deep breath, closed her eyes and jumped.

Amy's free fall jolted to a halt. Air gushed from her lungs. Blood rushed to her head. Nausea swept over her, and she found herself dangling in midair. She gasped for breath through the heavy skirt that covered her face and held her suspended in the tree. Her first hysterical thought was that her full-breasted body was all that had kept her from being hanged by her own skirt—hanged as surely as if a rustler's noose had been slipped around her neck by some eager vigilante.

In desperation, Amy managed to pull the offending skirt down far enough to clear her face and to see the limb on which her garment had snagged. She yanked on the worsted suiting, but it held fast.

Reprimanding herself for her imprudence, Amy felt for the limb overhead, but her own weight held the material taut against the branch and she could force no slack to free herself.

She attempted to swing her small booted feet back up to the main trunk of the tree, but there was too little room to maneuver. She fumbled with the buttons, but with her skirt turned wrong side out and enveloping her, she remained imprisoned.

Straining the muscles in her arms, Amy tried to pull herself upward. She was quickly exhausted from the effort and let her body fall limp. The sudden drop of her weight caused a slight rip in the material. With a new thrust of energy, Amy lifted herself up again and again, but the small, hopeful tear near the double-stitched hem of the closely woven material widened ever so slightly.

It was ridiculous, but she couldn't get down. She hung like a sack of freshly dug potatoes airing on a barn rafter.

Sultan neighed softly, presenting Amy with a new ray of hope.

She called for Sultan to come to her, but the black gelding did not seem to understand that she wanted him to walk beneath the tree. Despite all her coaxing, he would come only so near and no further. Each time the Arabian came near Amy's swinging torso of white petticoats, he snorted, shook his head and backed away.

Tears of frustration stung Amy's eyes. It was ludicrous, but she was only three feet from the ground, and it might as well have been a hundred. Exhausted, Amy hung there, her face perspiring from her efforts, her waistband straining against her breasts and her white cotton underskirts billowing in the light wind.

Sultan snorted at the sound of hooves, the creaking of a saddle.

"You look like a half-skinned rabbit."

"You!"

Colby Grant sat on his strawberry roan, his arms folded across the saddle horn as if he had been watching her for some time. He pushed back his Stetson and grinned just as the sun peeked over the banks of the Arkansas to dance across his golden head and the mustache above the smirking mouth.

Amy dropped her hands to hold down her petticoats. Why did this man always appear when she was in these inane predicaments? Where was her father, anyway? Amy closed her eyes and prayed that Colby Grant would go away.

"Looks like you need some help, ma'am."

"I don't need your help. Just go away," she hissed. She tugged on the skirt again.

He moved his horse nearer. "Mind telling me what you're doing up in that tree?"

Amy flailed her feet at him. "None of your business. I said go away. At least you could be a gentleman and turn your back while I get down."

"You sure you don't need some help?"

"No," she hissed, "and get off my property."

The left eye narrowed, and then he shrugged and reined the roan toward the smoldering campfire.

Amy continued to jerk on the pinioned skirt and heard another small rip. She'd soon be free, and without Colby Grant's help.

Colby dismounted and tied his horse to a blackjack sapling. With his roweled boot, he banked the dying embers of the campfire and rolled a couple of river stones into place. He added a few sticks of wood. From his saddlebags he withdrew a pot and strolled down to the river to fill it, seemingly oblivious to Amy's predicament.

"Are you going to hang around there all day?" he asked as he passed her on his return trip. Served the little missy right. He'd let her suffer a little while longer. Maybe it would take some of the starch out of her.

Amy ignored his taunt and continued to tug on her skirt between sidelong glances at Colby Grant.

He unwrapped an oil-papered bag and cut off a slab of meat which he carefully sliced and placed on suspended sticks over the coals. When the water began to simmer in the pot, he dumped in the contents of a fruit jar.

The aroma of fresh coffee and side meat sizzling over the fire made Amy's mouth salivate and her shrunken stomach rumble. She was mortified.

Colby strode back to the tree and peered up at her with that brazen right eye. Her hair had fallen around her shoulders and the morning sun put blue highlights in the dark tresses. Crissy's hair had shone like spun gold.

"Breakfast about ready, ma'am."

Amy turned her head away.

"Of all the stubborn, mule-headed, obstinate females I've ever seen, you take the cake." He shook his head and grinned. "Or maybe you prefer bananas? Fresh out of 'em, ma'am."

With a torrent of anger flooding over her, Amy exerted every last ounce of energy at swinging her body toward the man. Her hands sprung open to claw at the smiling face just out of reach. Her laced boots fanned the air in a futile attempt to strike the man with her feet. Her billowing petticoats rose and flared to reveal her black cotton stockings. But she didn't care—

Ri-i-p-p-p-p!

In the midst of Amy's tirade, the skirt tore free of the branch and dropped her with violent impact on her back to the hard ground at Colby's feet.

He bent over her. "That was a fool thing to do. You all right, Miss White?"

She couldn't talk, her throat constricted, and she writhed on the ground as her lungs gasped for air.

"Lie still," he ordered.

Amy watched in horror as a knife appeared in his hand. She was powerless to fight the man as he forced her over on her stomach and yanked up her shirtwaist.

Oh, dear God, not Colby Grant, too?

Whoo-oo-o-sh-h-h!

Air rushed gratefully into Amy's burning lungs.

Colby placed a hand on her throat. Her pulse raced wildly under his touch.

"Take it easy, ma'am. Don't get in any big hurry."

As her breath became even and her mind clear, Amy realized that the man had sliced through the staves of her corset—her best corset. Amy tried to sit up and cover herself. The light shirtwaist over her unbound bosom seemed to be intact, but her shredded riding skirt left her underskirts in view. She could no longer fight back the tears.

Colby reached over for her blanket and wrapped it around her.

"I feel terr—terrible. I hurt—hurt—all—over," she said between sobs.

Colby's strong arms cradled and held Amy close. "Sh-h-h. It's all right now," he whispered, his lips near her ear, a hand caressing her hair.

Amy's tears subsided to an occasional sob. She could breathe once more, but she did not want to move. She didn't want to leave the comfort of Colby Grant's embrace, to escape the warmth of his protective arms. She only wanted to lie here and rest, to inhale his distinctly male odor of cigar and wood smoke.

Colby sniffed; his mustache twitched. He raised

his head and sniffed again. "Gol' durn—the meat's burning!"

Abruptly, Colby's arms released her, and in her blanket cocoon, Amy found herself dumped unceremoniously onto the ground. She struggled to free her arms as Colby retrieved the meat from the fire, and she blatantly laughed when he singed his fingers. It served him right.

"Not too bad." He grinned as he offered her a tin plate with the sizzling slices of side meat and a chunk of hardtack. In his other hand was a tin cup of steaming coffee.

Amy shook her head. She would not eat this man's food. He had laughed at her, was still laughing at her. He had slashed her garments and he had let her fall. Bananas, indeed! "The big ape!" she muttered.

"What was that ma'am?" He looked down and laughed at her again. "May not be the Harvey House, but the coffee's not bad." He drank noisily from the cup.

It smelled heavenly. Oh, if only she *were* in the rail station at Topeka waiting at the Harvey House to be served a proper meal at a properly appointed table and escorted by a proper gentleman. Instead she was on this barren frontier in complete disarray and the captive of this wild man who stared at her most of the time out of one brazen blue eye. But the coffee smelled wonderful.

She licked her lips. "Well, maybe some coffee."

He whipped a kerchief out of a hip pocket, wrapped it around the handle and offered her his tin cup.

Amy eyed the offending cup and hesitated.

"Sorry, I don't carry a spare. Unexpected company will have to make do."

"Company," she snorted. "You're on *my* property—"

Colby withdrew the cup and took another sip.

It smelled so good. Amy licked her lips. "But I'm willing—I'm willing to overlook . . ."

The arrogant smile galled Amy as Colby handed her the cup, but she held her tongue.

"Careful. The cup's hot," he said.

Slowly and with deliberation, Amy turned the cup around to drink from the opposite side. Wonderful! She took another sip and closed her eyes to breathe in the heavenly aroma.

Her eyes flared open as she felt his large hands envelop hers and gently take the cup away. She flushed under his bold gaze and looked away as he carefully drank from his side of the cup. He offered her another sip without releasing the cup. She couldn't protest. He handed her a bite of meat and she ate from his fingers. She drank more coffee and bit a mouthful of hardtack that was surprisingly tender. She fought to keep her breathing even, to regain her senses. She was obviously delirious from her fall.

"Where—where did you learn to cook? This is tasty."

"Survival, Miss White." Colby sat back on his haunches, his muscles bulging. "Survival. Old Eliza made sure I understood the rudiments."

"Old Eliza?"

"A cook I once knew in Alabama."

"Alabama? Your drawl doesn't sound that Southern. More like Texas or out West someplace."

He nodded. "I've done a spot of traveling, but I was born in Alabama. After my father died from an old leg wound he suffered in the Civil War, old Eliza was the only family I had left. She took care of me. Made sure I ate my grits and vegetables, took care of—" He had started to say "Crissy."

Amy thought she could detect a wistful smile beneath the mustache as his voice trailed off, low and reverent.

"And your mother?"

"Never knew her. She died when I was born." He

cut a piece of side meat in two. "You sure ask a lot of questions."

"I don't mean to be impertinent, and you may not think I would understand, but I do. I'm—I'm an orphan, too." She accepted the bite of meat with her fingers. "My parents died when they headed out West, and my father—Mr. White—and his wife, Hannah, adopted me. They're the only parents I've ever known." She tilted her head and raised her chin slightly. "My biological parents were French," she added as she daintily put the meat into her mouth.

The corner of his eyes crinkled and as his right eye wandered over her, she could feel her cheeks becoming feverish. She could imagine how she looked with unruly hair, her face most likely smudged with dirt, and a nose that was perhaps too patrician. She reached up to position a curl over the birthmark.

"French, huh? *Parlez-vous français?*"

"Oui, monsieur." She laughed. Perhaps he wasn't as uncouth as she had first supposed. *"Est-ce que votre famille est française?"*

He shook his head. "You lost me, ma'am. The few French words I learned in N'Orleans aren't exactly the kind you use in polite company."

Amy wondered if he had understood her blasphemies at the Kansas line. She reddened and changed the subject.

"What happened to Eliza?"

Colby got to his feet and turned away from Amy. "She was freed after the war, of course. So when . . ."

He had started to say "Crissy" again, but he didn't want to answer any questions about Crissy. He took a big breath. "Anyway, Eliza took a passel of kids with her and headed north. Eliza never had any youngsters of her own, but she mothered every pickanin around."

"So you just—just drifted, I suppose, after that?"

"In a manner of speaking." Colby bent over and

plucked a tiny blue flower from the prairie grass and offered it to Amy.

Amy caught her breath at the touch of his large hand. "And just where did you drift?"

"Well, as I said, I spent a spell in N'Orleans." Colby reached up to the throbbing left eye. "And then I drifted, as you put it, over to Fort Smith for a while, where I heard about The Run. Missed out on the 'eighty-nine Run at Guthrie. I figured this was my last chance to see history in the making."

The rattling of doubletrees, traces and hames on a team of horses clattering into the valley interrupted them. Colby rose to his feet, his right hand automatically falling to the butt of his Colt.

"Hallo-o-o-o, there! Seen a lone gal around—"

Amy struggled to her feet, remembered her state of undress and hugged the blanket around her as a wagon drew toward them. The pair of grays came to a stop, raising dust over the campsite.

"Papa! Thank God!" Amy cried.

Sultan neighed in recognition as the rotund man with white hair set the brake and scrambled down. Alfred White's derby sailed to the ground, his round sack coattails flapped over a wrinkled vest, and his narrow tie and stiff collar were askew as he ran toward Amy.

"Amy, lass," he said. His brow furrowed in his perspiring ruddy face as he wrapped his arms about her. "Been mighty worried about you." He stepped back to hold her at arm's length and saw the sorry state of her attire.

"What happened here?" Alfred drew his paunchy form up straight and gave Colby a hostile stare.

"I'm just fine, Papa."

"Well, you surely don't look it." The old man cocked his head and glowered at Colby. "Am I supposed to be grateful that my little girl looks like she's been— been—"

Colby laughed.

"Truly, Papa, I'm fine. There—there was just a little accident—"

"Accident? What kind of accident?"

"I—I fell out of the tree." She pointed to the cottonwood.

"What in tarnation were you doing up in a tree?" He turned toward Colby and asked again, "What was she doing in a tree?"

"Papa! I can explain." But she really didn't want Colby to know how she had been frightened the night before by the skunk at the campfire. It would give him something else to laugh about. "It—it seemed safer than the ground and—and I was afraid I'd fall off Sultan."

Alfred shook his head. "I knew it was a mistake to let you make the run, lass."

"I'm perfectly fine, Papa, but what kept you?"

"Broke an axle about twenty miles back and after it got dark I knew I'd never locate you. I came on at daybreak. But when I didn't find you where you expected to be, I started getting worried. I checked every section along the river. I was sure beginning to think I'd lost my little girl."

She laughed. "You should be proud of me. We're now homesteaders."

"You did it? You really did it?"

Amy glanced at Colby as she nodded. He shook his head as if he wasn't hearing right. "Yes, Papa, we did it."

Alfred clasped her in his arms and said, "But I still think I was a damn fool to let you—"

"Papa!"

He threw up his hands. "Just look at yourself. You look like you've been hogtied and—" He scowled at Colby.

"Papa, this isn't Mr. Grant's fault. In fact, you should thank him for running off some claim jumpers." Amy couldn't believe she was defending Colby.

"Thank him?"

"Papa!" said Amy sternly. "He saved my home-stead."

"I saved *my* homestead, you mean," Colby interjected quietly.

Alfred looked at Amy, to Colby, and then back to Amy.

Amy flushed. "We do have a slight problem, Papa." She fought for control. "We—we both staked this place—" She stopped, grasped the folds of the blanket binding her feet and raced for the tree. She halted midway. Colby Grant could have taken the marker at any time. Feeling foolish, Amy turned back to the men.

"Papa, what do the regulations say about homestead-ing?" She looked smugly at Colby.

"Well—uh—well. You just have to drive a stake in the ground, that's all, and have a witness—"

"There!" She turned to Colby. "That settles it. I had a witness and you didn't."

"What witness?" Colby asked.

"You!"

Colby's mouth gaped.

Amy turned to her father. "I could use my trunk. I'm afraid these clothes . . ." She let her state of disorder speak for her.

"Lass, you are a sight."

"I'll give you a hand, Mr. White," Colby said and followed Alfred to the back of the wagon. Alfred dropped the tailgate and tied back the canvas. Colby boosted himself inside.

"You've got an army printing press back here—a Washington," she heard Colby say with surprise.

Her father beamed. "Ordered it all the way from New York. Solid iron and brand new. Cost me a hundred and fifty dollars. Best press there is."

"Can't argue with you there, Mr. White. It operates

on the toggle-jointed bar principle, doesn't it?"

Her father nodded, and Amy wondered how Colby Grant knew so much about presses.

Amy heard metal scraping on the wagon floor and watched as Colby struggled to lift out the metal trunk with its barrel-stave top and crossbar slats.

"Is this the one?" he asked when he had wrested the trunk free of the wagon and placed it on the ground.

Amy nodded and announced with pride, "Papa is starting a newspaper in New Ponca."

Colby seemed flushed from overexertion.

Alfred replaced his derby and straightened his coat lapels. "First copy will be on the streets of New Ponca next Thursday."

"Think there'll be court legals to run by then?" Colby asked.

"Hope so, young man. Wasn't for the government running all that court stuff, a man could go broke running a newspaper."

Both men laughed at her father's joke, and Amy wondered if perhaps Colby Grant had been an apprentice at some time during his years of drifting from place to place. But he certainly wasn't a young man, as Papa had called him. Colby Grant was at least thirty and maybe older.

Colby offered her father coffee and one of his cheroots as Amy searched through her trunk for a change of clothing. She heard them talking about the race, about the hordes of desolate people scouring the countryside for homesteads and the fact that both men had purchased certificates for lots in the new town from Mr. Barnes. She couldn't understand why Colby had taken her declaration of ownership without further resistance. But he and her father seemed to be getting along quite well.

She heard Colby say, "When I came back through town last night there was some talk about a protection association."

"You mean there are some yahoos contesting Barnes's right to build a town?"

"Well, guess his runners weren't the first to stake it. Think some of them crossed over from the Osage."

"Didn't think that was legal."

"Guess the court will decide that. Unless they decide to sell out to Barnes. So far they aren't selling."

"What do you think will happen?"

Amy saw the smile spread across Colby's face.

"There are some 2,500 certificate holders and two homesteaders. What do you think will happen?"

Her father laughed.

With clean clothing and a towel in her arms, Amy tapped her foot impatiently until Colby took the hint. He carried his soiled utensils to the river, rinsed them and repacked his saddlebags.

With the cumbersome blanket still wrapped about her person, Amy headed toward the river.

"No hurry, Mr. Grant," Alfred said. "I'll be heading for New Ponca shortly. If you'll wait up a minute, we could ride in together," he suggested.

"Papa, I trust you will give me time to freshen up." Her father could be so exasperating.

Colby grinned at Amy. "Much obliged, Mr. White, but I think I'll mosey on in."

"Well, we'll see you in town." Alfred said. "Won't hurt to rest the team a spell."

Colby shook hands with her father again and mounted up. He tipped his hat toward Amy, then spurred the strawberry roan toward the west. With a touch of sadness she didn't understand, Amy watched the denim-clad figure on the ugly horse move further and further away.

"Nice fellow," Alfred said and winked at Amy.

Turning on her heels, Amy walked with burning cheeks to the arbor of trees along the riverbank. The blackjack and cottonwood trees would lend her a bit of privacy as she attended to her *toilette*. She dropped the blanket and placed her fresh clothes on it. She unlaced her boots, stripped off the ruined shirtwaist and riding skirt, pulled the destroyed corset from under her chemise and stepped into the water.

The river water was cool and invigorating, a relief from the mid-morning sun bearing down on her bare shoulders. She waded in up to her chin, shed the rest of her undergarments and tossed them on the bank. Using her rose soap sparingly, she cleansed her body of yesterday's dust and grime and rinsed her dark hair until the tresses hung sleek and shiny down her bare back.

Refreshed, Amy let her body drift slowly about in the cool stream. She listened to the drumming of a red-bellied woodpecker and the sweet trilling of a chickadee. She watched as a monarch butterfly dipped into a blooming thistle and flitted away. A ground squirrel with swollen cheeks switched his bushy tail and scurried out of sight. Overhead, cumulus clouds drifted slowly by as Amy floated effortlessly in the cool waters.

Her peaceful reverie was interrupted by a large covey of quail rising from the riverbank in a blur of beating wings. Something had disturbed them.

"Papa?" she called softly, lowering her glistening body modestly into the stream.

A twig snapped, leaves on a bush trembled, and the birds fell silent.

An Indian stepped into the clearing.

Chapter Four

Amy screamed.

It was not the same Indian who had helped Bat accost her yesterday, of that she was certain, but he was no less menacing.

The man wore a soiled blanket around his bare shoulders. A lone feather stuck out of a large and misshapen black hat. The man's eyes bulged out of their orifices. His mouth was twisted and his nose was flattened as if someone had bashed in his face. Dark braids swung down on his chest, a chest as light as a white man's, but it bore grotesque scars, and his stomach protruded over worn leggings and a breechcloth. His knees were bent in a crouch as he stared at Amy.

"Go away!" she screamed, thrashing the water and treading away from the bank.

He shook his head and rubbed a gnarled hand across his cloudy eyes. "*Nng-g-gh-ha*," he grunted, and fell to his knees on the ground and in a quiet, guttural voice asked, "*Tonde Xtha? Tonde Xtha?*"

The old Indian held out his hands to her, and his eyes seemed to plead with her.

"Get out of here!" she hissed.

The Indian raised his arms and appealed to the sky. *"Wa' kon tah'. Wa' kon tah'."*

He was praying, Amy was sure of it, but the man had no right to be here. She was bathing, and he was invading on her privacy.

She slapped at the water with her fists. "Go away, you filthy beast. Get out of here!"

Another Indian, much taller, younger and darker, but dressed in denims and a plaid shirt, stepped into the clearing, a scowl on his pocked face.

"Papa! Papa!" Amy screamed. "Bring your gun!"

The old Indian shuffled to his feet and repeated the words, *"Tonde Xtha?"*

"Papa!"

The tall Indian, whose glossy black hair fell loosely to the top of his shoulders, grunted a guttural command and turned to leave. The old one shook his bowed head, but reluctantly followed, sliding through the trees as quickly and as quietly as he had come.

Alfred came crashing through the timber with his Springfield rifle.

"I'm coming! I'm coming!" He puffed into the clearing and swung the rifle to his shoulder looking for a target. When he found Amy safely treading the water in mid-river he let the gun barrel drop.

"What in tarnation, lass? You sounded as if you were in trouble."

Frantically, Amy waved a bare, wet arm and pointed down river. "They went through the trees."

"Who went through the trees? Not Grant?"

"No, of course not, Papa! Indians. They—they were spying on me."

"Spying on you? How many of them? Did they have guns?"

61

"No-o-o-o. Well, maybe they weren't spying. There were two of them. The old one kept staring and saying something I couldn't understand. He was horrible-looking, Papa. He was almost nak—well, he didn't have on many clothes. Just leggings and—and a blanket," she sputtered.

"Sounds to me he was harmless enough. There are Osages, Poncas, Otoes and even some Kaws around here. Suspect they're not much different from the Sioux or Omahas around Milford. Just more of them."

She slapped the water with her fist. "I was bathing. They were trespassing on my land."

"Not sure but what the Indians figure is we're the trespassers, lass." His eyes scanned both banks of the river. "Whoever they were, they seem to be gone now. You probably scared them off with your caterwauling. Now get out of the water and get dressed."

Resignedly, Amy quickly toweled off, with her father standing guard a discreet distance away. Calmer now, she talked about their plans as she put on a clean white waist and a skirt of pink and gray gingham over fresh undergarments.

"I think I should like to build our house near the river, Papa," Amy said as she coiled and pinned up her damp hair. "Perhaps at the edge of this arbor."

"If you'll look around, lass, you'll see some high-water marks on some of the trees. See where some trash has lodged in the lower limbs? Bet this river can really get out of its banks."

"Well, maybe on top of that bluff that overlooks the valley."

"Wouldn't be anything between you and the North Pole up there. The wind is liable to blow you clean off the cliff."

"Well then, against the bluff, there where the valley begins to lift."

"When are you planning to build all this? And with what?"

Amy laughed as she buttoned the lined, elbow-length cape of matching plaid around her shoulders. "Someday. It would be modest at first, of course, but later, when the newspaper is flourishing, we can build a really fine house."

"Mr. Grant might have something to say about that." He shook his white-tufted head. "Let's quit the daydreaming, lass, and get to town."

Amy placed her marker and her registration papers in a large knitting bag with her beaded purse and dug out her pink parasol. "Speaking of Mr. Grant, I'll have to go to Perry. I want to file on my claim before he does."

Her father tied Sultan's reins to the back of the wagon. "I can't have you gallivanting around alone. Not after those renegades attacked you. Besides, I need to get in to New Ponca and see about my lot."

"Now, Papa, it won't delay you that much to take me to the rail station at Cross. I'll take the train to Perry and you can go on to New Ponca. I would certainly be safe on the train."

Alfred pulled the gold watch from his vest pocket. "It'll be noon before we get to Cross. By the time you get back from Perry it may be dark. No time for a young lady to be out and about. I think I've let you take enough chances as it is. You might not be so lucky next time."

Amy shuddered at the memory of her attackers, but was insistent.

"The Santa Fe makes six runs a day from Cross. There's bound to be a livery where I can leave Sultan. And when I get back from Perry, I'll ride Sultan to New Ponca. That should be before sundown. Please, Papa."

"I ought to have my head examined. If your mother was alive . . ." He wiped his watery eyes and blew his nose on his handkerchief.

"Papa," Amy said softly, "Mother would be so proud of us. Really she would." She reached over to kiss his ruddy cheek and detected a faint whiff of liquor. It was on the tip of Amy's tongue to chastise her father, but she didn't have the heart. Poor Papa, he still desperately missed Hannah. Amy would say nothing now, but when she returned from filing her claim at Perry, she would find his stashed bottle.

On their drive west, they passed several groups of weary and jubilant settlers pitching tents on new homesteads, piling stones at corner boundaries, or raising crude canopies of brush as shelter from the hot winds and blazing sun bearing down relentlessly on the virgin prairie.

Gregarious by nature, Alfred White braked the wagon to exchange a few polite words with his new neighbors, but as time went on, he acquiesced to Amy's suggestion that a friendly wave would suffice for now and kept the team moving.

The government-designated town of Cross was a city of chaos. The air cracked with whips as angry wagon masters maneuvered loads of lumber, hardware and other badly needed supplies through the crudely laid-out streets thronged with people and their conveyances. Poultry and livestock of every description added to the noise and confusion.

Cross was a town primarily of tents. Here and there were new frame buildings put up by the government, and more were under construction. A boxcar on a siding served as the depot and telegraph office. On one of two sets of tracks adjacent to the Santa Fe depot, the southbound train puffed black smoke as a burly fireman worked with a tender to load coal and fill the tanks from a leaky water tower. On the crowded platform, anxious passengers milled around impatiently.

"Round trip ticket to Perry for my daughter here," Alfred said, putting a dollar through the cage.

"Sorry. Sold out." The station agent reached to pull down the shade.

"But I must have a ticket," Amy protested.

"Sorry, ma'am. No seats left. And I don't think you want to ride in the baggage car with a coffin."

"A coffin?" Amy's small gloved hand went to her throat.

The railway clerk in the cage nodded. "Fool man dropped his wife out the train window yesterday to stake a claim. Found her dead on the track this morning with her legs—"

The blood rushed from Amy's face, and the clerk left the rest unstated.

"She can have my seat in day coach, Henry," an authoritative voice announced.

Amy turned to a man in an expensive gray cassimere suit with a satin vest. Over his arm hung a gold-tipped black cane. Beneath the fashionable square crown hat, his face was clean shaven except for thin black eyebrows and neatly clipped sideburns. His eyes were dark and level with Amy's. His nose was almost delicate, and his thin lips quivered nervously as he smiled at Amy.

Amy lowered her gaze. "That's very kind of you."

"Mr. Kane, I thought you were in a big hurry to get to Perry," the ticket agent said.

"Permit me to introduce myself." The man bowed slightly to Amy and addressed her father. "Silas Kane." He tipped his hat, revealing a handsome head of dark, wavy hair.

"Alfred White. And this is my daughter, Amy," her father said, taking off his derby.

"If you will permit me, Mr. White, I will gladly relinquish my seat to your lovely daughter," he said with proper decorum.

Amy flushed and tipped her parasol to hide the glow in her face.

"Henry, I'll ride in baggage." He put his ticket in Amy's gloved hand.

"Mr. Kane," her father said, offering his hand. "That's mighty fine of you. I sure do appreciate it."

"My pleasure," he said.

"*Vous êtes bien aimable,*" Amy said, her cheeks warm under his smiling appraisal.

"My apologies, Mr. White. Imagine suggesting the baggage car to a lady as genteel and sensitive as your daughter."

Alfred cleared his throat. "Well, she's not all that sensitive—"

Amy interrupted her father. "Are you sure Sultan will be safe at the livery?" She smiled at Mr. Kane. "I left my mount in their care. Do you suppose he'll be all right?"

"I'm sure of it. In fact, I'll see to it personally, Miss White." He doffed his hat and quickly faded into the crowd.

"He must be some powerful man," her father said to the man called Henry in the ticket window.

"He's a banker. Up from Guthrie or Oklahoma City. Hear tell he's going to open up a bank in that town they're calling New Ponca," the station agent said before he closed the window.

The train whistle puffed impatiently and shrieked a warning. The conductor called, "All aboard for Perry, Guthrie and Oklahoma City."

With Amy on his arm, Alfred pushed through the jostling crowd of weary settlers and surly misfits.

"Why I let you talk me into these things, I'll never know."

"Oh, Papa, don't be such a fuddy-duddy." She gave her father a light kiss on his perspiring cheek and took the porter's hand as she mounted the steps into the passenger car. Her folded parasol dangled from her wrist, and her gloved hand grasped the handle of the knitting bag with the precious marker and flag.

Amy wasn't sure she had made the best of bargains with Mr. Silas Kane. She entered the rail car to find it crowded with settlers, littered with cigar butts and stifling hot. Cinders and tobacco smoke settled into the coach. Nausea rose in Amy's throat at the smell of burning coal and perspiring bodies in close quarters. Her seat on the hard oak bench next to the window offered little respite, as hot cinders from the engines flew by as the train charged down the track. Amy settled back to watch the countryside sweep past. Here and there, corrals and fences were springing up on the barren prairie. Plows had turned a few furrows, and the first layers of sod houses dotted the landscape.

"That's the town they're calling New Ponca," a freckle-faced cowboy sitting next to her shouted over the train noise.

Scores of tents dotted a barren landscape. Dust spiraled into the sky. Horses, men and a few wagons were a blur as the train raced by.

"Not much, is it?"

Poor Papa.

An hour later, the Santa Fe screeched to a halt at the Wharton station in Perry where a freshly painted sign hailed the government town as the "new metropolis of the southwest." The town teemed with more tents, wagons, horses and people than she had seen at Cross. Passengers shoved, pushed and gouged their way off the train and onto the station platform and then to a string of filing booths on an open lot nearby. Amy raised up her gingham skirt slightly to reveal the tips of her shoes and walked rapidly to the end of the shortest line that snaked around the west side of the depot. She opened her parasol. Not only did it give her some respite from the heat, but its pointed staves kept people at a distance.

The line moved slowly, and Amy's embroidered handkerchief was soaked with moisture when two hours later she faced the man inside the filing booth. The clerk beneath a green eyeshade barely looked up as Amy shoved her registration papers through the bars. The man, his sleeves stained with ink in spite of arm garters, scanned the report.

"Hmm-m-m, you say Section 25, Township 26, Range 3, East?" He thumbed through a heavy ledger, already thick with filings.

"Yes, that's right," Amy said, looking down at her marker.

The man flipped through the pages of the volume. "Here it is." He looked up. "Ma'am, there's already been one filing on that section."

"But I have the corner marker to prove it's mine." She pushed the flag and corner marker into the barred window.

"You're not s'posed to dig up the marker," he said wearily.

"I was afraid someone would try to jump my claim."

"Mark the lady's filing down."

Amy turned to find Silas Kane smiling at her. Her hands fluttered nervously to the high collar of her shirtwaist.

"Probably some cowpoke trying to do this fine lady out of her property." Kane winked at Amy, and she quickly hid her crimson face beneath the parasol.

The man in the booth shook his head. "Well, I'll tell you. A Mr. Grant filed on that section earlier today." His face brightened. "I see that's the name of your witness. Be you the future Mrs. Colby Grant?" His look was hopeful.

"Of course not," she stormed. "My name is Amy Elizabeth White. My father is Alfred White, and Mr. Grant is trying to steal my homestead."

The man in the cage frowned. "Well, he did file first. And it appears he has you down as his witness."

Amy gritted her teeth and closed her eyes. She must not make a scene with Mr. Kane standing at her elbow.

"Now see here, my good man," Silas began. "This man Grant is obviously a bad sort, and certainly a liar."

The man sighed. "Well, I'll mark your filing down, Miss White, but you can figure on a court trial. Of course, you know that by law you're required to make improvements on the one-hundred-sixty-acre homestead within six months, and if you live on it for five years, it'll be yours—" he looked down at the filing book— "or his."

Silas Kane stepped forward and gently moved Amy aside. "The man Grant is most likely a drifter and it's quite probable that he will abandon the premises before the end of the year."

The man frowned. "Well, it won't be the first parcel to be contested," he said and handed Amy the filing papers to sign. "That'll be fourteen dollars."

Amy handed the money through the window.

Silas Kane cleared his throat. "Miss White, should you need an attorney, I would suggest Mr. D. J. Donahoe, who is opening an office in New Ponca."

"You've been a great help," Amy said as they walked away from the filing booth. "My father has bought a lot in New Ponca. We'll be starting the town's first newspaper. If we can ever repay your kindness . . ."

"I'm very pleased to be of service, Miss White," he said softly. "Nothing to repay me for." Silas touched his hat with the tip of his cane. "However, perhaps you would be so kind as to share some refreshments with me until the train leaves for Cross?" He bowed slightly and offered his arm to Amy.

She hesitated. Silas Kane was the first respectable man she had met in this new country. Certainly, he was a gentleman compared to Colby Grant.

"Oh, but Mr. Kane, I'm already indebted to you."

"If I have offended you . . ." His thin eyebrows knitted and his eyes pleaded for forgiveness of an unknown offense.

"Oh, most assuredly not, Mr. Kane. It's just that—"

"We both have to wait for the northbound train, Miss White. And an unescorted lady . . ."

Amy's mind raced with indecision. Unlike the smirking Colby Grant, Mr. Kane was a true gentleman. And he couldn't really be called a stranger. He would be their banker in New Ponca. And she *was* thirsty. Amy tilted her parasol to one side and took his arm.

Kane's hand closed over Amy's gloved one as he directed her to a nearby brush arbor. A board nailed to a corner post proclaimed it to be Kate May's diner. He took out a pristine white handkerchief and wiped the top of a keg before offering Amy a seat. He ordered tea and a bowl of stew for each of them.

"Sold out of stew and eggs 'fore daylight," the woman in the apron said. "I got beans and cornbread."

Kane scowled and apologized for the meager fare.

This was no shy, bumbling cowboy, or a rough-hewn Colby Grant, thought Amy. Mr. Silas Kane was a man very much accustomed to being in control. He was obviously a successful businessman, a prosperous banker, a man to be respected in the new town.

His attire and demeanor were those of a gentleman. He smelled of bay rum, not campfire smoke or tobacco. He wore his suit with the aplomb of someone accustomed to the better things in life. His tie was straight and the stiff white collar buttoned in spite of the afternoon heat. He laid his napkin across his knees instead of tucking it under his chin. His hands were small and clean. His nails were manicured.

Amy thought of her own bark-scraped hands and in her embarrassment removed only one glove for their repast. She nibbled on her cornbread and found herself telling Silas about her part in The Run, to which he expressed mild disbelief. Amy carefully made light of her adventure and skipped over the incidents of the two men who attacked her and her run-ins with Colby Grant. And of course, she didn't tell him about the ridiculous incident of the tree, or the Indian who watched her bathe. Oh, no! A gentleman of the stature of Mr. Kane would never have understood that a lady could get herself in such predicaments.

"You were very fortunate to have staked a claim, Miss White. Having been part of the 'eighty-nine Run at Guthrie, I know that something like this always draws riffraff, the down-and-outers, all kinds of shady characters, whom I'm sure you've never encountered. A lady of your position cannot be too careful, however."

"I—I suppose not."

He smiled. "There will be ladies coming out soon to be with their husbands." Silas Kane colored, as if he had read Amy's thoughts. "I'm—I'm not married, Miss White, but it's a well-known fact that a town cannot survive without well-bred women such as yourself."

Under his smile of approval, Amy rose with relief when she heard the conductor's call to board the northbound train.

Silas did not ride in the baggage car on the return trip. He escorted Amy to her seat in coach and sat down beside her. Attempts at conversation were limited by the noise of the other passengers and the churning wheels of the locomotive.

On arriving at Cross, he escorted Amy to the livery and insisted on driving her to Ponca in his carriage with Sultan trailing along behind.

"You amaze me, Miss White," Silas said. "How you manage to look so cool in this heat is a mystery to me. You don't know what a pleasure it is to be in your company. You're like a breath of fresh air on a hot, sultry day, I must say."

Amy's heart beat a little faster.

"Your voice," he continued. "I can't quite place it. New England, perhaps? You have such eloquent diction."

"I—I'm a graduate of Miss Stevens's school in Boston," Amy said, flustered by his compliment. "And I'm of French heritage."

"Of course, I should have known." His smile made the pulse in Amy's throat race.

"Do you speak French, Mr. Kane?"

"No, my dear. Though I'm an admirer of Maupassant."

"Oh, really, Mr. Kane. He's one of my favorite authors." She blushed. "Of course, Miss Stevens would never let us read all of Maupassant's works."

"Indeed, indeed, Miss White. I seem to recall he was quite a romantic. Or am I thinking of Alfred de Musset?"

Amy's cheeks glowed as she recalled being caught by the head mistress with a copy of *Mimi Pinson* under her bed covers, and she quickly sought a way to change the direction of the conversation.

"This is very desolate looking country, Mr. Kane. Far more severe than I had supposed. I wonder if there is a future for any of us here."

"It may sound immodest, Miss White, but I would not invest my money if I didn't believe in the future of this town." He patted his breast pocket. "A man from the territorial governor's office met me in Perry today and issued a temporary charter for my bank in New Ponca. There's money to be made in this town—lots of money." He smiled at her. "For those with foresight, of course."

"Of course." He left no doubt in Amy's mind that he was a man of foresight.

Silas warmed to his subject. "There are other men of foresight, even brilliance, I dare say. Take Mr. Barnes.

B.S. was a very successful furniture manufacturer from Michigan before coming out here. And I'm sure he expects to make a second fortune. I understand he traversed the whole of the Cherokee Outlet in a buggy looking at the government-planned townsites. Seems B.S. was unimpressed and decided to build an entirely new city."

Amy arched an eyebrow. "Why did Mr. Barnes pick this site? Why here?"

Kane smiled patronizingly. "The availability of water, of course. There's the B&M Ford on the Arkansas River, and the railroad. Of course, the Santa Fe only stops at Cross and the Indian reservation down south, which is quite frustrating when you see it pass by without stopping, but I have no doubt that it will stop at New Ponca one day."

"Isn't the station at the reservation called Ponca?"

He nodded and smiled. "Not for long, however. Mark my words. We—Mr. Barnes and I—are men of persuasion." He placed his hand on hers and squeezed it lightly. The soft down on her arms rose in response.

"It sounds so adventuresome, Mr. Kane. And so—so—"

"So visionary?" he suggested. He smiled at her.

"Yes, that's the word. Visionary."

Silas Kane's matched team of bays trotted along briskly in the late afternoon sun, and in minutes they came within the sight and sound of New Ponca.

Amy's expectations of the new town, embellished in her mind by Silas Kane's vision, were shattered when the carriage rolled down the wide grassy strip of prairie lined with tents, wagons, carts and horse-flesh. Silas reined around a surveyor's transit, and a man bent on one knee pounded a stake into the ground that bore a crudely painted sign of "Grand Avenue." The dust, the chaos and the noise over-whelmed Amy.

Even as Amy watched, tents proliferated like mush-rooms on both sides of the broad lane. Unlike the government towns of Cross and Perry, no wooden structure graced the skyline of New Ponca. Not one tree or bush broke the horizon to lend protection from the searing winds or the glaring sun in the western horizon.

Wagons loaded with lumber and supplies rumbled down a broad lane, cutting long ribbons of death in the dry grass. Fancy rigs and homemade carts careened around donkeys braying in mutiny. In the melee it was hard to tell whether riders on horseback were only half-crazed or fully drunk, but all was mayhem.

Sounds of construction came from every direction. Carpenters pounded nails into wooden frames lying on the ground. A blacksmith's sledge rang against an anvil molding a shoe. A mallet knocked the cork out of a new keg of brew on a tailgate saloon. Men unloaded crates under stretched canvas and brush arbors and were immediately in business behind barrel-keg barriers.

On a knoll a few yards south of the bedlam, the Indians in their brightly colored shawls and blankets watched from their pony-drawn wagons at the unruly scene of a town rising from the dust.

Amy shuddered and searched the impassive faces, but found no one she could identify as her intruders at the river. Her eyes were drawn to a tall and imposing Indian sitting rigidly erect in the seat of a spring wagon, his headdress of eagle feathers setting him apart from the others. Around his neck he wore a bear-claw necklace, and on his chest was a breast plate of bone beads and porcupine quills. In his hand he held a spear tied with feathers.

"That must be White Eagle," Silas offered. "Maybe we can convince the old buzzard to change the name of the Ponca rail station to honor himself." He pursed his lips. "White Eagle Station," he mused. "I like it. Bet

74

ol' White Eagle will agree for a couple of ponies."

Amy swallowed the feeling of panic. She wanted desperately to see Silas Kane's image of this new town, to see her own vision. She wanted to see a building bearing the sign of *The Ponca Democrat,* with her father's new Washington press, his boxes of type, flats of printing paper and a barrel of ink waiting inside.

She wanted to see real streets, with boardwalks where you chatted with decent folks. Buildings with doors to open for shopping and doors to close at night for safety. Instead, animals and people milled around in the middle of a dusty and barren prairie under the dark, watchful eyes of Indians in full war regalia.

Amy closed her eyes. There would be so much to do to transform the rubble on the prairie into a livable town. And the weariness overwhelmed her. What had she done to her father? She had foolishly uprooted him from a home he had known all of his life, expecting him to start over. He was not a young man. If anything, Papa was a crushed man. Was it possible to forge a new life out of this—this nothingness? Or was she a dreamer? Were they all dreamers? Or drifters, like Colby Grant?

She looked over at Silas Kane. His eyes were bright, his thin smile wide as he waved a hand and called out greetings to faces he recognized.

No! Silas Kane was no dreamer, nor a drifter, and neither was Amy Elizabeth White! She would make the dream a reality. She would do whatever it took to forge a new life here. She would not go back to Milford, Nebraska, where they called her father a drunk and refused to acknowledge her existence or accept the teaching skills she had to offer.

Amy Elizabeth White was no longer emotionally numb. Her equilibrium had returned. She raised her chin, looked straight ahead, and the vision began to take shape in her mind.

Chapter Five

"Amy! Mr. Kane! Over here!" Alfred White called and then turned back to the man standing beside a wagon load of lumber.

Silas maneuvered the carriage over to Alfred's wagon and helped Amy down.

"Seventy-five cents a square foot, Mr. Keck? Sounds mighty steep to me," Alfred said.

"That includes the construction. Take it or leave it." Keck shrugged.

Alfred's frothy eyebrows gathered on his forehead. "That's more than I'd planned on."

"Could we pay you the rest of it in installments?" Amy asked.

Keck shook his head. "Wish I could, ma'am, but don't reckon the lumber yard at the reservation would give me credit."

Silas cleared his throat and smiled at Amy before he spoke to her father. "If you'll permit me, Mr. White, maybe I can be of service. You can be my first customer." He reached inside his jacket for the bank's charter papers.

Alfred shook his white head. "I don't know. I hadn't figured on having to borrow money."

Kane went on. "A very reasonable rate of interest, I assure you. This town needs a newspaper, and Miss Amy has told me of your plans." He smiled at Amy.

Alfred turned back to Keck. "I still say you're too expensive."

Keck rubbed his bald head and smiled. "I can start today, and when they finish the surveyin', we can move it onto your lot. You'll be in bizness."

"How long you figure that'll take?"

"Wal, Mr. Barnes said it would take another two days to complete the surveyin' for the townsite. Then we can draw for our lots. They've already built a platform for the drawin'."

"That would make it the twentieth," Alfred calculated. "That gives me only one day to get my first edition printed." He raked a hand through his white hair and replaced the derby. "Well, Mr. Keck, I guess you'd better get started." He looked over at Silas. "That is, if Mr. Kane will loan me the additional money I need."

"Your handshake is all I really need, Alfred," Silas said as he offered his hand.

Alfred turned to Amy. "You're looking pretty tuckered out. I hear there's a hotel over on what they're calling First Street. You might want to check it out. Just a tent, but—"

Kane interrupted. "More like horse stalls with canvas for walls. Twenty-five cents a night and no privacy. Cots are extra. I rather think Miss Amy will find it quite uncomfortable there."

Alfred grinned at Amy. "Beats a tree."

Amy's face reddened at the puzzled look on Kane's face. She prayed her father would not explain and said hurriedly, "I think I'd rather stay with you in the wagon,

Papa. It may be cramped, but I'll feel safer." She went to the back of Kane's rig and untied Sultan.

"Extra! Extra! Git yer paper heah!"

For a moment Amy thought she was dreaming, but she recognized the hawker with a stack of newspapers under his arm as Danny Rhodie, the thirsty young waif in tattered knickers at the starting line south of Arkansas City.

"Jist five cents," Danny hollered. "Special edition! Git yer paper heah!"

Amy dropped Sultan's reins and retrieved her chatelaine purse from her knitting bag.

"It must be an Arkansas City paper, Papa," Amy said as she handed Danny a coin.

"No, ma'am," said the grinning freckle-faced boy. "It's the new *Ponca Republican*."

With heart racing, Amy glanced at the paper's headline:

CHEROKEE STRIP RUN DRAWS THOUSANDS

She quickly scanned the masthead of the two-page edition. On the back page, in the upper left-hand corner, under the heading of *Ponca Republican* and in bold agate, she read: *Editor, Colby Grant.*

The heat flamed in Amy's face. Her breast rose in quick jerks as she sought air for her suffocating lungs. The fury boiled up from the cauldron of her stomach to become a bitter gall in her throat. And she remembered the mysterious manila package strapped on the back of Colby Grant's ugly roan.

Silas furrowed his brow and reached out a hand to steady her. "Miss White, are you all right?"

Still clutching the *Ponca Republican* in her hand, Amy nodded. She was not in the least suffering from vapors as Mr. Kane supposed. She was furious, enraged! And only with effort did she withhold the unladylike words rushing to escape her tongue.

"Where—where is he?" she hissed through clenched teeth to Danny.

"Who?"

"Grant—the editor, where is he?" She grasped the boy's shoulder.

Danny winced. "His tent's o'er yonder." He pointed, his eyes wide and his freckles bright in his ashen face.

"Let me see what you've got there, young fella," Alfred said goodnaturedly as he took the newspaper from Amy's hands. "Well, I'll be damned!"

For once, Amy did not admonish her father for his blasphemy, but demanded of Danny, "Take me to Mr. Grant."

"But he ain't—"

Amy held Danny's arm in a viselike grip and marched down the street. Her skirt kicked up dust as she took long strides, forcing Danny to hop every other step to keep up with her.

The sun was low on the horizon, but Amy easily spotted Colby Grant's tent through the haze of dust. Large block letters printed on the light canvas proclaimed it to be the home of the *Ponca Republican*.

Without hesitation, Amy entered the tent with Danny in tow. Colby wasn't there. On the ground lay his bedroll and the manila paper which had hidden the newspapers during the race. In frustration, Amy kicked the wrapping paper to one side.

"He doesn't even have a press! How could he have printed a newspaper?" But she knew the answer. The *Republican* had been printed in Arkansas City. "Where is that—that—"

"I tried to tell ya," Danny said. "He's gone to Ark City to get his press. He hired Mr. Jason's ox team an' said he'd be back t'night or t'morrow."

Amy let her breath out slowly and relaxed her grip on the boy, who inched away from her. "I'm sorry, Danny.

It's not your fault. It's Mr. Grant who—who—"

She wheeled away from the boy and stalked back to her father's wagon.

Silas produced a folding stool from his rig and insisted that Amy sit in the shade of the wagon. "It's been a long and trying day, Miss White. You must be exhausted."

"She just needs to simmer down a little," Alfred said as he slipped on a pair of narrow reading glasses to sort through a drawer of type on the tailgate.

"Colby Grant is a scalawag of the first order!" Amy's fist punctuated the air.

Peering over his glasses at Amy, he said, "Breaking that axle yesterday sure stirred up the type."

"It's obvious the paper was printed in Arkansas City, Papa," Amy huffed, rising from the stool and retrieving Sultan.

"I'll have to order some new E's in this California type," Alfred said. "Must have gotten too dry, and when the load shifted, the corners splintered."

"Papa!"

Alfred continued looking through the type.

In exasperation, Amy turned to Silas. "It's not really a New Ponca paper." She tied Sultan to the back of her father's wagon. "How dare he pass off that rag as a newspaper?"

"Now, now, Miss White," Kane said. Even though the air had begun to cool, the man was sweating.

"Colby Grant must have heard about our plans in Arkansas City and—and—"

"It's a free country, lass," Alfred finally responded. "I wouldn't worry too much about it. Competition is good for a town. If what Kane here says is right, this town's going to be plenty big enough for two newspapers."

"Grant is getting even with me for staking my claim on what he considers to be his homestead," she said to Silas.

Kane stared at his hat as his fingers inched around the brim.

"He's a scalawag!" she repeated. "Mr. Kane agrees with me."

Kane cleared his throat. "Well—uh—I haven't met the man, Miss White, but I certainly do sympathize with you."

"Amy," Alfred said looking over his glasses at his daughter. "You're not making sense. He carried the paper in with him. How could he have known that out of all the quarter sections in the Outlet you'd both stake the same one?"

"He—he heard about our plans—we made no secret of them—and he followed me and—and—" Amy knew that her words were as lame as her persecution of the man, but glared at her father defiantly.

Silas wiped his perspiring face with a handkerchief and put on his hat. "Miss Amy, it's terribly warm. I think there's a lemonade stand down the way. It would give me a great deal of pleasure if you would join me."

Amy felt her cheeks color from embarrassment at Kane's attempt to diffuse the situation. She retrieved her parasol and silently accepted his proffered arm. She was not making a very good impression on Silas Kane, obviously one of the new town's foremost citizens.

The clamor on the street prohibited conversation, and by the time they had walked to the far end of the dusty thoroughfare named Grand Avenue, Amy had recovered her civility.

The lemonade, surprisingly cool, was served to them in tin cups by Danny Rhodie's mother under a canvas awning tied to her wagon.

"Good, ain't it?" she said.

"It's as cool as if you had ice, Mrs. Rhodie." Amy smiled.

"'Tis ice. Me and Danny spent our last nickel on it. Wrap it in tow sacks 'n cover it in straw and ye be s'prised how long ice will last." The thin lips smiled with pride. "And I got 'nother load of ice comin' t'night or t'morrow. Mr. Grant's bringin' it."

The lemonade suddenly tasted sour, but Amy forced herself to swallow. When their drinks were finished, Silas escorted Amy back to her father's wagon and bade her good evening. She wasn't sure if he really had some business to attend to as he said, or if he feared another display of her dour disposition. She would not want to discourage Mr. Kane.

As the banker walked away, Amy turned to her father with an apology. "I'm sorry, Papa. My French temperament, I suppose."

"More than likely Hannah and I didn't apply the rod often enough, lass." Alfred sighed and embraced her.

"Oh, Papa, I love you. And you know you never laid a hand on me." She patted his jowl "But sometimes I wonder how life can be so cruel. Look at these people." She waved her arms. "When I see all the pain and suffering mirrored in their faces, I'm not sure we— they—have anything to look forward to. It's worse than in Milford. And we—they—have so many hardships, so many obstacles ahead of us."

"Well, it's not your fancy boarding school, that's for sure," Alfred said, surveying the turmoil about them. "Hope! That's what it's all about, Amy. And birth! You're watching the first gasps of a new life, Amy, and that's always painful."

Amy laughed and hugged her father. "And this baby—our baby—will survive and thrive?"

Alfred grinned. "Speaking of survival, how about supper? Our light's about gone and I'd like to save the oil lamps."

"And we're getting low on water."

"We can get some tomorrow from Water Billy. Though at twenty cents it's cheaper to buy a shot of whiskey."

"Whisk—whiskey?" She turned her back and rummaged in their sack of meager food supplies, trying to conceal her anxiety. "Twenty cents for water? We'll not pay twenty cents for anything to drink. Not when I've got a whole river full of water." She hoped her father hadn't bought another bottle.

Alfred must have read her thoughts. "Don't fret, lass. I've had my fill for a while."

She smiled and kissed her father on the cheek.

After sharing a meal of cold boiled eggs, jerky and hardtack with her father, Amy spread his pallet beneath the wagon and climbed up to her bed in the wagon box between the seat and the bulky hand press.

She threw back the blankets on the feather bed stashed there and stretched out her long limbs. She wriggled her toes that peeked out from under her hubbard night gown and heaved a sigh of relief. Her ill-treated body ached with weariness, and the day's heat still radiated from the canvas-covered wagon. Dust from the restless ribbon called Grand Avenue sifted down on her. Oh, what she wouldn't give for a bath in the cool waters of the Arkansas on her own homestead.

Waiting for sleep to claim her, Amy listened to someone mistreating a piano down the road and the occasional whoop from a successful gambler. Far into the night a wagon rumbled past, and she wondered if it could be Colby Grant with his press. Her fists knotted in frustration. The man had lied to her. By omission, she admitted, but nonetheless he had deceived her about his intentions here in the Outlet. She must not underestimate the determination behind that golden mustache and easy smile of sincerity or those daring blue eyes masked with innocence. Tomorrow she would go to the river for water and begin proving up her homestead to establish ownership before that despicable Colby Grant could claim the land by default. With that resolution, Amy fell into an exhausted sleep.

*   *   *

Early the next morning, Amy acceded to her father's demands and asked young Danny Rhodie to accompany her in a rented rig out to her homestead. The boy wasn't large enough to offer much physical protection, but his presence would perhaps keep strangers away. Amy had smiled and offered the young man a shiny new dime, but his reluctance had not been overcome until she mentioned he could fish and maybe swim in the river.

On their way, Amy stopped at different homesteads on the pretext of meeting her neighbors to study the fences, corrals and even a soddy in its early stages. Never in her life had she made anything other than a fancy bonnet or a new shirtwaist, but with her father's tools that she had brought along she was determined she and Danny would erect some kind of structure on her new homestead. There must be no doubt of her ownership.

While Danny baited limb lines in hopes of catching a fish for his mother, Amy marked several tall cottonwoods she thought would serve her purposes. With a crosscut saw they felled the trees and with Sultan's help dragged the timbers to the west property line.

The youngster proved to be fairly skillful with the ax and quickly notched the logs as Amy dug the holes. Sweat rolled down her face and saturated her clothing as she struggled with her task. Only by jumping repeatedly on the shovel with the weight of both boot-shod feet was she able to pierce the hardened ground.

When the hole was three feet deep she stopped and walked twenty paces north. Breathless and perspiring heavily, she handed the shovel to Danny.

"Your turn."

"Whut we buildin'?" Danny asked.

"A gateway."

Danny looked around. "But ye ain't got no fence."

"We *don't* have a fence," she corrected. "That will

come later," Amy puffed as she shoved against a log. "This is the grand entry through which everyone will one day pass to reach the ranch house." She straightened up and laughed at the freckles in the puzzled face. "The ranch house will come later, too." She upended a log in the three-foot hole and asked, "Don't you have dreams, Danny?"

"Ma says hit don't do no good to wish fer somethin' ya can't never have." He attacked the digging of the hole with unusual vigor.

Amy shaded her eyes from the mid-morning sun and watched in painful silence at the child diligently shoveling the dirt. It wasn't fair. Danny should be making kites and slingshots, kicking rocks or playing marbles, not building gateways and digging post holes like an old man.

Taking turns, they dug two more holes before they rested. Danny ran to check his fishing lines while Amy retrieved the lunch basket from the rig.

"I got 'im. I got 'im, Miss White," Danny squealed, holding up a catfish flopping at the end of his line. "They et the other two grasshoppers, but I got this 'un."

Amy clapped her hands in appreciation. "I'm proud of you, Danny. You're quite a fisherman." She spread their meager lunch of biscuits smeared with sorghum molasses and butter as Danny secured the fish with a string through its gills that would allow it to swim until they headed back to town.

After their lunch, Amy allowed Danny to wade in the river. "But no swimming so soon after your meal, Danny." Amy resisted the impulse to pull off her boots and join him, but settled for washing her face and repinning her hair.

When Amy and Danny resumed work, they set four notched posts, two on each side of what Amy insisted would be the roadway. Four logs were hammered, wedged and pounded between each set of posts. By late afternoon, they fell wearily to the ground and gazed proudly on a structure that somewhat resembled a ranch entrance.

"We need a board o'er th' top," Danny said, "with th' name of yore ranch on it."

"Name?" Amy hadn't thought about a name.

"Yeah. Whatcha gonna name it?"

Amy slumped to the ground, pulled the soiled cotton gloves from her badly swollen hands and softly touched the blisters. "I'm too tired to think, Danny."

"How's 'bout 'Miss Amy's Ranch'?"

"Did you know that Amy, or rather '*je t'aime,*' means 'I love you' in French?"

Danny's face reddened. "Maybe we better find 'nother name."

Amy laughed. "Well, we'll leave the name for later. We've done a good day's work. It's time to go home."

"Can I go swimmin' ag'in? Please? I ain't so clean and I shore don't smell too purty—"

"I'm *not* so clean," Amy corrected.

"You, too? Then ain't cha goin' swimmin'?"

Amy laughed. "We do need a bath, don't we?" She got to her feet and took his hand. "If you won't tell anyone, I will go swimming with you."

"You will?" Danny jumped up and down with glee.

Amy laughed. "But you have to turn your head when I get in and out. You promise?"

"I promise," he said solemnly and crossed his heart.

Amy quickly shed her boots and outer garments and dove in.

After an invigorating swim, Danny helped Amy fill a milk can with water from upstream before they headed for New Ponca.

Twilight had fallen when they arrived in good spirits, their clothes still somewhat damp, to face a concerned Alfred White.

"I was beginning to worry—"

Amy tied the reins and jumped down from the rig. "Oh, Papa, you should see it," she said, hugging him. "We built the ranch entrance and—" She laughed. "I know. Danny's already reminded me. We don't have a fence—yet. But the gateway is *magnifique*."

Alfred took her hands in his and said, "Feels like corncobs. Who's going to hold hands with you if you keep this up, lass?" he asked teasingly.

Amy blushed. "Has Mr. Kane been by?"

Alfred nodded. "And Colby Grant."

She jerked her hands away from her father. "What did he want?"

"To buy you out."

"Never! My homestead is not for sale."

"Said he'd pay you two hundred dollars. That's a lot of money. You could buy several lots in town and I wouldn't have to worry about—"

"He might as well have offered a thousand, Papa. I'm not selling." She turned back to Danny, thanked him for his help and smiled as she watched him skip happily down the street with his well-earned dime and the catfish on his string.

"Fine boy, isn't he?" Alfred said.

Amy nodded. "But his grammar is atrocious." She moved to the back of the wagon and began preparing supper. "One of the first things this town must have is a school."

Tuesday, it rained. It was a real gully washer. The dusty streets turned to mud and hampered the surveyors who were determined to finish their work and let the lot drawing begin. The Indians stayed in White Eagle and the weary settlers holed up in their tents for some much-needed rest after rescuing perishable goods from their leaky wagons.

It was impossible for Alfred to move his press, even if

he had had a tent to protect it. Amy sadly piled Hannah's beloved quilts on top of the Washington to ward off the rain, and hoped with a vengeance that Colby Grant's tent leaked like a sieve.

Wednesday, the drawing began. The skies cleared and the sun bore down relentlessly, turning the prairie into a steaming cauldron. Homesteaders slopped through the muck and mire to Grand Avenue between Third and Fourth streets. Amy held her skirts up out of the mud and wished she dared wear dungarees. Her shoes were beyond redemption.

Barnes climbed onto the platform in knee-length river boots and a dark brown cheviot suit to make a speech about the destiny of the town and the great task that lay before them. He announced that an organization would be formed called the Ponca Homesteaders Association.

"We've got a few people who claim they staked this four square mile in The Run." The crowd booed. "We know that's not true. But when dealing with dishonest claim jumpers, we want to be prepared to defend what's rightly ours."

The crowd cheered, and a few men fired their revolvers into the air.

"We will conquer. Ponca will prosper. We will have churches and schools . . ."

The Santa Fe blew its whistle and roared down the track at the west end of town.

Barnes raised his voice, " . . . and some day a railroad."

The settlers hooted and hollered their agreement, but were impatient for the drawing to begin.

"C'mon, draw now, speak later!"

"Git on wit' it!"

Barnes cleared his throat. "The rules are this," he said. "Eight blocks have been set aside for parks and a school. The school property is located on the east end of Grand Avenue and we've put a park right north of that. Now, no homesteaders will be allowed to build on those properties. Each certificate you purchased is worth one town lot or two residential lots. Each lot is twenty-five feet wide."

He produced three cardboard boxes. "Now, we've put the numbers of the certificates in this box and the description of the lots in the other two boxes. We'll draw a number, and the certificate holder has the option of drawing from the town or residential box. So when your certificate number is called and you've got your legal description, step up quickly and mark your lot down."

He pointed to the map nailed up behind him.

"The clerks will record your lot number and the legal description in one of these ledgers and then give you a receipt for your certificate. Now, let's commence the drawing."

He looked around at the crowd below him. "Have we got a youngster who can draw out the numbers?"

Danny, his freckles bright with embarrassment, and a tow-headed girl eight or ten years old wearing a red pinafore were lifted onto the platform.

"Well, now," said Barnes. "We thank you, young man, but I guess it's ladies first." Danny scrambled down and faded into the hurrahing crowd.

Congratulatory cheers went up with the drawing of each certificate. One of the first numbers drawn went to Silas Kane, who was granted a lot on the south side of Grand Avenue at Second Street. He beamed and waved at Amy, who ducked under her parasol at the grinning faces turned toward her.

Harry Koller, waiting with a load of lumber shipped down from Ark City to Cross, drew the second lot in the middle of the block on the north side of Grand between Fourth and Fifth Streets.

"Let's go, men," he yelled as he jumped from the platform and into his wagon. "We got a hardware store to build."

Peter Pearson, a small bearded man who planned to move his Arkansas City hotel in sections to the new town, drew a lot on Second and Cleveland.

The southeast corner of Third and Grand went to Will Chase, who found he had competition from W. E. Scott, another druggist who landed across the street and three lots west. The attorney, D. J. Donahoe, secured a lot at Fifth and Grand.

George Brett, with plans to establish an implement store, selected two lots on North Fifth for a family home, but "anyone wanting to sell a downtown lot, come see me."

Saloon keeper Mike Daley drew the northeast corner of Second and Grand. Fred Baldruff, the baker, received a lot on Grand between First and Second Streets, next to Tuck Myatt, who ran a tent grocery and held a 160-acre homestead just west of the new town.

As more numbers were called, the din around Amy and her father increased. Carpenters raised small crude buildings on newly drawn lots as wagons rolled down the street with loads of lumber from the sawmill at the Indian reservation south of town.

All day long, numbers continued to be pulled from the box with few breaks for the weary clerks or the little girl in the red dress, but by late evening Alfred's number had not been called. Amy knew that the walls of a structure had been built and carpenters were waiting to throw the frame building up on Alfred's site. But without a lot, nothing could be put into place. The press would remain in the wagon. It was too heavy to move twice. And tomorrow was Thursday, the day publishers went to press if they wanted theirs to be the legal paper of a community.

"Folks, it's getting late," Barnes announced. "We've still got twelve hundred certificates to pull out of that box. That's about half of you. I know you're anxious, but we've worn out this little girl. And to tell the truth

I'm pretty tired myself. This is the last certificate we'll draw. We'll start again in the morning."

The crowd groaned as the little girl, now sitting on a three-legged stool, wearily pulled out the last number.

"Number 1213."

A cheer went up on the far side of the platform, and Amy's heart saddened as her father's shoulders drooped.

"Tomorrow, Papa." She steered him toward their wagon.

"Wait, Amy. I want to get the clerks' list of the lot owners from today's drawing." He got out his pad and pen.

Amy breathed a sigh of relief. She had prayed her father would shake his grief and find renewed interest in publishing. If that was all she had accomplished by coming to the Outlet and enduring its hardships, every minute of agony was worth it.

The smile on Amy's lips faded when she saw the certificate holder of the last drawn number mount the platform. It was Colby Grant. Seething, she watched him mark an X on the map at the southeast corner of Grand and Fourth Street. There was just no justice in the world. Maybe Danny was right. Dreams were foolish.

The noise of saws and hammers continued through the night under the glare of campfires and coal oil lanterns. By morning, a weary Amy looked out of the wagon to find a changed horizon. The tent city boasted a sprinkling of frame buildings. Some were only lean-tos, but here and there more ambitious structures were being raised with false fronts and roofed porticos.

Amy dressed quickly and joined her father at the platform with other anxious certificate holders. Alfred's number was the second to be called, and Amy eagerly climbed the platform with her father to look over the map of the remaining lots. She had preferred a lot on Grand Avenue, but the choice was now limited, so

Alfred was grateful when he received a lot on North Second, just off Grand.

"That's too far west for my liking," Alfred said.

"It could be worse, Papa," Amy said. At least it wasn't next door to that despicable Colby Grant's *Republican* newspaper.

On leaving the platform, a jubilant Alfred White directed his team of grays to his lot and waited impatiently until Keck and his helpers laid the prefabricated floor of the building in place. With a half dozen helpers, Alfred skidded the Washington hand press out of the wagon, down the planks and onto the new floor. Only when the heavy contraption was positioned as he wanted would Alfred let Keck's carpenters resume their work.

Alfred tossed his coat aside and donned a green eyeshade and began to handset type for his first edition. Amy watched with awe as his fingers flew from the type cases to the composing stick. Carpenters worked around and over him, nailing up walls and roofing the building, but Alfred's concentration never faltered.

By late afternoon the first edition of the *Ponca Democrat* lay in the iron chase ready for printing. Below the masthead were four galleys of eight-point type. One story recounted The Run. Another listed the results of the first day's lot drawing in the new town of Ponca. The other two columns were filled with large ad type soliciting subscriptions for the *Ponca Democrat.*

"No time to proof, Amy. We'll have to let the typos stand."

Alfred tightened the form and pounded the type with a mallet to push down any uneven letters and then placed the form on the hand-levered press. Amy took off her cape and donned a printer's apron. She spread the ink as Alfred placed on the press each ready-print sheet, with worldwide news on the reverse. Sheet in, lever down, lever up, sheet out. Ink. Sheet in, lever down, lever up, sheet out. Ink.

Seven hundred copies were printed and stacked before Alfred fell against his new wall and let his rotund body slide to the pine floor. He rubbed his left arm. "Enough for the first issue."

Amy collapsed against the type case with the ink roller in her hand. Never had a newspaper been put to bed with such speed. Never had she felt such pride. And never had she been in such disarray.

Taking off the apron, she fanned her bodice, wet from perspiration. She wiped at her neck and face and was horrified to realize her face was smudged with ink.

"Mr. White," yelled Keck, "the sign's ready to go up."

Alfred huffed to his feet, grabbed a handful of papers and followed Amy out to the muddy street. In black Roman type, in freshly painted letters three feet high, in a frame twenty-two feet long, were the words PONCA DEMOCRAT.

Alfred put the newspapers down on the stoop and opened his arms to Amy. "We did it, lass," he said softly, tweaking her cheek. "We did it."

Amy kissed his ruddy jowls beneath the misty eyes and felt a tear slide past her lashes.

"Center it and put 'er up as high as you can get it," Alfred directed.

Arm in arm, Amy and her father watched proudly as the carpenters raised the sign and nailed the braces into place.

"Congratulations!"

Colby Grant in his dirty Stetson and ink-stained dungarees strode up with a stack of papers under his arm and offered his hand to Alfred.

"That's quite a day's work, Alfred." He picked up one of the papers and closed his left eye to scan it.

"That's five cents," Amy snapped, smugly noting the scar on his right earlobe.

Colby's eyes crinkled and his lips twitched beneath

his mustache. "How about an exchange? No sense in trading coin."

"That's right," Alfred laughed as he accepted a nickel from one of the workmen who had picked up a paper.

The small stack of papers went rapidly, and Amy rushed inside for more.

"Have a delivery boy?" Grant asked.

"Haven't had time to think about that," her father said.

"There are plenty of people waiting to read our newspaper," Amy interrupted. "All we have to do is put them outside the front door."

"Why not let Danny peddle your papers?"

"He's your carrier," Amy hissed, wishing it weren't true.

"Starting next week, I'm putting out a morning paper. You have an evening paper. Danny can carry them both. And he needs the money. His mother's not doing all that well."

Amy couldn't argue with that.

"I think that's a fine suggestion," Alfred said. "But aren't you afraid I'll scoop you?" he grinned.

Colby threw back his head and laughed. "A true newspaperman." He put a hand on Alfred's shoulders. "I'll take my chances. I figure it'll be a lot cooler putting out a newspaper in the middle of the night than in the middle of the day. Besides"—he grinned at Amy—"I'm a night person."

"I'll just bet you are, Mr. Grant," Amy said.

With another shake of Alfred's hand and a teasing smile at Amy, Colby walked away. She shivered in the warm evening sun.

News of the *Ponca Democrat's* first edition spread fast, and all seven hundred copies of the newspaper sold within an hour.

Amy counted out thirty-five dollars. "Enough to order ready-prints from Western Union Newspaper," she said to her father. "But we'll have to print more copies if we're going to make any money. I'm sure we can sell three times as many next week. We do have the better newspaper."

With her breasts filled with pride, Amy picked up the *Ponca Republican* resting on her father's type case. She wondered how many copies Colby Grant had printed. And what could he have possibly written that would best her father's paper? Her mind had barely expressed the thought when she saw they had been scooped.

"Oh, how I detest that man!" Not only had Colby Grant printed a complete list of lot owners from the first day's drawing, but he had reported on the election of provisional city officials, which had been held following the drawing while her father was hand-setting type.

Bulletin
The esteemed B.S. Barnes has ben elected mayor, which ths editor deems to be quite proper. City clerk wil be W.E. McGuire. Those elected to serv as councilmen are F.P. Adam, W.M. Randall, J.L. McCarty, P.I. Brown and A.C. Foy.

It was only one small paragraph and it was full of typographical errors, but it was enough. The exhilaration swelling Amy's heart for the day's triumphs vanished. She crumpled the *Ponca Republican* into a wad and tossed it in the trash.

Chapter Six

The southwest winds blew gently over the parched plains of the Cherokee Outlet and sent the yeasty smells from Fred Baldruff's bakery drifting slowly into Amy's consciousness. She yawned and stretched her limbs, feeling wonderfully rested after her first night's sleep in Pearson's Globe Hotel.

She relished the early morning coolness and the silence that she knew would be all too brief. The unrelenting heat would return with the sun's first rays, and the calm would be shattered by the sounds of construction as more buildings rose and tents were felled.

With the first peck—peck—peck of the hammers and the ding—ding—ding of the anvil at Stacy's blacksmith shop, Amy placed her feet on the bare floor, yawned, pushed her unruly hair away from her face and listened for a moment.

No sounds came through the door of the adjoining room, but she hadn't really expected any. Her father would be in the *Democrat* office by now, having left early for his breakfast at Mrs. Rhodie's tent cafe.

Amy agreed that the woman offered the best food in town, but women rarely frequented Mrs. Rhodie's. Her small tent cafe was a bit rustic with its wooden benches and communal table, but it was considered to be the stronghold of the town fathers.

Amy took pride in her father's inclusion in this small, elite group of men. Men such as Barnes and Silas Kane. Then there was George Brett, who owned the implement store with its plow points, hay rakes and broadcasters ready to tame the virgin soil.

She should include Jim Hutchins and F. D. Foutz who had teamed up to build a frame building for their Ponca Cash Store. And of course, Harry Koller, whose hardware store had been the first structure raised in the city. And she must not forget Tuck Myatt and Poke Adams, who had each opened grocery stores—Amy laughed—if tents with a bag or two of cornmeal, a bucket of sorghum molasses and a few bottles of warm soda drinks could be called stores. Everyone seemed to be waiting for shipments from Chicago and Kansas City.

Everyone seemed to be dependent on the railways. Even her father. Today she would drive her wagon to the rail depot at Cross and pick up the ready-prints for tomorrow's edition of the *Ponca Democrat*.

Amy sighed. To be fair, she supposed she should include that despicable Colby Grant on any list of town fathers, but his influence as editor of the *Ponca Republican* would wane when the superiority of Alfred's paper became obvious to everyone.

All in all, Amy saw the town fathers as a curious and unlikely gathering of men. Some dressed in three-piece suits that boasted of previous success. Others wore patched overalls or faded denims of the open range. But whatever their fortunes or failures of the past, each man had ventured into the new territory with optimism and determination.

Amy hugged herself at the thought of her father's renewed vigor and interest in the newspaper. His melancholy moments had been left behind in Nebraska. And there was no evidence he had sought solace in the whiskey bottle. Perhaps, just perhaps, the new beginning she had determinedly sought was within their grasp.

"And you're wasting this beautiful morning, Amy White," she reprimanded herself as the light filtering in her narrow window cast a pink glow on her body.

Amy attended to her *toilette* at the small washstand with its stoneware pitcher and basin. Looking in the small hanging mirror, she pinned up her dark hair, careful to pull a wispy curl across the mark on her forehead. She dabbed toilet water on each wrist and slipped into a gray bodice and navy skirt. She smoothed the coverlet on her cot and checked the lock on her trunk with her homestead papers and then shoved the large carrier aside.

It was a nuisance not having door locks, but Peter Pearson, the hotel's owner, had assured them they would be forthcoming. The hotel interior had been almost totally dismantled before it was moved in three big sections from Arkansas City to New Ponca, and so it was a matter of sorting out keys for the rehung doors and hauling down the rest of the hotel supplies. The hotel keeper had promised Amy a chest of drawers, curtains for the window and, best of all, an enameled bathtub for the room across the hall.

It would be heavenly to immerse herself in a tub of warm water, to scrub away the dirt ground into her pores and moisturize her thirsty skin. Not that bathing in the Arkansas was something she'd give up entirely, but soon the river would be too cold.

With the slim hope that Mr. Pearson would surprise her with eggs for breakfast, Amy pulled the door closed and backed into the hall with her parasol and beaded handbag.

"Mornin', ma'am."

Startled, Amy whirled to face Colby Grant.

He tipped his Stetson. A faint smile played on his lips when he removed his long, thin cigar.

Amy's thoughts darted to the trunk with her filing papers. The lock would be no match for someone with the strength and cunning of Colby Grant. She dared not hesitate. Perhaps he would think she carried the homestead papers on her person.

"Mr. Grant," she said curtly and moved quickly down the hall to the outside stairway.

"Miss White?"

She stopped at the top of the landing and forced a big sigh. "What is it, Mr. Grant?" She fought against the urge to lower her head and avoid the probing blue eyes.

"Have you been out to the homestead?" Colby raised a boot to the railing and tied the lower string of his holster to his right thigh.

Amy swallowed twice at the bulging muscles in the tight dungarees. "I'm—I'm going out to my claim today. Not that it's any of your business."

"I wouldn't go alone, ma'am." After what she'd been through with those claim jumpers, Colby thought she might have enough sense to be cautious. But unlike Crissy, Amy White didn't have a cautious bone in her body. Not that it had done Crissy any good to be careful.

"And just why shouldn't I go to *my* homestead?"

"Wiley Hines, the marshal over in the Osage lands, says Ben Cravens and his renegades are terrorizing the homesteaders northeast of town. Rustling cattle and setting fires. Might not be wise."

"I'll decide what is wise and—"

"You're being mighty stubborn." The morning sun glinted off his mustache.

"I suspect you're the only renegade I have to worry about."

With the cheroot clamped beneath his teeth, Colby folded his arms across his chest and leaned against the railing. He squinted his left eye shut and shook his head.

"Short memory, huh?"

Amy stared at the pine flooring in her embarrassment. "I suppose you want me to thank you again for ridding me of those claim jumpers."

"Gol' durn it," he said, rising. "I might not be around the next time you need help." He hadn't been around for Crissy. He had been too busy with other things. And now she was dead, and so was the man who had killed her. Colby's hair had grown over the bullet wound on his left temple, but the wound inside was still festering. "I don't need your thanks, Amy."

She fought against the heady aroma of his cigar. "Mr. Grant," she said with emphasis, "you hardly fit my description of a knight in shining armor."

His left eye narrowed beneath his Stetson. "And I suppose Silas does." Now why in the hell did I say that? he wondered.

"Silas—Mr. Kane is a gentleman!" Amy snapped open her parasol. The staves sprang dangerously close to Colby's face and his good right eye.

With a sniff of dismissal, Amy turned, her skirts sweeping down the stairs as quickly as her weakened knees would permit. She heard Colby chuckle and his spurs jingle softly as he followed her with catlike steps. Her legs threatened to dissolve into mush as she entered the door of the Globe dining room.

You're not responsible for her, Colby told himself. You vowed never to take on that kind of responsibility again. No matter how much you care about someone, you can't always protect them. No commitments, no strings. It was safer that way.

100

Relieved that Colby had not followed her into the restaurant, Amy took a seat at a vacant table for four. Women in the Territory were still so few that for a minute the noisy chatter from men seated in the restaurant hushed. Amy averted her eyes and waited for them to resume their conversations.

A woman in a starched white apron over a faded blue dress served Amy the breakfast plate of heavy biscuits, watery gravy and weak coffee. Amy passed up the mush.

"Do you mind if we join you? You seem to be the only lady being served."

A large-bosomed woman in a black tailored suit with a lace tie at her throat towered over Amy. The woman's dyed-black hair was pulled severely away from her face into a tight bun. On either side of her stood a blond young lady, each dressed in identical plaid novelty cloth, but there the similarities ended.

The young girl with the milky, opalescent skin scowled and lowered her pale blue eyes to the handkerchief she twisted in her hands. The other, with just a hint of freckles across the sunburned bridge of her nose, smiled with her eyes and mouth as she scanned the Globe dining room.

The older woman cleared her throat.

"I'm—I'm sorry. Please join me. I'm Amy White."

"White? Your father publishes the *Democrat?*"

Amy nodded.

Thin lips smiled. "So pleased to meet you. I'm Mrs. Horace Carrington. May I introduce my daughters Naomi and Rachel?"

"Oh, how wonderful to meet you at last. I met Mr. Carrington the day of The Run."

Naomi's eyes rolled up to stare at the ceiling as she offered a limp hand. "Pleased t'meet you, I'm sure."

Rachel's full mouth widened into an impish grin, and her clear eyes met Amy's as she took her seat.

"Welcome to New Ponca," Amy said cordially.

"I declare, Miss White, this is a terrible town, if you can call it a town." Mrs. Carrington huffed as she seated herself. "Not at all what I expected. But I take my marriage vows very seriously. And when Horace insisted on coming out here, there was nothing I could do. Absolutely nothing."

"I think it's exciting," Rachel said with a grin.

Amy decided she liked the girl.

"You would," sneered Naomi. "Momma cried and cried, but father was so mean."

The large woman flushed.

"Father said it was a great opportunity," Rachel said defensively.

"I suppose Horace is right. And I don't want to give you the wrong impression, Miss White." She paused to smile primly at Amy. "But it's such a hardship bringing my lovely daughters to this place. They should be coming out this year."

"And would have," Naomi whined, "if we'd stayed in St. Louis."

"I'm glad," Rachel said. "All that fussing with dressmakers and planning what you're going to wear to this tea and that—"

"You're going to end up an old maid, Rachel," Naomi hissed, "and I'll not wait for you, even if you are the first-born."

"By two minutes," Rachel laughed.

"Girls! We do not discuss such things in public," Mrs. Carrington sighed. "Although, Miss White, I'm sorry to say there does seem to be a shortage of proper young gentlemen around."

Naomi's eyes scanned the room. "They are so ill-dressed, so—so illiterate and uncouth."

Her mother nodded in agreement. "I'll simply have to find a way to convince Mr. Carrington to send our daughters back to St. Louis to stay with their Aunt

Myrna." She paused for a gulp of air. "There are no schools or churches here in this Godforsaken place. To think I left behind my lovely home to come here. I did, however, insist on bringing my best china and my lovely tea service. I packed them ever so carefully, but I suppose they will only gather dust in this—this town."

Amy found herself defending her new home. "Well, Mrs. Carrington, I'll admit New Ponca isn't much at the moment. But when you look at how much has been accomplished in less than a week, I think you have to be optimistic."

"You mean it was worse than this?" Naomi demanded.

"We only arrived yesterday on the Santa Fe," Mrs. Carrington explained.

Amy put down her coffee cup. "A week ago there was nothing but a sea of tents. Mr. McGuire is pushing efforts for a Presbyterian church. And land has been set aside for a school." She looked at the pouting Naomi. "And as for social gatherings. Well, we can start a ladies' club, can't we?" she challenged. "I hear Mrs. Hampton is having a piano shipped in. Her home on South First will be finished soon, and I should think it will be quite suitable for entertaining."

"I've taken piano lessons for four years," Naomi said.

"Well, we must have a recital. Do you play, too, Rachel?"

Naomi laughed. "Hah! Her? Her head's always stuck in a book."

"Well, we can start a literary group and study club," Amy suggested.

Caught up in Amy's enthusiasm, Rachel clapped her hands. "And what about a riding club? Father promised me a horse."

Naomi groaned. "I'd rather start a Bachelor Girl's Club."

"Well, I suppose we could organize such groups," Mrs. Carrington said, frowning, "but begging your pardon, Miss White, with the exception of yourself, I'm afraid we haven't met a decent lady in this town."

"Well, in truth, I don't know very many ladies yet, either," Amy said. "But I have met Laura Hampton and she's a most gracious lady. And Minnie—Mrs. W. E. Scott." She smiled. "Her husband has a drug store. And there's Arvella and Myrtle Smyth whose father is a carpenter and farmer just south of town. And Maud and Jeanette Barnes, daughters of the town's founder."

Naomi groaned.

Amy folded her napkin and rose. "We'll have to have tea one afternoon and discuss just what we can do to enliven this town for the young people." She smiled. "Now, if you'll excuse me, I must attend to some business for my father."

Amy hoped she had not been too defensive about her town, but she was just as sure that with time New Ponca would boast of social clubs, schools and churches of the finest order. The pride Amy felt in her new home put a spring in her step as she headed for the *Democrat* office.

"Papa, have you written tomorrow's editorial?"

Alfred wiped his ink-stained hands on his apron. "Been too busy. Something on your mind?"

"Well, yes. Schools."

Alfred pushed up his spectacles and wiped his sweaty eyes. "You're thinking of Danny?"

"Not only Danny, but all the other children, like that little girl in the red dress at the drawing."

"The Myatts' daughter?"

She nodded. "And more families are arriving every day. At breakfast, I met Mrs. Carrington and her two daughters—twins."

"Bet Horace was glad to see them." He handed Amy a scrap of newsprint and a thick editing pencil. "Promoting a school for the town will make a fine editorial. You write it."

The Santa Fe blew its whistle and churned through the west end of town rattling the windows of the building.

Alfred frowned and raised his voice. "And then I'll set the type while you go to Cross and pick up the ready-prints from the rail station."

"Me? You want me to write the editorial?"

"I don't see why not. You wanted to be a teacher, didn't you? And you've got more schooling than most people in these parts."

Amy pulled off her gloves and perched on a stool at the counter. How should she start?

The children of this town need a school.

What else should she say? She chewed on the pencil. What was it Papa always said? Tell them who, what, where, when, why and how? Writing was harder work than she thought.

She reread her sentence. She had the "who" and the "what."

She started again.

This town should thank Mr. Barnes for his foresight in setting aside lots on which to build a school.

That took care of the "where."

If New Ponca is to prosper, its citizens must find some way to build a school now. We cannot wait for the town to grow. We cannot wait until all of the other buildings are finished.

So much for "when." Now for "why."

We have a duty to the children of this community. We have a responsibility to the town. Today's scholars are our future leaders. What kind of town will New Ponca be in twenty or thirty years if our children are not taught how to read and write and cipher? What kind of community will we have if we don't instruct our children in the principles of citizenship? What mistakes will future leaders make if they have no understanding of history, of accounting or economics? How sad and dreary this town will be if appreciation for music and the arts is lacking in our citizenry?

Now for the "how."

They would need teachers, but it would sound too self-serving to include her own qualifications. There would be time enough to submit her teaching credentials once the school was built.

"How?" was the unanswered question. Volunteer labor wouldn't be a problem, but funds would be needed for lumber, roofing materials and windows. For books and pencils, desks and blackboards. There were so many things to buy. Certainly her own resources were meager and there were too few men such as Silas Kane and B. S. Barnes who could give a significant amount. Well, she'd leave out the "how." Maybe her editorial would be read by some generous benefactor who would provide the "how."

Quickly she ended the editorial.

In moving to this wilderness, we have all made many sacrifices and faced many hardships. The adversities and difficulties are not over, but surely a tiny portion of our thoughts and efforts can be focused on a school for the town's children, for the town's future. Surely the 1,200 people who call New Ponca their home, and the number grows each day, can find the ways and means to lay the foundation for tomorrow's leaders.

Amy sighed. She was not entirely satisfied with her efforts, but she handed her notes to her father. "I'm sure you can say it more eloquently."

She fiddled with her gloves, straightened papers on the counter and fussed while watching out of the corner of her eye as he read it. She wanted his approval, but she just couldn't get down on paper what she was feeling inside. And worst of all, she couldn't figure out how to make a school for New Ponca a reality. Admiration for her father's journalistic expertise grew.

Her father peered over his glasses at her. "I may just give you a job. It's a fine editorial, Amy. I'll put your name on it."

"Oh, no, Papa! You mustn't. It—it might not receive the same acceptance. It might not seem ladylike and—and—"

"Ladylike?" he bellowed. "I never know whether you're being a lady, a farmer or a carpenter these days."

"Don't forget 'delivery boy,' Papa," she teased as she walked out the door.

Arriving in Cross, Amy oversaw the loading of the ready-prints and wired the Eastern news syndicate to double their order next week. Instead of heading the team of grays south to Ponca, Amy reined them east, toward her homestead. The arbor on the Arkansas River would offer a cool respite from the midday sun. Besides, she would not let Colby Grant frighten her away.

A smile played on Amy's lips as she reined the grays at the gateway she and Danny had erected. It might not be the strongest, straightest or most flawless entryway she had ever seen, but it was certainly the most satisfying.

Danny was right. She had to think of a name for her homestead.

Slowly, Amy drove the team through the archway of the new timbers and headed for the arbor. Wagon wheels turned over the fertile grassland, crushed bouquets of dried thistle, bare ground—bare ground?

Amy yanked back on the reins. The sod had been plowed and carried away, leaving an angry bare spot. The area was not large and the prairie grass would soon reclaim it. But she was furious at the rape of her land. Amy followed the trail of furrows and wagon-wheel tracks, her eyes roving the horizon for people, for horses, for Colby Grant.

Amy knew what she would find before she reached the clearing some hundred yards north of her arbor. In the side of a small hill were the beginnings of a soddy.

She tied the reins to the wagon brake and jumped down. On closer inspection, she saw the structure was half soddy and half dugout. Someone, and it could be no one else but Colby Grant, had dug some ten feet back into the hillside. A heavy ridge pole braced with smaller logs held up the roof. In front of the dugout, newly cut sod had been laid three bricks high around the log framework. Openings had been left for a doorway to the east and and a window to the south.

"So Mr. Grant thought he could scare me away, did he? He thought he could build a home on my homestead and I'd roll over and play dead. Well, Mr. Grant, there's plenty of good red blood in my veins, thank you."

Amy put her body weight against the logs framing the doorway and shoved. The rough bark picked up her sleeve. The post was buried deep and held firm. She kicked at one of the sod pieces baked into rock hardness by the September sun. The sod dislodged and fell inside. She shoved another sod brick, and another, and another. When she was satisfied with her destruction, she remounted the wagon and drove into New Ponca.

Amy helped her father unload the ready-prints as she raved and ranted about Colby Grant's latest maneuver to claim her homestead. To her chagrin, Alfred voiced little concern.

Leaving the empty wagon at the livery, Amy returned to the hotel. Mr. Pearson darted out of the dining room as she started up the outside stairway.

"Miss White, the bathtub got here today. Want me to send up some hot water?"

Amy brushed at her dusty sleeve. "I look that disreputable?"

The man pulled at his suspenders and guffawed. "You never looked prettier, Miss White, but you said to let you know—"

"Yes, of course, Mr. Pearson. You don't know how I'm looking forward to a real bath."

"You and everyone else in this hotel. But I told 'em you got the first crack at it."

"I appreciate your thoughtfulness."

"Well, I'll send Hennessey up with the water."

Amy ran eagerly up the stairs and to her room. A quick glance told her that nothing had been disturbed. The trunk remained untouched. She supposed if she had to choose between locks on the doors and a bathtub, she'd take the latter. Quickly, Amy slipped the pins from her tresses and let her long dark hair flow around her shoulders. She dug out her wrapper and crossed the hall to the bathroom, pausing a moment to read the sign on the door: KNOCK BEFORE ENTERING.

She rapped on the door.

"C'mon in," Hennessey answered. The black man poured in the last pail of hot water. "Ah's got it all ready, missy," he said through the rising steam.

"Thank you, Hennessey."

Amy looked around the room. The enameled tub looked huge, long enough to recline in and deep enough to sink luxuriously up to her neck. There were no faucets, no running water, but the drain was piped through the floor. A cane chair with a ninety-nine-cent price mark on its oaken back had been placed before a dressing table on which fresh towels and a bar of camomile soap lay. In one corner was an upholstered commode.

Amy tested the water and found it deliciously warm. She propped the chair under the doorknob, draped her wrapper across the seat and undressed. Placing her skirt and bodice on the dressing table, she sat on the commode and removed her stockings, camisole and other undergarments. These, too, she stacked neatly.

Rising, Amy pirouetted around the room. She blushed as she caught sight of her naked reflection in the mirror. Anticipation of the bath had swollen the tips of her small, firm breasts. The tawny skin was smooth and taut on her flat abdomen. Her waist tapered to softly rounded hips. A dark luxuriant heart of ringlets nested between her long, slim legs. She thought of Colby Grant—No! She thought of Silas Kane. What would he think of her body? Was she too heavy in the hips, too small in the breasts? Amy shook her long mane, lifted the curls from her face and frowned at the birthmark. Had Silas ever noticed the flaw?

"Oh, dear. I forgot my lotion." The White Lily formula seemed to make the dark spot on her forehead lighter, less noticeable, and its pleasant fragrance would perfume her bathwater.

Donning her wrapper, Amy removed the chair and cautiously opened the door. She looked up and down the vacant hall and darted into her room. She wrestled the trunk away from the wall and searched through it for her miracle cream.

A chair scraped across the floor in the adjoining room.

"Papa, is that you?"

The door opened. "Getting dressed for supper, lass?"

Amy hugged her father. "As soon as I have my bath. A real bath, Papa. Mr. Pearson's tub came today."

"Well, I don't know if you'll condescend to sit down at the same table with a dirty old windbag like me."

She laughed and wriggled her nose. "Well, if I don't find my White Lily, I may smell more like camomile soap." Finding the fragile bottle, she locked the trunk again.

"I'll see you downstairs, lass."

With her lotion in hand, Amy peered into the hallway

and without hesitation entered the bathroom door.

"What th' hell—!"

"You!" Amy sputtered.

Colby Grant reclined in the tub, water up to his armpits, a cheroot in his mouth and a shot glass of bourbon in his hand.

"You're in my bathwater!" She stomped her foot and clutched the wrapper to her breast.

He blew a ringlet of smoke into the air and grinned. "You forgot to knock." His hair was damp and looked more auburn than gold. Droplets of water glistened on his bronzed shoulders.

Amy turned her head. "This was my bathwater. I had gone across the hall to get my—" she felt dizzy—"my clothes—my clothes are over there. See?" She turned to face him again. He had laid aside his cheroot and shot glass and was vigorously soaping his arms and chest.

"Want to wash my back?" The damp mustache twitched.

Trembling, Amy shook her fist. "How dare you?"

A smile spread across Colby's face, and his brazen blue eyes roved over Amy's thinly clad body. "I wish I did dare."

"You're drunk and if you don't get out of my bathtub, I'll—I'll—"

"You'll what? Tell the management?" He laughed and placed his bar of soap on the floor by the tub. "And just how are you going to explain being here in the first place?"

"Get out of here this instant!" Damn Colby Grant! And Mr. Pearson for not having locks on the doors. "Get out of my bath!"

Colby placed his arms on the rim of the tub. "Are you sure?"

"Yes, I'm—" Amy sucked in her breath and found her gaze meeting daring blue eyes. Colby's muscles bulged at the shoulders and rippled across his chest. His knees bent and his arms straightened. Water splashed on the floor. And then his upper torso was rising slowly out of the water. Rivulets raced down through the ringlets on his chest to his narrow waistline. There was a glimpse of white skin, a navel, a thin line of hair running down—down to—

"No!" She found the strength to turn away. "Please wait! I'll just get my clothes and—and—" She shut her eyes and took a step toward the dressing stand to retrieve her clothes.

"Watch the soap!" Colby cried out.

But it was too late. Amy felt her bare foot slip out from under her. Her eyes flew open, her arms flailed the air, and her dark tresses fell across her face. The bottle of White Lily clattered to the floor. She cried out just as Colby's upper torso sprang out of the bathtub to catch her in his wet, strong arms.

"Let me go." Over Colby's shoulder, the mirror reflected his wet buttocks, his strong thighs rising out of the tub. She closed her eyes and tried to shove him away. The force of her energy threw Colby off balance. His feet slipped in the tub and he fell back into the water. With a cry, Amy fell in after him.

"Damn!" Colby whispered.

Still locked in Colby's arms, Amy raised her head above the waves of sloshing water and gasped for breath. She could smell the camomile soap, feel the throbbing in his throat and the firmness of his jaw. A wispy, damp curl from his mustache tickled her ear. She trembled as he placed his lips against her cheek.

"Are you hurt, Amy?" he whispered.

Sputtering and gasping for air, she shook her head.

Beneath her, Colby's body convulsed. His lips twitched beneath the mustache that rained droplets of water, and then his deep, rumbling laughter erupted.

Amy struggled against the strong arms clutching her to him. She felt the water drip down her nose as her hands pushed against him. It was a ridiculous scene. She fought to restrain herself, but a titter escaped, a giggle bubbled up until her body convulsed with laughter.

They clung to each other, their wet bodies racking with laughter, their lungs gasping for oxygen.

"I guess—I got—my bath—after all," Amy said between gasps.

When the hysterics subsided, Amy's head rested on Colby's shoulder, her arms across his stomach. She quivered and his muscles tightened. The water rippled gently. Amy found she did not want to move. The water was warm and soothing, and through her sodden wrapper, Colby's hands gently massaged her shoulders.

Colby turned the docile Amy to face him. His lips brushed against the dark spot on her forehead. He nibbled at her nose. Yep, you took whatever life offered you and savored it for the moment. And sometimes life's offerings were pretty spectacular.

"Where in the hell did you get those smoky gray eyes?" he said huskily. "Every time I look at you I feel like I'm having to fight my way out of some damn cloud."

Amy started to tell him how his own bold, daring gaze made her weaken, but his mouth sought hers and she found herself responding hungrily.

"Let me bathe you," he whispered. He eased the wrapper off Amy's right shoulder and kissed her in the hollow above her breast.

Amy fought to recover her senses. What was she doing in this bathtub with a man—a disrobed man—the man who was trying to steal her homestead—the man who was building a soddy on her land? She struggled against Colby's embrace, against the strange desires awakened in her.

"N—no," she said softly.

Colby's strong arms released her. But when she

did not move, he lifted her bodily out of the tub without rising.

"You'd better get out of here," Colby growled softly.

Amy was shocked by her reflection in the mirror. The sodden, transparent wapper revealed every curve of her body. Water from her hair and body pooled on the floor at her bare feet. She looked like a drowned rat.

Amy snatched a towel from the dresser and gathered up her clothing. "You are the most despicable man I have ever met. You—you are a thief, a liar and probably a cheat. And—and you should be ashamed of that rag you call a newspaper. Ha! You can't even spell!" With her free hand, she turned the knob on the door.

"P-r-o-v-o-c-a-t-i-v-e," she heard behind her.

She whirled to face Colby and hissed through the open doorway. "And you are i-n-s-u-f-f-e-r-a-b-l-e!"

"Why, Miss Amy, what's happened to you?"

Amy turned to face Silas Kane. A frown creased his brow and comprehension flushed his face as his eyes left Amy's water-soaked attire to the bathtub where Colby was relighting his cheroot.

Chapter Seven

Amy slammed the bathroom door behind her and faced Silas Kane. A vein in his pallid temple ticked nervously. His thin lips pursed and dark, narrow eyebrows arched and knitted. With a scowl, he observed her damp, unruly hair, the dripping sleeves of her thin wrapper, the towel she hugged about her. From behind the bathroom door came the baritone strains of "Oh, Susannah."

Amy's hand went to her throat. "I—I forgot to knock."

The boisterous soloist sang louder. "I come from Alabama with a banjo on my kne-e-e-e."

Silas raised his gold-tipped cane and shook it menacingly at the bathroom door. "He should be horsewhipped!" Silas hissed. His cane punctuated the air with each word.

"Horse—horsewhipped?" Amy edged toward her room, clutching the towel around her soaked body.

"For dashing water on a refined lady like you." He tapped his cane near the puddle at her feet. "I assure you, Miss White," he said, his voice rising, "there are a few gentlemen in this town who would—"

Amy backed slowly into the room, leaving a wet trail on the floor.

Kane's face reddened. "My apologies." He squared his shoulders, shifted his eyes to the bare rafters overhead and exhaled audibly. "I shan't detain you any longer. I'm sure you want to dress. Your father has graciously accepted my invitation for the two of you to join me for dinner." He tipped his hat and turned on his heels and walked toward the outside stairway.

In the safety of her room, Amy put her face in her hands. Tears of humiliation seeped through her dark lashes. To be caught in such a disheveled condition, in such a compromising position, and by Silas, had to be the most embarrassing moment of her life. A nervous hiccup shook her body. And yet Silas had found a logical explanation for the ridiculous scene. She pinched her nose and held her breath to stifle a hysterical giggle. Incredulously, Kane had concluded that Colby had thrown water on her, that she had been an innocent victim.

It served Colby right. The despicable man had dared to kiss her, to—to—

Amy's fingertips moved delicately to her swollen lips and up to her wet temples, to the blue birthmark on her forehead. The downy hair on her body tingled at the memory of his wet mustache against her skin, his strong arms embracing her. Even now, the rosy tips of her breasts were erect and hard. She closed her eyelids and could feel his kneading hands on her shoulders. She inhaled deeply and the sweet aroma of his cigar came wafting back. The sensual laugh that rumbled deep in his chest, before it tumbled out of his moist, demanding mouth, echoed in her ears.

"Amy?" Her father knocked on the connecting door.

"Just a minute, Papa. I'm not dressed." What was she

doing standing here in wet clothing thinking about that contemptible Colby Grant?

"Well, Kane suggested we eat a little earlier than usual since Doc Taylor and Olin Keck are organizing the Freemasons tonight. So let me know when you're ready."

Panic gripped her. Colby would surely be there. How could she go downstairs and face those unsettling blue eyes, the ravishing mouth beneath the debauching mustache? How could she bear to sit in the same room with a man who knew she had touched his sun-bronzed skin, or knew that she knew the tan faded to pristine whiteness at his waistline? It would be unbearable.

"Papa, would—would you mind if I dined alone in my room tonight?"

"You feeling all right?"

"I'm fine, Papa. It's—it's been a long day. And—and the hot bath made me very sleepy."

"Well, I'll send Mabel up with a tray. But Kane's going to be disappointed."

Amy felt a moment of regret, but she couldn't appear in the dining room. What if Silas confronted Colby? What if her lie was exposed?

Colby had plenty of reason to want to humiliate her. He would do anything to get his hands on her homestead. He wouldn't wait to seek his revenge when he discovered she had tried to destroy his soddy.

She shuddered to think how far he might go to rid his *Republican* newspaper of her father's competition. If Colby regaled his barroom cohorts with scenes from their bathroom encounter, if he humiliated her with the scintillating details, she would never be able to hold up her head. No matter how hard she toiled for the benefit of the town, no matter how deserving, she would never command respect. The malicious gossip would be tantamount to being tarred and feathered and run out of town on a rail. All she had struggled for, all the miseries suffered in the run, the tortures she had inflicted on Sultan, the dangers she had faced from the claim jumpers, all would have been for nought. But worse than her own degradation would be watching her shame nullify her father's accomplishments and destroy his rekindled spirit.

Amy covered her face with her hands and blinked back hot tears. She heard her father's door close and his footsteps fade in the hallway. With a painful heaviness and despairing numbness, she shed her damp garments.

The rap on the door startled her. That couldn't be Mabel. Perhaps her father had returned. Amy draped a towel around her nude torso.

"Amy, it's Colby."

Her hand halted on the doorknob. What was he doing here? Did he think she was some easy trollop? Quickly, she shoved the heavy trunk in front of her door, the metal strips scraping against the floor.

"Amy, I want to apologize." His husky voice was deceitfully mellow, low and barely audible through the soft pine door. "I know you're in there."

She dried her body with harsh vigor, the towel leaving her skin feeling raw.

"I'll leave your beauty lotion here by the door. Not that you need it," he chuckled softly, "but you left it in the bathroom."

The rogue! She bit her tongue and quelled the burning desire to hurl disparaging epithets through the door. Her fists knotted in anger, her naked body shook, and fury pounded at her temples. Amy heard Colby's footsteps move away from her door. Her anger gave way to relief, and something else. Disappointment?

"*Mon Dieu,* Amy Elizabeth White," she berated herself. "How can you romanticize about a man so abhorrent?"

Nevertheless, lethargy weighted her arms as she slipped on a cambric gown and slid beneath the sheets on her cot. She was still staring at the ceiling when Mabel brought her tray of corned beef and cabbage, and the bottle of lotion she had picked up outside the door.

Amy let Mabel fuss over her. "I reckon you're coming down with something," the woman said as she plumped the pillow and straightened the coverlet. "Eat all your meat," she commanded as she placed the tray across Amy's lap. "You'll feel better tomorrow, you'll see."

But she wouldn't feel better until Colby Grant was off her homestead and out of her life. Finishing her tray, Amy slipped out of bed and retrieved the homestead papers from the trunk. Until there were locks on her door, she had to find a better hiding place.

She rapped lightly on her father's connecting door. Satisfied he was downstairs, Amy tiptoed into his room and to the wooden trunk at the foot of his bed. It was unlikely that Colby would search her father's things. And unlike her smaller trunk, it couldn't be carried off by one man, not even a man as strong as Colby Grant.

Amy quietly opened the trunk and began removing its contents. If Colby Grant was brazen enough to search Papa's trunk, he'd surely be discovered before he could get to the bottom of it and find the homestead papers.

Her father's clothes took up the top two-thirds of the trunk. Beneath them, Amy found Hannah's Bible. It fell open to the family record.

In fading black ink, Hannah and Alfred's marriage in August of 1870 had been noted and in the column for births was the lone notation. "Amy Elizabeth White, approximately two years old, adopted June 5th, 1877, Milford, Nebraska."

In the column for special events, someone had written the story of her parents. "Pierre and Mimi Loutrec, parents of a small child, now known as Amy, died of consumption in Milford, Nebraska, in June, 1877, while traveling with a wagon train headed for California."

Amy wondered what her life would have been like if her parents had lived. Would there have been brothers and sisters? She would have liked that. Would she have liked California? They say the sun shines every day. But she would miss the colorful months of fall, the blankets of snow in winter and the smell of the rains before jonquils burst through the ground in spring.

She sighed and set aside the Bible. There were fading pictures of Hannah and Alfred on their wedding day, a picture of Hannah holding a child in her arms and one of Alfred holding a toddler with dark hair on a pony. Amy smiled. Alfred and Hannah had been loving and tolerant parents.

Amy picked up a small box. Something inside rattled. She opened the lid and unwrapped white tissue paper to reveal a string of mussel shells. Puzzled, Amy held them up to the light. The nacre inside each shell shimmered with the iridescence of mother-of-pearl.

"How lovely," Amy whispered as she straightened the sinew strands at each end. She couldn't remember Hannah ever wearing the necklace, but Alfred must have made the ornament for Hannah during their courting days. Carefully, Amy rewrapped the shells in the tissue paper and placed them back in the box.

With the sound of footsteps in the hallway, Amy quickly hid her homestead papers below the box of shells, replaced the pictures, the Bible and her father's clothing. She crept quietly back to her room. It would take a thorough search by that despicable Colby Grant to find her homestead papers now.

The thought of Colby Grant brought back her frustration. She paced the floor until bedtime, relieved that her father did not disturb her when he returned from the Freemasons' meeting. But sleep came in fitful spurts with dreams of Colby Grant's arms holding her close as an angry Silas Kane looked on, and then laughter rumbled out of Colby's throat as he raised his arm in triumph with the coveted homestead papers clutched in his hands.

After a long and restless night, Amy entered the *Democrat* office in a foul mood. She snapped at Danny who came in jingling coins in his pocket and handed her Colby's morning paper. She gave the *Republican* a cursory glance and tossed it aside with a flagrant insult that sent Danny shuffling warily out the door.

She was short with her father, responding to his running commentary with curt disinterest as they prepared the afternoon edition of the *Democrat*. All she could think of was how to rid herself and her homestead of Colby Grant. And short of cold-blooded murder, she had thought of no solutions.

When the last sheet was pulled from the press, Alfred wiped his ink-stained hands on spoiled newsprint. "Something bothering you, lass?"

"No," she sighed.

Amy untied her apron and turned away. Most of her wrath and trepidation had dissipated with the hard labor of the afternoon, but the feeling of impending doom was hard to shake.

Alfred pulled out a clean handkerchief to clean his glasses and dry the sweat from his ruddy face. "Go back to the Globe and rest a spell, lass. I'll see you at supper time."

"I am a little tired, Papa. Will you ask Mabel to bring up a tray again tonight?"

The white bushy brows frowned. "Maybe I'd better have Doc Taylor take a look at you."

"Doc Taylor? What on earth for?"

"You seem to be under the weather. Barking at me one minute. Mum as a clam the next. Eating your meals in your room—"

"I don't need a doctor, Papa! Can't a woman be—be—" She ran out of the building and down the street before the threatened tears could spill.

Amy's mood carried over through Friday. She avoided any further questions by letting her father believe that her monthlies had come upon her. She stayed away from the homestead for fear of running into Colby Grant. And she hadn't heard from Silas Kane. Perhaps he knew the truth. Perhaps everyone knew.

By Saturday evening, Amy was as angry at herself as she was at Colby Grant. "Amy White, it's your word against his," she admonished her distraught image in the mirror. "You're not going to let him run you out of town, are you?" She raised her chin, straightened her spine and took a deep breath. "Then it's time to stop hiding in your room like a miserable coward!"

With staunch fortitude, Amy entered the Globe dining room that evening on her father's arm. The Carrington family greeted her warmly. Several men at the counter nodded politely with no sign of having any knowledge of her humiliation at the hands of Colby Grant.

Frank McCarthy strode over to their table. "Haven't had a chance to tell you, Alfred, but that was a fine editorial." The livery owner clamped his hand on Alfred's shoulder. "You can count on me."

Alfred stood to greet the man, his thumbs stuck in the pockets of the vest covering his broad expanse. "Guess you're the last to hear, Frank. I wish I could claim the credit, but the accolades go to Amy."

"Papa, you promised." A flush of pride rose in her cheeks.

"I promised not to put your name on it and I didn't." Crow's feet crinkled around the edge of his spectacles.

"Right fine piece, Miss Amy." McCarthy smiled.

"I—I think everyone agrees that a school is important, but it will take money . . ."

McCarthy amplified his voice. "Listen up, folks," he said to the room full of diners. "This little lady thinks we ought to have a school, and seeing as how I've got a couple of young'uns, I'm going to start the fund with ten dollars." He pushed several worn bills into Amy's hands. "Now, the rest of you ante up."

"Here's my five, Miss Amy. Wish it could be more," said the carpenter, Olin Keck. "And maybe the Masonic Lodge can help. It's the kind of project Freemasons like to tackle."

Men rose from tables and counter stools to pile ones and fives before a flustered Amy. At Mrs. Carrington's urging, Horace handed Amy a few singles. Brother Jim McGuire reckoned as how a school came before a church. "'Sides, there's no school on Sundays. Perhaps, we can have services in the schoolhouse."

"What's going on here?" Silas Kane closed the door and tipped his hat at Amy.

"Miss Amy's collecting money for the new school," someone said.

"Fine cause. Fine cause."

Amy smelled his bay rum fragrance as he flicked imaginary road dust from his coat lapels. She smiled at the young banker.

"I'll add a hundred dollars to that," Silas said, hanging his cane on the back of a chair at Amy's table.

The dining room fell silent. Amy was embarrassed. She appreciated his donation, but his largess had fallen like a shadow across the conviviality of the room. Men whose meager offerings had been given in the passion of the moment, without thought of next week's food and lodging, turned away to reprimand themselves for their illogical generosity.

Distressed by the awkward stillness in the dining room, Amy got to her feet. "Thank you, gentlemen. Mr. Kane's gift is appreciated, but most of us can only give a small amount."

Colby Grant entered the dining room. When he saw Amy, his eyebrows arched and a smile played on his lips beneath the twitching mustache. He touched the brim of his hat in greeting and walked to the serving counter.

Momentarily flustered, Amy started again. "Most of us staked our last dollar to come to this new land and start a new life."

Colby sat down on a stool and pushed his Stetson back on his head. He rested his elbows on the counter behind him and stretched his long legs in front of him and looked at Amy with a slight twitch to his mustache.

Amy quivered at Colby's impertinence and tried to recoup her thoughts. "The school. We—we don't have much, but we have something worth more than money. We have talent. Mr. Keck is a fine carpenter." She turned to Horace Carrington. "And you have nails and hinges that we'll need to build the school." She smiled at Frank McCarthy. "And you can haul lumber from the sawmill."

Amy's vision swept the room to stop briefly on Mrs. Carrington and Mrs. Hampton. "We can sand and paint, make curtains." She laughed nervously. "We will need some money, of course, but if we each give a little, we can have our school."

Nate Hampton shoved back his chair. "My family is staying at the Lewis Hotel while we're building our house, so I'll spread the word over there."

Peter Pearson, the owner of the Globe, stepped out of the kitchen. "Here's some fruit jars to hold the donations. We can set these up in stores over town."

Amy's vision blurred with gratefulness. "Thank you. Thank you," she whispered.

Kane rose to stand at her side. "I see we're going to raise more money than one should be carrying around, so tomorrow I'll open an account in the name of the New Ponca School."

Colby lifted his well-worn Stetson and waved it in

Kane's direction. "And Kane will pay top interest, I'm sure."

The challenge from Colby was unmistakable. The diners held their breath.

Kane's eyes hardened at Grant's effrontery. "Of course. Of course."

Amy smiled defiantly at Colby as Silas took his seat. With that announcement, the festive air of the room was restored. Men cheered and shook Kane's hand or slapped him on the back. Women and children clapped their hands.

Amy felt proud to be a part of the town. Her smile took in every man, woman and child in the room, but her gaze rushed past Colby Grant lest she find those deep pools of blue mocking her, destroying her shored-up confidence.

Colby swiveled around on his stool and gave his order to Mabel.

Drained, Amy eased herself back into her chair. She basked under Alfred's fatherly pride while Kane counted the odd assortment of bills.

"Well, Miss Amy, it looks like we're building a school. We have one hundred and forty dollars."

Amy's enthusiasm wavered. It would take five or ten times that to erect a school building. And Colby Grant hadn't offered a dime. Well, what had she expected from that—that—one-eyed, despicable, claim-jumping, soddy-building, lady-molesting bushwhacker?

On finishing his coffee, Alfred offered a cigar to Kane.

"Hate to pass up a good smoke, Alfred," Kane admitted, "but I thought a walk in the fresh air might do Miss Amy some good."

"Good idea. Maybe some exercise will put some color in those cheeks."

With one quick glance at Colby's rigid back, Amy took Kane's arm.

For Amy and for most of the settlers, the hour after dining was the best time of day. The sun waned on the horizon and the harsh winds calmed. A hint of autumn chased away the day's searing heat and a semblance of order settled over the town.

The around-the-clock noise and confusion ceased as carpenters laid down their hammers and saws. The forge cooled and the anvil at Stacy's Blacksmith fell silent. Drovers reined in their teams in front of tent cafes to fill their plates with hearty stew and cornbread.

The signal for the evening procession came when Chief White Eagle ordered his elk-horn chair removed from in front of Paley's saloon and loaded aboard his wagon. Most of the other Indians joined him as he abandoned the town for the day.

Townsfolk poured from their rooms to stroll down dusty lanes or on the occasional boardwalk past the latest construction. Shop owners closed their doors and joined the parade. Lone settlers abandoned their tents to jaw at railings or join thirsty ranchers for a friendly drink at the bar. Farmers and wide-eyed children raised dust as they rolled past in their spring wagons on their way home to half-finished soddies and dugouts. A piano in Paley's saloon tinkled softly and a dance hall girl in red taffeta lounged wistfully against a swinging door.

For a while Amy could believe she lived in a progressive municipality somewhere in Kansas or Missouri instead of a struggling frontier town thrashing violently with pangs of birth.

Amy sighed audibly.

"Penny for your thoughts," Silas asked.

Amy blushed. "I was just thinking how beautiful the night is. How calm and peaceful it seems." And how the cool air lessens the smell of the open latrines, she thought to herself. Silas patted her gloved hand. They both knew that this halcyon period would be brief.

At the first hint of darkness, when lanterns flickered

into life, the calm would be fractured. "Camp Town Races" would come hammering from the ivories. Thirty-dollar-a-month cowhands would stampede into town looking for Saturday night thrills—whiskey for parched throats, a royal flush at a poker table, and a stolen kiss from painted lips. As the night wore on, voices would rise and raucous laughter would erupt as inhibitions were dispelled. Contesting homesteaders would glare at each other over shot glasses of raw liquor colored with tobacco juice. The age-old battle between cattlemen and sodbusters would erupt from brazen taunts into drunken brawls and flying missiles. Unhealed wounds of the Civil War would surface and bullets and fists might fly. It was then that the decent folk would scatter to the safety of their homes, however modest or crude.

But for this brief hour, you could believe you lived in a civilized world.

"Hello!" Mayor Barnes offered his hand to Kane and tipped his hat to Amy as he hurried past.

"Good evening, Barnes." Kane greeted the man with a smile.

Amy marveled at the lack of animosity between the bankers. It was more than civility. Kane had supported Barnes wholeheartedly, knowing from the first they would be competitors.

Would she ever get to the point that she could feel the same way about Colby Grant? Not as long as that insufferable man was on her property!

Kane offered his hand in greeting to Will Chase who was just stepping out of his tent drugstore.

"Starting the store building next week, Silas," he smiled. "Sure appreciate the loan."

"My pleasure, my pleasure."

Kane introduced Amy to Col. George Miller and his son Joe, both of whom were in range clothes with high-domed Texas hats, and pistols on their hips.

"Just came in to wet our whistles before Joe heads for Mexico," the colonel drawled in a voice as leathery as his face.

"Bringing up another herd?" Kane said to the man who appeared to be little more than Amy's age. "Need a draft?"

"Much obliged," the colonel interrupted, "but Joe's been goin' down theah for nigh on ten years by himself. Reckon his word is good 'nuff for most folks." He smiled at Amy. "Just heard, Miss Amy, that you're trying to build a school. I believe in education. Helped the Poncas set up their boarding school a few years back."

"Oh, Colonel," Amy gushed. "I'd be most grateful for your support."

Amy and Silas walked on down the street and met the Nate Hampton family. Kane and Mr. Hampton talked about the prudence of credit to particular homesteaders while the two ladies chatted.

Mrs. Hampton adjusted her stylish bonnet. "Oh, Miss White, our house is almost finished and I'm having a tea next week. I do hope you can come. Carry Nation has promised that she and David will be here."

"Carry Nation? I'm afraid I haven't met all the homesteaders."

"Oh, she isn't a homesteader. Leastwise not of the Cherokee Strip. They homesteaded last year over in Day County near Seiling. But they are very well known in Kansas and Oklahoma Territory for their missionary work. I'm sure you'll find them quite interesting. Especially Mrs. Nation." She turned to her husband and laughed. "Of course, Mr. Hampton thinks she's far too outspoken for a woman."

"I'd be delighted to come." Amy smiled, relieved once again that Colby Grant had shown a small streak of decency and no gossip had reached Mrs. Hampton's ears.

"By the way, Miss Amy," Nate Hampton interjected. "Fine thing you're doing about the school."

Splintering glass from across the street cut off Amy's reply. The night's first saloon fight reminded them all that the hour was getting late. The Hamptons said their goodbyes and picked up their pace as they fled toward the Lewis Hotel.

With Amy's hand resting lightly on his left arm, Kane turned north off Grand Avenue and headed back to the Globe Hotel.

"It seems everyone's singing your praises, Miss Amy."

"Hun-gha!" A stooped figure smelling of drink and urine loomed from the shadows of the alley, his hand outstretched, a blanket around his bare shoulders, braids falling beneath a black hat with a single feather.

"Oh-h-h!" Startled, Amy drew closer to Kane. She recognized the scarred face and the flattened nose of the Indian who had trespassed on her land at the river.

"Away with you," Silas said sternly as he waved his cane and took a step to move around the Ponca.

Another Indian stepped from the shadows and blocked their way. It was the old Indian's companion.

"Give him money," the tall, young Ponca with the long straight hair and pocked face ordered. He was still wearing the plaid shirt and cowboy denims. But now, Amy was so near she could see that his scarred face was much darker than the old Indian's, almost the color of mahogany, and his solemn dark eyes were set deep above high cheekbones.

"Shines White hungry."

"Most likely thirsty," Kane snarled and waved his cane. "Away with you!"

The old Indian threw up his hand, yanked off his feathered hat and grunted. *"Tonde Xtha. Tonde Xtha."*

The tall Indian stepped forward. His eyes narrowed

and a slight smile played on his lips as he stared into Amy's face.

A noticeable shiver went through her and she stepped back.

Silas swung his cane. "Get back, you dirty, stinking Indian!"

The swarthy face darkened, the brooding eyes sparked like flint. His shoulders tensed and hands slowly drew into a fist as he stared at Silas defiantly.

"No, Roughface." The old Indian's voice was guttural. He pointed to his own forehead and shook his fingers as if they were hot.

Roughface's eyes flitted to Amy, and for a moment the pocked face relaxed. But then his eyes darted to Kane. He sneered and spat on the ground, narrowly missing the toe of Kane's patent leather shoe. Like quicksilver the two Indians slid into the shadows.

"Disrespectful animals!" hissed Kane. "Are you all right, Miss Amy?"

Although somewhat shaken, Amy nodded. She thought she had become accustomed to seeing Indians. She had learned to ignore their stoical faces and veer around them as she went about her daily chores, but she could not shake off the chill that sheathed her now.

"Roughface certainly is an appropriate name," Amy said, shivering.

"They're filthy people. It's a shame the smallpox epidemic of a few years ago didn't wipe out all of them."

Amy shuddered.

Kane added, "We can't have those heathens hanging around town scaring folks to death. It's time we had some law and order here. I've already talked to Barnes about hiring us a lawman."

"Oh, Miss Amy?" a young girl's voice called.

Amy turned to see the Carrington family approaching. Rachel waved her arms to get Amy's attention.

"Momma, she's embarrassing me," complained

Naomi who trailed behind her parents.

"You'll never guess what's happening?"

"What's happening, Rachel?"

"A box supper to raise money for the school."

"A box supper?" Amy looked at Kane and back to the Carringtons.

"Horace," Kane asked, "what's this about a box supper?"

"Well, Colby Grant has suggested we hold a box supper as a fund-raiser for the new school," the hardware man said. "I'm on the committee to help set it up. You can read all the details in the *Republican* next Thursday."

"A box supper? Isn't that a marvelous idea, Miss White?" Rachel asked.

Amy couldn't resist smiling at the young girl's excitement.

"Father." Naomi tugged at Horace's arm. "I simply won't go unless you promise to buy my box. I would be humiliated if no one selected mine."

Grand Avenue suddenly erupted into a roar of confusion. Dust churned from the thundering hooves of cow ponies. Colt .44s cracked the air. Imitation war whoops rent the skies.

"Must be the Blocker outfit. I heard they'd just finished with roundup," Kane shouted over the noise.

"Hurry, girls. It's time to go in," Mrs. Carrington fussed.

Amy smelled cigar smoke and looked over Rachel's shoulder. She lowered her gaze at the sight of the mustache beneath the Stetson.

"Oh, Momma, must we go in now?" Rachel pleaded. "I want to look at the horses." But the girl's eyes were on Colby. "Evening, Mr. Grant."

"Ugh!" Naomi grimaced. "Sometimes, Rachel, I would swear you are twelve years old instead of sixteen."

Rachel shifted her gaze from Colby to her sister. "Miss Amy likes horses. She rides Sultan all the time."

"Well, I—I—" Amy didn't really want to get involved in any discussion that involved Colby Grant.

Colby smiled at Rachel. "Miss White's Arabian is a fine horse. As fine as any you'll find at the races tomorrow."

"Races?" But Amy's voice was drowned out by another brouhaha erupting on Grand Avenue.

Colby took Rachel's arm as they strolled farther down Second Street away from the din. "That bunch of mangy rawhide down on Grand right now isn't worth your time, Rachel. Wait until tomorrow. At the big race, you can see some of the finest horseflesh in the country."

Rachel's overt adulation for Colby Grant surprised Amy. She supposed his lean-hardened frame, his bold, blue eyes and of course, his white Stetson and that golden mustache that seemed to dance on command would cause many a young lady to have the vapors. But Amy was no schoolgirl with post-puberty stirrings of romance. Perhaps she should warn Rachel, who obviously couldn't see the arrogance in the man's sensual mouth or the ruthless determination in that handsome, firm jaw.

"What race?" Amy asked Colby directly, ignoring Kane's tug on her arm.

"Would have sworn that Danny brought you a paper this morning, Miss White." He brushed down his mustache. "Jim Kennedy has invited a stable down from Independence, Kansas."

Amy battled to maintain a stoic expression. She would not give Colby the satisfaction of hearing her admit she had not read the *Republican* or that she was upset by being scooped again.

"Well," Kane said. "I'll put my money on Kennedy's filly, Black Silk. And I've seen his trotter, King Okla, in action. Who owns the Independence stable?"

"Eliza Carpenter."

"Well," Kane said, smiling confidently, "doubt if she has anything that can best what Kennedy's got with that sire of his."

"Symboleer's the best all right," Horace agreed. "And Golden Girl and Linen are fine brood mares."

"Horace—Horace," Mrs. Carrington pleaded, "this—this indelicate conversation . . ." she finished lamely.

Colby grinned at Kane. "I haven't seen Kennedy's stock, but Eliza Carpenter's a fine judge of horse-flesh."

"She's a woman, truly?" Rachel clapped her hands. "Do you know her?"

Colby nodded and smiled down at Rachel. "She's got the best racing stable in the country."

"Heard she ran a whorehouse," Kane whispered to Horace unaware that Amy overheard.

Horace looked uncomfortable.

"A stable is a stable, gals or horses, eh, Horace?" Kane added in a low voice. "And she's a nigger," he said loud enough for everyone to hear as he spat on the ground.

The bone in Colby's jaw worked back and forth. His mustache bristled angrily.

"Oh my! Oh my!" Mrs. Carrington murmured.

"Is Eliza Carpenter a slave?" Rachel asked.

Colby took Rachel's hand in his. "She was, but she was freed after the war. When her former owner died a number of years later, he left Eliza two of his finest horses."

Kane gave Carrington a knowing glance.

Colby grinned at Rachel. "And Kane's right. Eliza is black as the ace of spades."

Amy wondered if Kane also was right about the woman being a madam. As the saloon girls on Grand Avenue chorused a rousing rendition of "Camp Town

Races," Amy supposed it was likely that Colby had even frequented Eliza Carpenter's establishment.

Colby continued, "Eliza had some fine horseflesh. And more importantly, she's got know-how and grit. Lots of grit."

"Well, I never heard of a nigger who . . ." Naomi's voice trailed off.

"Naomi! Say 'colored,' please," Mrs. Carrington admonished as two riders raced down Grand Avenue firing their pistols in the air. "Horace, I do think it's time to go in."

"I'll go along with you, if you don't mind," Colby said.

"We're not in a hurry, are we, Momma?" Rachel asked.

Mrs. Carrington smiled at Colby. "No. No, I suppose not. This end of the street seems calm enough."

Kane once again took possession of Amy's arm and maneuvered her down the street toward the Globe Hotel, quickly outpacing the Carringtons and Colby Grant.

"Mr. Kane," Amy said when they reached the landing at the top of the stairway. "It was a lovely evening."

"I'm glad you enjoyed the fresh air, my dear." Silas paused to check each lantern for fuel as they walked down the dimly lit hallway. He seemed as reluctant as Amy for the evening to end.

"It was quite a pleasant stroll until—" Her thoughts were on Colby Grant.

"I do apologize for the harassment by those savages."

"The Indians? Yes, of course." She lowered her gaze. "But I was not really alarmed, Mr. Kane. I feel perfectly safe in your company."

Silas polished the curve of his ebony cane self-consciously. "Miss Amy, may—may I kiss your hand?" He removed his hat and looked both directions in the hallway.

"Oh—h," Amy's heart fluttered. Thin lips brushed her glove.

He cleared his throat. "I realize I've known you only a few weeks, Miss Amy, but I think you know that I'm beginning to care very deeply for you."

Amy's pulse quickened. Unlike Colby's unsettling and irascible embrace, Kane's request was one of genteel behavior. He was truly a well-bred gentleman, discreet in manner and deportment.

"I would like to request you call me Silas." He cleared his throat again. "In private, of course. I would not like to compromise a lady, but I would pray that you would think of me kindly. You are a most refined, most respected lady, and I'm sure you are not unaware that I am appreciative of your—your comeliness."

Amy felt the heat rise in her cheeks.

"I believe I'm a gentleman of some stature and means, so it behooves me to posture myself with some discernment." His fingers inched slowly around the brim of his hat. "I shouldn't wish you to think I am being too presumptuous or expeditious, but I would be most grateful if you would consider—"

Boldly, Amy reached out to still his hands.

Kane stepped nearer.

With bated breath, Amy waited for him to continue.

The landing door opened and they leaped apart like guilty adolescents.

Colby Grant loomed in the doorway. He broke his long stride when he saw them. "Good evening—again!" He touched the brim of his hat in passing, well aware he had interrupted something between Amy and the banker.

Amy's eyes smarted in exasperation. She saw the mocking mustache and the sensual, teasing lips turn up in one corner.

Colby took his time walking down the hallway to his room as he whistled that infuriating tune of "Oh, Susannah."

When Colby closed the door, Amy smiled encouragingly, mentally urging Silas to continue, but the moment was lost.

With a slight bow, Silas cleared his throat one last time and bade her good night. With quick steps, Kane moved down the pine-floored hallway, his cane grasped tightly in his fist. Only then did Amy realize that her own hands were knotted in frustration.

Chapter Eight

Amy closed the door and pirouetted about the room. Silas Kane, the most eligible bachelor in town, wanted to marry her. She was sure of it. And he might have actually proposed if not for Colby Grant's ill-timed entrance.

A pox on the man!

She caught her reflection in the mirror above the washstand. Silas Kane had called her comely! Had he, too, thought of her eyes as smoky, gray clouds? When he pushed back the curls on her forehead, would he find the birthmark repulsive, or would his tender caress tell her the blemish didn't matter?

Amy reprimanded herself. Wanton and bestial urges dictated Colby Grant's actions. A man of discreet propriety such as Silas Kane would never call attention to the ugly, dark spot. He would pretend it did not exist. And rather than selecting one feature to compliment at the exclusion of others, Silas had told her she was comely.

A smile played on her lips as she undressed and crept into bed. But Amy's sleep was tormented by dreams she could not recall.

After a restless night, Amy found the Sunday church services in the tent on South First Street especially tiring. She also found it hard to enjoy the rare treat of fried chicken at the Globe dining room. An afternoon nap held far more allure than traipsing down to the west side of town to watch the horse races in the hot afternoon sun. But she thought it highly probable Silas would find the opportunity to make clear his intentions of last evening when they were so rudely interrupted by Colby Grant.

Just the thought of that despicable man's name was an irritation. And Amy was infuriated that she'd been the last to learn of the races. Not that she would have entered her beloved Sultan, anyway.

The black gelding had ridden his heart out for her the day of The Run. She did not relish putting him through such torture again. But Sultan did like to run. With ample preparation time, her five-gaited Arabian would have shown Colby Grant's colored madam a thing or two.

When Silas called for her, Amy pinched her tawny cheeks to heighten the color, smoothed the collar of her white embroidered waist and donned her gray cape before opening the door.

"Miss Amy," he said with a formal bow.

"Mr. Kane." She took his arm and wondered if he would get down on one knee when he proposed.

She thrust her pink parasol aloft on the landing and on descending the stairs, lifted the flounce of her gray walking skirt to step into Kane's open rig.

When they were settled comfortably against the quilted upholstery, Silas forced his bay into the already crowded street. He maneuvered the buggy west on Cleveland Street through the throng of townsmen, cattlemen and Indians to a knoll across the railroad tracks on the west end of Grand Avenue. The nearest wagon was sixty feet away and down the slope in front of them.

From their vantage point on the west side of the track, they could see the pre-race activities, the start of each heat, and barring a nose-to-nose finish, they could easily determine the winner of each race at the north end of the racing track which ran parallel with the railroad. They also had the advantage of being slightly above the discordant din and restless crowd. Nevertheless, the excitement of the afternoon was contagious, and Amy began to enjoy herself.

A rope had been strung across the dirt roadway to serve as a starting gate. Perspiring race organizers accepted entry fees at a raw-lumber booth. An announcer's box stood high above the crowd. Sulky drivers in their colored silks exercised their trotters. Perched atop quarter horses, seasoned jockeys tested the length of their stirrup irons. Homesteaders stood confidently by steeds that had served them well in The Run. Cowboys in range denims slouched across cutting ponies, and bare-chested Indians waited in the shade under the bellies of their piebald paints. Bookmakers waved their pads in the air and touted odds to indecisive bettors. In lieu of gold or paper money, wagers were accepted on pistols, plowshares, and buffalo robes.

Silas lifted Amy's hand to his lips. "I specifically chose this spot for us, my dear."

Amy's heart skipped a beat and she turned her undivided attention to Silas.

"Miss Amy." Silas cleared his throat. "Dear, Miss Amy, I—I would—"

The soft snick-snick-snick of rolling wheel spokes clipped the grass on the rise of ground behind them.

Silas released Amy's hand. They sat rigidly as a sulky pulled alongside.

A black woman wearing a billed cap and a numbered

cloth on the back of her green racing silks reined up. The unsmiling woman nodded but didn't bother to wait for their acknowledgment. She gathered up her billowing skirts and stepped down from the racing cart. She was a large woman, nearly six feet tall.

So that was Eliza Carpenter!

Hooves pounded up the slope. Colby's strawberry roan danced on his back feet before coming to a halt. Colby bounded out of his saddle, a racing cloth on his back bearing the number 33.

Silas frowned. "I had thought we might have some privacy."

Amy felt her spirits wilt as surely as the collar of her embroidered waist. Silas Kane had obviously selected this particular knoll in hopes it would afford him the privacy to pursue his intentions without interruption.

But like a weed in a pea patch, Colby Grant had popped up once again.

"Eliza!" Colby tossed his Stetson on the ground. The sun glinted off his hair and mustache.

"Massa? Massa Colby, is that you?" Eliza Carpenter shaded her eyes. A broad expanse of teeth gleamed against her dark skin.

"Now, Eliza," Colby said as he wrapped his arms around the big woman and lifted her off the ground. "Don't give me any of that darky nonsense."

Silas fiddled with his gloves. Amy shrunk back into the plush seats of the rig. Colby must, indeed, have been a valued customer of Eliza Carpenter's.

Not wishing to appear to be staring, Amy averted her eyes to the trotter standing in show-barn stance, head held high, a banded tail cascading into flaxen waves down to his golden fetlocks.

For once, Amy was in agreement with Colby Grant. The black woman did know her horses.

"Now, Massa Colby, you know I ain't never been no boot-licker," she admonished when her feet were back on the ground. "But you know you and the colonel wuz always special."

Silas cleared his throat and placed a gloved hand over Amy's.

"Forgive me, my dear. I do believe I see Mr. Kennedy over there."

He wrapped the reins around the brake and stepped down, ignoring Colby and the black woman. "If you don't mind, I should like to wish J.A. luck," he said to Amy.

Amy did mind, but Silas was already moving toward the melee down below.

Eliza Carpenter pushed back her cap to reveal a close-cropped head of tight, dark curls peppered gray. With dust or age, Amy couldn't be sure.

"You're beautiful as ever, Eliza."

The black woman pulled a bandanna from her pocket and rolled the whites of her dark eyes. "I cum up here lookin' for a fresh breeze and I gits hot air." She rolled the whites of her dark eyes.

"I see you're making out all right," Colby grinned.

"Shore am. Thanks to the colonel, rest his soul."

"Is Esther with you?"

The black woman ducked her head. "Ain't exactly the place to bring a—a—" She raised her head and grinned. "Sides, ain't I nuff of a s'prise?"

Colby laughed.

Amy quickly lowered her parasol and turned her head away. She didn't want Colby Grant to accuse her of eavesdropping. But who was Esther? Was she one of the—the girls?

"Where are you camped?" Colby asked.

Eliza's mouth spread. "I got a 'nother surprise for you." She poked him in the ribs. "Ain't camped nowhere. Rode in early this mornin' from mah place on t'other side of the reservation."

"You made The Run?"

"Yep," she cackled. "Snuck up on it from the south side. Got a contester for mah land, but I's hangin' on for now."

"But I thought you had settled down for good in Independence."

"Trying to git rid of me? Ah'm finding you folks real friendly."

Colby's deep voice roared into laughter. "You mean the Territory's ripe for picking."

"Biz'ness kinda slim up in Kansas," she said solemnly.

Amy pursed her lips. And so she's bringing her girls to New Ponca. Colby Grant would no doubt be her first customer.

"Sides," Eliza went on, "the grass is greener and higher on this side of the line."

"I'm afraid you'll find the pocketbooks around here mostly filled with bent horseshoe nails and spittle, Eliza."

Amy raised a white-gloved hand to her moist upper lip. She wished Silas would return. She would like to find another place from which to watch the race. She raised her parasol slightly.

The colored woman wiped her thick neck with the bandanna. "Tell yuh the truth, Massa Colby, ah ain't getting any younger." She stared off into the southwest skies. "Always figahed ah'd end up in some cotton patch with a stone for a marker. This looks like as good a place as any to be buried in. The ground's hard enough the varmints won't be diggin' up my bones."

She scuffed the ground and cackled. "Now don't go lookin' at me thet way, Massa Colby. I aim to live a long time. But I been thinkin' 'bout slowin' down a bit. Some days, this ol' darky finds it's a passel of trouble gittin' in an' out o' bed. Glad I got Esther."

Colby Grant turned his lean body toward Amy at the sound of her choking cough.

"I thought I recognized that bumper shoot." He took Eliza's arm. "C'mon. I want you to meet someone."

To Amy's relief, Silas chose that moment to return, stepping into the rig without so much as a glance at Eliza and Grant.

Amy quickly averted her eyes from Colby and the black woman.

"Another time, Eliza," Colby said.

"Ladies and gentlemen!" a megaphone blared. "Welcome to New Ponca's first horse race." The announcer waited for the cheering to subside. "We have six races for you this afternoon. Six races. And the first harness race is about to begin. Will the trotters please line up?"

"King Okla's the favorite, I'm glad to report," Silas announced loudly as he straightened his coat.

Colby frowned. "Maybe we'd better get in our places, Eliza."

"Some people don't know their rightful place," Silas said under his breath to Amy.

"You ridin' in this race?" Eliza folded up her skirts and mounted her sulky.

"Against you?" Colby laughed and shook his head. "Just the free-for-all."

"You still crazy, ain't ya, boy."

"Crazy enough to lay out ten bucks on your trotter." Eliza laughed. "Whew! Maybe you got some smarts after all." She turned the sulky around and headed down the slope.

Colby retrieved his hat, mounted his ugly roan and followed the dark woman without a backward glance.

"I do apologize, Miss Amy," Silas said.

Amy smiled forgivingly. "It must have been hard to find Mr. Kennedy in the crowd." She unbuttoned her cape and let it slide down her shoulders, revealing the lovely embroidery of her lawn blouse.

"I was speaking of that nasty scene to our left. I find

the mixing of races as offensive as you do, my dear," Silas said. "But one must learn to ignore a great many distasteful things today."

"I agree." But Amy's thoughts were on Colby Grant who had once again thwarted her hopes for a proposal by his untimely appearance.

Silas turned his attention to the trotters now lining up behind a pacing wagon. "Let's try to enjoy the races."

The megaphone barked from the high box, "May we have your attention. The course has been marked for five lengths—the quarter mile, half mile, five-eights, seven-eighths and one mile. And we want to thank Water Billy for spraying the street to cut down on the dust today."

There was a round of applause.

"Our first race of the afternoon," the announcer continued, "will feature the trotters in a five-eighths of a mile heat. That's five-eighths of a mile. And we have five entries. Trotters, take your places, please."

Eliza Carpenter gave Colby Grant a thumbs-up sign and moved her sulky onto the race track where four other harnessed carts waited.

"Who's in the yellow silks?" Amy asked.

"A homesteader by the name of Ford from Perry. He hasn't got a chance." Kane rubbed his hands together. "The red and blue sulky is drawn by a Nancy Hanks offspring from Muskogee. This one's named Little Nancy."

"Nancy Hanks? Didn't she set a new record of 2:04 at the Terre Haute, Indiana, races last year?"

"Right, you are, Miss Amy." His face registered surprise. "Quite an achievement for a six-year-old. Made old Forbes a mint."

"I think I read that Budd Doble is her trainer."

He patted her arm. "It's refreshing to know a lady who reads something more than the society page in a newspaper." He removed his hand. "Just as long as it's not carried too far."

She blushed. Below, the cart wagon started to move. Nose to nose, wheel to wheel, driver eyeing driver, the five trotters and sulkies followed. Speeds increased and the pacing vehicle veered off. The crowd roared, each spectator cheering on his favorite.

Kennedy in his blue and white silks was the first to break formation with King Okla.

Silas lifted his cane in salute, a pleasant smile on his face.

"Who owns the yellow and blue sulky that's moving up?" Amy raised her voice over the clamor. Eliza Carpenter was apparently outclassed by all but the horse from Perry, lagging in the rear.

"That's Molly Miller's bay. Young Zack's driving," Silas shouted. King Okla was still in the lead, followed closely by Little Nancy.

The two lead sulkies had passed the quarter-mile marker when Eliza Carpenter made her move. With a flick of the whip, the flaxen-maned horse took off in a dazzling display of speed. Moving front and opposing rear legs in perfect unison, he quickly passed the Miller cart. At the half-mile marker he was nose to nose with Little Nancy and King Okla. The crowd went wild.

Silas stood up in the rig. His hat caught on Amy's parasol and fell at her feet. The multitude below exploded into screams of pandemonium. People shoved aside their neighbors and swarmed onto the track for a better view.

In another few seconds Eliza Carpenter's sulky had broken the blue ribbon on the north end of the track and the race was over.

Silas slumped down in his seat, his perspiring face livid. In the resounding clangor, Amy couldn't be sure, but she thought she heard Silas blaspheme. She reached down and retrieved his hat. He jammed the derby back on his head without comment.

The green silks flashed brilliantly in the hot afternoon

sun as Eliza Carpenter made her victory run back to the starting line. Colby ran onto the track. When Eliza reined the horse to a stop, he swooped her from the cart.

The announcer looked down on the crowd and raised the megaphone. "Mighty fine race. Mighty fine. The purse of thirty dollars goes to Eliza Carpenter and her trotter, Sunrise." There was polite applause.

"The next race," the announcer said, "is for quarter horses only. Quarter horses only. Following this race there will be another harness race. This time for the pacers. Our fourth race will be a special match between Kennedy's Black Silk and Ford's Hangman. The sixth race of the afternoon—the one everybody's been waiting for—is the free-for-all. A mile-long race for anything that's got four legs. No goats, please."

The crowd laughed and whooped their approval.

"Now, let's get on with the quarter-horse race. We have twelve entries. They're going to run a three-quarter mile for win, place and show. The purse is worth a total of fifty dollars."

The multitude cheered again.

"Take your places, riders."

The crowd settled down to a hum. Kennedy walked out with Gold Medium and gave his jockey some last-minute instructions. A red-headed jockey in yellow silks held tight rein on Ford's nervous Lancer. The Muskogee stable was again represented, and Amy saw the yellow and blue colors of Colonel Miller's 101 Ranch.

Five more horses with denim-clad jockeys had joined the lineup when Eliza Carpenter came onto the track leading three quarter horses. Behind her billowing skirts trailed three small black boys in green silks and numbered cloths.

The spectators fell quiet. Kennedy pushed through the line of spectators. "We can't have this," he yelled. "Three horses from the same stable?"

Colby Grant's deep voice boomed out as his Stetson

moved through the throng to the track. "She paid her entry fee on each one of them."

The crowd began to buzz. The megaphone was lowered as Kennedy and Colby, with his flapping numbered cloth on his back, converged on the race organizers below the announcer's stand. After lengthy and animated gesturing and a review of the registration forms, the announcer raised the megaphone.

"Sorry for the delay, folks, but I think we've got it ironed out now. The entry fees are in order."

Silas nodded his head. "Money is money. Doesn't say how you have to earn it to spend it."

Amy blushed.

On the track, Colby assisted Eliza in lifting the small jockeys into their saddles.

"You pickanins git in there and ride like fools," Eliza yelled as she walked off the track with Colby, the number 33 waving on his back.

A titter ran through the spectators.

Amy felt overcome with nausea. The nerve of Colby flaunting his black madam before her—before this crowd.

"Are we ready?" The announcer looked across the line.

"We're ready, Mr. Starter, when you are."

The throng stood motionless and silent. The quarter horses strained their heads forward. The gun fired and they were off.

"Gold Medium takes the lead going into the first quarter, followed by Lancer, Walkaway a-a-a-nd the Colonel is moving up fast. And he-e-e-ere comes Plantation Baby and Green Hornet."

Silas slammed his cane down on the rig's splash board. The bay quivered and Amy flinched.

"It's Plantation Baby at the half-mile marker. No! It's the Colonel. And here comes Green Hornet in third place. I don't believe it, folks, but this seems to be a race between horses of the same stable."

The crowd roared.

There was no mistaking this time. Silas Kane said, "Damn!"

The announcer made it official. "It's Plantation Baby, the Colonel and Green Hornet in that order, folks. All from the Carpenter stables. How about that?"

When the crowd settled down, he announced a short intermission. "The next race, the pacers in harness, will begin in ten minutes at three-thirty, followed by our fifth and sixth races."

The crowd cheered.

Kane got out of the buggy and paced with his hands in his pockets.

Amy couldn't sit still another moment. It was too much. Colby Grant and his black madam needed to learn a lesson.

"Silas," Amy said when he had walked back to the rig. "I should like to return to the hotel."

"Miss Amy, they'll be running the next race soon. Maybe I can recover—" He flushed. "I can't cross the track."

"Oh, stay, please." Amy touched his arm. "It will be much easier, and quicker, for me to walk back than to fight through the crowd with the buggy."

"If you're ill, I should accompany you . . ."

She lowered her eyes. "Si—Silas." It was the first time she had called him by his first name. "I'm afraid I must be excused."

"Of course, of course. But did you realize, my dear, that you called me—" He cleared his throat. "I like the way you said 'Silas.'"

Amy hesitated. Was he thinking of last evening? Did Silas want to discuss their future? She stood hesitantly, her emotions divided.

"Don't let me delay you," Silas said, offering her a

hand out of the rig. "Leave before the next race blocks the track."

Amy nodded and turned away.

"Amy, you forgot your cape," Silas called.

She did not turn around. She walked quickly across the uneven ground, hoping she did not appear to be in flight. As she pushed through the crowd on the west side of the track, she saw Naomi and Rachel Carrington waving to get her attention. She hid behind her parasol and kept walking, crossing the track to the other side, where she nodded to the Nate Hampton family as she elbowed her way through the throng. Once she was through the crowd and out of Silas Kane's sight, Amy picked up her skirt and ran toward the livery.

"Amy! What's wrong?"

"Nothing," she yelled as she ran past her father. "I'll explain later, Papa."

Amy ran down Grand Avenue, past the saloons and Myatt's tent grocery. She rounded the corner at First Street and down to Cleveland. She raced by the Globe Hotel. There was no time to change. She sprinted down to Third and flew across the street to McCarthy's livery stable.

From the tack room, Amy raced to the stalls. Sultan whinnied softly when she slipped on his bridle. Quickly, she threw on the blanket and cinched down the girths of her English saddle. The narrow walking skirt made mounting difficult. But she stepped on a salt block and leaped into the saddle. She turned Sultan out of the stall and loped out the livery doors.

She could hear the crowd cheering for the winner of the harness race. No doubt one of Eliza's pacers had bested Kennedy's Gold Lace. The match race was next, and it wouldn't take too long to run that mile. But common sense caused her to check Sultan's stride. She wanted her black gelding warmed up and ready to run, not exhausted and spent.

In a fast trot, Amy guided Sultan down West Cleveland to First Street, turned north to reach the end of the town proper and then crossed the track and circled back to the crowd.

The crack of a gun and a roar from the crowd signaled the start of the fifth race, Kennedy's thoroughbred against Ford's.

"It's Black Silk in the lead," the announcer yelled. "Now Hangman. At the half-mile marker it's—it's— Folks, it's too close to call."

Amy forced her way to the registration booth on the west end of Grand Avenue and slid off Sultan's back.

"Three-quarter-mile marker and it's still nose to nose all the way, folks," the megaphone blared.

"I want to enter the last race," Amy yelled at the man in the booth whose eyes were riveted on the track.

The noise of the crowd crescendoed.

The man in the registration booth craned his neck. "Who won? Who won?"

"I said I want to enter the next race!"

"Too close to call," the announcer cried. "We're waiting to hear who won."

"Registration is closed."

Amy grabbed the man's shirt front. "The race hasn't started so you have to register me," Amy shouted.

"Black Silk," someone yelled, and the crowd around the announcer's stand roared.

"It's not official, folks," the announcer bellowed. "But it looks like Kennedy's Black Silk. Yes, here he comes down victory lane. Let's give him a hand, folks. Our congratulations to both Mr. Kennedy and Mr. Ford for the show put on by these fine horses."

The man in the registration booth pushed Amy's hand away. "Ladies aren't running in this race."

"This lady is running." Amy wrapped Sultan's reins about her wrist and unbuttoned her skirt. She had the man's full attention.

"Now, wait a minute." His face reddened.

She unpinned a coin purse hidden at her waist and shoved it at the man. "Here's the entry fee."

The man fumbled with the catch, but finally opened it. "It's two dollars, ma'am," he said meekly.

"Take it!" she ordered. "And give me a number."

He withdrew the bills and returned the small purse.

She replaced the purse, rebuttoned her skirt and grabbed the numbered cloth out of the man's hand.

Number 55. There would be 54 other horses out there, including Colby Grant's.

"You must be crazy, lady. You could get hurt, and there's no way you can win!"

Amy pinned on the number and remounted Sultan, snugging her leg around the horn. She might be crazy, but Sultan had taken her through The Run safely. And the only horse she wanted to beat was number 33, Colby Grant's strawberry roan.

"Well, ladies and gentlemen," the announcer called out. "This is our sixth and final race of the afternoon. I hope everyone has enjoyed themselves up to now and will go home safely after this next race. We've got a lot of horses entered, so you'll need to pull back away from the track if you don't want to get trampled."

The crowd moved back a few steps.

"We need more room," the announcer called out as more horses moved onto the track and spilled out on the trampled grass.

"Back," he called. "Back, back."

Free-for-all was an apt name for the race. Moving to the starting line were sun-leathered cowboys on cutting ponies and range broncos. A number of Indians held plaited-grass reins and waited to spring onto their unshod ponies. Trained jockeys maneuvered their steeds to outside positions. Frontier gentry on thoroughbreds minced across the track to wait alongside a few settlers with sway-backed nags. There was even a burro ridden by a long-legged clown to delight the youngsters in the crowd.

Amy recognized young Zack Miller on a chestnut stallion. And riding a sorrel was the freckled-face cowboy she had met on the train to Perry.

She gasped when she saw Roughface, the Indian who had accosted Silas.

Dressed in denims and shirtless, Roughface stood beside a bare-backed pinto. Streaks of red blazed across the savage's cheekbones. Splashes of black and white were painted on his broad, mahogany shoulders and arms. Roughface placed his hands on the rump of his pony. When he leapfrogged onto his pinto, muscles rippled and undulated. He looked like an eagle in flight.

Their eyes met, and before Amy could look away, a thin smile broke the stoic expression on the savage's face. She shivered and wondered where his friend Shines White was.

"What in tarnation do you think you're doing?" Colby Grant rode his ugly roan into line next to Amy.

"If I'm that offensive to you," Amy hissed, "move your horse."

"You know what I mean. This is a killer of a race, Amy."

"It's 'Miss White' to you." She raked at the strands of hair falling about her neck.

Colby glared. "Where's Alfred?"

"This is the last warning, folks," the announcer blared. "If you don't move back you're going to have a horseshoe imprinted permanently on your forehead."

"Where's Alfred?" Colby insisted.

"Where's your Eliza?" Her voice mocked. "Or sweet little Esther?"

"Esther?"

"If you're worried about how embarrassing it's going to be to lose to a woman, Mr. Grant, then perhaps you

should pull that ugly mare of yours out of the race."
Amy rewrapped Sultan's reins around her left hand and
took a good grip on the saddle horn.

"Alfred ought to take a horsewhip to you. And if I
had half a mind, I'd do it myself."

"Quiet! Quiet!" the announcer called. The starting
gun was raised.

"Amy, for the last time—"

The pistol fired. Sultan and 53 other mounts plunged
into the race. Colby and the ugly roan were a half
step behind.

"They're off," the announcer boomed over the noise
of the crowd.

The chaps of the rider on the left raked against Amy,
the rowels on his spurs snagged her skirt. Sultan veered
to avoid an outlaw's heels, and for a horrifying second
Amy's body lifted free of the English saddle. Fiercely,
she clung to the pommel and righted herself. Her hair
fell across her face, and she flung her head to one side
to restore her vision.

"Pull out before it's too late," Colby yelled as the
roan moved up on her right side.

"No-o-o-o!" Her teeth rattled. Her ears rang with pain
from the noise.

A bangtail cut into the left side of Sultan. The
gelding faltered, jarring Amy again. Colby's roan moved
slightly ahead.

"Go back, Amy! Go back!"

A quarter horse crowded between Amy and the
bangtail. She saw the jockey in red and white silks,
but she did not see his thrashing crop until she felt its
cutting edge on her left earlobe and shoulder.

Amy screamed, but to the crowd it was no more than
the piercing whinny of a panic-stricken horse. She clung
to her saddle out of fear of the trampling hooves behind
her. The blood from the wound splattered across her
face and down the bodice of her embroidered waist. She

could taste the saltiness of her own blood. She could feel its stickiness on her left shoulder and breast.

Colby glanced back, his body stretched flat across his roan as they passed the half-mile marker.

Amy saw his eyes widen, his body bolt upright at the sight of her blood-streaked face and bodice.

"My God! Amy!" he shouted. "You're hurt!" He pulled back on his reins. He didn't see the foam-flecked mustang wheel and vault into the air in front of him.

"Colby!" Amy screamed and yanked back on Sultan's reins.

A panic-stricken sorrel pounded into the melee. Colby's strawberry roan had nowhere to go and the three horses collided.

Colby kicked loose of his stirrups and tried to roll away, but his left leg was pinned under his downed mare. The crazed sorrel lay kicking the air. Colby threw his arms over his head and hunkered low as thundering hooves came pounding toward him.

"Colby!" Amy kicked Sultan in the flanks, and with a quiver in his withers, the obedient Arabian leaped ahead to shield Colby from the oncoming charge of horses. In the thunderous pandemonium, Amy threw back her head and shrieked like a she-bear protecting her cub. And then an eagle swept down on her.

Roughface leaped from his pinto and raced to her side. He pried her hands free from the pommel and lifted the screaming Amy down from Sultan's back, his strong, mahogany arms sweeping her up and away from the flying feet of the downed horses.

Other men ran onto the track. "Get out of the way, Injun," someone yelled.

"Woman safe now," Roughface said. He cradled her in his arms.

"Git yer hands off her, I said," a burly man yelled at Roughface. "Somebody get Doc Horner or Doc Taylor."

The Indian gently laid the sobbing Amy on a blanket someone had provided and let the crowd push him aside.

"Colby!" Amy cried.

"Somebody find Alfred. It's his girl."

"Colby!" Amy wailed.

If Colby hadn't been so worried about her—if he had never looked back—he would have seen the trouble ahead. He could have avoided the crazed sorrel.

Amy tried to sit up. "Colby?"

"Now, Miss Amy, you just lie back." Doc Horner turned to the crowd. "Get back! Give her some air!"

Amy tried to wrench away. "I want to see Mr. Grant."

"Doc, I think she's in shock," someone said.

"Is he all right?" she pleaded.

"What's that, Miss Amy?" Doc Horner asked as he wiped her face with a damp, gauzy cloth.

"Colby Grant? Is he—is he—" The swabbing alcohol on her earlobe and shoulder smarted.

"Grant? Knocked out for a time, but he's okay. Just bruised, I think. Now let's worry about you."

"I saw it all." The voice that came from behind the crowd around her sounded like Silas Kane. "That man Grant caused it all."

"No." Amy tried to push herself up on her elbows.

"Now, Miss Amy, you've got to be still."

Amy heard a soft whinny and knew it came from a horse lying on the track where it had fallen. She could see its hind feet jerking spasmodically in the air.

"Please," she whispered. She turned on her side and squinted through the glaring sun.

A sob of relief escaped her lips when she recognized the silhouette of Colby's muscle-hardened body. He stood facing the horse, with his back to Amy. He beat his Stetson against his breeches. Dust motes showered the sun-red sky as he put on his hat.

Amy lifted her hand to shield her face from the sun.

"Hold her arms down!" Doc Horner ordered.

She fought against the strong hands forcing her arms to her side, pushing her back on the ground.

Doc Horner dabbed more alcohol on Amy's ear and shoulder.

She struggled to see through the blinding red sun.

"Be still!" Doc Horner growled.

Amy could see Colby's upper torso as he took an unsteady step forward to stand before the blurred outline of a downed animal. Slowly his left hand reached down for the Colt. The animal nickered softly. Colby eased the gun out of his holster.

"No-o-o-o!" Amy screamed.

The gun fired.

The legs of the injured animal jerked, then stiffened.

Amy's body went limp.

"Let me through," Silas Kane demanded.

Colby, favoring his left leg, walked toward Amy. His large frame blocked out the sun and she could see his face. He squinted his left eye shut. The right one was hardened steel. The mouth beneath the golden mustache was grim. The smoking revolver dangled from his hand.

Amy turned her head away in shame.

Chapter Nine

Amy clamped her hands over her mouth to smother the screams in her throat. *Mon Dieu, pardonnez-moi,* but she loved Colby Grant. And he had loved that ugly roan. And because of her, the mare had to be killed. Colby would never forgive her. He could only hate her. He would not stop until he had forced her off her homestead, ruined her father's newspaper and run her and Papa out of town. Tears spilled down her face to mix with the crimson stains on her clothing.

Silas Kane pushed through the crowd with his cane and peered over Doc Horner's shoulder. "Miss Amy?" He stumbled back at the sight of her blood-soaked waist. His face was ashen.

Alfred arrived breathless from running. He bent down on one knee, puffing. His white brows knitted in concern.

"Amy—Amy, lass, where—where do you hurt?"

Amy clung to her father's hands, rocked her head back

and forth, but she could not speak through her sobs.

"Looks worse than it is, Alfred," Doc Horner said. "There's a small cut on her left ear and a laceration on her shoulder, but the artery wasn't cut. Just a lot of blood."

Alfred breathed a sigh of relief. "It's going to be all right, lass," he soothed.

"No, Papa! It—it will nev—ever be—"

"Let's get her to the hotel," Doc Horner ordered.

"Give us some room here," Kane growled at the curious spectators.

"Will someone take her horse to McCarthy's livery?" Alfred asked.

Amy offered no resistance as they lifted her into a carriage. She felt light-headed and clung to her father during the ride to the hotel. Doc Horner followed in Kane's buggy.

Shouldered between her father's and Silas's arms, Amy staggered up the stairs and into her room. Mr. Pearson sent Mabel rushing up with hot water and fresh towels. Mabel removed Amy's blood-stained clothing and helped her into bed. Doc Horner washed the ear and shoulder wounds with an antiseptic and examined her chest and limbs carefully.

"No broken bones," he announced. "But we better put a few stitches in that shoulder. Don't want you to have an ugly scar, little lady."

He worked quickly and there was little pain, but Amy couldn't stem the flow of tears.

"There now! By the time that bandage comes off, you'll be good as new." He put his suturing scissors back in his black bag. "Might be a tiny scar, but no one will ever know if you dangle one of them pretty curls by your ear."

Amy tried to laugh, but her voice broke into a sob. A curl for her forehead and a curl for her ear. But there were no curls to hide the ache inside, and no bandage large enough to cover the wound she had inflicted on Colby.

"Now, Miss White." Doc Horner took a vial out of his bag and asked Mabel for a glass of water. He measured five drops into the water and forced the bitter laudanum down Amy's throat. When he had repacked his bag and Mabel had taken her blood-spattered clothing away, her father and Silas reentered her room.

"Are you sure she's going to be all right?" Alfred's voice was barely audible.

"Rest is what she needs, and that opiate I've given her is already taking effect," Doc Horner said. "She'll feel much better in the morning."

Amy listened to them talk about her as if she were deaf. The laudanum might put her to sleep, the stinging of her wounds might ease, and the scars would probably fade, but no amount of sleep would erase the memory of Colby in the red haze of the horizon standing over his strawberry roan with his smoking Colt.

"It was a fool thing for her to do, Alfred," she heard Silas say. "I had no idea she planned to run in the races, or I would have stopped her."

"Kane," Alfred sighed. "You can't stop Amy from doing what she's going to do. Even that fancy boarding house back East couldn't take that willfulness out of her."

Amy's eyelids were heavy. She was finding it too much effort to stay awake.

"I expect all we can ever do with Amy is be there when she needs us."

Kane lowered his voice. "With your permission, Alfred, I intend to do just that."

What did Silas say? She wasn't sure, but she was floating now and maybe it didn't really matter.

When Amy awoke the next morning, she felt a stiffness in her back and an irritating prick in her shoulder when she turned on her pillow. Her throat felt raw and her eyes seemed puffy. The Sunday afternoon race came rushing back. She buried her face in the pillow, ashamed. Colby Grant would never forgive her.

Alfred entered the room, his face drawn, his brow furrowed.

Amy wanted to reassure her father that physically she was fine, but she didn't know how to tell him that she was upset, not for injuries received but for injuries inflicted. She pushed back the covers to rise.

"Best you stay in bed another day." Her father's hands restrained her. "Doc Horner left more laudanum to help you sleep."

Amy sighed and let her body go limp on the bed. It was the course of least resistance and she could delay having to face Colby. She closed her eyes.

Alfred kissed her cheek. "I've asked Mabel to look in on you from time to time and see that you take your medicine."

Amy slept on and off most of the morning. But there were dreams, disturbed images floating through her mind. She kept seeing the race and the renegade horse in front of Colby, the collision, hooves trampling Colby, the horse lying helplessly on the track, the gun in Colby's hands. She dreamed that an eagle had hovered over her and picked her up in his talons and flown away with her. There was a vision of an old Indian creeping into her room, but she had not been afraid because the apparition reminded her of Shines White. And once she dreamed she heard Colby's voice outside her door asking Mabel how Miss Amy was feeling. But it had all been a horrible collection of illusions, because Colby could only hate her now.

After the lunchtime rush in the hotel was over, Mabel came up with a tray. She tidied up the room while Amy picked listlessly at her food.

"Miss Amy, you wanna keep this ol' wilted flower?" Mabel asked.

"Flower?" Mabel placed the wild aster with its limp and fading blue petals into Amy's hand.

"Who—?"

"Don't know, Miss Amy. It was here on the washstand."

The simple wildflower was something Colby Grant might have done. She remembered the morning he had fed her breakfast—but that was before the race—before his beloved roan was slain.

Silas? No, Silas would have imported a bouquet from Arkansas City if he had thought of bringing flowers.

Maybe her father had placed the flower there.

Mabel clucked over how little Amy ate, helped her into fresh bed clothes and stirred up more powders for her to drink. "You just rest, Miss Amy," the woman ordered and left the room.

On Tuesday, Amy refused to stay in bed in spite of the heavy mood she could not shake. But she knew that sleep would only bring back the dreams of the race, of Colby and his strawberry roan.

What she wanted to do was write an editorial for next Thursday's edition. It would be an apology. Not that she expected Colby to recognize it as such. But there was nothing else she could do. No way to put the .44 cartridge back in Colby's revolver. No way she could breathe life back into that strawberry roan.

When Amy arrived at the office of the *Democrat,* Alfred was leaving to make his rounds of potential advertisers. "Don't overdo it, lass."

"It was only a scratch, Papa." She kissed her father on his ruddy cheek. "I'm fine, Papa. Just fine." She fingered the small bandage on her ear.

"Are you sure? I thought I'd call on the Brodboll Real Estate," he said. "He and his partner, Mr. Soligny, seem to be busy enough selling the leftover town lots. Maybe they'll take a four-by-four ad." His face was grim as he walked out the door.

Amy watched through the doorway as her father walked down the street. The lack of advertising for the *Democrat* was becoming a major worry. Newsstand sales were sufficient to pay for ready-prints, but without advertising, there would be no profit. That should make Colby happy.

Amy sat down on the stool at the counter and began to compose her editorial for next Thursday's paper.

The Evils of Horse Racing

Last Sunday afternoon's horse racing has served to remind all of us of the evils of this so-called sport of the kings. Maybe we should remember how many kings have enjoyed the sight of human blood-letting.

The door to the *Democrat* office opened. A frail woman in a faded bonnet walked in hesitantly with two spindly-legged toddlers in tow.

"Miss? Don't want to be no bother, but—"

"Yes?" Amy smiled. "Would you like to place an ad in the classified section?"

"No'm." The woman looked down at the floor. "I cum to see if you got a—a job." She raised her head and looked pleadingly into Amy's eyes. "Ironin', washin' or cookin'. I'd do anythin'. My young'uns are hungry."

"Are you homesteaders?"

"We lost our claim. We wuz goin' back to St. Joe to mah folks, but Ezra—he done lost the money at the horse races."

"Well, I don't have any work, Mrs.—?"

"Miz Johnson."

"As I said, we don't have any work for you, but"— Amy grabbed a piece of paper and began scribbling— "take this to Mr. Pearson at the Globe Hotel." She handed Mrs. Johnson the note. "He'll give you a good meal. And you might ask him about a job."

"Thank you, miss."

As the three stepped out the door, an Indian moved aside. Amy wasn't sure, but it looked like the old Indian, Shines White.

She sat down at the counter to finish her editorial.

The cost of horse racing is shameful in its waste of man and beast. But death and injury are not limited to the race track, but spread like a plague into the community by virtue of the open gambling that is allowed at these events. Families are becoming destitute and going hungry because of wagering their last few dollars.

A shiver ran through Amy's body. Someone was watching her. She could feel it. She turned to the window in time to get a brief glimpse of rheumy eyes in a shadowed and gnarled face just before it withdrew from sight.

Shines White! What did the old Ponca Indian want? Strange, his appearance no longer frightened her. Amy supposed she was getting used to seeing him hanging around on the streets every day with his tall friend, Roughface.

Roughface! How ironic that it had been Shines White's towering friend who had pulled her free in the melee at Sunday's race. Well, she didn't have time to worry about Roughface or the old Indian. He was apparently a harmless, if curious old man. She returned to her editorial.

I, for one, am deeply sorry I was ever a party to Saturday's horse racing event. The most immediate and progressive thing this town can do is to plow a wide furrow across each end of the track to put an end to this senseless activity that brings more dust, more violence and more heartache into the Territory.

The editorial wouldn't bring back the strawberry roan. Nothing could rectify that. But perhaps it would raise the consciousness of the townsfolk and put an end to the races.

Shines White peeked through the window again. When Amy rose, he stepped back out of sight.

"If I ignore him, he'll go away."

Amy took her editorial and moved back to the type cases. She was terribly slow at setting type, compared to her father, but he had been so busy lately, it was the least she could do.

She heard the door of the office open and turned to see the blanketed Indian. Something fluttered from Shines White's hand to the counter before he slipped back toward the door.

"Stop!"

Shines White cowered, but halted and jerked off his tall, feathered hat.

"What do you want?"

He turned and motioned with his hands.

Amy picked up the sheet of paper. It was a handbill advertising a sale in Ark City. She didn't understand.

Shines White motioned for her to turn it over.

On the backside of the handbill was a pen-and-ink drawing.

"Why, it's Sultan." Her Arabian horse, drawn in meticulous detail, was flying in a spiraling cloud. On his back was an Indian maiden. The drawing astonished her.

"It's—it's beautiful," Amy whispered.

Shines White hung his head in modesty.

"Where did you get this? Who drew this? Did you steal it?"

The old Indian straightened. "No steal." He fingered his ear and neck and pointed to Amy.

She touched the small bandage on her neck.

"For you. Make you feel better."

Amy flushed self-consciously. "For me? You drew this for me?"

Shines White nodded and beamed.

Amy looked again at the picture. Sultan, with the Indian maiden on his back, seemed to be flying away in the picture. A chill went over her. What did it mean?

"Sultan? Are you going to steal my horse?"

Roughface stepped through the door, a scowl on his face.

Startled, Amy gasped.

The dark face stared at her defiantly. The eyes narrowed. The lips sneered. "We go!" He ushered Shines White to the door and stopped to look back at Amy. "Shines White no steal."

"But the picture—an Indian maiden riding Sultan into the sky . . ." She had not meant to offend, but Sultan was very dear to her.

Shines White's cloudy eyes filled with tears. His hands moved as in sign language and spiraled up into the sky.

"Shines White's squaw rode horse to Great Spirit."

"But that's Sultan. That's my horse!" She pushed back her hair in frustration.

Roughface's eyes burned into Amy as he scanned her face. "Maybe so." The tall Indian followed Shines White out the door.

"Wait!" Amy called to Roughface. "I want to thank you—" She went to the doorway. But the two Indians moved down the dusty street without looking back. Roughface held Shines White's arm to steady his tottering steps. A young Indian girl in a red sack dress trailed behind. She looked back with dark, glowering eyes at Amy and spat on the ground.

Amy gasped and shrank back from the insult as her father walked up.

"An Indian attack?" Alfred peered over his glasses at the group ambling down the street. "I'm surprised you didn't yell at the top of your lungs."

Flustered, Amy smiled sheepishly. "They brought me a drawing."

Alfred chuckled. "Maybe you've made a conquest. I think that's the old Indian that Mabel ran off in the upstairs hallway yesterday."

Had Shines White brought her the blue prairie flower?

"Will you look at this, Father? It's a beautiful drawing of Sultan."

Alfred frowned. "That looks like your face on that Indian maiden."

Amy took the drawing out of her father's hands. There was a likeness. But the woman's skin was dark, and long braids flowed down the back of a buckskin dress with fringe and beadwork.

"Roughface said it was a picture of Shines White's wife who had, quote, gone to the Great Spirit, unquote." Amy explained. "And look, Papa, I hadn't noticed before, but there's an empty cradle board on her back. Poor woman, she must have lost her baby, too."

"Hmm-m-m-m." Alfred frowned.

Amy laughed. "I first thought they planned to steal Sultan."

"Indians draw all kinds of hocus-pocus things about the Great Spirit. Wouldn't read anything into it if I were you."

Her father's frothy brows knitted together as he turned the pages of his ledger. "I guess we'll start doing some job printing, Amy. Brodboll doesn't want to run an ad, but said he'd like to have some handbills printed listing some of the town lots he's got for sale."

"Well, that's fine, isn't it, Papa?"

Alfred nodded his head. "Means longer hours since we can't afford to hire extra help."

"I'll help."

"I know you will, and you do."

"Papa, I've written another editorial—"

"Good, good. Now you better go back to the hotel and rest, lass," he said.

Amy frowned. Her father hadn't even asked about the topic of her editorial. He was worried. Quietly, she put on her cape and started for the door.

"Oh, Amy?"

"Yes, Papa?"

"How are you and Silas getting along?"

Amy flushed. "Fine, Papa. Fine."

She fled out the door before he could ask her to explain. She wasn't ready to tell her father that Silas had almost proposed to her. And Amy didn't know what she would say when he did. Silas had all the virtues a woman looked for in a man—respectability, leadership qualities, refined manners, and financial stability. Silas would protect her, clothe her well and take pride in her being by his side. But she wished just once he would do something reckless and daring, such as throwing his cane aside, taking her in his arms and passionately kissing her.

"What's the matter with you, Amy White," she admonished. "No respectable woman would want a man who would throw her into a bathtub and attempt to make love to her."

Silas Kane would be a steadying influence on her life, someone she could count on after the passion of youth had faded away. And besides, Colby Grant was a despicable man just waiting, she was sure, to get even with her for the loss of his horse, just waiting for an excuse to throw her off the homestead.

"Stop it!" Amy said aloud. The ambiguous feelings

she had for Colby Grant would best be reconciled by forgetting about the man.

Amy walked slowly back to the hotel. She hoped her father would not be angry that she had charged the Johnson family's meal to their account. His concern over their finances was greater than Amy had realized. Well, she would just forgo lunch. When she returned to the *Democrat* office, Alfred seemed in better spirits.

"Barnes and his Board of Trade were just here."

"And—?" Amy slipped off her cape.

"They've voted to boycott the town of Cross."

"Boycott?"

"Yep! A good thing, too. Can't be two major cities in the Strip a mile apart. And we aim for New Ponca to be the survivor. We've all decided that what we can't buy from merchants around here, we'll wait and get it in Arkansas City."

"But what about the mail and the ready-prints we have to have?" Amy protested.

"The boycott won't go into effect till November first. That's the date the Santa Fe has agreed to drop our mail sacks at the reservation depot south of town."

"Seems a little ridiculous to me, Papa. Cross is a mile away and the Indian depot is at least two miles south."

"What's a mile? Besides, it's the only way to make our point."

"You mean you're hoping to force Santa Fe to build a station here?"

"Sure do." Alfred smiled. "Billy Thomas has agreed to let us use the front end of his furniture store for a post office, and Tom Noble said he'd deliver it for ten cents a family."

"And the ready-prints, too?"

"Well, we'll still have to go after them, but we'll get them at the reservation depot, not from Cross. Be sure you wire the new address to the Newspaper Syndicate next Wednesday."

Amy nodded. "What can I do to help you now, Papa."

"Not a thing, lass. Not a thing." His fingers were flying through the type cases as he set this latest piece of news into print. "Why don't you go back to the hotel and rest awhile."

"I'd rather ride out to the homestead."

Alfred shook his head. "I still think you ought to sell your claim to Grant."

"Never!"

"I don't like you going out there alone."

"It's perfectly safe. David Reynolds lives on the next quarter, and he leaves his wife alone out there all the time."

Alfred peered over his glasses. "You haven't heard?"

"Heard what?"

"Somebody poisoned the spring at the Reynolds place and Mrs. Reynolds died."

"Oh, no!" Amy's mouth pursed. "He's not giving up, is he?"

Alfred nodded. "Takes the heart out of a man when he loses his lifelong mate."

Amy put her arms around her father. "I know, Papa," she whispered.

"The only thing worse than losing your wife is losing your child." Alfred looked at her meaningfully.

"I'll be careful. I promise."

"See that you do. And don't forget the Starr gang tried to hold up the Santa Fe last week."

"Pshaw, Papa. They want gold, not me."

"And I suppose it's of no concern to you that Clyde Maddox is holed up west of town. He's just as bad as the Starr gang."

"Oh, Papa, he's sweet on the Logan girl."

Alfred laid down the type stick. "Go on," he shooed. "I can't outtalk you, even if I had the time."

Amy laughed and buttoned on her cape. She didn't

bother to change her clothing but went straight to McCarthy's livery stable to saddle Sultan and rein him toward her homestead, not without feeling a little guilty. Colby Grant would never be able to ride that ugly roan of his again.

Sultan cantered easily down the trail toward the Arkansas River. Amy marveled at how quickly the season was changing. The cooler October air filtered out the rays of the noonday sun. Prairie grass had ripened to a golden yellow, and seeds from wild oats shattered as Sultan cantered by. Cottonwood trees quivered in silver, and blackjacks boasted Jacob's coats. Amy took a deep breath to inhale fall's splendor.

Smoke!

Amy raced Sultan toward her homestead. When they bounded over the rise she saw the flames licking up the side of the timbers of her gateway. A strange dark horse, its bridle reins tied to a scrub oak, pawed the ground in fright. A figure bent over the largest blaze fanned the flames with a blanket. All of hers and Danny's hard work was going up in smoke.

"No-o-o-o!" She reined Sultan to a halt in front of Colby Grant.

Amy slid off the horse and attacked Colby with flying fists.

"Amy—"

"You couldn't poison the Arkansas so you decided to burn me out!"

"Amy—"

"Don't! Please, don't!" She begged. "I know I deserve it after what happened," she wailed, "but please . . ."

Colby dropped the blanket and grabbed her hands. "Hysterics won't help."

"I don't blame you," she sobbed. "You have every— every right to hate me."

"What the hell are you blubbering about?" He dropped his smudged hands and freed her.

"I know you want revenge for what happened at the races, but to set—set a fire . . ."

"You little fool!" His bared his teeth beneath the sooty mustache. "Why would I want to burn—"

"Because you know you're going to lose your claim to me."

"Lord o' mercy, woman. My soddy's on fire, too!"

"But—but if I win the claim, the soddy would be mine."

"Amy—"

"But you don't have to do that, Colby. If you want my claim that badly—"

"Amy!"

"—if it will make you feel better about your horse—about the race, you can have it. The claim is yours." She turned away in shame.

"Have you finished yet?" he shouted through the smoke. "I've been trying to put out the fire, not start it!"

"Put—put it out?"

"Stop wasting time!" he ordered. "Take this blanket to the river and soak it." He shoved her toward the river. "Maybe we can save the gate yet."

Too stunned to ask any more questions, Amy hiked up her dark skirt and ran through the smoke to the river. When she returned with the heavy wet blanket, Colby handed her another. Amy started back to the river and stopped. "This looks like my blanket—" She glanced over at Sultan tied to a bush. His back had been stripped of his saddle and his blanket removed. She looked over to find Colby beating at the flames. "—and this is my fire," she finished lamely as she sped toward the river.

The afternoon sun faded in a haze of smoke as Colby beat the searing fires around the gateway and the soddy.

Amy repeatedly ran to and from the river, her bodice

and skirt quickly becoming a mixture of mud, soot and water. Her arms ached with the weight of the soaked blankets, her throat dry from the smoke and flying cinders. Her hair tumbled from their pinnings. But she willed herself on, numbed herself to the pain.

Colby's yell finally penetrated the haze of her mind. "Let the prairie fire go," Colby shouted. "It'll burn itself out when it reaches the river. I think we've got it contained on this side."

Amy collapsed in an exhausted heap and cradled her head in her arms. The air was still thick with smoke and flying ash. Her lungs were raw and her skin seared from the flames. Amy raised her weary head just in time to see Colby racing toward her like a madman.

She screamed as he forced her back and prone on the ground. She flailed her feet and her arms in protest, but he rolled her over and over in the blackened grass.

"Why—why don't—why don't you just—shoot me?" Amy said between gasps of air when Colby had lifted her to her feet. She struggled against the hands gripping her shoulders.

"My God, woman! Your skirt was on fire." He picked her up in his arms and walked to the river. "I'm not taking any chances. 'Sides, we can both use a bath."

Bath? Amy struggled. She remembered their last bath. And then she ceased her thrashing, nestled her face against the golden mustache that smelled of smoke and waited for the water to envelop their bodies. A smile played across her dry lips as he waded into the river.

He dropped her unceremoniously into the water. Amy screamed and flailed her arms. "It's freezing!"

Colby laughed. He stripped off his shirt and used it to scrub his blackened hands and face.

Amy sank deep in the water and washed the cinders from her hair. "Ouch!" She had forgotten about her ear and shoulder.

Colby drew her to him. "Better let me take a look."

The bandages were soaked. "You could get an infection. We better get out and dry."

Disappointment flooded over her. She wanted him to take her in his arms, to kiss her hungrily, to caress her— But things were different, weren't they? For a while, the race to save her gateway and Colby's soddy from the searing flames had made her forget that they were destined to be foes. It was no longer just a battle over homestead claims, or competition between newspapers. Colby's mare was dead, just as dead as any feeling he might have had for her.

Amy turned her head away from him.

"I won't touch you, Amy."

His words confirmed her thoughts.

"But you should get out now," he said quietly.

Amy nodded and trudged to the shore under the weight of her wet clothing on Colby's arm. He sat her on a rock in the sun and leaned back against a tree. His muscled chest with golden hairs shimmered in the afternoon rays.

"You're some lady," he said quietly.

Amy flushed. Dare she ask Colby to forgive her?

"Mr. Grant—"

"Isn't it about time you started calling me by my given name?"

"Col—Colby," she swallowed. "I'm so sorry. I—"

He looked at her and grinned. Or was it a sneer? She couldn't be sure.

"I—I'm sorry about the soddy and—and the race." Oh, God, how could she make him understand how sorry she was about the ugly roan?

"A couple of new timbers and the soddy will be better than ever. That fire dried out that sod better than the sun. Better brick than ever."

He obviously did not want to talk about the race, or having to put down his strawberry roan.

"I wonder who—?"

Colby shrugged. "Could have been Ben Cravens. I've seen signs of someone crossing down river."

"Papa said Cravens was running a moonshine still and selling to the Indians."

Colby looked up at Amy. "And to some of the saloons in the Strip."

"That—that stuff is poison, isn't it?"

"Depends on how many rattlesnake heads."

Amy shivered. "Seems to me that the deputy sheriff, Carr, isn't doing a very good job."

"You hadn't heard that Carr's missing?"

"Missing?" She supposed Colby had scooped her again.

"Had four hundred dollars on him when he left his wife on Summit Street in Arkansas City last Monday. Said he was going to the rail station to check out the latest word on the Dalton boys."

"And they haven't found the body?" Amy shuddered.

"No, but they'll find it in some gulch or floating in the Arkansas."

Here in this sheltered arbor, Amy had almost forgotten how dangerous the Territory really was.

"There's talk," Colby went on, "of hiring a gunslinger to keep the peace in New Ponca. It would be a mistake."

"A mistake?"

"Gunslingers shoot and ask questions later. Lot of innocent folks could end up dead."

Like innocent mares end up with .44 slugs, Amy thought.

"I—I'm sorry, Colby, about—" A horse nuzzled the back of her neck. "Go away, Sultan," she said without turning. "Mr. Grant—Colby, I'm—I'm trying to apologize—"

The horse nudged her forward and she stumbled toward Colby. She turned, "Sult—" But it wasn't her horse at all. It was Colby's ugly roan.

"I—I thought she was dead!" Amy squealed. "I thought I had caused—"

"A torn ligament, maybe, but not dead."

"But you shot her."

"Shot her?" Colby shook his head. "I put down the other fellow's mount. Said he couldn't do it. Mighty hard thing to do when it's your own horse."

Amy bit her trembling lip and blinked her smarting eyes. She reached up and hugged the roan. "I'm so glad to see you." She kissed the mare's muzzle.

"Oh, to be a horse," Colby sighed, fingering his mustache.

She laughed. "What's her name?"

"No name," he said.

"That's a ridiculous name for a horse," Amy sputtered.

Colby's laugh rumbled up from inside and spilled out over the arbor. He held out his hand. "I don't know why we keep fighting, Amy. Can't we call a truce?"

"Truce!" Amy agreed.

They rode back into town together, their clothing smudged, Colby's shirt tied around his waist and Amy's hair flowing freely down her back. She felt free of all burdens, free of all worries, but her heart told her she wasn't free of Colby Grant.

When they turned the corner of Third and Cleveland to stable their horses at the livery, Amy saw Silas Kane on the stoop of the Globe Hotel. His face was grim.

Chapter Ten

"Amy, when you're at Cross today, don't forget to tell them the shipping order goes to the rail depot at the Ponca Indian Reservation week after next." Alfred stared down at his ledger and took a deep breath. "And we better cut back on the number of ready-prints."

"But, Papa, we're hard pressed to have an extra edition to save for our files—"

Alfred raised his green eye shade. "We'll just have to make do, lass."

"Is it that bad?"

"I'm afraid so." He buttoned his vest as he strode to the doorway and looked down the street at the false-front buildings. "No one has any money, and it's a mite hard to barter advertising."

"Papa—" The Santa Fe whistle interrupted Amy. She slammed down the black editing pencil. The train churned past the town without stopping six times a day and was a constant irritation. "Papa, maybe we should move the paper to Cross. The boycott may not work."

Her father raised his frothy eyebrows. "The boycott must work! And there's a lot more underfoot to convince Santa Fe to stop here."

"What do you mean, Papa?"

"Colonel Miller of the 101 Ranch and the Soldanis and Blocker outfits from the Osage have promised to build holding pins for cattle shipment if Santa Fe will move the rail siding to New Ponca. I just hope it comes in time." Alfred shook his head again. "No, Amy. We're staying. We've got the right kind of people here to make a good town."

The bell on the door tinkled. "Good morning." Silas Kane put his hat and cane on the counter in front of Amy.

"Hello, Silas," Alfred said. "You're out early."

Silas pursed his lips and cleared his throat. "Miss Amy."

"Silas." She lowered her eyes to the galley proof. Had he overheard their conversation? Did he know how poorly they were doing? Well, they still had a few days before their next installment was due.

"Miss Amy, I know you're busy," Silas said, "but I just heard about your fire and wish to offer my condolences."

"It wasn't the most pleasant experience I've ever had. Thankfully, Colb—Mr. Grant and I put out the fire before too much damage was done."

Silas frowned. "You looked in terrible disarray when you rode in yesterday evening."

Amy smiled. Silas was jealous.

Alfred came over to the counter and put an arm around Amy. "Fighting fires isn't exactly a social event, Silas."

"Of course, of course. I couldn't agree more, Alfred," Kane said, "and that's why I think you should forbid Miss Amy to go back out there. Renegades were setting fires all across the Territory yesterday, and they're not likely to stop anytime soon."

177

Alfred looked at Amy and frowned. "Then it wasn't an isolated incident?"

"Of course not," Silas said. "They fired the Rayburn place, shot up the Mayberrys' and . . ."

"Any idea who's behind it?"

Silas shook his head. "Marshal Hines suspects Ben Cravens and his bunch from the Osage."

"But why?" Amy asked. "They don't want to farm."

"That's the point, Miss Amy. They're villainous thieves, desperadoes. They don't have to have a reason. And they tend to view this side of the Arkansas River as their private real estate."

"And outside of the marshal's jurisdiction," Alfred added.

"Precisely," Silas said. "And I don't like the idea of Miss Amy going out there alone."

Amy thought of Colby Grant and laughed. "I'm seldom alone."

Silas Kane's dark eyes flashed. "It's foolhardy, Miss Amy." He shook his head. "Alfred, I should think you'd insist—"

Alfred interrupted. "Silas, I've talked until I'm blue in the face."

Amy reached for the glue pot. "I will not be run off my homestead."

Kane appealed to Amy. "My dear, let's look at this logically. In the first place, Grant will surely win title to the land in court."

"That remains to be seen," Amy said. She put the glue brush into the pot.

"In the second place, just how do you think you're going to put ten acres into cultivation? That is a requirement to obtaining title, you know, even if you beat Grant in court."

Amy slopped the brush onto the proofing galley. Glue spattered, and Kane yanked his hat off the counter.

"Silas," she said quietly. "I believe I have a year to lay in a crop."

"And you, Miss Amy, are going to plow that ground and—?"

She raised her chin. "Why not? Certainly other women have."

"I warned you, Kane," Alfred said.

Silas licked his lips. "Of course, I—I do admire your determination, Miss Amy. Indeed I do. You have that true pioneering spirit. It's—it's just that I hate to entertain the thought of your being out there where you might run into one of those renegades. I'm truly concerned about your safety, Miss Amy," he finished lamely.

"Thank you, Silas. But it will take more than a few miscreants to scare me off." She mustn't be angry with him for wanting to protect her.

Amy put the galley proofs on Alfred's desk and wiped her hands. "If you'll excuse me, I must get to Cross. We do have a paper to put out today." She pulled on her gloves and fastened the light cape about her shoulders.

"Aha!" Silas smiled and bowed slightly. "I anticipated your trip, Miss Amy. My buggy is outside."

"*Merci beaucoup.* How very thoughtful of you," she said. "It will save me from having to hitch up the grays."

"And I'll feel better," Alfred said. "With those ruffians in the territory, I'd rather not have to worry about you today."

With Silas at her elbow, Amy stepped through the doorway and came face to face with Shines White, who snatched off his black hat and smiled his snaggle-tooth grin.

Silas raised his cane. "Get out of here!"

Amy stayed Kane's hand. "No," she said. "He means no harm." She smiled and nodded. "Good day, Shines White."

The old Indian's failing eyes lit up and he ducked his head shyly as he stepped aside.

Across the street, Roughface stood poised to rescue his old friend.

In the brisk morning air, the bay trotted north on the well-worn lane to Cross. The open buggy rolled along smoothly, kicking up dust that gradually dulled the shine on Kane's patent leather shoes.

"I couldn't help overhearing that business is slow for Alfred," Silas said.

Amy dipped her parasol over her face.

"I would like to offer my help," he continued. "Another loan, perhaps?"

Amy forced a smile. "We're already indebted to you, Silas. And I'm very grateful for your offer. But we haven't made a dent on the first loan. How on earth could we ever repay a second one?"

Silas shifted the reins and took her hand. "Miss Amy, I'd like to think that it's all in the family?" He lifted her hand to his lips.

A chill ran up her spine. A few days ago she would have jumped at the chance of Silas proposing to her, but now—now that she and Colby had declared a truce— she wasn't so sure. She was being silly, of course. Silas surely didn't think of her as collateral for her father's newspaper loan, but she was beginning to feel as if she were. Slowly, she withdrew her hand. "Thank you, Silas, but—"

He raised his chin and twisted his neck as if his celluloid collar were too tight. "I don't want to rush you, Miss Amy, but propriety demands of single young ladies—"

"Propriety?"

Irritatingly, Silas cleared his throat. "Many gentlemen might not be as understanding as I am. One could have gotten the wrong impression yesterday evening. You must admit your attire was—was quite—"

"Disreputable?" she offered defiantly.

His face reddened. "And it was not the first time. You seem to have quite a few run-ins with Grant. I would think you would keep your distance."

"Silas! Are you suggesting—?" She snapped the parasol shut.

"Now, now, Miss Amy, I'm not impugning your character. But I would not like the people of this town to think ill of you. Or your father." He reined up before the Cross depot. "I'm sure you will be more careful from now on."

Amy did not wait for Silas to help her down from the buggy. She was too angry. And yet more was at stake than her own pride, or even her own heart. Her father and the future of the newspaper had to be considered.

She greeted Henry Little, the rail agent, and sent her wire for ready-prints, wincing inwardly when she reduced the number by two hundred.

Henry frowned when she dictated that the prints be left at the rail siding at the Indian reservation. "You people are really going to do it, huh?"

Amy swallowed the knot in her throat.

"Now, Henry," Kane said. "When they move this siding down to New Ponca, you'll be glad."

Henry shook his head. "I hope you folks are doing the right thing. Me? I don't really care." He shuffled some more papers. "Miss Amy, would you mind taking along Mr. Grant's ready-prints? Sent word he'd be late today, and I hate to see 'em sitting out on the siding all day."

"Yes, of course we'll take them." She looked at Silas. "That is, if you don't mind."

Silas scowled but waved permission with his cane.

The silence was deafening on the ride back to New Ponca. Amy deliberately tilted her parasol away from Kane. When the heat of the midday sun forced him to peel off his dark coat, she struggled to keep from laughing. It served him right for chastising her. Propriety, indeed! Why couldn't you do anything you wanted to do, anything you were big enough to do? Why were the rules different for women? She sighed. As much as she resented Silas Kane's attitude, she knew society dictated that well-behaved young ladies didn't run around the countryside unchaperoned. But why was it any different for her to ride to Cross with Silas than it was to ride from the homestead with Colby? But Amy knew there was a difference. Silas Kane had made his intentions quite clear to everyone in town by dining often with her and her father. She had attended the races with Silas and accompanied him on evening walks on Grand Avenue.

And you would never come back from a ride with Silas looking like a drowned rat, a laughing drowned rat at that, Amy White. It was unfair to take her frustrations out on poor Silas. She was being swayed emotionally by Colby Grant and the freedom she felt in his presence, the way his laugh came so easily from the sensual mouth beneath that golden mustache . . .

She shivered. Truce or no truce, she mustn't forget that Colby Grant wanted her homestead. And to rid himself of her father's newspaper competition. Why was it so hard to remember that he was a calculating, self-serving, reckless, wanton, sensual . . . ?

She took a deep breath. Silas was a man who looked to the future, who foresaw great things for this country, and for himself. And she could be a part of that. It would be *folle* not to consider Silas Kane a formidable catch. He was a respected and honorable man, albeit a little too logical perhaps, a tad too pretentious at times, and boring—Well, not boring, but reserved. He could do with a touch of Colby Grant's humor.

"Don't you agree, Miss Amy?"

"I'm sorry, Silas. What was that again?"

"I said there's room for only one paper in New Ponca."

Amy gasped.

"Alfred's, of course." He smiled. "And I'm here to assure you of that." He patted her hand.

She trembled from his insinuations, but as they neared the town of New Ponca, Amy couldn't resist a tweak at Silas.

"Perhaps you would like to don your coat once again. Propriety, you know."

"Yes, yes. Of course."

Silas stopped the loaded rig in front of the office of the *Democrat*. "Miss Amy, I apologize if I have upset you. It's just that I'm concerned about your welfare, and about our future—"

"Danny, let's get these unloaded," Alfred said as he stepped through the door followed by the boy.

"Half of those belong to Colby Grant, Papa," Amy said.

"Don't you worry about them, Miss Amy," Silas said. "I'll take them over myself."

Amy nodded agreement. She didn't want to run into Colby. Her feelings were still too confused.

"Oh, Miss Amy," Silas called out as she entered the *Democrat* office. "I shan't see you this evening. Meeting of the Board of Trade. But I'll call for you Saturday evening to attend the box supper."

"I don't recall being invited," she teased, but Silas wasn't listening.

"Hurry up, there, boy." He scowled at Danny. "I haven't got all day."

Amy stood at the counter and stared out the window at Silas and her father talking animatedly. Why was Silas so certain that some other gentleman hadn't asked her to the box supper? Someone like Colby Grant. Of course, she wouldn't have gone with Colby, but why did Silas have to take her for granted? Wasn't there an ounce of romance in the man?

Amy White, she scolded inwardly, you're not a schoolgirl, for heaven's sake. You're eighteen years old. It's time to control your adolescent impulses. Silas Kane is a respected businessman with a fine future ahead of him. You can't throw all that away for a man who drifts with the wind, no matter how silver his tongue is or how bewitching his eyes are, or—

She raked her hands over her eyes. "Stop it!" A bundle of ready-prints crashed to the floor. Amy blinked to clear her vision. Danny ducked down into his oversized shirt.

She laughed. "I'm sorry, Danny. I didn't mean you."

The boy looked around at the empty office.

"I was talking to myself, Danny. Isn't that silly?"

Danny's freckles reddened. "Yessum. Uh—I mean, no ma'am."

"Well, run along now with Mr. Kane and deliver the ready-prints to Mr. Grant."

Thursday morning, Amy waited for her father to return from his breakfast at Mrs. Rhodie's cafe and for Danny to bring the morning *Republican.* But it was Colby Grant who stormed through the door.

With each step, his boots threatened to cave in the pine flooring. He slung the paper on the counter in front of her. "I wanted you to have one of the few legible copies, Amy."

His voice was sarcastic. His eyes were steel blue. The lips under the mustache curled into a snarl around his aromatic cheroot.

"Why—why, what do you mean?" Amy picked up the paper. The print was smudged and barely readable.

"The next time you think about doing me a favor, don't!" He threw his cigar out the open door. He moved closer, shaking his finger in her face. She could smell the strong odor of whiskey on his breath.

"I don't understand. I thought we had agreed on a truce, Mr. Grant." She took a step back.

Colby seized her arm. "Truce?" He lowered his voice to an almost inaudible hiss. "You are an avenging she-devil! And—and—" Steel blue eyes became molten and his voice dropped to a whisper. "And I'm drowning in those eyes again."

Amy felt powerless to move under his hypnotic gaze.

Colby seized her by both shoulders and put his mouth over hers, roughly.

The mustache tickled her upper lip. His mouth, so savage at first, softened and his tongue probed hungrily. Her lips surrendered and a wondrous sensation surged through her heart.

Abruptly, Colby pushed her away.

Amy grappled for the counter stool and sat down.

"Oh, you're a treacherous one," he said adjusting his hat.

"Mr. Grant, I believe you're drunk," she said breathlessly. "A despicable, boorish drunk."

"Drunk? If I had good sense, I would be!"

"What are you talking about?"

"Ask *your* Mr. Kane!" Colby slammed the door on his way out of the office.

Bewildered, Amy slumped over the counter.

Young Danny peeked cautiously around the doorway.

"Danny, what happened?"

"Mr. Kane said he had t'get a load of water fer the bank. And Water Billy's hose got loose and sprayed Mr. Grant's papers."

"Oh-h-h, no-o-o, Danny! How on earth could that have happened?"

Danny fiddled with his cap and looked at the floor.

"Mr. Kane said it was an accident, but I told 'im thet keg wuz full already."

Amy hid her face in her hands. How could Silas have let it happen? Surely it was an accident. And how could Colby think otherwise?

"Thank you, Danny," she said. She touched her bruised mouth and felt again the heat of her own desire.

For the next half hour, Amy poured over the *Republican,* determined to read every smeared word.

Colby's front-page editorial boosted the new school. A committee had been selected to seek voluntary contributions from nonresident lot holders for the planned school. The Homesteaders Protection Association reported on its efforts to stop the harassment of settlers by fires, poisoned water and gunfire. The Board of Trade announced another meeting to discuss ways to promote the town.

Above a report listing the names of claimants going into court in Perry over homestead disputes was a crudely drawn cartoon showing a cow with two contestants. One pulled at the horns and one pulled on the tail. A lawyer, sitting on the stool, milked the cow.

Amy's fists clinched the newspaper. Colby knew that Silas had encouraged her to hire the attorney D. J. Donohoe to defend her right to the homestead.

Colby Grant! That insufferable, despicable man, that wanton heathen, that—that drunken excuse for an editor was publicly ridiculing her. Anger so clouded Amy's vision that she had trouble reading the article about the box supper scheduled for Saturday under the arbor on the school lot.

When she calmed down, Amy sat down to paraphrase Colby's words, setting type on her own article about the box supper. She put the article in the form, making room by taking out a filler about Eli Whitney inventing the cotton gin 100 years ago.

When Alfred returned to the office, she rolled up her sleeves and inked the type as they printed Thursday's edition.

Friday afternoon, Amy attended the tea at Mrs. Hampton's new home. Mrs. Barnes and her daughters Jeannette and Maud were seated on the new divan of upholstered tapestry. Amy sat next to Doc Taylor's wife on one of the crude benches brought in for the meeting. Mrs. Keck shared the cane chairs at the kitchen table with Mrs. Smith, whose young daughters Arvella and Myrtle were on the floor at her feet.

Mrs. Hampton introduced Carry Nation, a heavily corseted woman in her mid-forties with a voice too large for the crowded room. Her daughter Charlien stood meekly at her side.

Mrs. Carrington, with Naomi and a reluctant Rachel in tow, were the last to arrive. "I feel silly in this sailor suit dress. We're a thousand miles from the ocean," said Rachel.

"Well, I think it looks smart," defended Naomi, patting the white piping around her own navy blue collar.

"Ladies! Ladies! Shall we begin?" Mrs. Hampton tapped her spoon against a fragile teacup. "I think this is a momentous occasion. Our first ladies' meeting in our new town. And I'm sure it won't be the last."

They clapped politely. "You have all heard of our guest today, Mrs. Carry Nation, who is going to tell us a little about her background and then explain how we can organize a women's Christian organization for our fair city."

Amy and the other women smiled in Mrs. Nation's direction. Mrs. Hampton fingered her notes. "She was born in Kentucky, the daughter of a plantation owner. She moved to Missouri where after the Civil War she married a surgeon and they had a daughter, Charlien." She paused to smile at the girl wearing a faded and outdated dress. Mrs. Hampton continued, "On her husband's death, our speaker married a Mr. David Nation, a man of the cloth. From that day forward, Mrs. Nation has been working for the Lord."

Mrs. Hampton looked at the faces of the women seated around the room. "I think her remarks will be encouraging to all of us who feel we are facing undue hardships in this new land. Her story should remind us to keep the faith."

"First of all, ladies," Mrs. Nation began, "let's pray for all the weak and God-forsaken men whose souls are doomed to hell unless their womenfolk can erase the scourges of this world."

The women shifted nervously in their chairs.

"Lest you think I'm too harsh, I should tell you my first husband was intoxicated on our wedding day. He was a Freemason, and that lodge of Satan ruined his character and our happy home."

Mrs. Keck, whose husband had organized the new Masonic lodge, fanned herself with her handkerchief.

"Drink," boomed Mrs. Nation, "finally killed him. And so I have vowed to God I would fight to the death the vices of men, fraternal orders of all kinds, liquor and tobacco."

Amy thought of her father's near ruination, and of Colby's drunken tirade yesterday. Well, he may not have been drunk, but he had been drinking. Would he have dared to kiss her if he hadn't been?

Mrs. Nation went on to describe how she had obtained a teacher's certificate to support her daughter and mother-in-law.

"Unfortunately, the devil was at work and I lost my job because the weak parents objected to my strict discipline and teaching methods, which were, I assure you, only in accordance with God's laws.

"My first marriage was cursed, and my poor daughter bore the brunt of it. She developed an ulceration on one cheek which destroyed the flesh and left a gaping hole. Doctors couldn't help. There were numerous surgeries. But I turned to God, and soon she was talking and moving her jaw. See for yourself."

She pulled her daughter to her feet and grabbed her cheek, cruelly, Amy thought.

The young girl wilted from embarrassment.

"Stand up, Charlien. Be proud God sent you a miracle and cured you of a curse bestowed upon you because of a drunken father and, I'm sorry to say, a mother too often distracted."

She allowed Charlien to be seated.

"Nine years ago," Carry said, "I dedicated myself to God and vowed to give Him all my time, means and efforts." She raised her chin and her voice. "The moment I made that decision I was filled with the rapture of God. My heart expanded with love and ecstasy, and I knew God had a special calling for me.

"I prayed for God to find me a husband, and in a few days I met Mr. Nation, an ordained minister. My prayers were answered, and we were married six weeks later."

Amy had heard that David Nation was twenty years older than his wife.

"But God still had trials for me to face. While serving as a correspondent, Mr. Nation was severely beaten and he thought it best to move to Kansas, where he took charge of a church.

"But I did not feel I was fulfilling God's plans for me. And last year we decided to homestead in Oklahoma Territory. Mr. Nation ministers to our flock at Jones Corner, and I do what I can by lecturing in schools and churches against the evils of Freemasonry and the vices of liquor and tobacco."

Rachel Carrington rose to her feet. "Is it true that you snatch cigars and pipes from the mouths of men?"

A mortified Mrs. Carrington yanked Rachel back to her seat.

Carry Nation's nostrils flared. "I'm not ashamed to admit it, young lady. Tobacco is vile! Cigarettes are coffin nails!" Her eyes narrowed as she gazed around the room.

Amy fought back thoughts of Colby's delightful-smelling cigars and her father's occasional smoke. She really couldn't see the harm.

"There are just two crowds, God's crowd and the devil's crowd. One gains the battle by can and the other by can't. I do not belong to the can't family.

"C—A—N are the initials of my name. Altogether, it reads Carry A. Nation." She stopped to let this soak in before continuing. "This is no accident, but providence. This doesn't mean I'll carry a nation, but an aroused heart and conscience will, and I'm the aroused heart and conscience of the people.

"I have a mission to perform here. While the Territory is not yet a state, and its constitution is still unformed, I want to lay the groundwork for total prohibition of liquor."

"Not even for medicinal purposes?" Mrs. Horner asked.

"Especially not for medicinal purposes. Liquor releases the lust in man. You see it every day on the streets. Drunken cowboys and worthless sots allowing their poor women and children to go without clothing and food because of Satan's liquor."

Carry Nation's eyes blazed and her religious fervor shook the lace-curtained windows behind her. "I have stood in front of saloons with picket signs and watched the idiocy of drink. And I must tell you, ladies, I'm finding it quite difficult to restrain myself. Mark my words, one of these days I'll take a hatchet and chop in half every keg of evil fermentation in every saloon in the West."

Several women fanned themselves with their dainty handkerchiefs. Rachel smothered a snicker, drawing the full ire of Carry Nation's eyes.

"The young"—she glared at Rachel—"the young must not be destroyed by lusts of the flesh. There are one thousand harms from improper touch and self-abuse."

Amy felt Colby's burning kiss on her lips.

Mrs. Carrington looked as if she were going to faint. Mrs. Hampton, her face crimson, got up and whispered in Carry Nation's ear.

"Yes, yes, of course," the evangelist murmured and cleared her throat. "Today, we are here to discuss another important project of mine. And that is organizing women into Christian groups throughout the Territory. We aid the less fortunate by washing, sewing and mending clothes. We hold bazaars and sell such items as bright calico clips to the Indians to raise money for our cause." The women visibly relaxed.

"And of course our meetings include Bible reading and discussion. No gossip allowed."

An organizational discussion followed Carry Nation's address, and Mrs. Barnes was elected president. The meeting adjourned, and Amy walked back to the hotel with the Carringtons.

Mrs. Carrington sighed. "I can't help but believe that God sent Carry to the Territory. In spite of all her frankness, she seems to have a calling for the Lord's work."

Amy remained silent. In her opinion, Carry Nation was too dogmatic, and perhaps a cruel person when it came to her daughter.

"Well," said Naomi. "Momma can have her religious meetings, but I think we girl's should start our own club. Don't you, Amy? I don't see a thing wrong with a little fun. Or a little gossip."

"For once, Naomi," Rachel said to her twin, "I have to agree with you."

"We could play parlor games. Invite the most eligible bachelors to taffy pulls . . ."

"Now, girls," Mrs. Carrington cautioned, "don't get too carried away."

Amy laughed.

"Oh, it would be only the very nicest young people invited, of course, Momma," Naomi said.

Rachel's eyes shone. "Like Tex Drummond and Quinton Smyth, Jay Lerner, and"—she turned to Amy—"your Mr. Kane."

Amy felt flushed. That was the second time Silas had been called *her* Mr. Kane.

Saturday afternoon, Amy carefully decorated the box of food prepared by Mabel at the Globe Hotel. She took some lace from her trunk and glued it down across the top. Down the center, she laced a blue ribbon. She wanted her box to be especially attractive and distinctive enough for Silas to recognize.

When Kane arrived for her it was early twilight and Grand Avenue was deceptively quiet. Settlers uninterested in the fund-raising event for the school loaded wagons with supplies. Barefoot youngsters walked the streets with sticks of licorice from Scott's drug store. Bonneted ladies wistfully eyed choice pieces of calico in the window of Jim Hutchin's store. At the hitching rails in front of the town's seventeen saloons, cow ponies switched their tails at flies and waited for their range-riding masters who were bellied up at the bars quenching their thirst in celebration of the end of roundup.

"I hope the box supper isn't ruined by hooliganism tonight," Amy said.

"Don't worry, my dear." Kane patted her hand. "Walt Nolan was voted in as police chief last night. He has vowed to clean up the town." He pointed to a middle-aged man in a black hat and a handlebar mustache walking down the street. The man's hands hovered above two heavy Colts on his hips. Black eyes snapped from alley to street, from wagon to buggy.

"He certainly looks imposing, and a bit tense," Amy said as they turned the corner and headed east on Grand Avenue, where they joined others gathering at the vacant school lot.

Lanterns hung from tree limbs to illuminate the coming darkness. Kane positioned their chairs near the front and placed Amy's decorated box with other adorned packages on a flatbed wagon serving as a stage for the night's festivities.

To Amy's delight, her father arrived with a frail but smiling Mrs. Rhodie on his arm. Danny hovered nearby looking solicitously at his mother's box as it was deposited with the others. Amy waved at the Carringtons, nodded to the Barnes family and the Hamptons. It seemed most of the townsfolk were participating. Including several saloon girls who arrived with fancy boxes and an odd assortment of escorts with uncomfortable grins on their faces. With luck, Walt Nolan's first night on the job as police chief would be a quiet one.

A pony wagon pulled up with a number of Ponca Indians. White Eagle waited for his elk horn chair to be deposited on the ground before he moved from the wagon seat. A woman, who Amy supposed was his wife, sat on a blanket at his side. The rest of the tribal gathering stayed in the wagon with their stoic faces and dark, curious eyes.

Amy was even more shocked when Hennessey, the colored porter at the Globe Hotel, arrived with Eliza Carpenter and a wooden bench. Colby's open invitation had been accepted literally.

And where was the illustrious editor of the *Republican?*

Almost as an answer to her question, Colby Grant

strode up to join Eliza and Hennessey on the bench. On his arm was a striking blond woman. Her light eyes faded into white, almost gossamer skin. Her hair, tied up in a fashionable bun, was as white as a powdered wig. Her dress of green satin stuck out like a sore thumb in the crowd of dark calico dresses and worsted suits of the towns people.

So that was Esther! Amy pursed her lips. To think that she had been savoring Colby's kiss in her memory, that she had almost turned down Silas Kane's invitation tonight. She glanced at Silas. His face was as grim as her own.

The real estate man, H. R. Brodboll, mounted the wagon bed. "Folks, if there had ever been any doubt about our having a school, this dispels it. We've got over a hundred pretty boxes from our charming womenfolk to choose from. And so's we can all eat before it gets too late, let's get on with the auction."

The crowd cheered.

"What am I bid for this one? Smells like chicken to me, folks." He raised the gingham-wrapped box in the air.

"Quarter!" It was the young cowboy with carrot-top hair. A shy smile spread wide over his face. Excited friends began beating him on his back, urging him on.

"Way to go, Tex."

"I got a quarter," yelled Brodboll. "Who'll give me a half. Quarter, quarter, quarter." He nodded to another bidder. "I got a half, half, half. Who'll give me a dollar?"

"Six bits."

He nodded. "Give me a dollar, dollar, dollar."

"Yeah!"

"I got a dollar, dollar, dollar. Anybody else?" He waved the box around. "Sold!"

The crowd hooted as the bashful Tex Drummond

claimed his box and took his seat beside a blushing Rachel Carrington.

Box after box was auctioned, most going for fifty cents or a dollar. The crowd loved it. The fun was in seeing how high a husband or a boyfriend would go to eat dinner with his wife or sweetheart.

And then Amy's box went up for auction. Silas stood up before Brodboll could ask for a bid. "Five dollars."

The crowd cheered, and Silas took a bow.

Amy's face felt as if she had been standing too near a lantern.

"Well, this *is* an auction," Brodboll said. "I've got five dollars. Anybody want to top that?"

The crowd held its breath, waiting for the auctioneer to declare the box sold.

"Seven fifty."

Amy recognized Colby's voice and sank lower in her chair.

The crowd clapped their approval.

Silas turned around to see the bidder.

Brodboll grinned. "Must be something mighty nice in this package."

Colby Grant, Amy thought, I will never forgive you.

"Eigh—eight dollars," Kane choked. His normally pallid face was livid.

The crowd hooted and cheered.

"I've got eight, who'll give me nine? I've got eight, eight, eight, eight—"

"Ten dollars!"

Amy's head jerked up. That was not Colby's voice.

The crowd gasped and grew silent. Amy scanned the gathering for the bidder. Near the wagon of Indians, Roughface stood with legs apart, arms crossed over a vest, open to reveal his mahogany chest. His eyes were riveted on Amy. Sprawled on the ground next to him, with his head resting on a wagon wheel, lay Shines White.

Humiliation burned Amy's cheeks. She chewed on her quivering lip and looked at Colby. His eyes held her gaze for a moment and then flickered.

At her side, Silas gripped his cane. His right knee tremored spasmodically.

The hushed crowd waited. Amy lowered her head.

"Fifteen," Colby said quietly.

After a tense moment of silence, Roughface turned his eyes away from Amy and walked into the darkness. Shines White scrambled to his feet and followed. Amy shivered.

Brodboll wiped his brow. "I've got fifteen, Mr. Kane."

"Twen—twenty—" Kane's voice caught in his throat. "Twenty dollars!"

The crowd laughed nervously. Colby took off his Stetson and bowed in Kane's direction, conceding defeat.

Brodboll cleared his throat. "Going, going, gone! Sold for twenty dollars!"

The crowd clapped politely.

With a smile frozen on her face, Amy forced her head erect as Silas walked quickly to the front of the crowd to take the lace-covered box. Why had Roughface humiliated her? What would make him do such a thing?

The rest of the boxes were auctioned off, and gradually the crowd regained its exuberance and conviviality. Alfred successfully won Hattie Rhodie's basket of food. A friend of the red-haired cowboy bought Naomi's offerings, and Amy heard the girls giggling, obviously having a good time. As expected, Hennessey, the hotel porter, was high bidder for Eliza Carpenter's preparations.

Colby bid on several handsomely wrapped boxes but let them go when the frustrated husbands and gentlemen friends reached their wallet limits. He had been the lone bidder for Esther's bright green box. Realization swept over Amy. Colby had deliberately upped the bids to raise funds for the school. He hadn't wanted to share her box at all!

She frowned pensively. Only Silas had wanted her offering—and Roughface.

When the ladies and their successful bidders began to pair off to share their food boxes, Ben Duvall brought out his violin and entertained the crowd.

White Eagle rose grandly from his chair and clapped his hands. "Good show," he said and then mounted his wagon and headed south to the Ponca reservation with his entourage.

Amy and Silas sat silently as she spread out the contents of her box between them.

"Golly, Miss Amy," young Danny said, sauntering up. His tongue licked his lips. "Whut ya got in thet box? Bet it must taste good, huh, Mistah Kane? Ya payin' out all thet money."

Silas choked on a rabbit leg.

Chapter Eleven

With the door ajar, a cooling breeze wafted through the *Democrat* office where Amy sat pensively at the counter. She needed a good, strong editorial for tomorrow's paper, but nothing seemed to come together. She sighed. If worse came to worst, her father could always use a canned one from the wire service.

"Good morning, Miss Amy," Rachel and Naomi chimed as they entered.

Amy rose to greet them. "You girls are out early today."

"Well," said Rachel, "we've been working on a list for our new Bachelor Girls Club."

"Only the very nicest young ladies, of course," Naomi emphasized.

"Oh, horrors!" Amy said mockingly. "You've come to tell me I've been blackballed!"

Rachel laughed. "Of course not."

"Momma says," Naomi interjected, "that since we are really too young to make good judgments, she and Mrs.

198

Logan will carefully screen all applicants."

"So she's come up with the criteria," Rachel added. "Will you take a look at it?"

"Of course." Amy sat down on the stool. "Let's see. Young ladies between sixteen and twenty-five." She clutched her throat and gasped. "Does that mean I get kicked out in seven years?"

"You'd be a spinster! And I know you and your Mr. Kane are going to be married by that time," Naomi scoffed.

Amy's face glowed with embarrassment.

"Let's see," Naomi continued. "What else? Must be white, Christian young ladies of genteel deportment and legitimate birth."

Amy frowned. "Does that include adoptions?" Amy thought of her own parents who had died coming West before she was old enough to remember.

"Well, it does, if you can determine your parentage. But not if you are a—you-know-what." Naomi blushed.

"A bastard," Rachel giggled.

"I'm going to tell mother," Naomi sniffed.

Amy laughed. "Well, it looks complete to me."

"Momma also wanted to know if you could print these up in an application form?" Naomi asked.

Amy bit her lip. "I'm afraid we'll have to charge for printing them."

"That's okay. Momma said to figure up what it would cost and let her know."

Amy smiled and nodded. "Now, girls, scoot. I've got to write an editorial."

Amy picked up the large leaded editing pencil. She chewed on the unsharpened end and stared out the window. A familiar deformed face peeked in.

"Come in, Shines White," Amy called and wondered where his friend Roughface was hiding. She wanted to give him a piece of her mind for raising Silas's bid at the box supper. Silas had been so angry, he'd accused her of encouraging Roughface.

Shines White shuffled in smelling of strong drink and urine. She looked at his soiled pants and turned her head away. "I'm quite busy."

The gnarled hands of the Indian placed his latest gift on the counter.

Amy jumped and tipped over the stool as she stumbled backward. "What's that?" At first glance it looked like a hornet's nest.

His rheumy eyes watered and his face beamed with his offering. "Bird nest."

Amy stepped back toward the counter. "A bird nest?"

He nodded.

"What kind of a bird nest?" Amy picked up the limb and examined the gray, closely woven nest. The texture felt almost like silk. The oval shape clung to the limb, and there was a small hole for an opening.

Shines White fingered his head and then pointed to Amy.

"You want me to guess?"

He nodded.

Amy smiled. "An oriole?"

He shook his head, and a craggy grin spread across his face.

Amy thought of woodpeckers. No, they nested in trees. Flycatchers? No, their nests were. . . . "I don't know, Shines White. What bird wove this?"

Shines White snickered and held out his hand.

"You want me to pay you?" Amy was flabbergasted.

The old Indian tilted his head almost coquettishly at Amy.

Amy laughed. "Will a nickel do?"

The Indian smiled.

Amy opened the cash drawer and was reminded of their waning fortunes. She dropped the coin into the dirty outstretched hand. "Now tell me the name of the bird, Shines White."

The old Ponca edged backward. "Weaver bird," he said, and with another toothless grin slid out the door.

"But what kind of weaver bird? I've been robbed." She screeched as Shines White waddled down the street toward the nearest saloon, closely followed by his friend Roughface.

She started for the door to stop the old Indian, but she couldn't revive the anger. Laughter welled up in her throat when she thought of the nickel Shines White had conned out of her.

She was still laughing at herself when her father returned from his rounds.

He tossed his bowler on the counter. "Well, you seem to be in better spirits than when I left." He spied the abandoned bird nest on the counter. "What's that damn thing!"

"Papa!" Amy tried to sound matter-of-fact. "I just bought my first piece of native art." She burst into a fit of uncontrollable giggles.

"You bought that damn thing? From that old Ponca Shines White, I reckon."

Amy held her sides as she collapsed in hysterics. Tears ran down her cheeks. "I'm sorry, Papa," she gasped, "for wasting a nickel on that thing."

Alfred shook his white bushy head. "I really don't like the idea of those Poncas hanging around here." He wrinkled his nose. "The whole office smells. And when I think of how you carried on the first time you saw that old Indian . . ."

Properly chastised, Amy sobered. "I know, but Shines White means no harm and he's so funny." She added, "Not that I'm laughing at the poor man, Papa. He has a good sense of humor."

"Doubt if they find much to laugh about, Amy, and I'm sure that money will go for liquor. But I have to give him credit for one thing—putting the first smile on your face since the box supper. I just wish . . ." He hugged Amy close and brushed the curls on her forehead to one side. He sighed.

"You wish what, Papa?"

He released her and sat down at his desk. "I suspect Kane is rubbing off on me, but he's right in suggesting it's best to keep some distance between yourself and the Indians, especially Roughface. He could get the wrong idea, lass."

Amy sobered at the thought of her humiliation when Roughface bid on her lace-covered box.

Chagrined, Amy excused herself to drive to Cross for the ready-prints. She wished she knew a way to solve their money problems. She had already made application to teach at the new school, but in spite of her credentials, the job was by no means a certainty. She headed the grays north. There would be only one more trip to Cross before the New Ponca merchants put the boycott into effect and began using the rail station at the Indian reservation to get their supplies.

Amy was relieved that Silas Kane had been conspicuously absent today. She wanted no accidents if she were asked to deliver Colby's ready-prints. She would deal with the man in her own way. She didn't need Silas's help. When Amy pulled the wagon into the Cross depot, she knew she wouldn't be delivering any ready-prints today. Grant was loading his wagon.

"Morning, ma'am."

Amy's heart fluttered. "Good morn—"

The porcelain blonde stepped out of the waiting room in a bright red dress.

Amy snapped her parasol closed and rudely brushed past Esther on her way to the agent's window. "Please send my usual wire, Henry, and remember, next week's order goes to the Ponca Indian depot," Amy said.

In the reflection of the glass, she watched Colby get

in the wagon beside the woman. He snapped the reins and the wagon moved south.

After completing her business, Amy pushed the grays to get back to New Ponca. How dare Colby Grant flaunt that woman in broad daylight? Carry Nation had been right!

Amy stormed into the *Democrat* office. She knew exactly what her editorial was going to say.

"What happened to that good humor?" Alfred asked as he and Danny unloaded the wagon. He dropped a bundle of ready-prints on the counter.

"There's nothing wrong with my disposition," Amy hissed, "that wouldn't be cured by one less newspaper in this town."

Danny followed Alfred back out to the wagon. "Wimmen," he said. "Can't figure 'em. One minute thar sweet as ripe blackberries and the next minute thar sour as persimmons and bitin' yore head off." Danny shook his head. "Don't think I ever wanna git married."

Alfred's laugh boomed out as Amy seized her pencil and began to write.

DEMON RUM

A most remarkable woman came to visit our fair city last week, a Mrs. Carry Nation from Day County, Indian Territory. Mrs. Nation is working effortlessly to prepare this land for future statehood through her unrelenting campaign to rid the Territory of Demon Rum.

Quite accurately, Mrs. Nation has pointed out that New Ponca has seventeen saloons and as yet, not one church.

The evils of spirits are all around us. We see them in the bleary eyes of the poor and destitute Indian, in the inebriated cowboys who shoot up our town, and in the shameful way otherwise upstanding citizens succumb to even more heinous acts due to the influence of liquor.

Mrs. Nation has reminded the good mothers and daughters of this community that it is our responsibility to protect our families from this affliction, at whatever cost and by using whatever means. Her proposal that the ladies of this town march on the saloons with a Bible in one hand and a hatchet in the other has my endorsement.

Amy signed the editorial with a flourish and put it on her father's desk.

"That didn't take long." Alfred straightened his glasses.

Amy buttoned the clasp of her cape.

"Always indicates strong feel—" Alfred read the editorial and lowered his glasses. "Carrying things a bit far, aren't you, lass?"

"I signed it," Amy said defensively. "No one will blame you, Papa." She started for the door, suddenly contrite. "Unless you think it will cost you advertising."

"No, no. Unfortunately, people like to read things that stir up a controversy. They'll be standing in line waiting to see what in tarnation you're going to write about next."

"Well, then," Amy smiled. "Maybe I better raise our ready-print order next week."

Alfred sighed. "Not just yet, lass."

As Amy worked alongside her father, her anger gave way to frustration and a deep sense of loss. Why were men so blind? Why couldn't Colby Grant see how much she cared about him? And why couldn't she accept the man as the scoundrel he was? Was he really interested in Eliza Carpenter's strumpet? Is that what Colby wanted? Some sickly-looking woman? She sighed. It wasn't fair that Esther's skin was so translucent and unmarred and Amy had to live with that dark birthmark on her forehead.

The next morning, Colby's editorial once again promoted a train stop at New Ponca. Amy nodded in agreement until she came to Colby's concluding paragraph:

> *Too many of us have suffered the losses of having to rely on irregular deliveries from Cross, or the helping hand of so-called friends who aren't as well-meaning as one would first conclude.*

Amy slammed down the paper. His editorial was a deliberate slap at her and Silas Kane for delivering ruined newsprint last week. Well, just you wait, Colby Grant, until you read *my* editorial on Demon Rum, she said to herself.

Amy and her father finished printing the last bundle of ready-prints, and then Alfred made his announcement.

"I'm going to have to ask Silas for an extension, Amy." He took off his ink-stained apron.

"Maybe—maybe things will turn around in a few days, Papa. Maybe someone will pay their bill."

Alfred slumped in his chair and stared at his open ledger.

"You could go to Mr. Barnes's bank and get another loan."

He shook his head. "Tried that." He looked her in the eye. "Since Kane holds the first mortgage, there's no collateral."

"What—what about the homestead?"

"Thanks, lass, but you don't have a clear title."

"Thanks to Colby Grant," she said with derision.

"Now, lass, you're not being fair."

Amy blushed. "Then go to Silas. He's offered to help."

"If I do, I don't want you to feel pressured."

"Me? Papa, don't worry about me." She laughed lightly.

"Just don't change, lass. I know you've been seeing a lot of Kane, but I don't want you to feel obligated."

"Papa, have you ever known me to do anything against my will?"

"Kane's got a lot of attributes a woman looks for in a man"—he swung around in his chair to face her—"but I've also noticed how the sparks fly when you're in the same room with Colby Grant."

"Colby? That insufferable—"

Alfred sighed. "All I'm asking, Amy, is that you keep this business proposition between me and Kane."

"I promise, Papa."

She kissed his temple. "You worry too much. Besides, what if I did decide to marry Silas? He's the town's most eligible bachelor." She slipped out the door and walked toward the hotel before the tears could escape.

Papa was right. Silas would press for an answer to his proposal. Not that she didn't want to be Mrs. Silas Kane. She did. But she did not want to feel she was hostage to her father's fortunes. She wished Silas didn't make her feel that her father's business affairs were so closely aligned to their relationship. There had to be another way to resolve their money woes. There had to be something she could do, something she could sell to make their payment. Something!

"Miss Amy."

She stopped on the stairs and waited for Mr. Pearson to catch up with her.

"Miss Amy, I'm so sorry . . ."

"Yes, what is it, Mr. Pearson?"

"We—we're awfully sorry, but we can't carry your account past this week."

Amy held onto the bannister.

"I spoke to your father last week, but—"

Amy sighed and nodded. "I'll take care of it, Mr.

Pearson." But now, she didn't know. She walked slowly up the stairs to the landing, mentally listing the items in the trunk—a few trinkets of worthless costume jewelry, her mother's tarnished silver-plated brush and comb set, the mussel shell necklace, some worn clothing, the homestead papers . . .

Amy knew what she had to do. She went to her father's room and opened his wooden trunk. She dumped out its contents unceremoniously and retrieved the papers to her claim. She held them to her breast. This was the one and only thing, outside of the newspaper, that had any real worth. And without a clear title, it was of value only to Colby Grant. There was no other choice. Her father and his newspaper were more important than her silly, naive dreams.

Amy walked quickly to the corner of Grand and marched east past the Red Dog saloon. She held her breath past the butcher shop and ignored the men standing in front of Brodboll's tent. She glanced at Kane's bank on the other side of the street, but did not slow her pace. She marched across the intersections at Third and Fourth, and stopped in front of Paley's saloon. She steadied her trembling hands clasped around the homestead papers, took a deep breath and marched next door to the office of the *Ponca Republican*.

Colby's shirtsleeves were rolled up to clean his press of the morning's ink. The smell of kerosene was strong in the small building. The late afternoon light cast shadows across the press, but left Colby Grant's mustache in glinting sunlight.

Amy sucked in her breath.

Colby turned, the smile on his face fading as he wiped his blackened hands. "Afternoon, Amy," he said curtly, his blue eyes hard.

She nodded.

"Did you come to apologize?"

"Apol—?" Any lowered her eyes.

"Yes! For being such a stuck-up little snob at the depot." He wiped his hands and walked over to the counter.

Amy lifted her chin. "I doubt that I have anything in common with Esther."

The mustache twitched. "Don't tell me you've never seen an albino before?"

"Albino? You mean Esther?" Amy was incredulous.

"It happens sometimes, a genetic short circuit." He put an unlit cheroot in his mouth. "She's black, of course, and the mother, who thought Esther was God's curse, or worse yet, the offspring of a white man, dumped her on Eliza Carpenter's doorstep."

"I—I'm sorry. I din't know she was black."

"Can you imagine how it must feel to be white in a world that is primarily black? Poor kid doesn't fit in much of anywhere. I try to be the big brother she never had." Colby shook his head.

"Yes—yes." Amy lowered her head. "I was unkind. If you'll convey how sorry I am—"

"Consider it done." The smile broadened.

Amy licked her lips.

"Something else I can do for you?" A smile played on Colby's lips beneath the mustache smudged with black ink.

Amy took a deep breath. "You once offered me two hundred dollars for my share of the homestead. Does that offer still stand?" The amount would not only pay the payment now due Silas, but wipe out the entire loan.

Colby stared at Amy and frowned. Perspiration dampened her face. The dark spot near her forehead seemed to pulse. And in her hands she clutched the homestead papers.

Any maintained her gaze and fought to keep her lips form trembling.

"That depends."

The despicable man was deliberately trying her patience. "On—on what?"

"Why? Why do you want to sell out now? Especially since you got me to agree to a truce?"

"Seems to me you've broken that truce."

"I've broken it?"

Amy gritted her teeth. He always sidetracked her. She steeled herself to look into his eyes. "Mr.—"

"Uh-oh, this is serious."

Her voice trembled. "Mr. Grant, do—do you want to buy my claim?"

He frowned. "Is Alfred in trouble?"

"Of course not," she scoffed.

He shook his head. "There's only one reason I can think of that would make you give up that place after all you've been through—your father."

Amy squeezed her eyes shut. He wanted her to beg. He wanted to squeeze the last shred of pride from her body.

"You proud little vixen," Colby whispered. He came around the counter.

"Don't touch me!"

He stepped back. "Amy, if Alfred's in trouble—"

"He's—he's not in trouble. It's—it's just that I have far too much to do to worry about the claim these days and—and Mr. Donahoe says I haven't much chance in court and—"

"Donahoe be damned! I don't want to buy your claim, Amy. But if Alfred needs a loan to tide him over—"

Amy's eyes flared. "You're not satisfied to get my claim," she hissed. "You want it all. You want the newspaper, too. You want to take away the only thing left for Papa."

"Now, Amy—"

"No! I was willing to give up the homestead," Amy said, "but I'll never let Papa give up the newspaper. I'll fight you until your newspaper is run out of town, Mr.

Grant." She whirled and stalked out.

Why did she ever think Colby Grant was a reasonable man, or an honorable one? Behind those seemingly compassionate blue eyes, that golden mustache with its teasing smile, was a very devious man, a man of extreme deception, who hid patiently behind his mask of friendship just waiting for the homestead and the newspaper to fall into his lap.

"Well, we'll see about that, Mr. Grant," Amy said to herself as she marched back to the hotel and put the papers back in the trunk, her eyes threatening to spill their tears. "With some help from Silas, you'll never get your hands on Papa's paper," she whispered. "Never!"

Silas joined Alfred and Amy for dinner that evening at the Globe Hotel. Alfred seemed restless and somewhat agitated throughout the meal. He spoke very little to the banker, who was in unusually good spirits, his dark eyes snapping below the thin eyebrows.

Amy's stomach fluttered nervously and she left most of her food on her plate. Having opened her eyes to Colby Grant's true nature, she eagerly accepted when Silas suggested a buggy ride before they retired for the evening.

"It's been a long day for Amy," her father protested. "Thursdays are always tiring. Perhaps you should turn in early tonight, lass."

"*Au contraire,* Papa. A ride in the cool night air will make me sleep better." Amy kissed her father's cheek. "Shall we go, Silas?"

Alfred followed them out the door and stood by as Silas assisted Amy into the buggy. When they headed east in the fading twilight, she turned back to wave to her father and saw Roughface lurking at the corner, alone and scowling as his eyes followed Silas Kane's buggy.

Amy didn't realize she'd been twisting her handkerchief until Silas stilled her nervous hands with his and smiled. She forced herself to settle back into the upholstered seat, clutching her wrap against the cool evening air. Dust sifted through the air even after they left the confines of the town. Grasshoppers in the dry prairie fields sang menacingly as the bay clopped down the dusty road.

"Do you suppose we'll get some rain?" Amy asked, trying to make small talk. "Everything seems so dry."

"If we don't get rain soon, there won't be much wheat for winter pasture. Am afraid a number of farmers are apt to lose their homesteads."

Amy thought she saw Silas smile.

He drove the buggy off the road just west of the twin bridges. He jauntily leaped from the rig, tied the reins to a railing and assisted Amy to the ground.

The twin bridges made for a lovely setting, and Silas had obviously been sensitive to that. Perhaps romance was just beneath the surface, waiting to leap out after they were married. He took off his derby and laid it with his cane inside the buggy. They walked across the south bridge where a small rivulet of water flowed under the planks.

"Miss Amy, I've already spoken to your father and I wait only your consent."

Amy found she had no voice.

"I think we would make a striking couple," Kane continued. "I would be most proud to have you serve as my hostess. Our lives were destined to—"

Amy turned away. "I—I understand Papa has asked you to delay repayment of his loan." She had to get it out in the open.

The light glinted off his dark eyes. "Yes, yes, he has." Kane rubbed the palms of his hands and smiled. "But that shouldn't concern you. One always accommodates members of the family." He cleared his throat. "And I assure you, Amy, that as my wife, you'll never have to worry about Alfred. The newspaper could be a most useful asset in the future. I do have ambitions beyond being a banker." Kane stuck his hands in his pockets and inhaled deeply. "Some day the Territory will be a state and I intend to run for political office. It would be most advantageous to have an editor supporting me."

"You will make a fine state senator," Amy said.

"Senator? I was thinking of governor."

"That, too."

"You will be the most envied woman in the state." He smiled. "As the wife of the governor, Miss Amy, you would be my hostess for the many soirees and parties that are so necessary to political life."

She turned and walked across the north bridge.

Kane trailed along behind. "Let's not be coy, Amy."

"Silas—Silas—" Where was that interfering Colby Grant when she needed him? She wasn't ready to give Silas an answer, but she knew she couldn't stall him much longer. If only her father could repay the loan on the newspaper before she and Silas were married.

Silly girl, what are you worrying about? Any woman in her right mind would be eager to wed Silas Kane. What sane person would pass up the chance to be first lady of this state? How could any woman think of turning down Silas? And for what, or rather, for whom? For a man who is treacherous, deceptive and wanton? Oh, God, yes, wanton.

Carry Nation was wrong. Lust didn't have a thousand faces. Just one, Colby Grant's.

"Miss Amy!"

"Yes, Silas." She turned to face him. The moonlight illuminated his dark hair; his pallid face and his narrow lips pursed with impatience.

She was glad her own face was in the shadows, that Kane's reserve would never allow him to touch her face and discover the tears there.

"Your answer?"

"I would be proud to be your wife, Silas." The lie came out in a whisper.

He clapped his hands. "Let's go tell Alfred."

"I'm—I'm sure he knows," she said. "But, Silas, I do ask one thing of you."

"And that is?"

"Papa needs my help so desperately right now, Silas. It would mean so much to me if we could—if we could wait awhile before making an announcement about our"—she swallowed—"about our betrothal."

He frowned as he pondered her request. "I don't believe in long engagements, Amy, but for the time being I will do as you wish." He took her elbow and steered her back to the buggy.

Without further comment or ado, Silas drove back to the hotel and walked Amy to her door. He solemnly planted his thin lips on her hand and walked away swinging his gold-tipped cane.

Amy sagged to her cot, shivering from an inner chill. A feeling of hopelessness swept over her; an agonizing pain stabbed her breast and pierced her unhappy heart.

Silas Kane had not even attempted to kiss her on the lips. He had not used the word "love." The man had made her feel that his marriage proposal was just another business deal. Would he be this distant, this cold in the privacy of their own home after they were married? Would Silas Kane ever awaken the passion lying dormant in her loins? Would his touch send her soaring into heights of feverish ardor? Would his lips dare to crush hers in a wild, uncontrollable urge of passion, as Colby Grant's had? She could not bear to think of it.

Amy's eyes were puffy the next morning when she walked into the *Democrat* office.

Alfred looked up from his ledger and said, "Silas told me at breakfast that you had agreed to marry him."

"Did—did he tell anyone else?"

His eyes scanned her face. "No. No, he told me quite privately. He said you wanted to wait on the announcement."

Amy smiled with relief.

"He didn't understand the delay." Alfred sighed. "Are you sure you're doing the right thing, Amy?"

"I am, Papa." Amy tried to put a lilt into her voice. "How many young ladies get proposals from men such as Silas Kane? He's ambitious. He has wonderful plans for his future and for New Ponca. What woman wouldn't want to be a part of that, Papa?"

Alfred's brow knitted.

"Silas"—Amy continued—"Silas offers stature and stability. I consider myself very fortunate. I thought you would be happy for me." She looked away from his soul-searching eyes.

"I haven't heard you mention the word 'love'," he said.

"Papa!" Amy feigned shock. "I never thought of you as a romantic."

"Lass, I have to ask about Colby Grant."

Amy turned away from her father and busied herself with straightening the clutter on the counter.

"Don't do this for me, Amy, or for the *Democrat*. We'll manage somehow."

"I'm marrying Silas," she said. After a long silence, Amy turned to find her father's head bowed. Ink-stained hands covered his face. She went to him and bent down to kiss the jowled cheek. She put her arms around his shoulders and comforted him. And she smelled the liquor on his breath.

"Oh, Papa," she wailed, and the tears flowed for what they had both lost that day.

Chapter Twelve

The first heavy frost of the season spawned wool sweaters among the citizens of New Ponca and spurred frenzied activity throughout the community. As fast as lumber wagons could unload, weatherbeaten canvas tents were replaced with small one- and two-room structures. Every coach and carriage from the Cross depot brought more wives and children to the thriving town of New Ponca. Hotels overflowed with families waiting to move into modest new homes and with voracious speculators who scrutinized the town for unexplored opportunities.

On Grand Avenue, the druggist, Will Chase, completed his two-story structure and proudly announced that henceforth the top floor would be known as the "Opera House." He invited Brodboll and his thespian recruits to stage a play for the town's gentry.

But construction of the school and the upcoming celebration to dedicate the building generated the greatest excitement in town. The 32-by-64-foot building took shape under the able hands of the town committee, and Amy confidently submitted her credentials for a teaching position.

If she could be hired as an instructor at the new school, she could repay her father's debt before she married Silas. She didn't want to marry Silas as collateral for her father's newspaper. If—*when* she married Silas, she wanted to come to him free and clear. Her pride demanded it.

Amy tried not to think of Colby Grant. Ever since he had refused to buy her homestead, she staunchly avoided the *Republican* publisher. When she saw him striding down the street in her direction, his Stetson cocked over one eye, she quickly crossed to the other side of the avenue. Invariably, he would pucker his lips beneath that sensual mustache and whistle that infuriating "Oh, Susannah."

Amy spent much of her free time at the homestead, where she picked pecans and currants and monitored the ugly roan's recovery. On days when Colby's replacement for his horse was tethered in front of the soddy, she would turn around and go back to town in frustration.

She tried to keep her mind busy working with her father at the *Democrat,* gradually adjusting to making runs to the rail station at the Ponca Indian reservation rather than to Cross, passing on news items to her father, and always being on the alert for a hidden bottle of spirits.

Her decision to marry Silas obviously bothered her father. He had staggered a couple of times lately while coming down the hotel stairwell, and she had noticed an unusual number of typographical errors in his typesetting. The shadow of the newspaper's debt burdened them equally. But she did not have the heart to rummage through his things in search of a whiskey bottle. If it took the pain away, how could she deny her father a few moments of escape?

She attempted to push her personal problems aside as frenzy began to build for the school dedication. Both the *Republican* and *Democrat* newspapers touted the planned celebration in every edition. The Board of Trade, in its zeal to promote the new town, sent flyers around the world heralding the schedule of events—Indian war dances, horse races and a variety of athletic games.

The townsmen spent hours, to the neglect of their own businesses, discussing ways to present New Ponca as a flourishing city. One such scheme involved shipping in a load of street lamps from a city back East that had switched to electricity. The kerosene-burning lamps were quickly erected on the major streets and did, Amy admitted, give off an aura of a real city.

The citizens of Cross did not sit idly by, but had begun to promote their own day of celebration—the sixtieth day of the birth of the government-sanctioned town. When the New Ponca townsmen heard that a German band had been hired at Cross, they contacted a half dozen bands and orchestras and received commitments from three.

It was suspected that citizens of Cross had been behind an effort to ban the Indians from participating in the New Ponca celebration. When Kane got wind of it, he wired the Indian Department in Washington explaining the activities and the role the Indians would play. In due time, permission was received allowing the Poncas to attend the celebration. The frenzied competition between the communities resulted in numerous frays and skirmishes as the heralded day neared.

Amy considered herself as patriotic as the next person, but Silas had become rabid in his support of the school celebration. He spent considerably more time at the *Democrat* than at his bank.

Looking over Alfred's shoulder, Kane read his latest

promotional flyer and smacked his lips in approval.

"Good! Good! Good! I have invited a number of people from Guthrie. Renfrow, the Territorial Governor, and a few others I think are important to the future of this town"—he turned to Amy—"and our future."

She smiled weakly. His gift last evening, a copy of Mrs. John Sherwood's book *Manners and Social Usages,* still rankled.

"It's important," Silas continued, "that the right people become aware of my—our activities. And I assume you have sent out news releases to all the newspapers in Kansas, Missouri and Arkansas."

Alfred nodded.

Silas rubbed his hands. "Great! Great!"

Alfred pulled off his printing shade. "Aren't you just a bit worried? Thousands could show up, Silas. Then what will we do? Where will we put them?"

Silas dismissed the concern with a wave of his hand. "We'll worry about that when the time comes." He looked at his black leather notebook. "Let's see, Will Chase has agreed to let us use the opera house for the banquet and ball, and Colonel Miller is donating the beef for the barbecue."

"Sounds like you and Mr. Barnes have it all figured out."

Silas frowned at the mention of his banking competitor. "White Eagle has consented to bring in some dancers for the day. And the colonel is rounding up twenty wild Texas steers for the Indians to chase down with bows and arrows."

"Real live savages, huh?" Alfred's voice was sarcastic.

Amy hoped Roughface would keep Shines White on the reservation.

Silas sniffed. "Just think of the impact." He waved his hand across an imagined panorama. "A new city so progressive through its fine leadership that in two months—two short months—we have twelve hundred citizens, the finest school in the Territory, an opera house, five mercantile stores—"

"—and," Amy interjected, "seventeen saloons, raw sewage running in the streets, a half-dozen knifings and shootings every week, and no jail for the drunks that fall on your doorstep."

Silas snapped the slim note pad closed. "You left out two newspapers," he reminded her through pursed lips.

Amy felt the heat in her cheeks. She must learn to control her temper.

Alfred winked at Amy.

"I shall call for you at six this evening," Silas said curtly. He walked out the door into the malodorous arms of Shines White in his feathered black hat. "Get out of the way," Kane snarled and looked back at Amy. "After we're married I'll put a stop to his hanging around here."

Alfred's fleshy jowls reddened. "As long as I'm editor, Shines White is welcome here."

Amy hugged her father as Shines White, oblivious in his drunken state to Kane's threat, dimpled his sagging jaw with a finger just before sliding down the outside wall to the ground. They watched as Roughface lifted Shines White to his feet and shouldered his weight as they staggered down the street.

Saturday evening, as Silas guided Amy down Grand Avenue, she felt as if her face would crack from smiling if she had to speak to one more citizen. The new street lights flared at each corner, and lanterns burned dimly in the living quarters of many stores. The tempo of a piano picked up and raucous laughter became louder.

Across the street, a handful of inebriated cowboys spilled out of the Red Dog saloon and swaggered down the boardwalk, cursing and kicking the drunks they stumbled over.

"We'd better hurry, Amy," Silas said as they passed Paley's saloon where five young range riders braced themselves against the building and checked their weapons. "The Blocker outfit," he whispered.

"I see the law is on duty," she said.

Across the street, Walt Nolan leaned against a railing and spun the cylinder of his Colt. Light from the street lamp glinted off his black mustache and the brim of his black hat as the cowboys mounted up.

The young ranch hands lined up their horses five abreast across the street. "Haiyee-ee-ee!" they yelled and started down Grand Avenue firing their guns at every light and lantern they saw.

Silas pushed Amy against the wall of the corner drug store.

Walt Nolan jumped on the nearest horse and followed the cowhands down the street, his own revolvers blasting.

"Someone's going to get killed," Amy protested.

"We've got to clean up this town," Silas yelled over the din.

"But those are just young boys. They're probably celebrating Halloween tonight instead of next Tuesday."

"Amy, you astound me. Those scoundrels are carrying guns, not jack-o-lanterns! It's going to be expensive to replace those street lamps."

"I know, but wouldn't it be better to lock them up than kill them? When are we going to build a jail?"

"This evening you have asked: one, when is the town going to build a sewer system; two, when is this town going to brick the streets; and three, when is this town going to build a jail? My, my, Amy. Perhaps you should be the politician," he said sarcastically.

Amy bit her lip. She knew she was far too outspoken.

She knew that as Silas's future wife she should be supporting his efforts, not carrying on her own crusades. She would learn, if she had to tape her mouth shut.

The next morning the whole town buzzed with the news that one of the Blocker cowboys had been killed by Walt Nolan.

"Nolan didn't stop at the city limits," the carpenter, Keck, protested to Alfred. "He followed them right on down to the river, shooting to kill."

"Good riddance, I say," Silas interjected.

"You mean Walt Nolan went outside of his jurisdiction?" Alfred asked.

Keck nodded. "That one knows no jurisdiction. He followed the Blocker boys clear past the Old Maid's Spring to the B&M Ford, aimed straight at them. One of the ponies went down, but the boy rolled out of his saddle and jumped on behind one of the other riders. By the time they got to the B&M Ford, one was dead in his boots. The others splashed through on a run and made it to the Osage side, but two of them were wounded."

Alfred sighed. "Well, that's the third one for Walt Nolan's Boot Hill."

"Well, the Blocker boys are a wild lot," Silas defended.

Fighting against interjecting her own opinions, which would no doubt infuriate Silas, Amy gathered her things. "I'm off to the Chase Drug Store. We're decorating the opera house for tonight's Halloween party."

She was the last of the members of the proposed Bachelor Girls Club to arrive. Naomi was directing the freckle-faced cowboy, Tex Drummond, in his placement of the large pumpkins. When he had finished he grinned and said, "This looks like a hen party, so I'm going to scoot." He tipped his hat and clamored down the stairs.

"Let's put corn stalks behind the pumpkins," Rachel suggested.

Amy picked up the rolls of orange and black crepe paper ribbon. "Where on earth did you find this?"

"Poppa picked it up in Kansas City on his last trip," Jeannette Barnes said.

"Oh, this is going to be so much fun," Rachel said to Amy.

"Rachel, did you bring the mirrors and candles?" Naomi asked as she stood on a ladder hanging a wreath of dried thistle and autumn leaves interwoven on a grapevine.

Amy removed a tack from her mouth and waved her hammer. "Lanterns will be safer than candles."

"I suppose you're right," Rachel said, looking down at the street. "Oh, there goes Mr. Grant. Looks like he's headed for the bank." With a sigh, she turned away from the window. "Are we going to play that silly game?" Rachel shifted a pumpkin to a corner.

"We don't have a cellar," Maud Barnes reminded the Carrington twins.

"What are you talking about?" Amy asked.

"I know," said Naomi, "we can use the outside stairway."

"Are we all wearing white?" Maud queried.

"Of course," all except Amy chimed.

"Will somebody please tell me what's going on?" Amy laughed.

"Well, at midnight," explained Naomi, "we each take a candle." She held it in her hand like a young Lady Macbeth. "In our left hand, we carry a mirror. Then we're supposed to slowly walk down the stairs backwards to a cellar." She smiled.

"And?" Amy looked from face to face.

"That's when we'll see the faces of our future husbands in the mirror," Jeannette said.

Rachel giggled. "It helps if a friend happens to be waiting down below."

"Like Tex," the girls teased.

222

Rachel blushed.

Amy laughed. "What if you see someone you don't like?"

"Close your eyes—"

A barrage of gunfire broke out on the street below. Screams rent the air and horses thundered down the street. Amy and the young ladies ran to join Rachel at the window. Amy raised the sash.

Walt Nolan on a borrowed bay was in hot pursuit of three galoots on horseback heading for the river.

"Oh, no, not again!" Amy cried.

"Get Doc Taylor," someone yelled.

Men crowded around the front of Kane's bank directly across the street from the drug store. Will Chase ran out to the street.

"What happened?"

"Robbery. Nolan's after 'em. But some poor fool got caught in the crossfire."

"Know who he is?"

Amy saw her father rounding the corner of Second and Grand, one hand holding down his derby and a note pad clenched in the other.

"Not real sure, but he's wearing a big hat. Let's turn him over."

"No! No!" Amy cried. Rachel had just said she saw Colby heading for the bank. She ran for the outside stairway. "Colby!" Amy screamed as she clattered down the stairs.

Will Chase stepped out of her way as she flew to the corner and into the mob gathered in front of the bank.

"Get back! Get back! Let the doc through!"

The crowd pushed Amy back against the window of the bank. She looked in. Silas Kane was crawling out from under a desk. Alfred stood on the bank's whittler's bench, trying to see into the midst of the throng.

"Let me through, please," she pleaded.

"Colby, please God, not Colby," she whispered.

Kane squeezed through the doorway to the street.

"He's a goner, folks," Doc Taylor yelled.

"Amy!" Kane pulled on her arm.

She shook off Kane's restraining hand and fought her way to the core of the crowd.

"He never harmed anyone but himself."

The voice belonged to Colby Grant. Amy wept with relief.

The crowd shifted to permit Amy inside the circle. Shines White lay on the ground, with his black, feathered hat in the dust. Roughface cradled the old man's body where a red stain spread across his bare chest with its hideous scars.

"Oh, Shines White," Amy said as she knelt down beside him.

Colby placed a comforting hand on her shoulder.

The old Indian opened his rheumy eyes and looked up into Amy's face with his shy, snaggle-toothed smile. "Ho, *Tonde Xtha*." His hand raised slightly in some kind of sign and then fell limp.

"What—what did he say?" she asked Roughface.

The tendons in the arms around Shines White tensed. The dark eyes in the mahogany face looked solemnly at Amy. "He say, 'I greet you, little Prairie Flower.'"

Alfred reached out to Colby to steady himself as he looked down at the old Indian. He shook his head. "No! No!"

Amy put her hands to her face and sobbed. Poor Shines White, in deathbed hallucinations, had mistaken her for his deceased wife.

Colby's arms went around Amy and helped her to her feet. The crowd, having no further interest in a dead Indian, dispersed.

"You're right, Father," Amy said softly. "He should have stayed on the reservation where he belonged."

Roughface lifted the body of the old Indian in his arms and walked down the dusty street alone.

Kane grabbed Amy's shoulder and turned her around. "This is no place for a lady." He glared at Colby.

Tears streamed down Amy's face as Roughface headed south with his heavy burden.

"It's just a dead Indian," Silas hissed.

"He—he was my friend."

"I'll see to him, Amy," Colby said. He picked up Shines White's hat. "I'll get the wagon and take him to White Eagle."

"I'll go with you," Amy said.

Dark eyes narrowed in Silas Kane's face. "The Halloween party is tonight. The announcement—"

"I'm sorry, Silas. This is something I have to do."

Kane glowered at Colby, but stepped aside.

Colby ushered Amy to the livery and within minutes they had overtaken Roughface.

With Shines White in his arms, the tall Indian marched with a stoic expression and unfaltering steps down the dusty trail. He showed no signs of fatigue, but when Colby halted the wagon, Roughface relinquished the body. He climbed up in the wagon and sat down by the old Indian and began a soft, mournful chant.

The wagon rolled south down the well-beaten trail. The flat prairie gave way to rolling hills with thickets of plum bushes and groves of pecan trees along the Arkansas River.

After a couple of miles, Sherbon-Waugh's lumber yard came into view near the Ponca reservation train depot. They passed the unpainted frame structures of the Indian agent's office and the tribal store.

Colby looked back, and Roughface remained unmoved, continuing to keen softly.

They rode on another three miles, past a scattering of log and frame homes. In the yards, strips of meat hung for drying with swarms of flies hovering.

Roughface grunted and motioned to Colby to pull

up in the yard of a white frame structure with a roofed porch.

"Chief White Eagle's home."

An Indian woman draped in a blanket stepped outside. Roughface spoke to her in Ponca. The woman went back inside.

"Go." Roughface directed Colby to turn right, past a large brick structure.

"The Indian boarding school," Colby explained as they passed schoolchildren with shaved heads playing inside the fence. "Lice," he added.

They rode past other frame houses, but none with the startling white paint of White Eagle's home.

Roughface silently directed them to a small log cabin, almost a hovel. He slid off the wagon, picked up the body of Shines White and carried him through the door.

Amy and Colby followed. The room smelled of urine, stale food and whiskey. Blankets were piled on a pole bed in one corner. A bowl of soured food rested on the wooden table. A stove in the center of the room was cold, the wood box empty. A faded tintype of an Indian maiden hung on the wall.

Roughface laid Shines White on the blankets. "White Eagle will come soon to paint his face."

"Pai—paint his—?"

"An Indian custom," Colby whispered.

Roughface took a knife from his waistband and, in a flash, cut his ankles above his moccasined feet, his arms below his elbows.

Amy let out a little yelp and clung to Colby as blood trickled down Roughface's limbs.

"Just nicks," Colby whispered.

Roughface raised a swath of his own hair above his ear and shaved his scalp, taking the short hairs and sprinkling them on Shines White's body. He began anew his soulful lament.

"We'd better go, Amy," Colby said gently. The keening echoed through the cabin and was joined by the wailing of men and women pouring down the dusty road to Shine White's cabin. In the distance, the sound of a drum beat out a dirge.

Colby helped Amy into the wagon, but she stayed his hand from turning the wagon back to town as White Eagle arrived.

An aide helped the old chief down from his wagon and handed him the clay pot with red paint and a brush. White Eagle started toward Shines White's cabin, but stopped when he saw Colby and Amy.

The imposing figure walked up to their wagon.

"Greetings from White Eagle," the chief said. "Visitors welcome, but busy now." He looked at Amy and paused. He smiled slightly, then turned back to the task ahead and entered Shines White's hovel.

Colby headed the wagon home. When the sun dropped to the horizon, he halted the wagon and stepped down to light the lanterns on the splash board and tailgate.

"When—when will they—"

"Four days," Colby said. "They'll set up a tent, smoke peyote for a while, give away everything Shines White had, have a feast and kill a horse."

"I forget, sometimes, how pagan they are."

"Nothing too pagan about it, as far as I can tell. They'll get up every morning and look out from the tepee flap in a different direction—north, south, east and west—and on the fourth day when Shines White hasn't risen from the dead, they'll bury him."

"But the feast—you make it sound like a celebration."

"It is. The better the feast and the more blankets, ponies or whatever the family has to give away, the more they are honoring the departed. Not much different from an old-fashioned Irish wake, I suspect."

Amy shuddered. "I guess I'll never know what caused

those ugly scars on Shines White's chest."

"The sun dance," Colby said. "They tie thongs through their skin and to a pole in the center of the dancing arena. The young men dance continuously until the skin rots or is pulled away and frees them."

"How awful."

"It's been outlawed. Shines White was one of the last. But the dance was an important passage for young men of the tribe. It proved their endurance, their manhood. And the hallucinations they had from weakness and delirium were considered messages from the Great Spirit."

They rode the remaining five miles back to town in silence. Only the fading drums and the hooves of Colby's team broke the silence. The stars grew brighter as the night came on, and Amy shivered from the cool air.

Colby unbuttoned his denim jacket and wrapped it around her, drawing her shivering body to his warmth.

She tensed at first, but when Colby made no further demands, she relaxed and let her head fall on his shoulder. She drank in the manly aroma of him, the warmth of his body, felt the muscles contract as her lips brushed his neck. Contentment spread through her and a soft sigh escaped her lips.

When they neared New Ponca and heard the Halloween revelers, Amy sat up primly and Colby buttoned his jacket. They drove up Fourth Street and turned left at Central. A handful of youngsters with lanterns and treat sacks were scrambling from one home to another. They watched as two older boys turned over the outhouse at the A. C. Smith home.

The wagon moved up Third Street. The buggies and carriages were parked and the fiddles were playing upstairs at Will Chase's opera house.

Colby reined the team left on Grand Avenue. Bryan Hiskins, with a sack of candy in one hand and a shotgun in the other, guarded his butcher shop. Staggering drunks spilled out of Paley's saloon under the watchful eye of Walt Nolan. Only when revelers were a safe distance away did they dare pierce the sky with gunshots.

Colby turned the wagon right on Second Street, and Amy saw the glow of the lantern in the window of the *Democrat.* Colby looked at Amy and she shook her head. He drove on to the Pearson Hotel and walked Amy to her door.

She stopped before entering. "I—I wonder if it would be permissible for me to attend the services." She raked back the dark tendrils falling around her face.

Colby looked into her face and smiled. "Amy, I think I'm beginning to understand."

"I know it seems strange, but Shines White was my friend. That's all. There's really nothing to understand."

Colby nodded. "I'll find out about the services, if you want."

"Good night, and thank you, Colby," she said softly and closed the door before she remembered she had wanted to ask him again to buy the homestead. She pulled open the door, but Colby had vanished.

Exhausted, Amy fell into bed.

Minutes later, there was a knock on her door. She recognized the harsh rap of a cane and did not answer.

Wednesday, the editor of the *Republican* stormed into the office of the *Democrat.*

"What in the hell is this?" Colby's voice boomed.

Amy gasped and stepped back from the counter.

His eyes were like steel, his muscles taut. The bones in his jaw ground back and forth. His fists were clenched around a piece of paper. This was not the same man who had traveled to the Indian reservation with her last evening.

"Kindly—kindly do not speak to me in that tone of voice." What had happened to the man who had held her so close, so tenderly, last night?

"I'll speak any damn way I want to! What the hell have I got to lose?"

"Please keep your voice down! They can hear you all the way down the street." Panic rose in her breast. Colby Grant was a madman.

"I don't give a damn if they hear me clear up to Ark City!" He rounded the counter with one huge step and moved menacingly toward Amy.

"Mr. Grant!" She took another step backward.

"Back to 'mister,' are we? Why in the hell can't you call me by my name?" He took an even bigger step.

"As you wish, Col—Colby," she said in appeasement. He was stalking her like some defenseless prey. She moved back to put the type cases between them.

His long arms reached across to seize her, and she stepped back behind the press. He feigned a move to the right, and she fled to the left and into his path. She stepped back and back until she was in the corner, his face leering into hers. He was acting like an animal. He had gone berserk. She told herself to keep calm.

"In—in the first place, Mr. Gra—Colby, I have no idea what you're talking about."

"The hell you don't!"

"Colby"—her lips trembled—"Colby, if—if it's about my taking a quick look into your soddy last week, I—I apologize. Honest, I do. But I just wanted to see how the repairs were coming along and—"

"I'm talking about this!" He shook the paper in her face.

"Let—let me see."

He handed her a piece of paper.

She began to read the familiar handwriting of Silas Kane.

Mister Alfred White, prominent editor of the Ponca
Democrat, has announced the betrothal of his
daughter, Amy Elizabeth, to Mister Silas Kane,
well-known banker and community leader . . .

Amy felt the blood drain from her face. "He promised
not to tell anyone yet," she whispered.

"And just how long were you going to keep it a
secret, Amy?"

"I—I—"

"You get a big kick out of watching me make a fool
of myself?"

"N—no."

"It's a lie, then. You don't know anything about
this?"

Amy stiffened her back. "Of—of course, I knew."
Heat crept up her throat and into her face. "I—I
just didn't know when—when Silas was going to
announce it."

"Isn't that supposed to be the bride-to-be's pre-
rogative?"

"I—I've been so busy—"

"Seems kind of funny to me that you'd announce it in
my paper instead of the *Democrat*." His eyes narrowed.
"Or maybe you like pouring salt in the wound."

Amy winced. "Well, well, of course it wouldn't be
proper to announce it in our paper first. I'm sure Mr.
Kane was thinking of the propriety of it all."

"Propriety be damned! All I want to know is if
you love him." His eyes sought hers, bore into hers,
demanding an answer

She gripped the edge of the press. "Love? Of course,
I lo—love him. Why else would I marry him?"

"Don't lie to me, Amy."

"You, *la grande* prevaricator, dare to accuse me
of lying?"

"I saw the look in your eyes when you thought I'd

been killed in that bank robbery. You weren't worried about Silas Kane then. You were worried about me. And last night, when you were cold and I wrapped you in my arms—"

"You're imagining things. You're mad!"

"Am I?" Colby interjected. "Yesterday, when we took Shines White's body home, I thought we shared something special."

Amy licked her lips. "We—we did, Mr. Grant. But not in the way you think. It had nothing to do with you. Shines White was my friend. And—and as far as being in your arms, I was vulnerable. I was cold and tired. You misunderstood my actions. But I'm not surprised. Your ego is so big you think all women fall for you. Silas Kane is worth more than your little finger. He—he's a gentleman. He doesn't yell at me. He doesn't try to rob me of my claim and—and he—he's going to be governor of this state some day. He—"

"Governor! Only if he can buy enough votes."

Amy bit her lips to still her quivering chin.

Colby stepped back.

She heard him take a deep breath.

"Is that what you want, Amy?" His voice was calm and husky. "Are you that ambitious? That you'd sell yourself—"

Amy slapped him.

Colby's eyes narrowed. He let the announcement fall to the floor and seized her arms. He pulled her body into his. His mouth found her lips.

She struggled, but he held her close, his mouth savagely claiming hers. Her knees weakened, her heart exploded in ecstasy, and her arms went around his neck as she responded hungrily.

"Oh, Amy, Amy, Amy," Colby whispered between kisses. "I knew it couldn't be true! Not when you love me. Not when you can kiss me like that. Not when we feel this much."

Amy clung to him, smothered him with her hungry lips.

He kissed her throat, the spot on her forehead. "Oh, God, Amy, I want you. And you want me. I knew you couldn't marry that toady banker. You couldn't kiss me like this and love Silas Kane!"

Slowly reality returned to Amy. Silas held the mortgage to her father's newspaper. She pulled away from Colby and turned her back to him. "Go away, Colby, and leave me alone." She took a deep breath to stem the quivering voice. "I don't love you."

"You don't what!"

"I—I love Silas Kane and—and I'm going to marry him."

Colby seized her shoulders in his huge hands and pulled her around to face him.

She held her head high and met his eyes without wavering.

"Amy, don't do this." His voice was low. "Whatever your reasons are for trying to hurt me—whatever it is that makes you say this—whatever hold Silas has on you, I can take care of it. After Crissy died I never thought I could feel this way again. That life doesn't have to be empty, that it could be good again."

"Crissy?"

"But you made me realize I need someone to care for, and someone who cares for me. Let me help you, Amy. Whatever your reason for this foolishness, I'll take care of it."

"Like you're going to take care of my homestead?" she hissed. "And who is this Crissy? Another harlot like Esther?"

Colby gripped her shoulders harder. "I thought you understood about Esther."

Amy did understand and she regretted the remark, but had lashed out to camouflage the deep, wounding knowledge that Colby was lost to her forever.

Colby dropped his hands from her stiff shoulders. The sensual mouth thinned beneath the mustache. The left eye narrowed. "You really don't know me, do you?"

"I know all I need to know."

He took a step toward the door and turned around. "Amy, one last time. Don't do it." He stopped at the doorway and looked back. "And for your information, Crissy wasn't a harlot." His voice cracked. "She was my wife." His voice became a whisper. "Crissy died from being savagely raped. The son she was carrying was taken from her stillborn."

Numbness swept over Amy. Her knees threatened to crumple. "I—I didn't know. I—I didn't think—"

Colby looked at Amy sadly. "No, you didn't know. And you never stop to think, Amy." He rubbed his left temple. "And for a while I thought you could make me forget that heartache, could heal that hole deep in my gut, but then you—" His shoulders drooped. "I should have known better."

Amy's heart shattered at Colby's pain. She wanted to reach out to him, to comfort him, to love him, but with her last ounce of composure, she said quietly, "I am sorry for your pain, but you have to get out of my life, Colby Grant. I love Silas Kane."

Chapter Thirteen

Friday morning, well-wishers filled the *Democrat* office and congratulated Amy on her betrothal to Silas Kane. Alfred lowered his green eye shade and waved aside all visitors as his fingers flew in setting type that Amy knew could have waited another day.

Jim McGuire stopped by with Cap Reppeto, closely followed by the Carrington girls.

"Heard Kane's a lucky man, Miss Amy." Cap grinned.

She modestly lowered her gaze.

"Oh, Amy," gushed Naomi. "It's so exciting."

"Do I get to be a bridesmaid?" Rachel asked.

Mrs. Carrington came through the door. "I thought I'd find you girls here."

"Oh, Momma, isn't it wonderful? It will be the first wedding in town," Rachel gushed. "But it may not be too long before there's another one." She giggled and looked at her sister, Naomi, who scowled.

Mrs. Carrington sighed, "I do hope that you and that Drummond boy don't get in a big hurry, Rachel. I so wanted you to go back East to school."

Amy's mouth flew open. "I didn't realize you and Tex were so serious, Rachel."

"His father has a fabulous ranch in the Osage," Naomi bragged. "So it won't be too bad having Arnold for a brother-in-law."

"Arnold?" Amy queried.

"She means Tex," Rachel said and turned to her sister. "I wish you'd stop calling him that, Naomi. He hates it."

"Girls, quit your bickering," Mrs. Carrington demanded. "Weren't you going to ask Miss White something?"

"Oh, yes, Amy, we want to give you a bridal shower," Naomi said beaming.

Alfred dropped his type stick. Type clattered on the floor.

"Papa, do you need some help?"

His face was flushed and sweaty. "No, no, just getting clumsy, I guess."

Amy hoped he had not been nipping again. "Oh, goodness, I don't know about a wedding shower." Everything was moving too fast. She needed more time—time to hear from the school committee about her job application, time to sort out her true feelings about Silas Kane, and Colby Grant. *Mon Dieu!* Why couldn't she get that man out of her mind?

Rachel tugged at Amy's sleeve. "Are you excited? We're going to invite everybody in town."

"Everybody that's important, anyway," Naomi added.

"But we thought you should suggest the date."

"Well," Amy flushed. "There's no hurry. Sil—Silas and I haven't set a wedding date."

"Oh? Why not?"

"Well, we both are so busy with the upcoming school

celebration and the many things Silas has going. Papa still needs my help here. And I need to prove up on my homestead."

"I should think you would sell your claim now," Mrs. Carrington said. "With all your new responsibilities, your place will be such a nuisance."

"I suppose so, but I should like to talk to Silas before you set a time for a shower. May I let you know later?"

Roughface appeared in the doorway.

Naomi edged over to be near her mother.

Rachel raised one hand in greeting. Amy was thankful she stopped short of saying "How."

Mrs. Carrington sniffed. "Of course. Come along girls. Mr. Hutchins has received a new shipment of fabric."

Naomi put her hand up to her mouth and said in an audible voice, "Won't you be happy, Amy, when you and Silas are married and you won't have to deal with just any and everybody?"

With a disdainful glance at Roughface, Naomi followed her mother and sister out the door.

Roughface sneered at their backs, then turned his dark, brooding eyes back to Amy.

Alfred walked up to the counter to stand alongside Amy. His frothy brows were furrowed. "What can we do for you, Roughface?" he said gruffly.

"Burial Saturday."

"Thank you for telling me," Amy said.

"Come early for feast."

She nodded, and the tall Indian slid out the door.

"You're not going, are you, lass?"

Amy looked at the painting of Sultan and the maiden, at the bird nest hanging on the wall, and nodded. "I want to, Papa."

"I don't like it, Amy, and I'm sure Silas doesn't."

"Silas doesn't own me—yet."

Alfred winced. He rubbed his left arm and turned away. "Is Colby going?"

"Don't bring up that man's name to me!"

Saturday morning, Amy harnessed Sultan to a rented buggy and drove south, not without trepidation. She heard the drums immediately on passing the rail depot. The cadence grew louder and the cacophony of mourning charged the air as she neared the tribal headquarters. Indians in wagons and buggies surrounded her as she neared Shines White's hovel. She wasn't really afraid, but she had to admit she had been more at ease with Colby beside her.

A deerskin tepee had been erected in front of Shines White's shack. The open flap of the tepee faced east. To the west, tables had been set up beneath a brush arbor. A large black pot balanced on stones over a blazing fire. The contents bubbled over and gave off a pleasing aroma.

Roughface came out to greet her, a smile softening his solemn, pock-scarred face.

"Come." He took Amy by the hand and drew her into the dark cabin. The tenor of keening softened at a motion from Roughface.

"Are these all relatives?"

"Grandchildren." When he saw the surprise on her face, he added, "Grandchildren Indian way. White man say, no kin. Shines White of my clan." With his hand at her elbow, Roughface guided Amy to the burial litter in the corner of the room.

Amy gasped and drew back when she saw Shines White.

Red paint covered his face. A band of black ran across his forehead, a stripe down each cheek and his nose. Short, dark hairs from mourners peppered the peaceful face of the old Indian. He was dressed in new buckskin pants, and on his bare chest were the Sun Dance scars.

The stiff, gnarled hands held a beaded fan of eagle feathers.

"Why—why—" she whispered.

"Red is sun, gift of life. Black band is sky. Stripes for four winds." Roughface pointed to the fourth stripe barely visible on the back of Shines White's head. Roughface looked into Amy's face. "Why you not cut hair?"

"Oh, but—" A knife flashed in his hand and he quickly snipped off the curl on Amy's forehead, sprinkling the hairs on Shines White's face.

Flustered, Amy reached up to find another curl to cover the birthmark.

Roughface stayed her hand and pointed to a young woman. "Jenny Headman."

The pretty woman, not much more than a girl, had a dark spot low, between her eyes, which she lowered at Amy's gaze. Amy wondered if the birthmark bothered the girl as much as her own did.

The air in the shack was heavy and pungent, and Amy wanted to leave, but she wasn't sure Roughface would permit it. A slight tremor went through her. What was she doing here with this savage man, anyway? The tall, dark Indian was an enigma. One moment Roughface was almost tender, the next savagely cutting her hair. Was she in danger, as Papa had feared? And why had she felt so compelled to come? To pay her respect to Shines White, or simple curiosity?

One woman stopped her keening and walked over to Roughface and held out her hand. Roughface dug out a coin in his pocket and handed it to the woman. She returned to her chair and began wailing again.

Amy's mouth gaped. "You—you have to pay that woman to mourn for Shines White?"

Roughface shrugged. "Good singer. Must sing loud to reach spirit." He ushered Amy from the cabin and to the arbor just as White Eagle arrived with his escorts.

"Come. Time to eat."

The chief was in full dress with his colorful war bonnet, a rattle in his hand and tortoise shells tied at his ankles.

Amy was surprised and relieved to see young Joe Miller of the 101 Ranch trailing along behind White Eagle's wagon.

Joe dismounted, said something to a young maiden looking adoringly up at him, and came over to Amy. "Miss White," he said, doffing his ten-gallon hat. "Surprised to see you out here."

"Shines White was my friend—in a way."

Roughface pointed to Amy. "Shines White say *Tonde Xtha Zhinga.*" He shook his head. "Maybe *zage.*"

Joe grinned. "Daughter? No kidding?"

"Maybe so."

Amy flushed and nervously pushed back the hair on her forehead.

"What—what is he saying, Mr. Miller?"

Joe stared at Amy's face and shook his head slowly. "I speak a little of the language, but I don't always understand."

Feeling threatened, the pretty maiden came nearer. Joe grinned and took her hand.

White Eagle raised his feathered pipe to the sky and all became silent. "*Wa' kon tah'*—"

Joe whispered the translation into Amy's ear. "We pray to the one who gives to man the sunshine, the clear sky from which all storms and all clouds are removed, we thank thee for this bounty of food . . ."

Amy listened to the prayer, which lasted almost ten minutes as White Eagle paid homage to Mother Earth and asked for protection of the Poncas in a soul-rendering cadence.

"Amen," he concluded. "We eat."

Roughface handed Amy a bowl and took her to the boiling pot. Joe and the Indian girl followed.

"Dig deep, puppy in bottom," Roughface said, filling his own bowl.

Amy shrank back.

Joe laughed. "That's one of the colonel's best beeves in there, Miss White." He ladled a soup of meat, squash and corn into her bowl. "Indians have a great sense of humor when you get to know them."

Roughface grinned broadly. It was the first time Amy had seen any expression other than a sneer or a brooding smile on his stoic, dark face. He was quite handsome when he laughed in spite of the smallpox scars.

Roughface handed Amy a piece of puffy fry bread and led her to a table under the arbor where White Eagle and members of the family were seated. The rest of the Indians squatted on the bare ground to eat their food.

Following Joe's lead, Amy cautiously sipped the stew and was surprised to find it tasted good. And the fry bread, similar to a pastry, was marvelously light.

When everyone had eaten, Roughface went into Shines White's house. He returned with an armload of blankets and began calling out names.

"Clara Bushyhead."

The woman went up to Roughface, shook his hand and accepted a blanket.

"Joe Miller," Roughface called out.

Joe solemnly accepted a blue and red blanket.

When all of the blankets had been depleted, Roughface brought out the pots, the table and the other sparse belongings of Shines White.

"This is the giveaway," Joe explained to Amy.

"Colby—Mr. Grant said they gave away everything in honor of the dead."

Joe nodded. "Problem is, Shines White didn't have anything. Roughface used his own money to buy all those blankets you see him giving away."

"I didn't realize they were relatives."

"Only in the Indian sense. Roughface belonged to the same clan—Standing Bear's clan."

"And is he the last of that particular clan?"

"Not at all, ma'am. The rest of the clan went back to Nebraska with Standing Bear. Guess he's an old man now, but hear tell he's still kicking."

"Amy White."

She was startled to hear her name called.

Roughface handed her the tintype of the Indian maiden she had seen on the wall of Shines White's cabin.

"Thank—thank you," she said quietly.

"We go now," Roughface told the gathering.

Joe took Amy's arm. "Where's your buggy? I'll ride out with you to the cemetery."

"I—I don't know if I should go—"

"You'll learn a lot. I promise you it will be interesting." He motioned for the Indian girl to follow on his horse.

Amy wondered about their relationship. The only white men she knew who had married Indian women were fur trappers who had drifted into Milford occasionally for supplies.

At the cemetery high on a hill overlooking the Salt Fork River, the Indians took the body of Shines White from the litter and placed it in a sitting position in a shallow grave facing east. A soft chant began. Secretly glad that she was not alone, Amy watched from the buggy as the Indians arranged a series of short poles over the grave and began heaping earth into a mound to cover the timbers.

Clay bowls of food were placed around the grave.

"The food will keep Shines White free from hunger in the afterlife."

An old worn-out horse was led to the grave.

"Close your eyes, Miss Amy."

Before she realized what was to happen, Roughface

quickly and deftly slit the throat of the dapple-gray horse. The animal slumped to the foot of the grave, kicked the air a few times and then went limp.

"Why? Why?" she whispered.

"So Shines White will have transportation."

Amy struggled to keep her equilibrium and fought down the nausea swelling up into her throat.

Roughface led a young girl, two or three years old, to the grave.

"No!" Amy protested.

"Sh-h-h, it's all right." Joe patted her hand.

The child with a small white feather in her short-cropped hair was lifted up to the top of the grave. Two men held her as she slowly walked the length of the mounded dirt and then was helped down.

"The child signifies that Shines White is going to be reborn into a new life."

The final ceremony was the lighting of the fires at the base of the mound.

"The fire," Joe whispered, "lights the way for Shines White's travel."

The Indians began to leave the burial grounds.

Joe took the reins of his horse from the Indian girl and mounted. "You're only about two miles from town, Miss White. You should be all right. I need to head back to the ranch." He tipped his hat, reached down and swung the Indian girl on behind and trotted off to the west.

Amy headed the buggy slowly north to New Ponca.

Roughface ran after Amy, trotting alongside.

Amy stopped the rig. "Thank you for letting me come."

"I tell you a story."

"I must get back." The images of Shines White's burial swam in her head. She wanted to get away.

Roughface restrained Sultan. "Long ago, on the Niobrara, I was small boy, maybe six summers. Ponca ordered to leave homeland in the north and come to Indian Territory. Ponca no want to go, but blue soldiers point guns."

"How awful."

"I remember long walk. No food, plenty storms. Many die. Shines White's wife die. Her name Prairie Flower."

"Yes, you told me the story once before. Shines White must have missed her terribly."

"Shines White say you Prairie Flower, come back to life."

Amy blushed. "I know. I'll cherish the tintype you gave me."

He looked at her. "Prairie Flower had baby. Baby not die. Baby have tattoo on head."

"Tattoo? Do the Poncas tattoo their babies?"

"Some babies. Babies of chieftain clan."

"So that means Mrs. Headman, the woman mourning for Shines White, is of the chieftain clan?"

Roughface nodded. "You have tattoo."

"I have—I have a tattoo?" Amy fingered the dark spot on her forehead. "It's a birthmark." She tried to laugh. "You've met my father, Alfred Whi—Alfred White."

Roughface could not know that her real parents were French and had died on their way to California.

"Maybe so."

Amy felt a chill. "I—I'm sorry, Roughface, but I must hurry on to town." She snapped the reins and Sultan moved smartly ahead.

Sunday morning, Amy walked to church with Alfred in a light rain. "Papa, tell me again about my parents. They were French, weren't they?" Amy felt the muscle in his arm tense.

"Of course, child. So dad-blamed French I couldn't understand a thing they said. Why do you ask? Not giving up on me after sixteen years, are you?"

"Oh, Papa. Of course not," Amy sighed. "but I wish I had known them."

Alfred patted her arm. "They were fine folks, Amy. Don't let anyone ever tell you different."

Amy and Alfred walked to a frame building still under construction between the corner saloon and the gambling house, both open for business. Silas Kane met them at the door.

The Carrington buggy drove up, and Amy waved at them to join them on their plank and beer-keg pew. But Mrs. Carrington turned her head and led her family to the front row to sit with the Duvall family. Naomi sniffed the air and Rachel stared at Amy without speaking. Mrs. Carrington whispered something to Mrs. Duvall, who put her hand over her mouth. She glanced quickly at Amy and looked away.

A chill went through Amy as she took her seat between Silas and Alfred. Had she offended Mrs. Carrington in some way?

Jim McGuire flipped through a hymn book. He looked at Amy and scowled slightly. Several pairs of eyes followed his. They, too, frowned.

Silas squirmed in his chair.

"I—I don't understand," Amy whispered. "They look at me like I have a plague." She pushed a curl over the birthmark.

"You did make quite a spectacle of yourself over that drunk Indian that got killed. What possessed you to go with Grant to take him to White Eagle?" he hissed. "No decent white woman . . ."

The services began with McGuire making the announcement that next Sunday's services would be held in the new school building. The people clapped. "Now, let's sing 'Amazing Grace.' "

After the church services, Silas attempted to steer

Amy to his carriage, but she slipped away from his ushering hand and walked over to the Carringtons getting into their buggy.

"Naomi," she said, smiling, "what can I do to help with the school ball?"

Naomi looked at her mother. "I—I think everything's taken care of, Miss White. I guess we don't need your help, thank you."

"Why so formal, Naomi?" Amy looked at Rachel, who ducked her head and bit her lip. A gnawing began in Amy's stomach. "Are you sure?"

Rachel looked at her mother pleadingly. "Couldn't Amy help us with the decorations?"

"What's left to do?" Mrs. Carrington said haughtily. "It will only take a minute to hang them, now that they're all made."

"But they're not all ma—"

"Rachel! I finished the last one last night," her mother insisted.

"Oh." Amy said. "Well, if there's anything else . . ."

"Horace, how long do we have to sit here in the rain?" Mr. Carrington flicked the reins and the carriage rolled away.

Smarting from the rebuff, Amy walked back to her father and Silas. "Oh, well. That will give me more time to help you, Papa." She turned to Silas. "Joining us at the Globe dining room?"

Monday, Amy read proof on her father's typesetting, but decided to return to the hotel when Colby came in to see her father.

"Alfred, have you got a minute?"

In her rush to leave the *Democrat* office, Amy almost stumbled over Roughface leaning up against the outer wall. "Roughface," she acknowledged curtly, wondering why he would still be hanging around now that Shines White was dead.

Colby followed Amy out the door. "Wait up, Amy. I need to talk to you, too."

"We have nothing to discuss."

"Oh, don't we?" Colby shook his head. "You are the most stubborn woman I ever ran into." He took a step toward her.

"Stay away from me!" Amy lifted her parasol menacingly.

Colby raised his hands in surrender. "I won't touch you. I just want to talk."

"There's nothing to talk about unless you're willing to buy my half of the homestead."

"I don't want to buy—"

"Then we have nothing to talk about."

"Are you sure?"

"I—I'm sure. I'm marrying Silas Kane. And—and the sooner, the better." Amy turned her back on Colby and marched toward the hotel.

Colby threw his Stetson on the ground.

Anticipating a hectic Thursday because of the school dedication activities, Amy made her run to the Indian rail station for ready-prints on Tuesday, a day early.

The agent handed her a basket of wires with her mail. "Miss Amy, looks like there's going to be thousands coming to help you people in New Ponca celebrate the new school building."

"Oh, my!"

"Santa Fe has had to order several special trains to Cross."

"I know. I don't know where we'll put them all," she said as she sorted through the stack. Among the wires she found one from the school committee! Eagerly, she tore open the envelope.

The committee has had a number of applicants for the position of teacher at the new school.

After looking over the academic requirements and the personal integrity of all candidates, we have decided to employ Mrs. Rita Caldwell for the first three-month school term.

"Mrs. Caldwell?" Amy's voice exploded through the depot. "It's not possible. I've much more schooling than she has."

But it did explain Mrs. Carrington's attitude toward her at church Sunday. With her husband on the school committee, she would have been aware that Amy had made application for the teaching job. She was obviously embarrassed and uncomfortable about Amy being turned down. But it did not explain Jim McGuire's attitude.

Perhaps Silas was right and her attendance at Shines White's burial had been offensive to the townspeople.

She returned to the *Democrat* office with the ready-prints and handed Alfred the mound of telegrams from groups of people accepting the town's invitation to dedicate the school.

"I warned Silas this might happen." Alfred shook his head.

Amy was half listening. "Has Naomi or Rachel been in?"

"No. No, they haven't." He put down the wires and sighed.

She re-read the school committee's rejection letter. She would have to marry Silas. There was no other way to help her father pay off his debt. Colby had refused to buy her homestead and she had been denied a teaching job. She was trapped.

What do you mean, "trapped," Amy Elizabeth White? Silas Kane is the most eligible, most attractive, most respected, most sought after, most—Any woman would be proud to marry Silas. So why did she feel as if an ugly, all-enveloping cloud were descending over her, squeezing every ounce of life out of her?

*   *   *

That evening, after an uncomfortable and almost silent dinner at the Pearson Hotel, she and Kane took their usual stroll down Grand Avenue.

"Good evening." Silas tipped his hat to the Duvall family and stopped. Ben nodded and gave Amy a big smile. Emma frowned and pulled impatiently at her husband's arm. "It's getting late, Ben."

To Amy she said, "So sorry we can't stay and chat."

Amy furrowed her brow as the Duvalls walked away.

In front of Myatt's grocery they ran into Jim McGuire, who nodded at a greeting from Silas and stepped quickly back inside his storeroom.

Kane frowned. "What's his hurry?"

Before Amy could ponder the rebuff, young Joe Miller hailed her from across the street. "Hello there, Amy."

Kane flinched. "He's very familiar."

Amy held out her hand to Joe and nodded to his brothers, Zack and George. "Thank you, again," Amy said. "Not only would I have been frightened at Shines White's funeral, but I would have never understood what was going on if you hadn't been there."

"No call for you to be scared," Joe said.

"I did find it quite unusual, and interesting."

Kane tightened his grip on Amy's arm. "We must be going, Amy." He tipped his hat and steered Amy down the street.

"That explains why everyone is being so cool to us— to you," he hissed.

"Why?"

"Attending that old Indian's funeral, of course. It's certainly not the kind of behavior I expect from the future Mrs. Silas Kane. I think you have an apology to make to these good folks for the way you've been carrying on with those savages."

"*Moi?*" Amy bristled. "*You* deal with the Indians. Well, maybe you don't. But everyone else deals with them, selling them things, things they don't need, like liquor."

"That's business. But we don't socialize with them."

"A funeral is hardly a social event. And I don't feel that I have to apologize for going to Shines White's burial. In fact, I found it quite informative, if somewhat gruesome at times. The symbolism incorporated in the ceremony was quite thought provoking. Especially when they killed the horse—"

"Sh-h-h!" Silas hissed as Mayor Barnes and his wife approached.

"Where are the girls Jeannette and Maud?" Amy asked.

"Playing charades with Naomi and Rachel and some young men friends," Mrs. Barnes said through pinched mouth.

"Oh, what fun! Silas, shall we join them?"

"We weren't invited."

"Oh, of course." Amy lowered her flushed face as the Barnes hurried off.

Silas marched stiffly on down the street.

Amy could feel his anger with each step.

"Your foolhardiness has once again proved to be a major embarrassment, Amy."

Amy bit her lip to still a retort.

They met the Carringtons and Silas intended to walk on by with a quick nod, but Amy stopped in the middle of the boardwalk determined to make the woman speak to her.

"How are you this evening?" Amy said.

Horace fiddled with his hat. "Hello, Silas."

Mrs. Carrington's big bosom heaved. "Miss White, have you visited with Mrs. Duvall?"

"Just briefly, a few minutes—"

"Well, I'm sure she told you" —Mrs. Carrington's voice hurried on— "that she's entertaining so much these days that we'll have to postpone your wedding shower."

Amy felt the heat rise in her face. Silas Kane's thin lips turned blue and twitched nervously.

"I most certainly do understand." She looked at the pursed lips. "Mrs. Carrington, I'm sorry if I've offended you."

The woman laughed weakly. "Offend me? No, no, *Miss White,* how could an Indian offend us?"

"I beg your pardon."

"Just how far are you going to carry this charade? Everyone in town knows you're an Indian."

"Indian? Mrs. Carrington," Amy gasped. "I thought you knew I was of French heritage." Amy laughed. "Just because I went to Shines White's funeral doesn't make me an Indian."

"With that skin, with that tattoo, you can't deny you're an Indian," Mrs. Carrington scoffed. "You had us fooled for a while, but you can be sure that the Bachelor Girls Club is not going to have an Indian as a member."

Silas coughed, and the vein in his temple ticked nervously.

"It's not true. It's not true." Amy turned to Silas, whose face had drained white. "Silas, it's not true." She turned back to the Carringtons. "Why are you being so malicious?" she demanded.

But Amy remembered the mussel shells in her father's trunk and a niggling doubt began to rise in her breast. "Let's go see my father, Silas. He'll tell you my parents were French and they died of consumption on their way west. Alfred and his wife adopted me. It's—it's all recorded in the Bible."

Amy ran into the *Democrat* office with Silas following reluctantly. "Papa, Papa! Tell Silas." She was crying.

"There's a rumor—a rumor going around, a malicious rumor."

Alfred slumped in his chair, his celluloid collar askew, his vest and shirt unbuttoned.

"I am—I am French! Tell him, Papa! Tell Silas I'm French!"

"Amy—" Alfred rested a hand on the left side of his chest.

She laughed hysterically. "Answer me, Papa."

"I wanted to protect you."

"Protect me? You—you mean it's true?"

Alfred bowed his head. "Shines White *was* your father, Amy."

"No! No, it can't be true!" Amy grasped the edge of the counter to keep from falling.

"I'm sorry, lass."

"How could you lie to me?"

Alfred shook his head. "We loved you, lass."

She reached up to her forehead and whispered, "It's not a birthmark at all, is it?"

"It was such a tiny dot when you were a baby, we thought it would go away." He looked up, pleading with her. "Your mother and I loved you. And that's all that counted."

"My mother? I don't even know my mother. And to learn—to learn that Shines White was my father . . ." She turned to Silas and laughed hysterically. "My father was a pitiful, drunken Indian."

"Oh, lass." Alfred massaged his chest. "I never would have agreed to make The Run if I'd known the Poncas had relocated here."

"How could you have let me live such a deceitful lie all these years?"

"Hannah and I loved you. You were the daughter we never had. And I don't think I ever knew Shines White was your father. But I stopped and talked to White Eagle today and he confirmed my worst suspicions that you were the daughter of an Indian princess, Prairie Flower. I didn't remember her name until I heard Shines White say . . ."

"An Indian princess, no less?" She laughed again. "Papa, don't make it worse."

Alfred stood up and staggered back against his desk.

Amy's upper lip curled and she turned to Silas Kane, who fingered the brim of his hat uncomfortably.

"Isn't that ironic? One drunk as a father isn't enough. I have to have two!"

"Don't, lass," Alfred pleaded.

Silas cleared his throat. "You're overwrought, Miss Amy. And quite understandably, but under the circumstances, I think we should delay our wedding plans."

"Wedding?" She laughed as one possessed. "What a grand joke on you, Silas. It wouldn't do for the future First Lady of the new state of Oklahoma to be Indian, would it?" She sneered. "I may be an object of ridicule, but you're going to be the laughing stock of the territory."

Silas Kane slapped on his hat, pivoted smartly and walked out the door.

Chapter Fourteen

Wednesday morning, Amy refused to open her door to Alfred, not even when he begged for her forgiveness.

"Lass, I'd cut off my right arm if I could change things. Please, Amy. Let me in."

How could Papa—Alfred—have lied to her for sixteen years? How could he have let her live a lie all her life? To protect her? No one could protect her.

She thought back to the people in Milford, Nebraska, and their whispered comments, their refusal to let her teach in the schools. They knew! Everyone knew but Amy. Even the girls at Miss Stevens's school in Boston must have suspected that Amy was an Indian.

"Look at that natural ability," they had said when she rode the fine thoroughbreds in their stables.

"Oh, don't you know, people of her race have inherent artistic talents," they had said when she finished a delicate flower arrangement.

And she thought they had meant French, not Indian. Had the invitations to their estates and plantations been excuses to show off a "tame Indian"?

How they must have laughed at her behind her back. A great horrendous joke on Amy. Everyone knew she was Indian but Amy.

Even her mirror had lied to her, because she had seen what Hannah and Alfred wanted her to see—a young French girl. Her trust in her adoptive parents had been complete. Their love had given her no reason to question them, no grounds to doubt her French heritage.

Amy left McCarthy's livery stable astride Sultan and rode slowly down Second Street. She passed Hiskett's busy meat market, the quiet office of the *Democrat* where Alfred had probably retrieved a bottle from his hidden cache, and the Red Dog saloon with its rowdy imbibers.

She reined Sultan left at Grand Avenue, ignoring the yeasty smells of Baldruff's City Bakery and the polite tip of Doc Horner's hat. She rode steadily eastward, past the raw frame structure housing Will Chase's drug store and opera house and Paley's saloon where a blanket-wrapped Ponca Indian lay curled in a drunken sleep. Next door was the office of the *Republican.*

Amy wanted to spur Sultan forward, to leave behind the town, its smells, its sounds, its people, but she resisted the impulse to prod Sultan into a lope and carefully paced the black gelding as they rode past the *Republican.* She fought to keep her eyes looking straight ahead, but through her peripheral vision she saw Colby standing in the doorway. Her humiliation was complete. She could not see, but imagined the smug smile that must be plastered on his face. As an Indian, her claim to the homestead would be null and void.

Sultan's measured pace pulled at Amy's nerves as they moved down the wide street past the other saloons, past Brett's implement store and Donahoe's law offices.

Amy reined Sultan around the water tower at the end of the dusty street and veered northeast to pass the new schoolhouse and a new two-room home where a washing hung proudly on the line.

Her breath came in ragged, shallow gasps as if some unknown monster were squeezing her chest. Her heart pounded in her ears. When she crossed the wooden bridge at Turkey Creek and entered open country, her last shred of control fled.

Amy threw back her head, her throat arched to the skies, and from deep within her came a gurgling, rasping, piercing scream that ripped through the silence of the fading November afternoon. Using the crop brutally, Amy raced Sultan across the dry grassland, through the scattering of cottonwoods, to the hidden arbor where the thicket of blackjacks and wild plum bushes nestled on the banks of the Arkansas. Her lathered horse, with foaming muzzle and flaring nostrils, walled its eyes at the strange creature dismounting, and then plunged into the sanctuary of the stream, his reins trailing.

Amy dropped exhausted to the ground, falling on the cool, sandy bank. Her knotted fists began pounding the soft earth—pounding, pounding, pounding!

Indian! Indian! Indian!

Amy screamed her disgust, her violation, to the skies. Jarring, maddening sounds clawed their way up and out of her throat and spewed out into the wilderness, one after another, again and again. Her ears roared with the sounds of her venomous words.

Finally, the vocal cords constricted in protest and the shattering cacophony drummed only in her frenzied mind until her thoughts became bile and gushed up from the caverns of her bowels.

The rancid spittle and her dehydrated body forced Amy to the stream. She crawled down the shallow, sandy shelf to the water, cupping her hands to draw the cold water to her mouth, once, twice, a third time, but the thirst and taste of bile would not go away.

When the ripples calmed, Amy stared down at the image of a stranger, some poor soul with a rent sleeve in her wrinkled gray jacket. A torn jacket revealing a tawny arm, a dark arm, an Indian arm. Some deranged person with unkempt hair, raven-black strands falling free of restraint around a tear-streaked face. The face—the face was of an Indian.

"There. See there? The mark! There, near the hairline." She pointed into the stream, and the image was reflected back to her. "You!" she screamed. "Yes, Amy White—you! You're an Indian. See it? See the brand?" she screeched. "Stupid, stupid Amy. French! Ha! You're a dirty, stinking Indian!" She peered into the stream again. The blue dot glared back at her. "Aaagh!" she croaked, teeth grating, grinding. She grabbed a handful of coarse sand and began scrubbing at the blue spot, grinding the gravel and soil into her forehead without mercy. Grinding, grinding, grinding.

Colby watched Amy ride east on Grand Avenue, her slender body stiff and erect in her confining, proper gray suit. Her long-lashed eyes wavered neither right nor left. Her chin tilted haughtily as always, the dark hair smoothed back in that gawd-awful chignon when it ought to be flowing down her shoulders. Outwardly, she seemed the same, but an uneasiness swept over him.

Leaning back against the newel post on the brand-new overhang of the *Republican,* Colby stared at the black Arabian and its rider until they veered northeast. He should feel relieved. Amy was heading for their homestead. He no longer thought of it as *his* any more, but *theirs.*

He watched as the dust of Sultan's hooves settled on the road. He was sure Amy was going to that small arbor along the river. He'd often followed her unseen to the homestead, afraid of the danger she might face at the hands of the Starrs or the Maddox gang. A time or two Amy had almost discovered him. He'd been careful to leave no signs of his own intrusions, especially at the arbor. He knew Amy well enough to know she would have promptly sought another haven. He liked knowing that she enjoyed this special place with him. Even if she didn't know it was his favorite spot, too.

Still, something gnawed at Colby. He tried to dismiss it. There was no cause to be concerned. Amy appeared to be taking the revelation of her Indian blood—well, stoically—like an Indian. Maybe that's what bothered him. Amy—the proud and spirited Miss Amy White—seemed not the least bit concerned that she was not a proper French lady, but a Ponca Indian.

It shouldn't matter. Labels were just flimsy cloaks of respectability for the true savages of civilization. Some of the most deranged and criminal minds he'd known could boast of lily-white skin. Scotch, Irish, German, Chinese or Negro. What did it matter? Certainly, it didn't matter to Colby.

But would it matter to Amy? Yes. To Amy it would matter.

And it had mattered to that obese, domineering old crone, Mrs. Carrington, and some of the other ugly, blackballing witches with daughters in the Bachelor Girls Club.

He could imagine how much pleasure they'd had in humiliating Amy, using her Indian heritage as a hatchet more vengeful than Carry Nation's.

And Kane! Why had she agreed to marry that slick, oily banker in the first place? He was an addicted gambler and a ruthless businessman. Surely, Amy had seen his true colors when he had humiliated her by calling off the wedding. Colby wished he knew how to make Amy see it had been for the best. She couldn't love Kane, not when every time she and Colby were together the air was filled with an electricity that defied all laws of nature, a magnetism stronger than both of them that drew them together, stronger than any force he had ever encountered before, stronger than his feelings for Crissy.

Colby went back inside the *Republican* office and retrieved his hat and coat. It wouldn't hurt to ride out that way. Sultan could throw a shoe or trip in a prairie dog hole. The sun would be down in about an hour, and the wind blowing from the north would bring a crisp chill to the Indian-summer days of mid-November. Maddox or the Starr gang might be holing up at the quarry again. She shouldn't be out alone.

Colby found Amy on the bank of the Arkansas. But she was not the Amy he knew. Her clothing was in disarray, torn and soiled. Her dark, luxurious hair fell wildly about her soiled face. She was crouched on the bank, her arms hugging her body as if in pain. She rocked and babbled. Her vermillion lips drooled with spittle. In her grubby fists, she clutched strands of loose hair. Sand clung to her raw and bleeding forehead.

"Amy," he whispered. He didn't want to scare her.

She continued her incoherent ramblings, the trance-like swaying, oblivious to his presence.

"Amy." He touched her shoulder lightly.

Her dark head jerked around, damp raven hair raging wildly around her face. Gray eyes widened and nostrils flared. Without warning, her body shot upward to a low, tense crouch. Clenched hands sprang open, tendons strained, fingers curved like talons of a puma in readiness for a kill. And then the wine-tinted mouth snarled open and a scream of madness rent the stillness of the fading afternoon as she lunged at him.

Colby staggered back as the force of the distraught woman slammed into him. Grasping fingers tore at his hair. Her nails raked at his face and entangled themselves in his mustache. Spittle sprayed his face, and sharp-toed boots cracked his shins.

"You little hellcat," he cried.

He caught the clawing hands and pulled the slender body into his. He snared the flailing limbs with his legs, using every sinew and muscle in his body to immobilize the wild creature.

As gently as possible, Colby pushed Amy's body to the cold ground cushioned with fallen leaves. He forced her onto her back and pinned her hands between her writhing body and his.

Amy hissed, spat and began anew the wrenching and hysterical screams, tossing her head back and forth.

Colby wanted to shake her back into awareness, but his hands were too busy. In desperation, he forced his head against hers. He clamped his mouth over hers and held on until the desperate need of air stilled her resistance and she fell limp beneath him. Colby slowly moved his lips from her trembling mouth. He relaxed his grip and inhaled slowly, gradually lifting his weight off her soft body.

Amy's chest heaved as she gulped for air. Her body jerked and shuddered until the rhythm of her breathing became even. She lay there whimpering, moaning softly between little sniffles, her long, black lashes hiding the smoky, gray eyes.

Easing away from her, Colby retrieved a flask from the saddlebags, untied the blanket roll and knelt down by the tortured woman. She looked small and vulnerable on the ground. The bodice of the blouse beneath the torn jacket shuddered with each soul-wrenching sob.

Wrapping one arm around her shoulders, Colby raised Amy to a sitting position and forced the mouth of the flask into the flaccid, ruby lips. Her eyes remained closed, but she frowned at the smell. She tried to move her face, but her chin was held rigid by his strong hands.

"No!" she hissed between clenched teeth, and with

renewed strength tried to twist away from him.

He threw his legs across her hips to hold her there, and poured the raw, burning whiskey into her mouth.

She gagged, coughed, tried to spit it out.

"Drink it," Colby commanded.

Amy held her breath as long as possible, spilling the liquid out the sides of her mouth until she was forced to swallow. She coughed and shuddered, then swallowed again.

"That's my Amy," he whispered softly, pouring more down her throat. "Sometimes it helps."

There were more dribbles of liquor, more quiet, calming words from Colby until her rigid body fell limp in his arms. Tears spilled from under the long lashes to mix with river sand and streak down her face.

"Don't cry, Amy. It's all right." Colby's strong arms cradled her quivering body, his huge hands lightly stroked the taut muscles in her neck. He caressed the tangled, raven mane, pushed strands of hair from her face, revealing faintly in the fading dusk the blue dot nestled at the widow's peak.

Amy shivered, her black lashes fluttered.

"You're chilled," he said huskily, and hastily wrapped the blanket around their bodies.

The warmth of the wool blanket, the heat of Colby's body next to hers, the soothing anesthesia of the whiskey, slowly thawed the chill in Amy's fatigued body and mind. There was no more rage. There was only hurt, injury, betrayal, and the safe haven of Colby's arms. Calm returned to her wretched mind. Reality was restored. If only this were reality. If only she could spend the rest of her days shielded by his warmth, borrowing from his strength. If only she could stay here through the eternities, where no one could hurt her, where no one would have to know she was Indian.

With her head burrowed in Colby's chest, Amy took a deep breath. She wanted to say she was sorry. Sorry that she was so weak—sorry that she had been so arrogant about her heritage, sorry that she wasn't French, but Indian. She waited for the rage to well up inside of her again, but there was no energy for it. For the moment all she wanted was to feel Colby's arms about her, to feel the muscles rippling in his back as he held her close, to smell the strange manliness about him. She didn't want to think about that other world out there. A world of hate, of envy, of prejudice. A world, God forgive her, that she had helped create with her own narcissistic vanities and prejudices.

She whimpered. She could never hold up her head in New Ponca. She didn't know if she could continue to live there. Her life would be completely different now. And the only world she ever really wanted was here in Colby's arms. If only she could stay here forever, feeling the soft, golden hairs of his mustache brush across her hungry lips, his strong body enveloping hers.

She wondered what it might be like to have Colby make love to her. But she would never know now. She was only an Indian. She couldn't bear to have that dream lost to her forever. She would never know what it was to be loved, wholly and completely, by this man whose overtures she had so often rejected. Never. Unless it was now. Here in this place.

Colby fought against the sensations of holding Amy in his arms. The heat of their joined bodies was too intoxicating, too threatening. He slowly moved away from her.

"Hold me," Amy whispered. "Make love to me, Colby." She heard him suck in his breath. "Please." *Oh, God, don't let him turn away from me.* She drew his arms around her.

"Amy. It's better you rest now." His arms tensed, his voice raspy.

"Hold me. Love me. Make it all go away," she whispered.

"Amy—Amy," he breathed. His heart quickened, but he forced his body to remain still. She was in shock. She didn't know what she was saying. The proud Miss Amy White would never have uttered those words.

"You don't know what you're saying," he said huskily.

She smiled at him and nodded. "Please," she whispered and lifted her dark head upward, kissed the raw wounds she had inflicted on his face and then sought his lips.

Hesitating, waiting for the rebuff he was sure would come, Colby placed his lips lightly on hers only to find her responding hungrily, demanding more. Her hands grasped his face, holding him there.

He groaned, feeling a stirring in his loins he had long denied, and drew her closer.

Her hands moved down his back, throwing his muscles into spasms as she naively kneaded and pulled his body into hers.

Burying his face in her raven hair, Colby trailed his fingers down her smooth, silky throat to the rising mounds beneath the thin lawn blouse. Tenderly he cupped his hands around her breasts, his fingers tracing the small, hard nipples rising up at his touch.

Amy shivered and sighed, and the electricity reverberated through his hands to the hairs on his chest and down through his yearning body. Logic cried out in Colby's mind to stop. Amy didn't know what she was doing. She was like a frightened fawn seeking a haven, an orphaned child, a wounded animal.

When he hesitated, she lifted her head and searched for his lips. Her body arched beneath him demanding more, and the pounding in his loins pushed him forward.

Gently, Colby laid her onto the blanket on the ground, cushioning her head with his muscled arms, pressing his lips to her left earlobe. "Are you sure, Amy? I've never wanted . . ." His heart beat wildly, his breath ragged. He never wanted anything so much in his life. But did he dare take advantage of her now when she was so vulnerable?

God, how he loved this proud vixen. How many times had he wanted nothing more than to hold her, to love her? Did she know how hard it had been not to have taken her before? And now—now that she wanted him, demanded him, was it just to vent her anger? To assuage her wounds? Dammit! He wanted to make love to her. How long could he lie their stiffly, not doing as she bade him, as he wanted to do, as he shouldn't do?

As if in answer to his unspoken questions, Amy pushed her breasts up into his hands again. He commanded his muscles to relax, but she forced her body even closer and nestled inside his arms. His body was as feverish as hers. His loins ached and muscles in his thighs knotted from the tension.

He groaned. He couldn't stop his hands from touching her, and as he caressed her, her lips parted and he lowered his head to taste the sweet dew of her lips.

Amy drank in the splendor of his kiss, heard his tortured breaths and found herself wanting to run her fingers through the hairs of his golden chest. She slipped her hands through his shirt, and felt a tingling in her fingertips as she touched the forest of gold. "It's so soft," she whispered. She quickly unbuttoned his shirt and pulled it aside.

A moan slipped from Colby's lips as her hands brushed his nipples, setting his senses on fire, awakening every nerve in his being.

Amy reached up and cupped Colby's face in her hands. "Make love to me, please," she prodded again. Her arms drew his head toward her own thick, luxurious mane. She pushed her breasts into his chest, her lower body into his loins. He groaned again. She purred softly as her fingers entwined the golden curls on his chest.

Colby knew he should stop her, but the tips of the long, slender fingers were electrifying, setting off sensations he didn't want to deny. He didn't want to stop her. He didn't want to stop himself.

She bent her head and kissed his nipples, and he moaned, clutching her to him. Then slowly, almost timidly, she moved her hands downward and with her finger drew circles around his navel, gently probing. He shuddered and was unable to force his mind away from his own mushrooming desires.

"Amy, are you sure?" In the moonlight, he saw her nod, and stilling his hands to be calm, he stripped off her gray, torn jacket, found the pearl buttons and began slowly to unbutton the waist, kissing each newly revealed spot as it gave way, the creamy throat and the tiny scar on her shoulder. He kissed the hollows between her arm and the soft, tawny mounds.

With each caress, Amy shivered and sighed, and the tremors vibrated through his hands to the hairs on his chest and down through his yearning body.

He tugged at the ribbons of her camisole, releasing her voluptuous body. Tenderly he cupped his hands around the firm, heaving mounds, his fingers tenderly tracing the small, rosy aureoles around each nipple.

"You're so young." He nuzzled her silky throat.

"I'll never be young again," she murmured brokenly.

Colby slowly eased her back down on the blanket, scarcely breathing lest he disturb the moment. The twilight had given way to darkness, but the night was even brighter with the moon overhead, and the rays reflecting off the river.

Amy saw his golden hair haloed in the moonlight, and she reached her arms up to hold the nimbus of her breast next to Colby's perspiring body. She purred and arched against him again.

He placed his hands on each bare mound and buried his face there. He smelled the sweetness of her, felt the richness of her breasts. His tongue encircled the rosebud tips and the virginal nipples awakening, rising to meet his teasing tongue.

Amy threw back her head, thrusting her throat upward as she moaned and writhed to his touch. Her hands clutched his head to her breast, and she wanted him never to stop. Her body cried out for deliverance.

His lips moved on down to her waist to encircle and dart in and out of the small hollow of life.

Amy's breath came rushing and panting into his ear as she reached for the waistband of her skirt.

Colby's hands stopped her. "Let me undress you, Amy," he said huskily. "God, how I've wanted to do this. To see"—he chuckled softly—"what in tarnation was hidden under all those skirts and petticoats."

As he fumbled with the catches, she placed her hand on his denim-stretched crotch. She found herself anxious for his touch, and her own hands found success with the buttons of Colby's trousers.

Quickly, helping each other, they shed their clothing, and when they were at last facing each other in the moonlight, they stretched out on the blanket and marveled in silence at the bounty of nature and their calling need of each other.

He was so golden.

She was so dark and richly beautiful.

His muscle-toned body was *magnifique,* leaner, harder and his maleness more voluminous than she had imagined.

Her long, tawny legs that merged into a thatch of raven blackness were more slender and shapely than he had ever envisioned.

He was man.

She was woman.

Their eyes drank in each other's splendor until their bodies, their yearnings could not be denied and they rushed ravenously into each other's arms.

Doves cooed in an evening dance of their own. The gurgling river flowed serenely on its journey south. The heavens were sprinkled with gold dust, and the Milky Way was rich and boasting as the cacophony of passion and the perfumes of ardor slowly faded into the night.

Chapter Fifteen

For a long while Amy and Colby lay curled up in each other's arms on the bank of the Arkansas River. They listened to the stream whisper past and watched the moon travel lazily across the canopy of stars above them.

Colby held Amy close as she nestled next to him, savoring her nearness, the musky-sweet odor of her body. He stroked the damp tendrils of black unruly hair and caressed her soft earlobes. In her tawny throat, he could feel her pulse beat slowly. He watched the even rise and fall of her breasts, the redbud tips now softly retired and asleep as Amy seemed to be.

The crisp air of the November night crept slowly into her senses, and she shivered. Colby drew her perspiring body nearer. He kissed the long lashes and the raw forehead with the hated blue mark. But when he touched the caste designation with his fingers, she flinched and pulled away from him.

"Don't."

"Amy."

She let out a single sob.

"Amy," he whispered. He wished he knew how to comfort her, how to protect her.

But he'd been unable to protect Crissy, and too late to comfort her. He'd gone to Birmingham for household supplies and seed for the spring planting of cotton. When he'd returned home to the plantation a few days later, Crissy's frail body and golden hair had been washed and dressed for burial. Her cold remains lay in the drawing room next to the small bundle that would have been their son.

"She was fragile. The man was brutal. The baby didn't have a chance," friends said in trying to console him.

Colby had sold the plantation and said goodbye to his loyal freedmen who worked his fields, and began his search for the man who had committed the dastardly deed. It had taken Colby three years and four months, but he had finally tracked him down in New Orleans and had killed him in a stand-off on a street in the French Quarter.

He fingered the small scar at his left temple and winced at the memories. The eye was dead, just as his heart had been until this raven-haired beauty had awakened it. Amy had rekindled his spirit and aroused in his breast a desire to live life to the fullest, to dare to enjoy its bounty while it was within his grasp.

Colby prayed he could shield Amy from all the pain and grief that life would apportion to her, but there were inner battles confronting Amy that he could not share, or bear. She faced a journey into reality. Somehow, she had to find acceptance for who she was, or there could be no peace in her heart. She had to embrace certain truths before she could go on with her life, before she could come to him with an open spirit.

Amy stirred. "Is the earth supposed to spin?" She tried to stand but was dizzy.

Colby steadied Amy and wrapped her shivering body in the blanket and carried her to his soddy. He kicked open the door and shuffled across the dark room until he found the bed. He laid her cocooned form on the thin cot and struck a match to light the kerosene lamp.

Through her lashes, Amy watched the golden hues dance in and out of the shadows of the room with its rough-hewn timbers and earthen bricks. Her eyelids were heavy and weariness crept into her limbs, but her heart and mind were strangely buoyant.

Colby unwrapped the blanket and pulled the remaining clothing from Amy's torso. He found a towel and moistened it in the basin. Carefully, he brushed away the sand from the raw skin on Amy's forehead. She winced.

"My lovely Amy." He draped the blanket over her shivering form.

She snuggled beneath the covers.

"I'm going to make you some coffee." He put kindling in the old iron cook stove.

She was asleep before the teakettle had started its soft whistle.

Amy awakened slowly to the smell of coffee and fatback. When the faint light filtered through the cracks in the timbers, she recognized Colby's soddy and remembered the night before.

Colby had held her close, his huge hands had caressed her tenderly, his arms had been strong and loving, his lips searching and demanding, his mustache soft and teasing. Her heart fluttered as she remembered how their bodies had come together in that final moment of rapture.

"Colby?" she whispered, listening.

Silence.

Amy sat up. A pain pulsed through her temple. She touched her forehead. It was raw and feverish. She slowly drove the sleep from her brain and rose from the cot. She shivered and wrapped the blanket around her naked body, and wandered over to the two-legged table nailed to the wall. Colby had pinned a note.

Sorry, my love, didn't want to wake you, but have a paper to print. There's coffee and bacon, and water in the teakettle if you want to wash up. Don't hurry back to town. I'll help Alfred with the paper.

The door of the soddy opened.

"Colby?" Amy called.

The early morning light silhouetted a woman in the entry of the soddy.

Amy shrank back. "Who—who is it?" She couldn't stand facing any of the women in New Ponca. She didn't want their ridicule. Being found here would be the final blow, stripping the last shred of dignity from her.

"Yo' awake?" The tall woman walked into the room.

"Esther! What—what are you doing here?"

"Colby sent me. He said yo' needed some clothes." She lowered her head as she handed Amy a sack.

Amy pulled out a skirt and waist. "These are my clothes."

Esther nodded.

"How—?" Colby must have gone to her room at the hotel and searched her trunk to find her clothes. Had he gone through Papa's trunk, too, and found the homestead papers? The conniving and contemptible man had made love to her, then left her at the soddy so that he could steal her claim.

Amy's shoulders sagged. She was being irrational. It no longer mattered. As an Indian, her claim on the homestead was invalid. And Colby had made love to her only at her request. He hadn't really wanted her.

271

After all, she was just an Indian,

"Yo' need somethin' to eat." Esther dished up the meat.

"No, thank you," Amy hissed. "I don't want anything from Colby Grant." What a fool she had been.

Esther picked up the waist and held it out to Amy.

She snatched it away. "I'm not helpless!"

"Yes'um." The tall, wispy figure faded out the door.

Amy dressed hurriedly and walked out of the soddy to find Esther saddling Sultan.

"Don't—!" Amy sighed. She was being bestial, taking her anger out on the poor woman.

"I'm sorry, Esther. Thank you." For the first time, Amy understood what it must be like for Esther, a white apparition in a black world, an oddity among her own people. At least Esther was a misfit because of nature, not because of lies and prejudices. And, God help her, she had been as cruel to Esther as Mrs. Carrington had been to her.

Amy mounted Sultan and headed for town. Her hair fell around her face, and she could feel the river sand on her face and body. Well, she'd give the people of New Ponca something to really gossip about.

Clouds of dust and a roar of voices greeted Amy when she arrived in town. She needn't have worried about what the townsfolk might think. They were too busy dealing with the hordes of visitors arriving for the school dedication. The road from Cross was filled with rented hacks rolling into the city from the first Santa Fe special with its nine coaches of excursionists.

People overflowed the town. They clogged the boardwalks and spilled out into the dusty streets. Men and a few women pushed and shoved their way through the few stores and numerous saloons which opened early to accommodate the demanding crowd. Shrill laughter mixed with the tinkle of player pianos and the clamor of raised voices.

Forcing a nervous Sultan through the din and clatter of the crowded streets, Amy passed the *Republican,* where people snatched Colby's newspaper from Danny's hands as fast as he could make change.

Colby would no doubt have published an additional supply of newspapers. Unlike herself and Papa— Alfred—, Colby had the money to buy as many extra ready-prints as needed.

The livery was surrounded by rigs, horses and new arrivals, but Amy urged Sultan through the horde to stable the black gelding and ran to the hotel.

She met Mabel coming down the landing with an armload of linen.

"Why, Miss Amy, have you been out riding this early in the morning? And you made up your bed 'fore you left, too? Sure wish I had your energy."

Amy rushed past her without a word and fled into her room. She could hear her fath—Alfred—moaning next door.

"It's all my fault."

"Take it easy, Alfred."

It was Colby.

Alfred wailed. "Poor Amy."

"Alfred, she's all right. I sent Esther out to the soddy to attend to her."

Amy went to the washbasin and washed her face and hands. She combed out her unkempt hair and then stalked into Alfred's room.

Colby smiled. "There you are."

Amy glared at him. "Don't speak to me." What had Colby told her father—Alfred? She looked down at Alfred on the bed. His clothes were awry and his face flushed. In his hand was a small glass of liquor.

"Drunk!" she said disgustedly.

Colby leveled his right eye at her. "Seems to me I remember someone having a nip or two last night."

"Doc Taylor," Alfred wheezed, "said a shot of whiskey might help."

"You made me drink that vile stuff," she hissed at Colby. Alfred's words hit her. "Doc Taylor? When?"

"Aww, he's an old fuddy-duddy." Alfred struggled to sit up. "Help—help me up, Amy. We—we've got a paper to put out."

Colby forced Alfred back on the bed. "If you keep on, Alfred, you're going to have a real heart attack."

A pang of sympathy hit Amy. "Papa—" Amy stopped. "Alfred, are you all right?"

Alfred nodded. "I've been so worried about you. Thank God, Colby found you."

Amy looked at Colby and sneered. "Oh, yes. He found me."

"Oh, lass," Alfred said. "If I had it to do over again, I would . . ."

Amy interjected, " . . . have told me the truth? Tell me the truth now, Papa—Alfred."

The fading eyes watered. He sat up on the side of his bed.

Colby took the whiskey and handed Alfred a cup of coffee.

"I never meant to hurt you, lass. I wanted to protect you."

"By—by lying to me?"

"When it became obvious that no one in Milford was going to accept you, Hannah and I decided it would be best to send you back East to school."

Amy laughed sarcastically. "What would Miss Stevens have thought if she had known I was Indian?"

"She did question your heritage, but we told her you were French. And our money was good."

Colby put on his hat. "You don't need me here. I'll go down to the *Democrat*. Danny can help me put out your paper." He turned to Amy. "You and Alfred need to talk. And then get some rest."

Amy watched Colby leave her father's room. "Do you trust him?"

"With my life." Alfred smiled. He straightened his suspenders.

"Alfred—" She didn't know what to say to this man she had called Father for as long as she could remember. Somewhere, secreted deep inside of her, buried in all of the anger at him for her life of deception, was a love she couldn't deny. But there was also guilt. If she hadn't pressured Alfred to come to Oklahoma Territory she might never have discovered the truth about herself, and he would not be in a fight for his life to save his paper. It was at her insistence that they had pulled up stakes and gambled their last dollars to make this new start. And it had all been for nought.

"Alfred—"

He buried his white frothy head in his arms. It hurt both of them too much to call him by his given name.

"Papa—"

"Oh, lass—"

He started toward her, but she shook her head and stepped back. "You say you love me, and that you only wanted to protect me, but how could you have let me live this lie? How, Papa?"

"Hannah and I loved you, Amy. You were a babe, less than two years old, when we got you. You were the child we never had. We loved you so much. That's— that's why you're called Amy. Hannah looked it up in a book. '*Aime*' means love or something like it in French. We certainly loved you." He cradled his face in his hands.

"Papa," she whispered. "I don't know if I can forgive you. I'm eighteen years old, a grown woman, and I don't know who I am or where I belong."

He nodded. "I'm—I'm sorry."

She tried to smile. "The townspeople have made it

clear I don't belong here. I guess the only place I really belong is the Ponca Indian reservation," she said ruefully.

"Don't say that, Amy," Alfred pleaded. "You belong here, with me. And in time, people will accept you for what you are—"

"An Indian?" She laughed.

"—my daughter, a lovely young woman, and nothing more. Nothing's changed, Amy."

"Oh, Papa, everything has changed."

"One good thing, though," Alfred said with a smile. "I don't see getting rid of Silas Kane as being such a bad change."

"But what will you do, Papa? Silas will surely call your loan."

"Don't you worry your pretty head about that. You just worry about making your peace with Colby. I know you love him, lass."

"Colby? Don't ever mention that despicable man's name to me again!"

"Methinks you protest too much." Alfred rose and put on his coat. "I'm going down to give Colby a hand."

"Colby—Colby said you should rest."

"I thought you didn't trust him."

"Papa, I find it very hard to have much faith in a man who has everything to gain by seeing that we're ruined in this town. We've worked too hard to let Colby Grant take it away from us now."

"You're beginning to sound bitter, Amy. And mark my words, that kind of thinking is like whiskey. It rots your guts. You've got to go on with your life and take the lumps that come with it. But you don't lay down and die like—like I almost did when I lost—when I lost Hannah."

"But how can I live in this town when people won't even speak to me?" she asked.

"There are plenty of kind folk here, Amy. Not all are

like Mrs. Carrington and some of the other tea-sipping gossips. Now, get some rest. You'll want to have enough energy to dance up a storm at the ball tonight."

"The dance?" She laughed. "I'm not going—" But Alfred was out the door before she could finish her protest.

After bathing and repinning her hair, Amy walked down to the overflowing hotel dining room. She was ravenous.

"You just sit right here, Miss Amy," Mr. Pearson said smiling. "Only right I take care of my regular customers first."

Amy's vision blurred at his kindness. She knew he was not ignorant of the gossip. "*Merci*—thank you, Mr. Pearson." She choked down a hysterical laugh. It was ludicrous to speak French.

After breakfast, Amy made her way through the crowd of early arrivals, now growing restless as they waited for something to happen. In droves they moved down the street, going from store to store, buying up everything for sale out of boredom, paying prices that were more than double what they would have paid in their own hometowns.

Amy pursed her lips in distaste. It was absurd for thousands of people to travel to this desolate part of the world to help celebrate the dedication of a simple school building. The promotional efforts of Silas and his Board of Trade had been a disastrous success.

Well, she didn't have to worry about Silas Kane anymore. And she would burn that ridiculous book of etiquette he had foisted on her when she got back to her room.

A part of Amy was sorry that all of the efforts of the Cross townsmen to jinx the celebration had failed. The small town was in a fight for its life. It had advertised its own celebration—Indians, bands, feasts—everything that New Ponca had boasted. But the visitors who had poured into the siding at Cross considered the small band that greeted them as part of the New Ponca celebration and stayed only long enough to find a conveyance south.

Someone jostled Amy. "Scuse me, ma'am." The gentleman doffed his hat as he turned to face her.

The woman on his arm asked, "Is that an Indian, Ernest?"

The man looked again at Amy. "A half-breed maybe. Kinda pretty, though."

"And we're not deaf, either!" Amy snapped and walked on down to the *Democrat* office.

Alfred leaned against a type case and tried to set type. Sweat or tears, Amy couldn't be sure which, fell from his flushed face and onto the metal type. She walked over and hugged him.

At half past one, the Santa Fe specials disgorged several thousand more tourists from Newton, Wellington, Wichita and Winfield, Kansas. Amy watched through the window of the *Democrat* as they joined the horde surging through the streets of the "progressive" city with its new street lamps.

When the last load of excursionists had poured into the city, the parade began on Grand Avenue.

Alfred grabbed his hat and Amy's arm. "Let's go, lass. We still have a paper to put out this afternoon."

Three bands marched from West Grand to the public square to the tune of "Marching Through Georgia." Colonel Miller and his sons followed the marching bands and dignitaries with twenty head of cattle destined for the Indian roundup and barbecue. Behind them surged more than 8,000 exuberant celebrants, a good number of them waving flasks or whiskey bottles.

At the park, the Ponca Indians waited. The women in their ribboned tunics tended fires under huge pots and prepared spits for the meat. Young men stripped to the waist and with lassoes in hand and knives between their teeth made ready to entertain the crowd by chasing the cattle on foot and slaying them for the barbecue. Amy saw Roughface, dressed only in a breechcloth, his muscles taut and ready, his mahogany skin oiled to a sheen.

The noise from the throng of people unnerved the cattle and two steers escaped, but eighteen head of cattle were quickly slain by the 300 charging Indians. The tribal women swept down on the carcasses to skin the hides and butcher the meat for the feast. At the sights and smells, the crowd quickly moved a safe distance away.

The wind picked up, and Silas Kane announced that the formal dedication ceremony would begin in the new schoolhouse. Only a hundred or so people were able to squeeze into the building. Hundreds of others spilled out on the porch and around the open windows to hear the speeches, but most of the town's guests headed back to the saloons.

Mayor Barnes welcomed the visitors to New Ponca and boasted of the progress made in sixty days. "From tents on a bald prairie to a city of schools and parks in less than two months. That's quite an accomplishment, and a testimonial to the people of this city."

The crowd roared its approval. At this point, Amy was sure the mob would celebrate anything. She wanted to leave, but the throng was so dense she was forced to stay at Alfred's side until Silas had introduced the speakers.

After two hours of oratory, the crowd faded away to join the majority of the celebrants surging up and down Grand Avenue looking for something to do.

Alfred and Amy pushed their way down the street.

"Well, hello, Henry Little," Alfred said. "Decided to close up the depot for the afternoon?"

"Booked solid. No tickets to sell." Little smiled sheepishly.

"How's the celebration going at Cross?" Alfred probed.

"Well, half an hour after the last train arrived, there wasn't anything but a yellow bull pup and a stray cat sleeping in the street."

Alfred slapped his thigh. "That bad, huh?"

"Even the Indian dancer they hired lit out after one drink. Mighty lonesome burg, so thought I'd get on down here and see what all the hullabaloo was about."

"Glad to have you." Alfred smiled. "And glad to see you're one of the few sober visitors we have today. Maybe Nolan had a good idea when he asked for Thatcher to come over from Blackwell to help corral this crowd."

Amy noted the throng was becoming more unruly every moment. There was no water, no shade and no place to sit down. Some shop owners, depleted of their meager supplies, closed their doors and stood guard to keep out the mobs who roamed the streets. Indignant celebrants accused saloon owners of serving watered-down whiskey. Runners had been sent to Ark City and the Osage in search of more liquor to satisfy the thirsty multitude.

In an attempt to keep the teeming crowd entertained, Mayor Barnes ordered the Indian pony and foot races to begin ahead of schedule. The drill team from the Ponca Indian school performed, and when all the entertainment had been exhausted, someone came up with the idea of a tug-of-war contest.

"Ah'll bet ya fifty dollars the east side wins," a fair-haired man called, waving a whiskey bottle.

"Ya gonna show me yore money, Shorty? Or are you just blowin' smoke?" someone yelled.

Shorty swaggered over to the challenger. "You callin' me a liar?"

"Nope. I'm callin' you a drunk. I jist don't think you got fifty dollahs on you."

Deputy Thatcher stepped between the two men.

"Back off, Thatcher. Nobody calls me a liar." Shorty shook off the officer's arm.

Thatcher licked his lips nervously. "I'll have to place you under arrest." The deputy pulled his gun out of his holster and cocked the hammer back.

The people trampled each other as they tried to get out of the way. Another deputy, Bob Burnett, lunged toward Thatcher.

"Don't! You'll kill somebody in this crowd."

The gun went off and everyone screamed.

Shorty fell face down on the dusty street. He groaned, then slowly began to move and to pat down his body. A lopsided grin spread across his drunken face. "He missed me."

"But he didn't miss Hennessey!"

Colby Grant stood on a dray wagon, looking down at the hotel porter. "Get Doc Taylor."

Amy wrestled with her desire to go to Colby's side and help him tend to Hennessey, but she saw Eliza Carpenter and knew she would only be in the way.

"Come on, lass," Alfred said. "Let's wrap up today's edition before they get so drunk they can't read the paper."

Alfred had set the last line of type on the last story and tightened the galley in the iron turtles when a loud gun blast sent Amy to the window.

"What's going on out there?" Alfred asked.

"Oh, my!" Amy put one hand across her eyes. "That's horrid."

Alfred joined Amy at the window in time to see Walt Nolan and one of his henchman slash the air with whips, forcing drunks to roll closer to the buildings and leave room for people to walk.

"I hope Silas Kane is happy."

Alfred stepped to the doorway. "Nolan, you're doing a fine job," he yelled.

"Papa?" She questioned her father.

Nolan strutted over to Alfred, a gun in one hand and a whip in the other. "That's what I was hired for."

"Yessir," Alfred said, "a fine job, but I was wondering if maybe we ought to move those who have passed out somewhere where they won't get trampled. Might be a state senator in that mess down there and we'd never know it till we started to bury him."

"Maybe you're right." Nolan holstered his gun. "Johnny, load up these guys and take 'em down to Stacy's livery barn and let 'em sleep it off in the stalls."

Amy smiled at her wise father.

"Have you heard how Hennessey is doing?" she asked.

He frowned. "Doubt if he makes it till morning. Grant took him down to Eliza Carpenter's place, down to his own kind."

"Thank you," Amy said curtly. She had never realized how much bias and prejudice dwelled in the hearts of ordinary men.

Nolan yelled out more orders and then pushed through the crowd, his lash threatening anyone within reach.

After the last copy of the *Democrat* had been snapped up, Alfred convinced Hattie and Danny to join him and Amy for the evening barbecue at the park. In spite of the mob scene, serving tables still boasted piles of savory meat, Indian fry bread, corn soup and boiled beans. Amy found the food unexpectedly tasty, and wondered what other foods the Indians might eat.

Alfred wiped his chin. "I believe we have sated ourselves."

"I'm not sated, but I sure am full." Danny rubbed his stomach.

Amy and Albert laughed.

When the Indians began their traditional tribal dances, Amy found her feet keeping time to the beat of the tom-tom.

Roughface danced with bands of feathers tied on his arms, a yellow roach rising out of his dark hair, and turtle shells at his ankles. He provocatively swooped his oiled body and gracefully dipped his wings in front of Amy as he moved through the ancient choreographed steps.

Amy looked on in fascination until she caught Silas eyeing her with a smirk. Defiantly, Amy began to clap her hands and nod her head to the ancestral rhythm vibrating through her body.

When the dances were over, Alfred and Amy walked Danny and his mother back to Mrs. Rhodie's small home.

"Ah thank ye fer bringin' us home. Lot of ruffians out theah."

Alfred smiled. "Breakfast in the morning?"

"I'll open up as usual," she said, "but iffen you come a mite early, the cinnamon rolls 'll be hot."

Alfred doffed his hat and steered Amy back to the hotel.

"You *are* going to the ball, aren't you?" Alfred asked.

"I think I'll stay in, Papa. I'm tired." Amy bit her lip. She had spent hours on the white gown she had hoped would impress Silas Kane and make Colby Grant envious. But now, how could she even show her face, to say nothing of wearing white, after all that had happened? The Carringtons had made it plain they didn't want to be in the same room with her—with an Indian. And Colby—

"Tuck your tail and hide, is that your battle plan?"

"That's not fair," Amy protested.

283

"Life isn't fair, generally," Alfred said. "You have to accept yourself for who and what you are, Amy."

"I'm an Indian," she breathed. "I'm finding it very hard to find any self-respect in that, Papa."

"But you're also my daughter, goldarn it! After sixteen years, doesn't that count for something?" His eyes pleaded.

"All right, Papa," she said softly. "We'll go to the dance."

Amy and her father joined the crush of dancers in the opera house over Will Chase's drug store as Doyle's orchestra struck up the grand march.

Standing against a wall, they went unnoticed at first, but then Amy's eyes connected with Naomi Carrington's as she danced near.

The young woman whispered to her partner and the couple behind them. Amy watched as Naomi's comments spread through the dancers around her until the heat in Amy's face was unbearable.

"Let's go, Papa."

Alfred glanced at his pocket watch. "It's near midnight, lass. There's a supper over at Kane's bank. Don't suppose you want to go."

"May I have this dance?"

Colby Grant, in his dirty dungarees, stood before her. "Sorry, but I've just come from Eliza's. Doc Taylor's done all he knows to do. I'll have to go back soon. Eliza and Esther will need me."

The relief that had first swept over Amy turned to indignation.

"Eliza and Esther," she hissed, "always need you." She wanted to cry out, *Can't you see I need you?*

Colby swung Amy out on the dance floor. "Do I detect a bit of sarcasm in those smoldering gray eyes?"

He pulled her close, and for a moment Amy could forget the ugliness in the world. For a sweet while she remembered the night before when he tenderly held her in his arms and passionately made love to her. She fought against the apprehensions creeping in about Colby's motives. It made no sense that he had been kind to her because he wanted her homestead now that her claim was invalid. Did Colby really care about her? Or did he only pity her? She had begged him to make love to her, but had he held her close and sent her into rapturous splendor because he loved her or pitied her? Did he think she needed the same kind of charity as he gave to all underdogs, to young Danny, to Eliza and Esther, to Hennessey?

Amy pulled away from Colby. "Why didn't you bring Esther?"

"Don't be cruel," Colby snapped. "You of all people ought to understand the prejudice in this town."

"Prejudice? This town?" she scoffed. "Why, they even sent a special request to the Great White Father for permission for *us savages* to attend today's big celebration. Remember?"

Colby spun Amy around on the dance floor until she was breathless, then drew her back into his arms. "Good thing you weren't reared as an Indian. They'd have cut your tongue out long ago."

Naomi, on the arm of her date, whirled by. She put her hand to her mouth and let out a war whoop. The other young dancers around her joined in with their own Indian yells. All except Rachel and her red-haired fiance, Tex Drummond, who looked embarrassed.

"Ignore them," Colby whispered. "They're just envious that I'm dancing with the most beautiful and desirable woman here."

Silas Kane with Jeannette Barnes clinging to him moved into Amy's vision. The twisted smile on his face mocked her.

She pulled away from Colby, who was trying to hold her on the dance floor. "Don't let them get away with it,

Amy," he whispered. "Hold up your head, dammit!"

"I can't!" Amy whispered. "Just let me go, Colby." She wrenched free of his arms and ran out of the opera house and down the stairs.

Naomi and her date looked down from the upper landing and laughed. "Why don't you go to the reservation and dance with your own kind?" Naomi yelled down.

Amy stopped on the stairs and looked up at Naomi, who put her hand to her mouth and let out a poor imitation of an Indian yell.

"Where's ya goin', squaw lady?" A drunk in tails and top hat fell against her, pinning her against the rail. He grabbed her hand and tried to pull her against him. "Wanna trade a blanket for a kish or two?"

"Get your hands off her." Colby threw the drunk over the railing and scooped Amy up in his arms.

"Let me go!"

"Colby!" A woman called as they reached the street.

Colby stood Amy on her feet. It was Esther on the back of a mule. At her side was Colby's ugly roan.

"You'd better come," the woman said softly.

Colby looked from Amy to Esther.

"Go, Colby," Amy said softly.

"Come with me."

She shook her head. "I'd only be in the way."

When Esther and Colby had been swallowed up by the masses, Amy made her way back to the hotel, stepping over sleeping drunks not yet picked up by Nolan's men. She rerouted around a crowd of unruly imbibers just as a woman screamed, "My God, his innards are coming out!" Amy fled as the man with the knife stared unbelieving at what he'd done.

Safe in her room, Amy tried to sort out her feelings. She could hear the revelers on the street and the music coming from the opera house. She supposed that now that they were fortified by the midnight supper, they'd dance until daylight.

She told herself it was all so frivolous. Parties were for the young and flighty, and her heart had lived a thousand years, and a thousand deaths. But she could not still the fury churning inside of her that the world she had envisioned for herself and Papa had been taken away. All the suffering Papa had endured over her insistence that they come to Indian Territory had been for nought. Without additional financing, the newspaper was doomed. And Silas would no doubt find it very advantageous to foreclose. Colby had won, after all, if only by default. And there was little she could do to stop it. She was a Ponca. Her father had been an Indian drunk, and somehow she had to learn how to cope with that cruel fact, and she had to learn who Amy Elizabeth White really was.

Amy knew what she had to do. Packing quickly, she took the string of mussel shells from the trunk and wrapped them in a change of clothing along with the tintype of her mother, Prairie Flower. She placed her homestead papers on the bed and left Alfred a note.

I'm sorry, Papa, but I must find out who I am and where I belong. Please don't come after me. I need time to sort out my feelings. I'm leaving the homestead papers with you. If Colby will buy my claim, take the money and put it on Kane's note.

At Stacy's livery, Amy stepped gingerly over drunken bodies and saddled Sultan. The train whistle blew, warning visitors the first coach would soon depart. She backed out of the way as inebriated men were loaded onto hacks for the short drive to Cross. For a moment, Amy wished she could melt into the crowd and go with them. But she couldn't go anywhere until she knew where she had been. And the answers could only be found with her own people.

The trail to the Ponca village was strewn with casualties from the town's celebration. Indians weaved back and forth on the road as they softly chanted native songs. A few gave up the fight and lay down to sleep along the trail. Others trudged slowly south.

"Are you alone?"

Amy stifled a cry of fright as Roughface rode his pinto up beside her, his woman on behind.

Amy nodded. "I'm going to my father's house."

Roughface nodded as if that were explanation enough and rode silently beside her on the road south.

Chapter Sixteen

A rooster crowed and smoke from a campfire drifted into Amy's consciousness. She yawned and stretched her arms to the ceiling, then froze at the sight of the bare rafters overhead. Her heart pounded as her eyes wandered around the lean-to. Her eyes focused on the tintype of Prairie Flower resting on the table and she remembered. Her arms fell limply to her side.

Amy shifted her body on the lumpy mattress and strained against the wool blanket that Roughface had given her last night. She wrinkled her nose. She had not noticed the foul smell of the blanket before. She had been too exhausted, too internalized to really notice her crude accommodations. She had only been grateful to Roughface for not asking questions.

For she had no answers. No answers for the way she felt Colby. No answers for Alfred. And no answer to the most important question of all—who was Amy Elizabeth White? But that wasn't her real name, was it? What name had her mother, Prairie Flower, given her?

The rooster crowed again, and Amy knew she was not only embarking on a new day, but a new life that might bring more unanswered questions. She threw off the blanket and dressed. Wishing for a cup of coffee, Amy looked in the small cabinet, but found only a small sack of ground corn.

She would have to find some way to feed herself, to tend to her needs while she learned about her people, about herself. She had only a few coins in her purse. She would have to find work of some kind. Perhaps the Indian agent could help her get a job at the storehouse. Perhaps she could teach at the Indian school.

She turned at the light knock on the door. "Come in."

Roughface entered with a cup of coffee and a bowl of steaming porridge. His woman waited just outside the doorway with a scowl on her face.

"Thank you." Amy sipped the hot coffee and smiled.

Roughface pointed to the woman. "Gray Dove."

Amy tasted the cereal in the bowl. "Thank you, Gray Dove. I'm afraid I've given no thought of how to care for myself." She laughed nervously. "That's quite naive, isn't it?"

Roughface shrugged. "I eat, you eat. I hungry, you hungry."

"Oh, but I can't expect to rely on your good graces the rest of my life. I thought I would go see the Indian agent, Major Wood, or the trader, Mr. Harsh. Maybe one of them could find me some work."

Roughface sneered. "You want to be a slave?"

"Slave? Of course not. Perhaps I could mind the store or teach at the school."

"Better you go with me."

"Go with you?" She looked at Roughface's woman. "Where?"

"Home."

"Home?" She flushed.

"North to Niobrara, to buffalo ground, to your grandfather."

Her heart quickened. "My grandfather?"

"Chief Standing Bear."

"But I can't just take off. I—I—"

She looked into his eyes, dark and brooding. "But—but how would we get there? I have no money for the train or the stagecoach." And she could not, would not, ask her father.

"We go in wagon."

"It—it would take a long time."

He shrugged his shoulders.

Amy sighed. "That's all I have, isn't it—time? Do you know the way? Do you have a map?"

Roughface ushered Amy outside. He stooped and picked up a stick and began to draw in the dirt.

"Ponca here." He marked an X. "Ponca here." This time he placed the X farther north. And then he began to draw in the rivers, naming them as he moved the stick north from Indian Territory. "The Arkansas, the Platte, the Niobrara."

"That's in Nebraska."

Roughface nodded.

Dust rose in the air as a rig came clattering down the lane.

Roughface hissed. "Major Wood."

The soldier jumped down from the buggy. "Roughface, Dovey," he acknowledged. "Well, well, well. If it isn't Miss White."

"Good morning, Major." She smiled, pushing back her unkempt hair. Unlike Roughface, Amy had no fear of the Indian agent. After all, she had exchanged pleasantries with him on many occasion in New Ponca.

He walked around Amy and then stared into her face. "Well, well, well. You sure had me fooled."

"I beg your pardon," Amy said. She despised the

man's superior attitude that made her feel small and worthless.

"You really are an Indian."

Amy raised her chin. "My mother was Prairie Flower, daughter of Chief Standing Bear. My father was Shines White."

"Maybe—maybe not. For all I know, you could be Apache, but you're not on my Indian roll, so don't expect to get rations."

"I expect nothing for free, Major. I'm intelligent and resourceful. I'm sure I can find a job here on the reservation."

"Sorry." He shook his head. "And you can't hang around here free-loading. The government won't stand for it."

Amy looked at Roughface. "What time will you leave?"

The agent looked at Roughface. "Leave?"

"We go to visit our brothers and sisters up north."

He sneered. "Well, don't expect me to give you any extra rations." He jumped back into the buggy and sped off.

Roughface turned to Amy. "We go before the next rising sun."

All day, Amy watched as the small band of Indians prepared for the trip north. They dragged out a ragged tepee and placed it on a travois, on which they tied bundles filled with their meager belongings. Roughface worked to repair a wheel on a dilapidated wagon, weathered gray and cracked from time.

Amy withdrew into Shines White's cabin and packed her mother's picture and the small sack of ground corn in her satchel of belongings. She had so little to contribute. She braided her hair like Roughface's woman, tearing the hem of her petticoat into strips to intertwine in the braids. With her hair pulled back from her forehead,

she knew the blue dot was conspicuous. She tied the
mussel-shell string around her neck. She wished she
had a mirror. Did she look like her mother, Prairie
Flower?

Early the next morning a light knock on Shines
White's doorway and Amy was on her feet. The sun
had not risen and the cock had not crowed, but it was
time to leave. She winced at the scrawny horses that
pulled the rickety old wagon, and the pony hitched
to the lone travois. The small group climbed into the
wagon. Amy followed on Sultan as they headed north.

Roughface and Gray Dove sat on the wagon box
seat. Riding in the back of the open wagon seat were
Johnny Cries-for-Ribs, a young mute, and Henry Grass,
a thin middle-aged man who coughed constantly. The
old woman, Alice, leaned against the flimsy wall of the
farm wagon clutching a baby cradle.

"Granddaughter," Roughface explained. "Mother ran
off with white man. She whore," he sneered.

Amy's throat tightened. Was she Colby's whore, too?
Why had fate been so cruel to throw them together?
White men might make love to pretty Indian maidens,
but they never married them. They abandoned them in
disgrace—and with babies.

When they neared the town of New Ponca, light was
beginning to rise on the horizon. As Roughface veered
the wagon toward the spring to fill the water jugs, Amy
reined up Sultan and dismounted for one last look at the
town she had helped to create. The Carringtons and the
others could never take that away from her. Tears began
to seep through her lashes for what had been lost, for
what might have been, for all the abandoned dreams.

She turned toward the east, toward the Arkansas
River as it swept around the bend past New Ponca.
She closed her eyes and in her mind walked through
the yellowing bluestem of her homestead to the arbor
where she and Colby had made love. For a moment, she

could even smell Colby's manly scent, feel his feverish body against hers, his hungry mouth on her lips, and her loins throbbed anew with passion.

She opened her eyes to the harsh light. "Danny was right. 'It don't do no good t'wish fer somethin' ya can't never have.'"

Amy tightened Sultan's cinches and began to remount. The gelding whinnied, and she turned to see Colby riding toward her. He brought the strawberry roan to an abrupt stop in front of her.

He grinned down from his saddle. "Well, you look the part." His eyes took in the mussel-shell necklace, the braided hair.

"This is who I am. It's not an act."

Colby frowned. "Is this what you want, Amy?"

"I can't fight it anymore, Colby." She mounted Sultan and reined him south. She did not want Colby to know where she was heading when she left New Ponca.

He followed. "So you're going to be a reservation Indian?"

"Is there a choice?"

"You know there is." Colby's arm reached out for her.

"Don't touch me! I'm not your—your Indian whore!"

A muscle worked in Colby's jaw as he leaned back in his saddle. "Well, I'll say one thing for you. You're acting like a savage. But you're more uncivilized than any Ponca I ever met. Maybe it will do you good to live on the reservation for a while. Maybe you'll learn how to be a human being."

"But I am an Indian," she sneered. "What's here for me? Who would marry me now?"

"Not all men are like Silas."

"Silas is a decent, successful businessman." Why was she defending him? Because she knew it irritated Colby?

"You want him? You want Silas Kane? After what we shared?"

Amy's eyes wavered. "Why wish for something you can't have?" She spurred Sultan into a run.

Stunned, Colby watched as the proud figure of Amy White rode off to the south.

"What's in that little fool's head." He shook his own. Life on the Ponca reservation south of town would not be easy, but she'd learn a lot, and maybe living a few days with her blood brothers would bring her to her senses.

Colby loped the strawberry roan toward New Ponca.

Amy rode south until she was out of Colby's sight, then circled back north. When she caught up with the slow-moving band of Poncas she wondered if the vagabond crew would actually reach the northern Ponca reservation. The pinto pony pulling the laden travois was old and graying, and the mismatched bays that pulled the creaking wagon with its wobbling wheels looked severely undernourished.

When they came upon the Chilocco Indian reservation, Roughface pulled the wagon down the mile-and-a-half lane toward the massive three-story limestone school building lying on the banks of Chilocco Creek.

"We stay here tonight."

Amy was disappointed they were still so near New Ponca. It would not be easy to escape detection if her father started looking for her.

The Indian-school superintendent was not happy to see the motley crew, but finally agreed to let them stay the night when they promised to be on their way early the next morning.

He looked curiously at their little band of seven. Amy kept her head down hoping her braids and dark skin helped her blend into the group. She did not recall ever seeing the man before, but many people knew her whom she did not know.

The man looked at Sultan. "Fine horse you got there," he said to Roughface. "Where did you steal it?"

"No steal."

So much for subterfuge. Sultan would easily be remembered.

The man's lip curled in disbelief, but he waved his arm. "You can camp just outside the gate."

Roughface unharnessed the horses while Gray Dove gathered stones and branches for a fire. She spoke a few words in sign language to Johnny. He went to the creek for water and poured it into a pot resting on the stones. Alice, with the baby cradle tied on her back, dug wild onions. Henry sat on his haunches near the fire and coughed. Only a handful of words were exchanged, all in Ponca, all foreign to Amy.

She felt useless, a burden to this poor band of Indians. "What can I do?"

Gray Dove did not answer.

"Please, I'd like to help."

Roughface walked up to her. "Rest. Long way. You are soft."

Resigned, Amy found a pencil and a sheet of paper in her satchel. She must write a letter to Papa. She did not want him to worry. She wanted him to understand the importance of this journey of discovery. She must learn about her people before she could learn about Amy Elizabeth White. But most of all, she wanted Papa to know that she forgave him and that she loved him.

When she had finished her letter, Roughface brought her a bowl of corn and onion soup. If not delectable, it was certainly palatable and filling, and it warmed her in the crisp evening air.

At nightfall, Roughface took the small tepee from the travois and swiftly raised the tattered canvas. He laid a tarp under the wagon and motioned to Alice.

The old woman grunted and rolled under the wagon with her blanket, placing the infant, still in her cradle, at her side.

Roughface motioned for Amy to enter the tepee.

Gray Dove said something harshly and glared at Amy.

Amy shook her head. "I'll sleep with Alice." It would be more important than ever that she be cautious in her attitude toward Roughface. She did not want to encourage him and draw the ire of Gray Dove.

Roughface shrugged and shoved Gray Dove into the torn tepee.

Amy crawled under the wagon as Johnny and Henry settled themselves overhead in the creaking wagon bed. She hoped the frame would not cave in on her and Alice, or the cradled infant.

Amy found it difficult to ignore the curious odor of the old woman, until she turned on her side away from Alice. With guttural sounds of lovemaking coming from the tepee, she watched the campfire gradually burn down. The flickering embers brought back memories of her first night on the Oklahoma prairie, of the red eyes of the skunk she saw in the firelight as she guarded her homestead, and she stifled a giggle, and then a sob.

She would not think about her lost homestead or Colby Grant. And she would not think about Papa. She pushed her fists into her eyelids. She must not let her mind dwell on what might have been. She must concentrate on discovering the real Amy Elizabeth White before she could think about the future. She only prayed that Colby would be generous and buy the homestead from Alfred to save the *Democrat* from Silas Kane.

At daybreak, Roughface handed Amy a handful of dried blackberries. She gobbled them down as Roughface reloaded the wagon and travois. When they crossed the river and rode through Arkansas City, Amy veered off to the post office to mail her letter to Alfred and then met Roughface at the livery, where she bought a bag of oats with her few remaining coins.

The small band of Poncas rode almost due north

under a warm sun across rolling prairies, golden with fall grasses. They passed through the small settlement of Winfield, then veered slightly northwest.

At midday, Roughface stopped in the shadow of a barren plum thicket while they nibbled on dried jerky and pecan nuts brought from the Ponca reservation.

In the next few days, they traversed around the big village of Wichita and made their way across numerous plowed fields to Newton, careful to avoid the stockyards a mile and a half west of the rail town.

Amy was amazed at how Roughface could accurately direct them to a camp each evening near a river or a stream, finding outcroppings or small knolls to help protect them from the wind, growing colder each mile they went north.

A routine had evolved so that few words were necessary when they stopped to camp. Only Henry Grass was idle, maintaining his vigil at the campfire, growing weaker with each coughing seizure.

Roughface tended to the animals while Johnny filled the pots with water from a nearby stream. Amy gathered wood and Alice looked for wild roots and berries as Gray Dove started the cooking fire, ever watchful of how close Roughface was to Amy.

Today, Alice found wild onions, rhubarb and sunflowers. She ground the sunflowers into flour to make something resembling hardtack. Gray Dove put a small chunk of meat and dry corn into the pot for soup. She placed the wild onions on a bed of coals to roast, turning them occasionally until they were done. They ate them by puncturing the onions to let the steam escape, then scooped out the centers.

After their meal, Alice dropped the wild rhubarb into a fresh pot of boiling water, changing the water several times to rid the rhubarb of its bitter taste. When the roots had cooled, she gave them to Henry to chew. Within minutes his cough had eased.

The next day they crossed cattle trails and small streams so vile with manure that even the horses wouldn't drink. Roughface finally found a spring of good water near Lindsborg, a Swedish settlement nestled in a series of gentle outcroppings called the Flint Hills. In the distance was a small soddy and a crude barn, surrounded by freshly plowed fields. A pair of mules stood next to a lean-to, seeking protection from the never-ending winds. A milk cow was tethered to a stake in front of the soddy.

The Poncas finished eating most of their meager supplies that evening. Alice had not been successful in finding roots or onions. And the limbs that Amy had brought back to camp had been discarded by Gray Dove with scorn.

"Sumac," Roughface explained. "Poison."

The satchel of food that Gray Dove carried in a sling over her shoulder was limp, and the burlap sack of oats for the horses held only a handful of gritty bran.

In the middle of the night, they all came down with diarrhea. Amy, embarrassingly enough, was the first. By morning, they were all too weak to travel.

In the afternoon, the settlers at the soddy became curious enough to venture out in their wagon. They came within shouting distance.

"Could you use some turnips?"

Gray Dove staggered over to retrieve the sack.

"Not much," said the thin woman whose face was wrinkled from days in the sun, "but you're welcome to the turnips. They're fresh. Just dug 'em." The woman licked her lips and looked at her full-bearded husband, whose hand rested nervously on a rifle in his lap.

Amy suddenly realized that the settlers were afraid of them. But could she blame them? Had she been any different the first time she saw Shines White? Couldn't they see they were a sick and scraggly group of seven?

She started to reassure the woman, to say thank you for the turnips, but Roughface grunted and motioned her to be silent.

He was right. It was best if no one knew she spoke English.

Roughface crawled into the back end of the settlers' wagon. "Milk cow."

The man's hand tensed on the rifle. His wife stayed his hand.

"We go in morning. Milk cow, now," Roughface repeated.

"Of course." The woman turned the team toward the soddy.

Roughface returned with a molasses bucket full of fresh milk. Gray Dove built a fire and poured in the milk, adding pepper and salt to season. When the milk was boiling hot, Roughface apportioned it evenly until the pot was drained.

By morning, everyone had recovered, but because of their weakness, they traveled only a few miles before making camp for a meal of turnips.

Near Salina they ran into a cold, drizzly rain, which further slowed their travel. Alice found a few wild onions to go with the last of their cornmeal to make a thin soup. Johnny stumbled over a bird's nest and the three tiny eggs were added to the pot. Gray Dove tossed in a handful of grasshoppers and beetles. Amy's stomach rolled, but she was so famished, she spooned down the soup with relish.

That night, sleep came quickly to the fatigued Amy. There were no lingering thoughts of Colby and Papa, and she no longer noticed the strange odor of her bed companion, Alice.

The Poncas followed the Smoky Hill River to Abilene and camped early in the afternoon on the outskirts of the boisterous cattle town. Misting rain fell on ground already saturated from earlier downpours. After setting up camp, the weary and discouraged Poncas found no onions and few edible roots. The area had been trampled into mud by the cattle herds heading for the railroad yards in Abilene.

Roughface went to the river and returned with a handful of cattails. He cut off the clump from which the roots grew at the bottom of the stalk and began peeling off the layers until he reached a tender portion. He cut the remaining three or four inner rings into small half-inch lengths and tossed them into the pot of boiling water.

Amy's stomach growled after the meager meal. The others looked just as hungry.

"I'm going into Abilene," Amy said.

Roughface objected. "Trouble."

"But we need food, and so do the horses. I may go hungry, but I refuse to let Sultan starve!"

Shivering from a quick bath in the icy stream, Amy dressed into her one change of clean clothes. She found a bed of mint and chewed several twigs to freshen her mouth.

Roughface continued to discourage Amy.

"You have no money."

"I'll find a way to get what we need." She looked over at the whimpering baby trying to find nourishment from a piece of dried leather in Alice's hand. Henry, weakened by lack of protein, lay prone in the back of the wagon. Johnny sat with his back to the wagon wheels with dull eyes staring into the distance.

"I'll find a way."

"Bad town, bad men. I go with you."

Grey Dove scowled.

"No, it's better if I go alone." She had passed for white once, she could do it again if it meant getting food for their small band and the horses.

"Take this with you." Roughface slipped a small, sharp knife into her hand.

The rain eased as Amy reached the edge of the town. It was near nightfall, which would be to her advantage. She dismounted and took the blanket from her shoulders and rolled it up. She saw Roughface lurking in the shadows. She hated to admit it, but she felt safer. Gray Dove, however, would be angry.

Amy undid her braids and shook out her dark mane. She swept it up in a chignon, careful to cover the caste mark. She donned the jacket to her riding suit and smoothed out the wrinkles as much as possible. She picked up Roughface's knife and with reluctance slid the well-honed dagger up her jacket sleeve, the hilt resting at her wrist.

Remounting Sultan, Amy raised her chin, squared her shoulders and took a deep breath. With a touch of her heels in his flanks, she urged her black gelding down the muddy street.

Amy trotted Sultan past the Abilene Hotel to the dimly lit mercantile building located between two noisy saloons. A half-dozen rowdies lounged in drunken stupor under the overhang.

"Wal, where did you come from?" asked a drunk cowhand hanging onto a saloon newel post as he watched Amy dismount.

"*Merci,*" she said, bowing her head to hide her face.

"Wal, mercy to you, lady. Oh, yeah. Mercy, mercy, mercy." The cowhand slid down the post and into the mud. Other cattle wranglers standing around hooted and laughed.

With a quick glance at the sign, Bailey's Mercantile, Amy scooted inside. So far, so good.

"Good evening, Mr. Bailey." Please, God, let that be the man's name.

"That's right," said the man across the counter as he looked up from his books. He smiled. "How can I help you?"

"Well, I'm quite embarrassed, really. I'm on my way

to Fort Riley to meet my dear husband—"

He guffawed. "Why, you must be Major Dowd's wife." He reached out his hands. "He's sure been impatient for you to get here."

Amy panicked, "Is—is he here?"

"No'm, I'm 'fraid not. The platoon left yesterday for the fort. Too bad he didn't know you'd be on that last stage."

"I'm sorry, too."

"Are you staying at the Abilene?"

"Yes, yes, I am, but I'm afraid I have a wee bit of a problem, Mr. Bailey."

"Wal, I bet we can fix you up, Miz Dowd, whatever it is."

"Oh, thank you," she breathed. "You know I couldn't bare to leave my fine Arabian horse behind, so we brought him along, tied behind the stage. But I'm afraid I have run out of oats—"

"Pshaw! That's no problem."

"And out of money," Amy added.

"Again no problem, Miz Dowd. The Army keeps a running tab here and we'll just add a bag of oats to it. Is there anything else we can help you with?"

"Well, there might be something else." She smiled sweetly. "The major hasn't had a home-cooked meal since we parted. Could I possibly have a few staples so that I can surprise him with my specialty the first night I arrive?"

The storekeeper frowned. "Wouldn't the officer's mess have everything you need?"

"Oh, but you see. I can't be sure," Amy said. "I don't need much, really," she hurried to say. "A small slab of bacon and a pound of beans would do nicely."

"Well, all right. I guess it will be okay." He wrote her order down. "Where do you want me to send it?"

"I'll take the supplies with me now, if you don't mind. My horse is right outside."

Bailey frowned.

"We—that is the Compton family I'm traveling with—will be leaving quite early in the morning for Fort Riley, and I wouldn't want the major to be disappointed my first night home," she said, giving him her most charming smile.

"Guess it's the least I can do for the major," Bailey said, resignedly.

He hauled out the sack of oats and tied the bundle behind Sultan's saddle. Amy accepted his hand in mounting and took the bag with the bacon and beans.

"Thank you very much, Mr. Bailey. The major won't forget this."

A drunk on the boardwalk raised up his head and sniffed. "I smell Indian." He reached for his gun.

Amy reined Sultan away from the hitching post just as the lumbering man got to his feet.

The man clamped a hat on a bald pate, white above the sunburned brim line. He had bowed legs, and his gun hung low, beneath a bulging stomach. There was an ugly red scar on his left cheek and a red mustache above a mouthful of broken and rotten teeth.

"I seen that black horse before."

Mr. Bailey sputtered. "What are you raving about, Bat? That's Major Dowd's wife."

"Not unless he's got a new one. His wife's ugly as homemade soap the last I saw of her. And she ain't Indian."

"Indian? That lady spoke French."

"She's highfalutin, all right, but take my word for it. She's a squaw."

"I've been hornswoggled." Bailey turned to see Sultan's heels fly out of sight as twilight turned to darkness.

"Don't worry, Bailey, I'll fetch her back here fer ye. I've been waitin' a long time to get even with that little hussy."

Bat grabbed the reins of his horse and swung into the saddle.

"Wait for us."

"Don't follow me, boys. That she-cat's all mine." They bellowed and guffawed as Bat spurred the horse into a run after Amy and her black Arabian.

Once Amy had left the town behind, she slowed Sultan to a fast walk and followed the river toward their campsite. In the dark, with only the light of a quarter moon, and a vigilant Roughface somewhere in the shadows, she felt more secure. And it was unlikely that anyone would bother to trail her, at least until morning, and by then their little ragged band would be long gone.

Do you realize, Amy Elizabeth White, that you have become a thief? She vowed to find a way to repay Mr. Bailey someday.

Sultan neighed softly and walked sideways in the trail.

Amy reached behind her saddle. The bag of oats had shifted. She dismounted, unaware she was silhouetted on the glassy surface of the river by the small piece of moonlight overhead.

"Whoa, Sultan. What's wrong with you?" Amy admonished as the gelding danced around. "It's not that heavy—"

She turned just as Bat's horse bolted into view and raced toward her. Amy ran toward the river, but the big, burly man dove off his horse and landed on top of her.

Amy screamed and struggled against the weight of the man's foul-smelling body. She brought her arm down in a straight line. The knife Roughface had given her slid down her sleeve and into her palm. She stabbed furiously at the man.

Bat screamed and rolled over. Blood gushed from several wounds on his body.

Roughface rushed to Amy's side and grabbed her hand before she could mistakenly stab him.

She shuddered and let Roughface take the dagger from her.

"We go," he said, jabbing the knife in the ground several times to clean it of Bat's blood.

"No! No, I can't leave him here." Amy looked down at the blood-spattered face and recognized her attacker as the man who had assaulted her on her homestead the day of The Run. "Oh, my God, Roughface. What have I done?"

"You killed bad man."

"God forgive me, but I didn't mean to kill him."

"Hurry, before white men come."

"I must go back."

"No go back. White men hang Indian."

Amy dropped her head. "You're right, Roughface. I can't go back, now or ever. No one would believe it was self-defense."

"I will take care of you."

Amy wasn't sure it really made any difference if she were hanged to death. She could never go back to Colby and Papa in New Ponca now. She certainly had discovered who Amy Elizabeth White was. She just hoped that Colby and Papa never learned what she had become—a stinking, dirty, thieving, murdering Indian. It was not a pleasant discovery for Amy.

Roughface did not wait until daylight to break camp. In the waning moonlight, they loaded up the wagon and the travois, snuffed out the embers of the fire and headed north.

Keeping to the sparse timber and refraining from building evening fires, the small band skirted Fort Riley, just north of Junction City. They stayed hidden in the willows during the daytime. A small piece of fat from the slab of bacon kept the baby in the cradle quiet and contented. They moved only at night, with the stars to keep them on course. Not until they had traveled up Buffalo Creek and were past Clay Center did Roughface permit them to build a camp and cook some much-needed food.

Gray Dove stretched the bacon and beans, which she parboiled with the wild onions and roots, to four meals. Only the bacon rind was left to throw into the pot when they camped on the banks of the narrow Republican River, just south of the Nebraska line.

The wind was cold, and patches of snow made the search for food more difficult. Trudging down the stream with her whimpering grandchild on her back, Alice collected dried rose hips to add to their meager meal. She located a bush of chokecherries, small red berrylike fruits, now dried into shriveled raisins. Amy found the fruit sour, and more pit than flesh.

Roughface did not let his band of Poncas camp that night, but forced them to keep moving. There was no moon, but stars reflecting on the white snow lit the darkness as they traveled, the horses struggling through drifts up to their hocks.

"I can't go much further. I'm freezing and I'm going to fall out of this saddle," yelled Amy as she rode alongside the wagon, clutching her blanket around her.

He looked at her English sidesaddle. "Not much good. Throw away. Ride like man."

"Throwing away my saddle won't keep me warm. Where are we?"

He pointed to the east. "Hastings." He pointed northwest, "Fort Kearny."

"How far?"

Roughface said nothing.

"Don't you understand? We're all going to die out here from cold and hunger." She motioned to the four huddled under the blankets in back of the wagon.

Roughface pointed to a faint glow in the northern horizon.

Amy spurred Sultan ahead and reined him to a halt at the top of the knoll. She looked down on a small Indian settlement. Wisps of smoke rose from the log huts and the tepees, offering warmth and possibly food to their little band.

For two days, Roughface and his small band rested and visited with the Pawnee. The tribe, dependent on government rations which always seemed to arrive later and later, gladly shared their lodging and dwindling food supply with the seven Poncas.

The women were especially curious about Amy. She had the caste mark on her forehead. Her hair was braided, although not very deftly. But she dressed and talked like a white woman. They listened with keen ears around the campfires as Roughface told Amy's story in words she could not understand, eliciting sympathy and friendly overtures from the Pawnee, especially from the women.

A young maiden pointed to Amy and back to Roughface. "His woman?"

Amy felt the color rise in her cheeks. "No," she said and looked at Gray Dove, whose sullen face made the Pawnee women giggle at their mistake.

Roughface joined the Pawnee the second morning in a hunt for food. They trudged through the deep snow and the treacherous sage flats, but returned at midday with one small deer.

Amy watched as the women worked quickly and deftly to skin the venison and wrap a chunk of it in oily parfleche for the Poncas to take with them. From their meager stores, the Pawnee gave them a cup of ground coffee and a small bundle of ground corn. And Amy remembered Roughface's words. "I eat, you eat. I hungry, you hungry."

Roughface and his small band said their farewells to the Pawnee and once again headed north. Nights were increasingly cold, and even when the snow ceased falling, the mornings were blanketed with fog so thick they couldn't see fifty yards ahead.

"Mother Earth warm. Snow cold. Make smoke," Roughface said.

At nightfall they reached the Platte River near Grand Island. Roughface insisted they cross before stopping to camp.

"But there's ice on the river," Amy protested. "We'll freeze to death if we get wet."

"Morning ice too thick and not thick enough. Cut hooves of horses," said Roughface, who drove the team forward. The wagon crunched through the thin sheets of ice, but crossed without incident. With caution, Amy urged Sultan to follow.

Roughface chopped down a small aspen and shaved back the bark on several chunks to quickly start a bonfire as well as a small cooking fire.

Gray Dove threw a scoop of coffee into a pot of boiling water. She cut off a chunk of venison and placed it on a spit across the fire.

Roughface dug through the snow to uncover a buffalo gourd, drying on a long trailing vine. He gingerly moved the gourd into the light of the fire.

Amy reached down for the gourd. "Tell me what to do, Gray Dove?"

The woman smiled.

Roughface grabbed Amy's arm. "Thorns!"

Gray Dove scowled.

Amy saw that the straw-colored gourd was not really covered with thorns, but with an almost invisible fuzz of short spines.

Roughface scraped the spines from the gourd, then chopped it open. He scooped out the seeds, which Gray Dove stashed in her food pack, then tossed the gourd into the pot. By the time they had dried their clothes in front of the bonfire, the pasty mush and venison were ready to eat.

The sun came out to warm them the next day. They traveled northeast until they crossed Shell Creek and then moved due north again. By nightfall they reached the Omaha agency. Crude log homes housed the Indians, and there were five or six small framed residences for the white employees, a blacksmith shop, a sawmill and a government storehouse.

Amy and the other Poncas were greeted warmly by the Omahas, who offered them nourishing meals and feed for their weary animals. There was much good talk with the Omahas, many of whom spoke English and could help Amy understand the stories being told. That night Amy slept in a real bed and in a building warmed with a wood heating stove.

In the morning the Poncas moved on. They followed the Elkhorn River northwest and veered away from the white settlement of Page to make their camp.

The next day they trekked northward along a small creek until they reached the lower ford of the Niobrara River where the stream was divided into islands with shallows and quick sands.

"Tomorrow," said Roughface, "you meet grandfather, Chief Standing Bear."

"Where?" Amy's eyes scanned the white horizon.

Fear creeped inside as she thought about meeting the man who had fathered her mother, Prairie Flower. In his ancient age, would Standing Bear's memory still be strong? Would he be able to tell Amy about her past?

"Our brothers here," Roughface said. He took a stick and drew in the snow the lower and upper fords of the Niobrara, and then another river. "Missouri," he said. Then he marked an X in the area between the two rivers. He drew another line above the Northern Ponca settlement. "Dakotas." He placed an X to the northwest.

310

"Fort Randall. Many soldiers."

Amy shuddered. She wondered how long it would be before the soldiers came looking for her after they found Bat's mutilated body. She was sure no one could readily identify her unless they came face to face with her in her civilized clothes. But there were few horses like Sultan, her black Arabian gelding.

"The soldiers," Amy said. "They will recognize Sultan."

"No worry," Roughface said. "You will have new pony tomorrow."

That night, under the wagon, Amy hunkered against Alice for warmth and wondered what her grandfather would think of her. She took a deep breath. Tomorrow would be the beginning of her new life. It would be like nothing she had ever known, but it could be the only life for her now. She could never go back to New Ponca and shame her father for what she had become. And Colby—Colby was lost to her forever.

At daybreak, Roughface hurried his band of seven to pack up and move quickly across the shallow ford of the Niobrara River. They chewed on the last of the cooked venison as they slogged through the snow northward.

By mid-afternoon the Poncas came to the upper ford, wide and full of quicksand islands and thin sheets of ice. On the other side of the Niobrara River, twenty or thirty Indians waited a few feet behind a tall and imposing figure with flowing gray hair.

"Our brothers," said Roughface.

The Northern Poncas waved and yelled their greetings as Roughface's band plunged into the icy waters and skirted the quicksand islands to reach the other side of the Niobrara.

"We've come home, Sultan," Amy whispered.

Chapter Seventeen

Tramping through the snow, Chief Standing Bear walked a few steps ahead of the other Poncas who hailed Roughface and his band as they climbed from the icy waters of the Niobrara.

Amy looked at the towering and stately old Indian and dismounted.

Chief Standing Bear stood wrapped in a red blanket with blue stripes over buckskin leggings and a chambray shirt. He wore a single feather in long, graying hair, a necklace of yellowing bear claws at his throat, and a wide beaded belt at his waist. The somber, strong face with an aquiline nose and square jaw smiled. The hollows in his brown, weathered cheeks deepened.

Roughface and the others jumped down from the wagon to greet their northern brothers with much chattering in their native tongue. Amy moved toward Chief Standing Bear, eager to tell him she was the granddaughter he had lost long ago, but Roughface restrained her.

"Must wait."

"But I—"

"Do not offend. The time will come."

With Sultan's reins in her hand, Amy walked with forced patience behind the group led by Standing Bear, who rested his weight lightly on a walking stick. Many shy and curious glances darted Amy's way. She lowered her head, feeling alone and vulnerable.

Would the Northern Poncas accept her? She had no place to go if they did not allow her to stay with them. Amy's skin was lighter than most of the Poncas'. Her dress and manner reflected her Eastern education and mores. Perhaps they would shun her or assign her to menial chores as Gray Dove had done because Amy did not know which roots were poison. Amy did not understand the words they spoke, or the signs of Mother Nature they interpreted. She had never tanned a buffalo hide or carried a bronze-skinned baby in a cradle on her back. She had lived her life as a privileged white woman.

What if her grandfather wanted nothing to do with the child of his beloved daughter, Prairie Flower? It was conceivable he might view Amy's presence as a constant and unhappy reminder of his loss. Perhaps he had forsaken Amy in his heart when he had been forced to leave her in the care of Alfred and Hannah White.

She prayed that Standing Bear would not show disgust when he discovered the woman she had become. She begged God to forgive her for being the selfish daughter who had brought her adopted father to Oklahoma Territory for unrealistic and unfulfilled dreams. She appealed silently to the heavens for pity on the haughty woman who had boasted of a false and ludicrous lineage. She petitioned God for mercy on the foolish woman who had impassioned Colby Grant to make love to her. But she dared not pray God to grant forgiveness to the desperate

313

woman who had slain another human being by her own hand.

She shuddered and drew the blanket closer as she trudged down the trail behind Gray Dove.

Two miles down the snow-covered path the Northern Ponca village came into view of the small band of Poncas and their greeting party.

A large brush arbor, its roof partially caved in from the snow, dominated the stretch of low land surrounded by rolling hills. Log cabins with smoking vents and sweating windowpanes squatted haphazardly around the arbor. One cabin sat a little to one side. A narrow path led to a large tepee covered in buffalo hides. Other lanes led from the cabins to patches of cornfields with stalks dying in snowdrifts. A couple of milk cows, a few ponies and mules pawed through the grass and grazed on wheat gleanings. A thresher, rusting plows and two spring wagons and three travois dotted the perimeter of the fields.

When they reached the edge of the village, wolflike dogs barked and more Poncas burst from their cabins gesturing excitedly. A few were dressed in tunics and leggings. Most wore white man's clothing—pants and vests and long calico dresses.

Children paused in their game of stickball to watch the procession, then dropped their sticks in the snow and squealed with anticipation of the food and games that visitors brought to the village. When they saw the thin, ragged clothing on Gray Dove and Alice, the frailty of Henry Grass and Johnny Cries-for-Ribs, and heard the hungry wails from the cradle on the old woman's back, they turned back to their games.

An old woman asked, "Have you eaten?" The words were always the first spoken to visitors, as Amy would learn later. Several women rushed to the cooking stones near the arbor.

Feeling like the vagabond she was and wishing she

had taken time to rebraid her hair, Amy accepted the invitation of a shy young woman who ushered her into a cabin.

"Warm your hands and feet," she said softly. "My name is Laura."

"Laura?"

The woman smiled. "It is the name they gave me at the mission school. My father calls me Little Wren."

"Amy White," she said and took the blanket from around her shoulders. She walked over to sit in the large cane rocker in front of the wood stove in the middle of the room, but the young woman motioned Amy to take the smaller chair in back of the stove.

"My grandfather's," she said of the rocker.

Amy rubbed her cold hands and looked around the room. Blankets were piled on the three iron bed frames and mattresses positioned against each wall of the cabin. Near one, a kerosene lamp and a worn Bible rested on a barrel keg. Above the beds, clothes and small wrapped bundles dangled from nails.

Through the doorway, Amy saw the wood cook stove with a steaming kettle and a counter with water buckets and sacks of beans, flour and coffee. Dried yellow squash and red and green peppers hung from the ceiling near the stove. Shelving underneath the counter held pots and pans and dishes. A pickling crock held spoons and ladles. To the right was a table covered with a red-checkered oilcloth and four chairs with rawhide seats.

"I didn't realize you lived so—" Amy stopped herself before she said "civilized." "Your home is quite comfortable."

Laura frowned. "Is it that bad with the Poncas in the south?"

"Yes—no—I mean, it was very bad on the trail," Amy finished lamely, suddenly aware that other than Shines White's hovel, she knew nothing about the way the Poncas lived in Oklahoma Territory.

Amy warmed to the young woman. "You see, Laura,
I have not lived as a Ponca, but as a white woman."
She raked back her dark hair to reveal the blue spot on
her forehead. "Until a few days ago I thought this was
a birthmark."

"I do not understand."

"It is a long story," said Amy, who drew her smoking
feet away from the stove.

"Forgive me," Laura said softly. "It is not our way
to ask questions. Sometimes I forget. My grandfather
Yellow Horse says the mission school sometimes breeds
bad behavior."

"You do not live with your mother and father?"

"They died of smallpox many years ago."

"I'm sorry."

"I do not remember them." She shrugged. "Come, I
hear the prayer. It's time to eat." She went into the
kitchen and returned with two bowls and two spoons.
"When we have visitors, we eat at the arbor." She
laughed. "Even when we have an early snowfall."

Amy liked the young woman, Laura—Little Wren—
very much.

Small bonfires around the arbor offered warmth to the
people who filled their bowls and sat on the benches to
eat their food. As Amy neared the boiling pot she turned
to Laura. "I know. Dig deep. Puppy in bottom."

Laura laughed. "You like our jokes." It was a
statement, not a question.

The stew, with real chunks of beef, potatoes and
corn, tasted wonderful to Amy, but she was careful to
eat slowly lest her shrunken stomach rebel. Between
bites, her eyes scanned the arbor looking for her travel
companions. The men sat across from the women, but
the children wandered wherever they wished. Amy's
grandfather Chief Standing Bear sat in a chair positioned
between the benches lining the edge of the arbor.

To the right of him several benches away, Johnny Cries-for-Ribs and Henry Grass devoured their food. She finally found Roughface sitting on his haunches, balanced steadily on his heels, his empty bowl on the ground. He talked low to an elderly man seated to the right of Standing Bear.

Laura saw Amy watching the two men. "He is talking to my grandfather Yellow Horse, brother of Standing Bear."

Amy located Gray Dove sitting near her and Laura with the young women of the tribe. Further down on the same side of the arbor, Amy saw Alice eating with a group of older women. At her feet, a youngster played with the baby cooing happily in her cradle.

Roughface rose and shook hands with Yellow Horse and returned to the kettle to refill his bowl.

When all had their fill of food and were laughing and chattering in their native tongue, Yellow Horse stepped over to Standing Bear. He squatted in front of the stoic leader and spoke at length.

Chief Standing Bear rose and walked across the arbor to stand a few feet away from Amy.

She trembled under his solemn scrutiny and nervously raked at the curls on her forehead.

He smiled. "Come."

Amy glanced nervously at Laura, who nodded and whispered, "Do not speak first. Show respect."

Amy followed the tall, elderly figure to the log cabin. She was joined by a somewhat fleshy woman dressed in a buckskin tunic and moccasins who frowned slightly.

"I am Suzette, wife of Standing Bear."

Amy studied the face of the woman in dark braids, whose brown skin was only now beginning to show the signs of aging. "You are my grand—?"

Standing Bear stopped and raised his hand, but did not turn around. "We will talk later. You must rest now. And I must study these things I have been told."

The cabin was furnished very similarly to Laura's, but there were only two beds, a double bed and a cot. Against the third wall rested a library table with a Tiffany lamp and a horsehair settee, as modern as any to be found in New Ponca.

Standing Bear spoke to his wife in Ponca.

"You sleep here," said Suzette and pointed to the cot.

Amy's heart fluttered with the questions she wanted to ask her grandfather, but she kept her countenance. She was learning she must be patient.

"I—I need to wash up."

Taking a small lamp from near the bed, Suzette ushered Amy into the kitchen. She poured steaming water from a kettle into a metal basin and left her.

Amy rinsed her face and hands. She had no more than wished for a change of clothing when Suzette had returned with a calico tunic.

Refreshed, Amy returned to the parlor. Standing Bear and his wife, Suzette, maintained their silence with averted eyes for several minutes. Amy got the message and retired to the cot, pulling the blanket up to her chin. Standing Bear sat in front of the wood stove in his chair and smoked his pipe.

When Amy closed her eyes, Standing Bear spoke again to his wife. Amy only caught the word "tepee" and then heard him leave the cabin. She waited for further sounds, for her grandfather to return, but in the warmth of the room and the comfort of the downy cot, Amy succumbed to her weariness and fell asleep.

Amy awoke to the low hum of Standing Bear's voice as he talked to Suzette. She did not move, but listened as the woman let out little cries of wonder as her husband spoke at length in his native tongue. When he had finished, Suzette went to her husband's chair and knelt at his feet. She rested her head on his aging knees and wept softly. Standing Bear put a hand on her shoulder. "*Wa' kon tah'* is good."

Amy remained silent until Suzette wiped her tears and rose.

"Good morning."

Suzette rushed to her side. "Granddaughter! Granddaughter! You have returned to us." She clapped her hands and turned to Standing Bear, who smiled at Amy.

"Welcome," he said.

Amy threw back the blankets and stood on the wood floor in her bare feet in front of them. Recalling Laura's warnings, Amy waited for Standing Bear to speak. She did not want to say the wrong thing, to offend. She must learn to think before she spoke.

"We thought you were lost to us forever." A tear slid down his weathered face.

"Grandfather," she said trembling, "I am happy I have come." She resisted the impulse to embrace them both, heeding Laura's advice about maintaining the dignity and decorum of the Ponca household.

In the days that followed, Amy began to learn about her people. With encouragement and guidance from her grandmother Suzette and her new friend Little Wren, or Laura as she preferred, Amy began to learn the ways of the Poncas.

She discovered that most of the food came not from the small fields around the village but from the government storehouse.

"We get rations of meat weekly, unless the snow is too deep. The young still fish our streams. And sometimes the men hunt for elk and deer. It is rare when guns or bullets are issued to us. But when the agent permits, the hunts are much like those of old.

"One portion of side meat, the brains and the hide belong to the man who killed the animal. The rest is apportioned to his helpers, including the stomach tallow and intestines, the back muscles and sinew. Your grandfather gets whatever portion of the kill he wants, but he often waives that right."

"It is a blending of old and new," said Amy.

Laura nodded. "But sometimes they are incompatible and trouble arises. Our life is very hard at times."

"I want to learn everything," said Amy.

Laura's dark eyes sparkled. "Come, you will have your first lesson."

Amy followed Laura to the arbor where a malodorous aroma rose from washtubs filled with water and new deer hides.

"Ho, Little Wren," a woman hailed.

Amy watched as the woman took a fresh skin from the tub and carried it to an area where the ground was hardened as rock. The woman slit the hide along the edges and then stretched out the skin and pegged it into the ground, fur side down. She then took a tool made of an animal bone and began to scrape the fleshy portion remaining on the skin.

"You want to try?" a woman asked.

By now, the entire village knew Amy's story, but not all were as enthusiastic about her arrival as Amy's friend Laura.

"Go ahead," said Laura. "I must go to the storehouse for more supplies."

Amy squatted on the ground and scraped awkwardly on the flesh remaining on the skin. To block out the stench, she took short little breaths through her mouth.

"Bear down!" Gray Dove ordered with obvious enjoyment at Amy's discomfort.

"Work faster!" said another.

For two hours Amy worked on the skin, her hands cold and heavy with lard from the hide, her fingers nicked and bleeding, praying with each passing minute that Laura would return and rescue her. But no one came to relieve her. When the skin was clean, a woman took the scraper from Amy's hands and poured fresh water over the deer skin to cleanse it.

"It must dry."

Laura returned and explained to Amy as they ate their mid-morning meal of corn soup that when the skin became hard it would be turned and the hair scraped off.

"When it is soft and of even thickness, it will be tanned with a mixture of dried animal brains and sage."

Amy forced the food down her throat.

"After drying, it will be kneaded with cornmeal to take out any remaining moisture. To soften the skin, we drive a post into the ground, fasten a small sinew loop to it, and the skin is run through the loop and pulled from side to side. It's done inch by inch and repeated three or four times to make the skin soft and pliable."

Not all of Amy's lessons were so work-intensive or so foul-odored. She also discovered the proper behavior of a Ponca woman, from such things as wearing the stripes on her blanket horizontally to sitting properly.

Only old women sat with legs stretched out in front of them. Girls and young women sat sideways and always to the left of any room they entered. They rested with knees bent and legs drawn back closely to the right. The latter admonition, Laura had explained, was a carryover from the time when the Poncas all lived in tepees. As overseer of her home, the mother sat next to the entrance so she could see who came and went, careful that her legs did not hinder their movement. Young boys were taught to sit firmly on their heels, never wavering, and be able to rise quickly and steadfastly to their feet.

There was even a proper way for a woman to rise.

"No, Amy, you do not jump up," Laura laughed. "You spring up lightly without using your hands, though it's permissible to place one hand on the ground when you first rise."

By watching her grandmother, Amy learned to move noiselessly in and out of the cabin, going about her errands in silence, keeping her garments in order, her hair neatly braided at all times. And she learned to walk a step or two behind her grandfather.

"Out of respect for the old ways," Laura had explained. "The women walked behind so the men could protect them from attack."

Amy tried her hand at grinding wheat and corn, although flour was readily available at the government storehouse. She practiced awkwardly with an awl and sinew to sew beads and quills on a scrap of material, while her grandmother worked deftly and expertly on a new dress for Amy. The skirt was of bright red broadcloth, heavily embroidered in colorful threads. Ribbonwork adorned the front of the short waist or tunic.

Amy found she preferred the loose tunics to her own more modern garments, enjoying the ease and freedom from her laced corsets.

She picked persimmons and helped her grandmother wash clothes in the large metal tubs hanging on the back wall outside of the cabin. She scrubbed clothes on the rub board with soap root until her knuckles were raw, rinsing her wash and hanging it on the fence behind the cabin until frozen dry.

Water for drinking came from a well near the arbor. Water for laundry came from the stream.

"Don't go to the river alone," Laura admonished with a glint in her eyes. "Young men haunt these places, lying hidden in the grass or among the bushes so they can seize the opportunity to speak with the girls."

Amy laughed. "How quaint."

Laura smiled. "Custom does not permit young men to visit girls in their homes, so they hide and wait.

Sometimes they'll even play a love song on a flute."

"Well, I won't have to worry about that. As far as I can tell, all the young men here are married, with the exception of Johnny and Henry."

Laura laughed. "I know. But in the old days men could marry as many wives as they could take care of."

"Polygamy? I would never share the man I married." She forced her thoughts of Colby from her mind.

"My grandfather Yellow Horse had two wives. Your grandfather Chief Standing Bear had three wives. Only your grandmother is living."

Amy sat stunned. "Didn't the women object?"

Laura shook her head. "In the old days, because of the many battles, there were always more women than men in the village. Taking a second or third wife was a way of caring for the women, so they did not object. So, be careful, lest a suitor catches you at the river and begins teasing you or playing a love song on the flute."

Amy laughed. She loved the girl talk. She had never known a relationship with a woman as this.

"The only other way an Indian may court a woman is for him to ask another to be his go-between and secure an interview for his friend with the chosen woman."

"I would never be chosen." She looked at her raw hands. "I'm not very good at tanning hides or quill work. I shan't worry. No one would want me." Colby Grant hadn't wanted her, had he?

"I wouldn't be too sure. It's a mark of honor to marry a woman with a tattoo." She smiled. "Come, we will find some tallow for your poor hands."

That night, long after the lamp had been extinguished, Amy heard the faint sounds of a flute at the window near her cot. She froze. Who could it be? It must be Laura playing a joke on her.

Her grandfather took his cane and pounded on the wall. "Go away!"

The flute faded away, and Amy gradually relaxed.

That night she dreamed that Colby was outside her window playing the flute. She could see him standing tall in the distance. Flecks of gold danced off his light brown mustache. He flexed hardened muscles as he opened up his strong arms to welcome her. His eyes, blue and warm, made promises with a teasing twinkle. She ran toward him, but he kept fading farther and farther away. He disappeared in the morning light, and with him, any serious thoughts Amy had about going back to New Ponca. Somewhere out there was a warrant for her arrest on charges of murdering that horrid man, Bat. Her only hope was to escape detection and pray that the law would not know where to look for her. Roughface had painted Sultan with whitewash to cover his beautiful black coat, decreasing her chances of detection. Her only sanctuary was here with the Northern Poncas. This was her present and future, and dreams of Colby were of her past.

In the following days, the sun melted the early snows, and trails became dry once again. Children ran races in the dusty roadway, and women gathered under the arbor with blankets draped across their shoulders to ward off the cold winds and worked on their beadwork and embroidery. The men sat on their heels telling legends and great stories of their own escapades which they hoped would one day become legends.

Laura translated. "A long time ago, the enemy Sioux chief came to make peace with No Ear, the Ponca chief. They sat around the campfire and smoked until No Ear asked the visitor to move away from him and nearer the campfire. The Sioux chief moved. After more talk, No Ear asked the chief to move again toward the fire. Again and again, No Ear asked the chief to move until the Sioux enemy complained he could move no further unless he moved into the fire and was burned. No Ear said, 'That is how the Ponca feel. We can move no further.' With that, the Sioux chief agreed to an honorable peace."

Amy laughed. "What a wonderful legend."

"There are many more." Laura smiled over her shoulder.

Someone was coming down the road in a rig.

"It's the Indian agent, Major Boyd."

"Major—Major?" Amy licked her lips of perspiration. "The Army?"

"He's in the Indian service, not the cavalry. He's brought the mail."

Major Boyd paid his respects to Standing Bear and a few of the other elders. "Got two letters here for an Amy White."

Standing Bear took the letters. "She is my grand-daughter."

"Is that right? Came up from the south, did she? Well, that explains the letters from Oklahoma Territory." He touched the brim of his hat. "I'll see you folks later."

Amy did not look at Standing Bear or at the major until the rig moved out of the village.

Standing Bear sent a young boy over with her letters.

One was from Papa, the other from Colby. She thrust the envelopes into the folds of her dress. "I will read them later."

Sensing Amy's hurry to read the letters, Laura left her at the door of Standing Bear's cabin.

Amy tore open the letter from her father.

Dear daughter,

I was relieved and grateful to get the short note you wrote before you left for Nebraska. I've worried every moment about the danger you may be facing. Word has been received that Roughface and his band made it without untoward peril, so I'll have to assume you are safe, too.

I hope you'll write me a letter and tell me all you are learning and if you are happy. I miss you every day. I miss your scoldings, your temper, your energy, and I miss your pretty face. (So does Colby, but I suspect he'll tell you himself in his letter.)

I pray you find what you are searching for, and praise God that you found it in your heart to forgive me for letting you live a lie. I only wanted to protect you, to keep you safe. Hannah and I loved you as our own.

Papa.

A tear fell and Amy wiped it away before it could smudge the ink. She folded the stationery carefully and put it in her pack of belongings hanging on the wall. With it, she placed Colby's unopened letter. Whatever he had to say was of no consequence now. Her life was here. She could not go home and shame her father by being arrested for murder.

"Oh, Papa," she whispered through her tears.

As the days passed, the winds grew colder and the snow fell more often as Amy learned more about her people and the tribal way of life. She attended a turning ceremony for a child who had reached puberty. Sitting between Laura and her grandmother, Amy tapped her feet to the beat of the drum which rested in the middle of the arbor surrounded by the head singer and the drummers.

"In the old days," Laura whispered, "the ceremony was held in the tepee and only in the springtime. Today, we use any excuse to get together for a party, for a feast and dancing."

The mother led her son to the edge of the arbor. She called out, "I desire my son to wear moccasins."

She dropped his hand and urged the child carrying new moccasins to enter the arbor.

Nonobi, the medicine man, wore paint on his face and a headdress of dried skin fashioned into a skull hat on which a ball of human hair was tied in front and an eagle feather tied in back. He faced the woman, who handed him some kind of payment.

"I desire my child to walk long upon the earth," the mother said. "I desire him to be content with the light of many days. We seek your protection; we hold to you for strength."

Nonobi addressed the child. "You shall reach the fourth sighting hill; you shall be bowed over; you shall have wrinkles; your staff shall bend under your weight. I speak to you that you may be strong."

Laying his hand on the shoulder of the child, Nonobi moved him toward a small campfire where a ball of grass had been placed to the west of the flame. On the east rested a stone.

"Grass signifies the land, the earth, and the stone is the hills over which he will travel," whispered Laura.

In a nasal tone, Nonobi began to sing to the four winds, asking for long life for the child from each direction of the earth. When he had finished, the medicine man lifted the child by his shoulders and placed his feet upon the stone. He turned the child completely around. He did this four times to signify the four directions. When he had finished, he placed new moccasins on the child's feet as the men around the drum sang and beat in cadence.

"When moccasins are made for babies," Laura whispered, "a hole is cut in the sole so the spirit world will not come for him. The child can say, 'I cannot go on a journey because my moccasins are worn out.' The new moccasins assure his family that he is ready for the journey of life."

Nonobi, the medicine man, lifted the boy to his

feet and made him take four steps in his new moccasins to signify a long life. Then he announced the child's name.

"Spotted Elk," he said. "Ye hills, ye grass, ye trees, ye creeping things both great and small, I bid you hear! This child has thrown away his baby name. Ho!"

Amy whispered to her grandmother, "Do I have an Indian name?"

Startled, the old woman thought a minute. "I do not remember what name your mother called you." She turned to speak quietly in Ponca to another old woman and then turned back to Amy. "Some say White Rose or Flowing Water. They do not know. I will ask Standing Bear."

At this point, Nonobi explained, and Laura translated to Amy, the taboo associated with Spotted Elk's new name.

"You must not kill, nor eat of the flesh of the great elk. To do so will turn you into a woman and you will be fit only to carry water and bring food to the warriors."

Quickly, deftly, Nonobi grabbed a tuft of hair from the crown of the boy's head, tied it and cut off the lock, putting it away in his parfleche case.

Amy gave a start, and Laura hid a smile with her hand and whispered, "They do not cut a girl's hair."

To end the ceremony and honor her son, the mother gave homemade gifts of blankets, baskets and trinkets to the singers and drummers and to special friends.

The drummers and singers began again, and the people rose to dance around the circle, the women in the inner circle wearing fringed shawls around their shoulders, the men dancing on the outside carrying rattles or eagle fans in their hands.

Amy reluctantly let Laura lead her into the ring, and was delighted when she quickly learned the simple two-step dance. Roughface made a point of dancing near Amy, smiling approval of her attempt to master the tribal ritual.

A few days later, Chief Standing Bear made an announcement. "In ten sleeps there will be a turning ceremony for my granddaughter who has returned from the dead, a celebration for the baby who came from the loins of my daughter, Prairie Flower. There will be feasting and dancing in her honor. Everyone is welcome."

For the next several days, Suzette worked feverishly cooking squash and berry pies in anticipation of the feast. Amy helped where she could and worried that her grandmother Suzette would go blind from sitting up so many nights to work in the dim light of the kerosene lamp to finish Amy's new dress.

The morning of Amy's turning ceremony, the women carried pies, breaded puddings and other foods they had baked to the arbor. They lit bonfires and prepared pots of stew and fry bread. Amy waited nervously in her grandfather's cabin with Laura.

"Do not worry."

"What if Nonobi drops me into the fire?"

"He will not drop you. He will not even lift you. You are too big. He will help you turn around on the stone."

Amy looked at her feet.

Laura laughed. "It will be a big stone."

"What name will he give me?" She fingered the mark on her forehead. "I do not want to be called something like Blue Spot or Dirty Face."

Laura hid a giggle.

When the time came, Suzette slipped a worn pair of moccasins on Amy's feet and walked with her to the arbor. When they neared the ceremonial area, she called out, "I desire my granddaughter to wear moccasins." She dropped Amy's hand and gave her a new pair of moccasins.

Nonobi, the medicine man, accepted payment from Suzette as she continued her ritualistic plea of long life for her Amy.

Amy trembled under the old shaman's gaze and wished she could be as certain as the old medicine man that she would reach an archaic age with wrinkles, graying hair and scores of grandchildren.

Feeling loose dirt in her torn moccasins, Amy walked with the medicine man to the campfire. The stone across from the ball made of grass was a large one.

Nonobi began his song to the four winds and laid his hands on Amy's shoulders. She turned carefully around as he directed her. On the fourth and final turn, Amy held her breath as she faced east and waited with apprehension for the name she would receive.

"*Tonde Xtha,* Prairie Flower," Nonobi announced.

A drone of approval reverberated around the arbor.

Amy wavered on the stone. She had not dreamed she would be given her mother's name.

"Ye hills, ye grass, ye trees, ye creeping things both great and small, I bid you hear! This child has thrown away her baby name. Ho!"

He turned to Amy. "You have been given the name of one who has gone to the heavens. You live in her spirit, in her likeness. It is proper you carry her name. But with this honor you carry a great burden. You must not shame her name."

Amy's heart quickened, and she wondered if Roughface would continue to keep her secret. She was sure he had never spoken of the slaying of the vile man, Bat, or she would not be receiving her mother's name now.

Nonobi cleared his throat, looking a little angry that Amy's mind had wandered. "I warn you again. You must not pick the wildflowers in the meadow, nor suckle their sweetness when you are thirsty. To do so will make you barren and turn your teeth black. And you will die early an old woman because you have no family to care for you."

For a minute, Amy was afraid the old man had forgotten and would grab her hair and cut off a lock, but her grandfather strode to the center of the arbor. Her grandmother followed with an armload of blankets for the giveaway.

Amy was pleased to see that Laura was given a white trade blanket with gold and green stripes.

As the one being honored, Amy sat quietly with her grandmother and grandfather as the drummers and singers called her new relatives into the circle to dance.

"I am very honored, Grandfather," Amy dared to whisper to Standing Bear. "I will try to be worthy of my mother's name."

Standing Bear nodded and continued to look straight ahead at the dancers.

Chapter Eighteen

Amy drew the deerskin robe over her muslin shift and left the back stoop of the cabin. Her moccasins made no sound in the early evening light as she moved over the new-fallen snow. She followed the path to the tepee with its seven lodge poles piercing the sky. She paused at the entry to listen for a moment before calling out.

"Grandfather, may I enter?" She opened the entry flap and peered in.

Standing Bear, his long, graying hair flowing around his aging face, sat with legs folded on a buffalo robe before a small fire. Wool blankets in bright colors with broad stripes made a pallet behind him. A clay pipe and a possibles pouch lay just outside of the circle of fire stones. The low flames licked at the dried willow sticks and cast tall shadows of the ancient one onto the canvas walls where a medicine bag with its sacred contents hung by a thong. Opposite the entrance, a gourd dipper rested in a trading-post bucket full of water.

Standing Bear turned toward Amy, a slight smile

stretching the leathery skin across his high cheekbones. He motioned with a frail hand for her to enter.

"Am I disturbing you?" When he did not answer, she said, "I will come another time," and turned to leave.

He raised his hand to stay her. His thin lips were blue with age or maybe cold, and Amy knelt to push warm blankets against the old man's back.

"Grandmother says you are ready to tell me about the Poncas—about my mother." She spoke softly, almost in a whisper. His dark eyes stared into the fire at a wisp of smoke as it coiled upward in the draft.

Amy sat down to the left of Standing Bear, folding her legs and drawing them to the right of her body as she had been taught, and waited for the old man to speak.

"Granddaughter, it is a long story."

"Grandfather, I have learned many things these many sleeps, but I am still ignorant of—of so many things. I want to learn about the old people—about my mother." She spoke softly, with respect, fighting the feeling of urgency within her. "I must know."

"You have been very fortunate to have lived as a white woman. You should go back."

"There is nothing for me there."

"The letters that have come for you—there is someone," he insisted, staring into the fire. "I see your heart withering inside of you."

Amy bit her quavering lower lip and raised her chin. "He is dead to me, Grandfather. I do not read the letters. He is a white man. I am Ponca."

"You are a human being. He is a human being. We are all of the same dust. We are of different colors, but our hearts are all the same. The judge for the Great White Father has ruled it so."

"Tell me about the trial, Grandfather."

"It is a long story," he said again. He closed his watery eyes and raised his head toward the heavens.

Amy waited.

After a long moment of silence he began to speak in the slow, canting way of his people.

"Many years ago—more seasons than I can count—the Poncas left the great waters of the west to live near the flowing waters of the Niobrara and Missouri in the Dakotas. When the white man came and the buffalo were no more, we made our home here. We raised our corn, our squash. We hunted the deer, trapped the beaver and snared the pheasant. Life was good. Our only enemy was the Sioux.

"Then one day, a missionary came and told us about the white man's God. This new Great Spirit was much the same as the old spirit, but better. We learned the white man's way of work. We plowed the land and sowed the grain. We reaped and threshed it. We sold what we did not need to buy things at Fort Omaha that we could not grow or make. We sent our children to the mission schools. We wore white man's clothing. We lived in log houses. We used our tepees for hunting trips, for sacred ceremonies."

His eyes fell solemnly on the medicine bag. "One harvest, the missionary told us our lands would be taken from us. He did not know how or when."

He bowed his head and licked his dry lips. Amy sprang lightly to her feet and brought the gourd to her grandfather. Standing Bear drank the water and continued.

"President Grant, the Father in Washington, sent men to tell us that the Ponca must move to Indian Territory. There was a great council. We refused to go. We told them that the land was ours. We had never sold it. Our homes were here. Our fathers and our children were buried here. We wished to live and die here. We told them we wished no harm to any man, that we would keep our treaties and live in peace. We told them they had no right to take our land from us."

Amy felt an anger well up inside, but she remained silent.

"They told us Indian Territory much better land. They said we could raise more grain and not work so hard. Then they asked the chiefs to go down and look at the land. They said we could take any land in Indian Territory we wanted."

Standing Bear paused and reached for his clay pipe. Amy waited patiently as he filled it with tobacco and herbs from his possibles bag. With deftness, his bony fingers captured an ember from the fire for his pipe. He slowly exhaled the first few aromatic puffs.

"We went to see this Territory, but we did not like what we saw. The land looked good, but when you scuffed it with your moccasin, there were many rocks. We could not farm it. We told them we would not bring the people to Indian Territory.

"The men grew angry and said they would leave us there to starve. They would not take us back to our lands on the Niobrara. I asked for money to send us home. They said no. I asked to go to see the Great Father in Washington. They said the Father had nothing to do with the matter."

He puffed slowly on his pipe. His fading eyes mirrored the pain of those days.

"There were two old men with us. Too old to travel on foot. I told the white men we would walk back to our homes, but that the old men could not. They took the old men and left us. It was winter. The rest of us started home. We slept in haystacks. We ate raw corn. We walked barefoot in the snow. We were weak and nearly dead when we reached the Otoe reservation. We made footprints of blood on the floor.

"The Otoe Indian agent had received a message from the wires on poles saying that we were runaways. He would give us no aid, but he allowed us to stay for ten days. We moved on, and in seven days we reached the

Omaha reservation. They are our friends and we speak the same tongue. They helped us send a message to President Grant. We asked if the Great Father had ordered this terrible thing. We waited three days and received no answer. The Omahas gave us horses and food, and in five days we reached the Niobrara. There was a feast to welcome us home."

Amy could not restrain herself.

"My mother, Prairie Flower, was she waiting here for you? And my father?"

He nodded, but his eyes clouded with age and memories.

"*Tonde Xtha* filled my heart with joy," he said finally. "I was not happy when she asked for the blanket ceremony with Shines White. He did not like to plow the fields. He only liked to fight. But he had strong medicine at the Sun Dance. And when he saved our horses from the raiding Sioux, I could not deny my daughter. He was a half-breed. His father was a Frenchman who trapped for furs."

"I really am part French, then? Papa, my adopted father, said Shines White was French, but I did not believe him."

"Yes, my granddaughter. Your papa told you the truth."

"Forgive me, Grandfather," whispered Amy. "I interrupted."

He smiled as he gazed into the fire. "In the pictures of my memory I can see you as a babe sleeping peacefully in a buffalo hide cradled on your mother's back."

The pleasant memory faded into a frown on the wizened face. "And then the soldiers came."

"Was there no resistance?" Anger flashed in Amy's voice. "Did you not fight?"

"We numbered only two thousand, including women and children. We had traded our weapons for plows. We could not fight. The day they came, about noon, I had just come from the field. Your grandmother Suzette was getting dinner. A man rode up and said an officer had given an order that we were to load up everything and bring it to the Agency building. I unhitched my horses from the plows and hitched them to the wagons and loaded in all I had. Many things I had to leave behind— the threshing machines, reapers, mowers and the mill. But the government had given them to us so I do not count them. But I had things I had bought with the grain and stock I had raised and sold. No man had a right to take them away. But I wanted peace, I obeyed. I took everything to the Agency. We raised our tepee on the Agency grounds, not understanding, but trusting the White Father to do right."

He closed his eyes. The scene of May 21, 1897, was still vivid in his mind.

"It was early morning. Pots of maize and maple syrup bubbled over the campfires. Mothers scolded children because they stirred up the dust with their game of shinny. Then we heard the bugles and the thunder of hooves as blue-coated soldiers entered the camp.

"A Major Walker said we had to leave at once. Our pleas to the Indian agent went unheeded. No argument would be heard."

"My people—"

"Our people did not understand. But there were many soldiers. The women dropped the tepees and loaded the travois. We had a few horses, a handful of wagons, but most of us walked or pulled travois. Much was left behind or destroyed."

"My mother, Prairie Flower—did she pull a travois, too?"

He shook his head. "She was weak with the white man's illness. Prairie Flower rode on my horse with you strapped to her back in your cradle. All the time, she coughed blood."

Amy recognized the symptom of consumption and felt

337

unexpected tears course down her cheeks as she thought about her mother's suffering.

Standing Bear ignored her tears. "It was late afternoon when the journey began. They herded us from our camp in South Dakota along the Niobrara south to the Nebraska border. The river was flooded and there was much danger, but we crossed before nightfall, losing many wagons and travois. Even the soldiers had problems. The Poncas saved many of the men and their horses from drowning.

"The days were long after that. We started with the rising of the morning star and stopped only after the sun had set in the west. The rains came every day. Food was scarce. We caught game where we could find it—rabbits, pheasants, even possums. We had no guns. Only rocks or slings."

He closed his eyes again. His lips trembled. His frail body sagged.

"Grandfather. Rest now. We will talk later."

He restrained her with his hand. "No, my child. I will tell the story this last time, and then I will rest."

He relit his pipe and picked up where he left off. "The rains came night and day, but we marched on. Our feet were heavy with clay. The wagons bogged down. Our old ones and the small children began to die. The medicine man did what he could, but it was not enough. At first, the soldiers let us stop to bury our dead the traditional way. But so many went to the Great Spirit that the soldiers buried them quickly in graves along the way."

"My mother?" Amy asked in a whisper.

Standing Bear bowed his head. "Prairie Flower was very low. She coughed all the time and there was blood in the spittle. She cried pitifully, and I begged them not to move her, to let us rest until she was better. But the soldiers forced us on. She was given permission to ride in one of the wagons, but it did not help much. She wept with every bump. Every turn of the wheel gave her pain. The rain did not cease, and I prayed for understanding of why the Great Spirit had deserted us."

He drew a red blanket across his frail shoulders.

"By the time we had crossed Shell Creek and reached the flats between the bluffs and the waters of Columbus, the roads were very bad. It took us all day to reach Soap Fork. In our weariness, we were as old men.

"The major decided to take the soldiers and return to Fort Omaha. They had horses. We had only our feet and a few wagons. Perhaps we could walk to Indian Territory, but we could not walk back home. We had come too far. So we went on.

"The Indian Agent Howard and Inspector Kimble went with us. There were more rains, but they were not so bad. But we marched to Ulysses. The next day we camped on the waters of the Blue. Prairie Flower was very low. I asked to stop, but the rest wanted to go on. So we marched on, following the Blue to Lincoln Creek."

He stopped.

"Lincoln Creek? That's near Milford, Nebraska," she whispered.

He nodded. "After the next sleep, the Great Spirit took Prairie Flower's last breath." He keened softly.

Amy bowed her head, her heart going out to her grandfather. Her soul aching for the mother she had never known.

After a time, Standing Bear accepted another drink from the water gourd and resumed his story.

"The women in the village at Milford were kind to us. They fed us. They bathed Prairie Flower and prepared her for burial in the white man's way. It was a Christian burial. She was buried in her quilled buckskin dress. She had spent many hours kneading the leather to make it soft, bleaching it to make it stone white. She had worked on the beadwork until her eyes rained blood. She wore it only at special ceremonies."

His eyes watered, the thin lips quivered, but he went on. "We camped at Milford for four days. Even though I permitted a Christian burial, I wanted to wait the rising of the four suns. On the morning of the fourth sun, when she did not rise from her bed as I hoped, I yielded her soul to the Great Spirit."

Amy reached for her grandfather's aging hand, but kept silent. He smiled at her.

"You were very sickly. There was no wet nurse. You were less than two summers old. I knew you would die. Shines White was grieving. He found a bottle of whiskey. He found many bottles after that. I asked what should be done about you, and he told me to do as I wished. He also knew you would die. So I gave you to a white woman who had been kind."

"Hannah White," Amy whispered.

"I know only that her name was White. It was same name as your father. It seemed fitting. I had lost Prairie Flower to the Great Spirit. In losing you, I hoped to give you life."

"Oh, Grandfather. Even with all those sacrifices, all those lost to you, you went on to Oklahoma Territory?"

He nodded. "I was only one chief. I could not abandon my people. We left Milford with saddened hearts but under sunny skies. But the sun did not last. That night, after we had camped, a giant storm suddenly came upon us.

"The wind roared from every direction. Every tent was blown away. It hurled wagons and boxes in all directions. We were as straws in the wind. We could not escape. We had nowhere to run."

He bowed his head. "Many were hurt. A granddaughter died from her injuries—the daughter of your mother's sister. The next day we sent her body back to

Milford to be buried near Prairie Flower's grave.

"I am glad the Great Spirit guided me to leave you behind. So many were hurt in the accident. We waited in camp for a white man's doctor to come from Milford to take care of the injured. While we waited we repaired our wagons and gathered our few scattered belongings."

"Oh, Grandfather. How awful for you." She wiped at the tears on her cheeks.

"We marched on. We crossed Wolf Creek with much hardship, with much loss. The Otoe agency gave us food and ponies. At Elm Creek, Little Cotton Wood died and four families rebelled and said they were returning to the Dakotas. The Indian agent rode nine miles on horseback to overtake them and bring them back.

"The weather changed. It was hot and humid. Our clothes were in rags, rotting from the many rains, and now they clung to us so that our skins could not breathe. We were tormented by green flies that attacked us and the horses in great numbers. The teams were exhausted. Sharp words were spoken between brothers. One man tried to kill Chief White Eagle for allowing the tribe to be brought into this trouble. I thought at first it was Shines White. But he was too drunk to fight with anyone."

Amy's thoughts drifted back to the streets of New Ponca, to the day of the attempted bank robbery, to the day Shines White, her true father, had been caught in the crossfire between Sheriff Nolan and two outlaw cowboys from the B&M Ranch.

"I went to Shines White's burial," Amy said quietly.

The old man nodded and placed a thin hand on her shoulder to comfort her.

He continued his story. "We moved south into Kansas, passing through Baxter Springs to reach Indian Territory. A terrible thunderstorm greeted us and once again we were drenched with rain. The homes we had been promised were not there. Not even a log cabin had been built for us. We had been brought to a wilderness without provisions and with no shelter."

He shook his head as if his memory had been wrong. "We raised our tents. We built campfires. But food was scarce. We were ordered to live on a small track of land on the Quapaw reservation until the Great White Father saw fit to provide us with permanent homes.

"We counted our numbers, and two hundred had lost their lives. The weather was hot, but our clothes stuck to us. It rained one minute and the next there was a fireball in the sky. By fall, many had consumption. We sold ponies, blankets and beadwork for money to go to Washington, D.C., to see why we were moved.

"They told us we had sold all of our lands and holdings to the government. I insisted on looking at the papers. The names on the papers were not the names of Poncas, but names of Omahas. We asked them to correct these wrongs. They said it could not be undone. We threatened to go to war, to kill the Sioux and the Pawnee who now lived on our land. The Indian office pleaded with us to keep the peace. They said that the government would provide permanent homes and give us money and goods if we would not fight. They would give us new tools, farm implements and livestock for thirty-five years."

"But that could never compensate for the loss of your homelands," Amy protested.

"We wanted to live in peace. We wanted to live by the teachings of the Great Spirit."

He paused to look at her, a hint of a smile on his thin, gray lips. "And our heads were not empty. The Father in Washington was a great warrior. His blue soldiers were many. The Poncas were few. We told them we did not want to live in this terrible land with the Quapaw. They agreed to let us select another land in Indian Territory.

"The chiefs of the tribe held a council. We talked to many. A man called Colonel Miller said he knew of a place with good grassland and rich valleys for farming."

"I know him," said Amy, amazed at how intertwined their worlds were. "He's a cattleman who rents land from the Southern Ponca."

"White Eagle and I visited the land where the rushing waters of the Salt Fork and Arkansas came together. It was as Colonel Miller said, so we agreed."

He paused to relight his pipe and puffed on it several times before he said, "It was a mistake.

"In the summer of the next year, we moved to the lands of the Cherokee Outlet. We were given 100,000 acres. Log houses were built for those who preferred them to tepees. Plows and tools were provided. They built a trading post where we could buy our own food and supplies. A boarding school for our children to learn the white man's words was planned."

Amy nodded. "I have seen the school." But she did not tell her grandfather of the shaven heads or the dilapidated houses in which many of the Southern Poncas lived.

"But all was not good, Granddaughter. After the rains left us in the fall, the waters in the Salt Fork became salty. It was not fit to drink. Food rations were promised, but there was never enough, or they came too late. There were no medicines. More of the people died.

"Families were scattered like quail on pieces of land called allotments. Whole families would be sick, and no one would know. People would die and the others would be too ill to bury them. They would drag them with a pony out on the prairie and leave them there. Many lost the will to live. Then came winter. The snows and cold were severe, and many more died of chills. When we counted the tribe, we numbered only seven hundred."

"Our poor people," Amy whispered.

"My last son died in his sixteenth year. I had lost all my children but one little girl. I was afraid she would die, too. When my son lay dying I promised that if he should die in this strange and foreign country I would take his bones back to the Niobrara for burial."

Standing Bear looked into the wall of the tepee for several minutes, remembering, before he continued. "I missed my son greatly. He could talk and write like the white man. He was a great help to me. I grieved because there would be no more chiefs from the Standing Bear band, and I wanted to fulfill my promise to him, to bury him on our father's land.

"I counseled with White Eagle, but he did not want to go back. So we drew a line on the ground. Those who stepped across would return to our lands on the Niobrara.

"There were only thirty members as we set out. It was the second of January when we slipped away in the middle of the night with the bones of my son in a box. We had few rations. I had ten dollars in money and Buffalo Chip had ten dollars. We had three covered wagons and one light spring wagon.

"After our rations and money ran out, we went without food for two days. I went to a white man's house and at first he did not understand. But he saw the poor ponies and brought corn for them. When my people saw the corn they took it from the ponies and put it into their own mouths. The white man understood and he fed us and gave us a few rations.

"We moved on. Other white men helped us. Some did not. Some were poor, too. Some were scared. We slept in haystacks and changed our course often, for I feared the blue soldiers would come for us.

"After ten weeks we reached the Omaha reservation. The Omahas and Poncas speak the same tongue, and we have many relatives among them. We wanted to go back to our own land, but the Omahas said, 'You have no plows or tools, you cannot go back.'

"The Omahas were sorry for the actions of a few of

their brothers who had deeded away our lands. They said, 'We will lend you seed and tools. We will give you land.'

"Many Poncas were ill, but we who were not sickly went into the fields to plow and sow our wheat. I was at work when the runner came and told us that the soldiers were coming to take us back."

Amy sat mesmerized.

"When I would not return with my small band to Indian Territory, General Crook put us into a jail at Fort Omaha. The general was a good man. He did not want to jail us, but he said he had no choice.

"Then General Crook went to a man who wrote words for the Omaha newspaper. He told the man he needed his help in freeing the Poncas. The government would not listen to him, but maybe the newspaper could tell about our problems.

"The man—his name was Tibbles—came to talk to us. He said he would write about our problems. Your grandmother appealed to him and said, 'My mother is buried on the Niobrara. My grandmother and another child lie there. My boy was a good boy and we tried to do what he wanted us to do—to bring his bones back home. We were preparing to bury him when the soldiers came. If we must go back south, let us have time to bury him at the old place.'

"The man, Tibbles, wrote about us. He went to the churches and spoke about our tribulations. The churches passed a resolution asking that we be permitted to stay with the Omahas."

"I have heard of Tibbles. He worked at one time for the *Omaha World-Herald,* then became a reporter for the Farmer's Alliance syndicate, I think."

"Because of this man, there was much talk in our favor on the streets, so General Crook held a meeting the next day. The Poncas put on their white man's clothes. We looked like citizens. Out of respect for a meeting with this important general, I wore my chief's costume. I wore my wide, beaded belt around my waist, and around my neck was the necklace of bear claws as a mark of my station.

"General Crook listened, but said he could do nothing, except provide us with food to go back to Indian Territory. But Tibbles did not give up on us. He talked to attorneys. They put the question to the courts of law as to whether the government had the right to imprison a man who had committed no crime.

"The government said we were not citizens, but wards of the government, and that we were not entitled to be thought of as citizens or human beings under the law.

"We went to District Court in Omaha. The government's man said bad things about my character. He said that I was the only chief who showed a bad spirit. That I was full of discontent while the other Poncas worked. He said they had expected me to run away, and since I had, they must discipline me. He said Indians cannot be permitted to leave the reservations at will and go where they please. If it was allowed, no Indian would stay on a reservation and before long the country would swarm with roving and lawless bands of Indians."

Amy shook her head at how anyone could see her grandfather as a lawless Indian.

"I said to them, 'In every tribe there are always two parties. Those who know it is necessary to work, to learn to read and write and count money, to be like the white man. It is necessary because the wild game is gone and with it our way of life.

"But there is another group who believe in the old traditions, who think the Great Spirit will be displeased if they live as white men. They want the old habits and religion. They hate to work. They want to lie in the shade in the summer and near the fire in the winter and make their women wait on them."

Amy thought of the Indians drunk on the streets of New Ponca.

As if Standing Bear had read her mind, he added, "White Eagle thinks the same way about these matters as I do.

"I told the judge, 'There is one God and he has made us of the same dust of the earth. He made me red and you white, and although we are of different colors, our hearts are all the same. I have committed no crime except I am Indian.'

"The talk went on for two days and one night. A week later, the judge ruled that it was not right for us to be in prison and ordered General Crook to release us. He said we were human beings."

Standing Bear paused in his story. An aura seemed to surround the old one as he straightened his spine, lifted his head with dignity and began to speak in a loud voice for the first time as if he were back in the courtroom.

"I said, 'In the old days, when the Poncas were wronged, we went on the warpath against the white man. We had no law to punish those who did wrong, but the white man has found a much better way. I have no more use for my tomahawk.' I placed it on the floor."

Standing Bear's body relaxed.

Amy remained silent until she was sure he had completed his story. Then she reached over and wrapped her arms around the frail but noble chief.

"I am so proud of you, Grandfather. And I am proud to be a Ponca," she whispered with tears filling her eyes.

"You must sleep now. Go to your grandmother in the cabin where it is warm."

"Come with me, Grandfather. You must be tired and it is getting cold."

He stoked the fire and laid on more willow sticks.

He tugged at the drawstrings on his possibles bag and repacked his pipe.

"It gives me pleasure to visit the ways of our fathers. I will sleep here tonight." He leaned back on the pile of blankets and closed his eyes.

Chapter Nineteen

Winter settled over the village of the Northern Poncas. Harsh winds raked the plains and brought heavy snows. It was the moon of little black bears—December.

Amy delighted in discovering the divisions of time the Poncas recognized. January was the moon when snow drifts into the tents. February brought the moon when geese come home. March, the moon of the frog. April, the moon when nothing happens.

She dropped her handwork in her lap and looked toward the morning light coming through the window. New snowfall was not expected. Her grandfather had not seen the horns turned upward in the quarter moon last night. This morning's cardinals forecast clearing skies and warmer temperatures. And if Nonobi's medicine had been good last night, Major Boyd would drive out from the Indian Agency with their delayed meat rations, and the mail.

Amy had written to her adopted father, Alfred, after much deliberation. She wanted to reassure him of her safety, but she did not want to encourage him to expect her back in New Ponca.

In her letter, she described the beauty of the Platte and Niobrara Rivers, but said nothing of her humbling experiences, of hunger and cold during her journey north. She did not mention she had stolen food or had killed a man.

She wrote Alfred of all she had learned, that she did, indeed, have French blood in her veins. She described her turning ceremony and told him of her new name, Prairie Flower. She did not tell him of the meager meals she and the tribe endured when weekly shipments of meat were delayed, or that the Ponca language was far more difficult than French.

Her letter narrated the warm reception she had received from her grandparents Standing Bear and Suzette, of her friend, Little Wren. She did not tell him of Gray Dove's sullen attitude toward her or of the needling she endured because of her frightful handwork.

Amy assured Alfred her black Arabian, Sultan, was in fine condition and related how the wind felt on her face as they raced over the sand hills. She did not tell him she combed the cornfields for leavings to feed the gelding. She did not write that Roughface had painted Sultan with white to look like a pinto in hopes he would escape detection by the occasional platoon of cavalrymen who stopped by their village.

She wrote how grateful she was for her education and how she felt her work at the mission school could make a difference. She told him her life with the Northern Poncas was a happy and satisfying one. She did not put in ink how much she missed her adopted father, or how her heart ached for Colby and for what might have been. She did not write her sleeps were interrupted by dreams of Colby with his golden mustache, his alluring blue eyes and his sensual mouth, or that when she ran to greet him with open arms, he faded away into the morning light.

And she did not tell him that she heard the flute at her window almost every night.

She had accused Little Wren—Laura—of teasing her, but her friend told her Roughface had been sighted sneaking around her grandfather's cabin. Laura's suspicions were confirmed when Gray Dove moved out of Roughface's cabin.

Amy could not avoid him. He had brought her to her new home, to her grandfather. She was indebted to him. She owed him her life. She could not offend him. It was not the Indian way.

"Horses coming," said her grandmother, whose keen ears had picked up the sounds before Amy or her grandfather had heard them. Standing Bear wrapped a blanket around his shoulders and stepped out the door.

Amy put down her quill embroidery work, which was showing some improvement, and went to the window. "It's Major Boyd and looks like someone's with—No! It can't be."

Panic squeezed her chest and the old feelings came flooding back. She wished she had combed out her hair and left it flowing down her back or smoothed into a chignon. She wished she had dressed that morning in her riding suit now cleaned and packed away. She did not wish to see the man. Why had he come?

Amy smoothed her tunic and pinched her cheeks. She admonished herself to hold up her head with dignity and honor. She was *Tonde Xtha,* Prairie Flower, granddaughter of Standing Bear, great Ponca Chief who had fought for citizenship for all human beings. She would not reject her people or her heritage, as the man getting out of the carriage had so cruelly rejected her when he discovered her true identity.

Silas Kane stepped through the door in a long overcoat. His eyes darted about the cabin as he adjusted to coming in from the bright sun. His thin lips curled into a sneer of contempt as he scanned the room.

His eyes focused on Amy and they widened.

"Amy? Amy White?"

"Yes, Silas, but my name is now *Tonde Xtha.* You may call me Prairie Flower, if you wish."

He licked his dry lips and nodded.

She must not forget her Indian manners. "Have you eaten?"

Her grandmother Suzette slipped out the entry to join Standing Bear and closed the door behind her, leaving Amy and Silas alone.

Kane took off his hat. "It's been a long journey to this godforsaken place. A cup of coffee would be nice." He put his hat on the library table and moved to the wood stove to warm his hands.

Amy went into the kitchen and returned with a tin mug. "*Pour vous!* It is hot."

Kane's lip curled. "You still speak French?"

"My father was half French."

Kane took a cautious sip. "The weather has been terrible. I've never been so cold in my life. And never hope to again." He took another drink of the coffee. "I hope to leave tonight on the stage from Fort Omaha."

"A long trip for such a short visit," said Amy. "Why did you come?" she asked harshly, then lowered her eyes. The man was bringing out the worst in Amy. She must hold her tongue, maintain the expected decorum and dignity of her race.

"This—this is not easy to say, Amy—"

"Prairie Flower."

He swallowed. "Pra—Prairie Flower."

It gave her great pleasure to see Silas stumble over voicing her Indian name.

"Prairie Flower, I'm willing—I'm willing to forget the past, if you are." A nervous tic pulsed at his pallid temple.

"I have just found my past," said Amy.

"I'm—I'm asking you to come back to New Ponca with me. I'm—I'm asking you to marry—marry me."

"Marry you?"

"No—no Indian has touched you, have they?"

"No, Silas. No Indian, as you say, has touched me." She didn't believe Colby had an ounce of Indian blood in him. She smiled at the small, pathetic man standing before her. How had she ever thought she could marry this man? "Go back to New Ponca, Silas. You don't belong here."

"And you do?"

"I am Indian, in more than just blood now. I love these people. I know what it is to be Indian, to suffer under the white man's dictates. I've learned the truth about the Great White Father who betrayed us. How could I ever fit in there now? I belong here with my people."

Silas trembled.

"You are an important man, Silas. What about your plans to be governor, perhaps a senator? You could not do those things if I walked on your arm."

"Amy, I'm willing—"

"Prairie Flower," she corrected.

"Prairie Flower, I'm willing to sacrifice—"

"Sacrifice? You do not know the meaning of the word." Amy spoke softly and without malice.

"You're—you're different, Amy." He looked at her braids at the simple muslin shift she wore. "Have they mistreated you? You even speak differently."

"Yes, I am different. Many things have happened to me since I left New Ponca. I have seen death and suffering, and many things you would not understand. But my people have not mistreated me. From them I have discovered how true human beings care for one another."

"Alfred—Alfred wants you to come back. Don't you

have any feelings for the man who reared you?"

"Papa" —her voice trembled— "is very dear to me. I worry about his health, about the newspaper and—" She raked her hand across her forehead.

Kane sneered. "Oh, don't worry about the newspaper. It's thriving."

Amy waited for Kane to explain, but he added nothing.

"There is no word in our language for 'love,' but I send my heart—*nonde*—to him."

Kane opened his coat. Sweat beaded on his brow. "I can't believe you are wasting yourself and all your education."

"I am not wasting my education, Silas. I work at the mission school, helping where I can. The more I learn about my people, the more respect I warrant, and the more I can do for them."

"Well, you've really gone back to the blanket," he sneered.

"That sounds like an insult, Silas."

"Forgive me. I let myself get carried away." Silas pleaded. "Must I beg you to return with me? I will lose everything if you don't."

"Lose everything?" Amy frowned. "What do you mean?"

Kane licked his lips. "I'm sworn to secrecy. But I'm in a little financial difficulty. Someone bought up my bank stock."

"Silas, I'm sorry. Truly, I am."

"If—if you don't come back with me, I will lose the bank. You hold my future in your hands, Amy—I mean, Prairie Flower. I beg you to come back with me. It was one of his conditions—that you had to come back with me as my—my wife."

Amy turned away from Kane to hide her confusion. Had Papa sent Silas Kane to bring her home? Was that the meaning behind Kane's earlier comment? Was Papa doing so well with the *Democrat* that he had turned the tables on Silas? Poor Papa. How could he believe that she could marry the man who stood before her begging her to save his bank by marrying him? Why would Papa want her to accept as her husband a man who had no values, a man who would trade personal happiness for worldly fortunes? Her shoulders sagged. Perhaps the old Amy would have. Her father did not know how much she had changed.

Amy turned back to Kane. "Go," she whispered. "Go before I cut out your tongue and your heart. You have insulted me and forced me to lose my dignity. You have stripped me of my honor."

Kane grabbed his hat. "I knew it was a mistake to come. You have become a savage like all the others." He rushed out the door, leaving it ajar, and climbed into the carriage with Major Boyd. "Let's get out of here."

When the rig had rolled out of sight, standing Bear and Suzette came back into the cabin. Amy sat on her cot, her head bowed over her embroidery, but she could not see the sinew or the brightly colored quills through the tears in her eyes.

"You have mail."

"Thank you, Grandfather." She took the letter from him without looking up. It was from Colby Grant. She shoved the envelope into the pocket of her shift and returned to her handwork. She would not read the letter. She could stand no more heartache.

"Granddaughter, you are not eating." Suzette scolded softly.

Amy took a bite of the oatmeal. "I'm sorry, Grandmother. I am being wasteful." But there was an emptiness inside that no amount of food would appease. Only Colby Grant could satiate the unfulfilled desires and dreams that consumed her. If only Colby had come to take her back to New Ponca, to ask her to marry him, instead of that pitiful excuse for a human being, Silas Kane. But Colby Grant had not come. And if he had, she could not have gone with him. She was wanted for murder.

It was a foolish dream, and it was time to put away foolish things. It was time to forget about the passion and ravenous desire that Colby raised in her being when he held her close to his heart. It was time to bury her old life and stride forcefully forward, to build a new happiness with her new family. She must become so involved in the welfare of her people that her earlier life would no longer invade her sleep. She must pursue her new life with as much fortitude and energy as she had exercised when planning her run into the Cherokee Outlet for a homestead.

A pang of concern rose in her chest. She'd had six months to prove up her claim. Three of them were gone. She hoped Papa had sold the homestead to Colby—

Of course! That's why Silas Kane had said her father was doing so well. Papa must have convinced Colby to buy her share of the homestead. *"Merveilleux!"*

"Poor, misguided Papa," she sighed. "He thought I loved Silas and could force the man to marry me." In her next letter she must tell him how wrong he'd been, that she did not love Silas and could never love Silas. She would tell him that she was happy with her life with the Northern Poncas. And she would promise to come south to visit him in May, the moon of planting. She would not tell him she would have to come in the shadows of the night, if she dared to come at all.

In spite of the growing cold and the many snowfalls, preparations were under way for the Christmas celebration. It was a strange intermingling of Christianity and the old beliefs, incorporating *Wa' kon tah'* into the white man's God.

In observance of the holidays, the Poncas made plans

for feasting and dancing and invited the neighboring Omahas to join in the week-long celebration. The village filled with much activity and growing excitement when the Omahas arrived and set up their tents and tepees.

The men of the two tribes worked together to reinforce the roof of the arbor. The women tied canvas to the sides to block the cold winds and built small fires until they were cozy inside. They pounded dried berries into their fry breads and made mincemeat, squash and persimmon pies. They sent their young to the woods to gather the buckets from the tapped maple trees. They cooked down the syrup into sugar for their baking and made a praline type of candy with pecan meats.

The men went out on hunting parties in search of deer and elk to supplement the meat rations from the Indian Agency. They were especially fortunate, returning with four stag deer, two dry does, twenty pheasant and a fat goose.

The pheasant and goose were cleaned and stored in a frozen snow bank for cooking on the feast day. The deer were skinned, the meat jerked and the skins worked for future moccasins and snowshoes.

In the evening, the drums were taken to the arbor and the singers took their positions. The Poncas and their guests, the Omahas, danced and got better acquainted with each other. When the drums became silent and most had retired, flutes filled the brisk night air as young men found new faces on which to shower their attention.

"Did I hear a flute at your window last night, Little Wren?" Amy teased.

Laura blushed. "It was only the wind. But I saw Roughface hugging the wall of your lodge," she goaded. "Did he whisper his love songs to you?"

As the adults of the two tribes went about their work, carefree children laughed and played pranks on one another. They cast shadow pictures on the wall with their fingers and told their own stories. They played cowboys and Indians. The Indians always won.

There were no thoughts of gifts to be opened on Christmas morning beneath pine trees decorated with tinsel and stars. Gifts were given to the children throughout the week, at whatever time their parents finished making them. For the boys, there were new whip tops carved from walnut or the ironwood tree. Little girls received dolls made of cornstalks dressed in scraps of calico beaded in minute detail.

Amy had been surprised and embarrassed when Roughface had given her a necklace of bone and quill, dropping it on a doeskin pelt behind her as she walked toward the river.

Little Wren had explained amidst giggles, "It is so you can say you found it on the prairie. There is no obligation."

Flustered, Amy asked, "But must I gift Roughface in return?"

Laura shook her head. "But it would be the polite thing to do," she said with dancing eyes.

"Do you think he would dare wear one of my pitiful skins?"

Laura laughed. "You are right. Perhaps he wants something more to warm his bed than warm pelts."

"Little Wren! Do not speak of such things."

"Is there another you desire?"

Amy took a deep breath and closed her eyes. She could feel Colby's arms around her, feel the heat generated from his muscular arms, the golden chest— She must put the memories out of her head. It was too painful to think of the past.

There was much storytelling during the week. The old ones gathered the children around them and told them of the "gajazhe," the little people who played in the prairies and woods and led people astray.

On feast day, the young were especially excited when the missionaries arrived. The Presbyterian minister and his wife distributed small bags of sweets and strange nuts and fruits—hazelnuts and almonds, large delicious apples and round, strange fruit called oranges with bitter skins and juicy flesh inside.

Afterwards, the Poncas and Omahas listened to the missionary as he read from the Bible. Following the retelling of the age-old story, there were long prayers and traditional church songs. And then the feast began. Everyone stuffed themselves, including the missionaries, who found it necessary to flee before the drums began to draw the Poncas to the dance circle.

The Poncas and the Omahas danced to the drums in their finest buckskin or ribbon dresses, with painted faces and elaborate costumes of eagle feathers, beaded breast plates and fringed leggings. Roughface, in his eagle costume, had danced in Amy's close proximity, regardless of how she moved around the circle. Everywhere she turned, he was there, with his mahogany shoulders rippling with each dipping and swaying motion.

Long after midnight, when the drums had been put away, the sound of flutes again fluttered through the night air. And Grandfather did not bang on the wall when the melodies from Roughface's flute filtered through her window.

When the week-long celebration ended, no one was sorry. Everyone had eaten too much and danced too long. The women were exhausted from their labors. The young were cranky from the constant activity, and the men were tired of their boasting visitors. But no one spoke such words. It was the Indian way.

Silence settled over the village as they waited the arrival of the moon of the snow drifts in your tent— January.

Amy ventured out only to care for Sultan. Meals with her grandparents were eaten in silence. Standing Bear spent more time in his tepee in deep deliberation. Suzette held her own countenance, working at her handwork and sighing aloud with her own reflections.

Perhaps, Amy thought, January should be the moon of new beginnings. The old year was dying and the new year was on the horizon. It seemed to be a time of introspection for everyone, a time of personal examination and preparation for the coming year.

Even Roughface seemed to have hibernated, for she no longer heard the flute outside her window. Perhaps he was studying on his own future. Perhaps he now realized he was wasting his time playing the flute at Amy's window, for she had been careful to do nothing to encourage him. It surprised her that she missed his nightly visits, so when Amy had not seen him for several days, she approached Gray Dove.

"He has gone on a trip," she said sullenly.

"Back to New Ponca?"

"The wind knows," she shrugged.

On the morning of the new, dark moon, Roughface loped into camp with six new horses. He rode straight to the lodge of Standing Bear and tethered them there.

At the evening meal, Standing Bear said, "I have found six new horses."

Amy avoided looking at her grandfather.

"I must make a decision. Do I accept them or do I send them back?"

Amy heard the flute again that night.

Over oatmeal the next morning, Standing Bear repeated, "I must make a decision, Granddaughter."

"It is your's to make," Amy whispered.

"But I wish only your happiness."

"Your wish is my happiness," she replied. "If you wish that I marry Roughface, Grandfather, I will do so with gladness and cheerfulness."

"Perhaps your heart lies in the south," suggested Standing Bear.

"No, Grandfather," said Amy. "I cannot go back to my old life. I am Ponca. I am *Tonde Xtha,* Prairie Flower."

"Are you afraid to go back?" he asked.

"Afraid?"

"You paint your horse colors to hide his beautiful black coat." He paused, "I have waited many sleeps for you to tell me."

Tears flowed down her cheeks. She could not withhold the truth any longer. "Grandfather, I killed a man."

Suzette uttered a cry.

Standing Bear nodded. "Bad man. Roughface told me. If you had not killed him, he would have killed you. *Wa' kon tah'* has forgiven you."

Relief swept over Amy that she no longer had to hide the truth from her grandparents.

"I have a decision to make," Standing Bear said once again. "I need your guidance. Have you nothing further in your heart to tell me?"

"I know of nothing, Grandfather." How could she tell him about her love for the white man, Colby Grant? It would serve no purpose to dwell on such dreams.

Standing Bear frowned. "Tonight, I will sleep in tepee with Great Spirit and wait for a dream to guide me." He left the table, placed a blanket around his shoulders and stepped outside.

Amy watched through the window as he entered the lodge of his brother, Yellow Horse, the grandfather of her friend Laura. In a few minutes Standing Bear and his brother came out and went into the tepee. A few hours later Yellow Horse left the tepee, bridled his horse and rode off toward the Indian Agency.

She joined Laura at the well where they filled their water buckets.

"Ho!"

"Ho! Where does your grandfather go?"

"He had an errand to run for Standing Bear."

Amy frowned. "Perhaps my grandfather needed tobacco for his pipe."

"I do not know. But I do know that I see six new horses in your pasture," Laura teased.

Amy blushed.

"You do not look full of happy spirits, Prairie Flower." Laura seldom called Amy by her Indian name. Her friend was concerned.

"It is a big decision."

"It is Standing Bear's decision."

"I know, but my grandfather is kind. He has asked my thoughts."

"And what are your thoughts?"

"All mixed up." Amy bit her lip to stop the trembling. "Can you keep a secret?"

"Keeping secrets are what Ponca women do best," Laura laughed.

"I'm serious, Little Wren."

"You are my friend, Amy. I will not betray you."

"I have been with another man, Little Wren. A white man who is lost to me."

Laura was quiet for a moment.

"I knew it. I shouldn't have told you."

"Sh-h-h, the others must not know your concerns."

Laura walked Amy over to a bench under the arbor and wrapped the blanket around both of their shoulders. "It is no matter with the Poncas. What went before has nothing to do with the future. Do not speak of it again."

"Grandfather has asked me if I have anything in my heart to tell him. Must I tell him about—"

"No, no," whispered Laura. "Standing Bear is not speaking of the flesh. He asks if there is another in your heart. Perhaps the white man."

"He is lost to me." There were some secrets she could not tell anyone, not even Little Wren. She could not tell her she had killed a man, that she could not go back to New Ponca for fear of being arrested for murder.

"Then you must marry Roughface. And have lots of babies. Now, dry your tears lest they be frozen on your face."

"Babies?" Amy laughed and wiped her face on the wool blanket wrapped about them. "Yes, I would like babies." Babies who would never have to be abandoned. Babies healthy and strong. Babies proud of being Ponca.

"Stop your daydreaming, Amy," Laura laughed.

"And we'd better carry these water buckets into the house, Little Wren, before they become solid chunks of ice."

In the evening, Suzette went to the tepee with food and water for Amy's grandfather.

"Granddaughter, you must sleep, too," Suzette said. "Perhaps you will dream of Roughface."

"Would it please you, Grandmother?"

"They are fine horses. And Roughface brought you back to us. He took good care of you on the long journey north from the southern reservation."

"You are right, Grandmother." But Amy did not dream that night. She did not sleep. Her grandmother and Laura had shared their feelings with her, but there was a raw emptiness in Amy's soul that would not be appeased with thoughts of marrying Roughface. Only when she thought of the children she would no doubt bear, did her heart smile.

When morning came, Amy had been unable to find any justification to reject Roughface.

"Grandfather, did you have a dream?"

"Yes, Granddaughter." He pushed away his bowl. "It was a disturbing sleep. I saw a raw land, a faraway land. There were no trees. On this land were flowers growing on the hillside. The flowers were bursting with sweet nectar, growing bigger and more beautiful every moment. And then someone—a man, I could not see his face, stopped and picked the brightest and the sweetest of them all. He carried the flower with him. Soon, it began to wilt in the man's hands. He threw the flower away, and I woke up."

"What did the dream mean, Grandfather."

"It could have many meanings, Granddaughter. Only you know the true one."

Amy bowed her head. If she were the flower, the man who had picked it and watched it wilt in his hands must have been Colby.

"Grandfather. I studied on the matter all night. The horses are fine animals. Roughface was my protector on the trail from the south. He is a good hunter. He will be a good provider. The Great Spirit has blessed me. It is my wish to marry Roughface."

She did not understand the troubled look on her Grandfather's wizened face.

Standing Bear stood to his full height. "So be it."

Suzette clapped her hands. "We must prepare your wedding dress. We must make plans for the feast."

"Please, Grandmother, I don't want you to go to a lot of trouble for me."

"You are my granddaughter. You have honored my lodge. We have six new horses. It is only right that we share our happiness with others."

Standing Bear raised a weathered hand. "The moon is in the wrong sign. We will wait until the moon is full in a fortnight."

"My husband," Suzette suggested softly. "Roughface may become impatient."

"He will wait for the fairest flower," he said and walked to the door. "It will give me time to see if any horse is lame." He turned and walked to the tepee.

Chapter Twenty

Wrapped in a heavy blanket astride Sultan, Amy loped easily over the sand hills and smelled the first promise of spring. Fresh humus peaked through the frozen earth. Ice on the Niobrara cracked and splintered in the morning vapor. Overhead, snow geese honked as they flew north in the brilliant blue skies. Below, snow-packed trails thawed into mires under wagon wheels and hooves.

Tonight, the late February moon would be full.

Tonight, there would be feasting and dancing.

Tonight, she would enter the wedding tent as Roughface's wife.

Amy cantered slowly back to the village below. Campfires glowed brightly as the women made preparations for the evening feast. Deftly and quickly, they raised the wedding tepee in front of Roughface's cabin.

Smaller than the ceremonial tepee of her grandfather, the wedding tepee of canvas was symbolic of an earlier time. After their first night as man and wife, the wedding tepee would be struck, and she and Roughface would move into his cabin. In the old days, the tent would have belonged to Amy, and the new groom would have moved in with her. But in the white man's world, ownership of the cabins was an example of the tribe's gradual journey from a matriarchal dominance to a patriarchal one.

Amy had wanted to help with preparations for the wedding feast. The idleness gave her too much time for reflection. And she must not think of Colby Grant. It was *folle!* It would be dishonest and unworthy of Standing Bear's honor if she went to another man's bed with her heart filled with Colby Grant. Roughface deserved more than that.

"You cannot help today, Granddaughter," said Suzette. "Today you are a free spirit. Tonight you are to be married. Go! Ride your black one and prepare your mind to become a wife."

A feeling of despair and melancholy weighted down Amy when she should have been filled with joy and ecstasy. Her ride on Sultan had not erased her despondency or lifted the shadows from her heart. Every time she closed her eyes and tried to imagine herself as the wife of Roughface, Colby Grant's face appeared before her with unspoken betrayal in his piercing blue eyes.

Down below, Yellow Horse rode into the village from the east. He had come from the road that led to the Agency. He dismounted in front of Standing Bear's lodge. The Ponca men seldom confided in their women, so she supposed that Yellow Horse had been to the Agency on an errand for her grandfather.

Amy slipped off Sultan's bridle and looked around the pasture. She did not see the six horses that Roughface had given to Standing Bear in exchange for Amy's hand. Perhaps they had wandered off to the wooded area to eat lichen.

"It will soon be spring," Amy announced as she entered the kitchen.

Her grandmother Suzette nodded and placed another piece of kindling into the wood box of the cook stove. Kettles filled with water began to simmer, and the old woman added ground herbs and spices to the various pots.

Amy leaned over and sniffed. "Acorns?"

"So feet no smell."

Amy laughed. "And this?"

"Chokecherries protect you from aching bones."

"Cattails?

"Make many babies."

"I hope there's no hurry," said Amy as she smelled another pot. "Rose hips."

Suzette opened a jar and handed it to Amy.

"What is it?" She sniffed and dabbed a bit of the oily mixture on her wrist.

"Sunflower oil and crushed mint."

"I'm going to smell like a spice garden."

Her grandmother smiled. "Smell good enough for Roughface to eat."

Amy's face reddened.

When the time came, Amy retired to the kitchen of Standing Bear's lodge, joined by her grandmother and her friend Laura. The table had been pushed aside for the washtub, and sheets of canvas draped on chairs on all four sides to provide the bride with a degree of privacy.

Laura and her grandmother poured steaming pots of water into the washtub while Amy soaked her feet in a basin filled with the acorn water. When the water had cooled sufficiently, she sat in the tub and cleansed her body with soap root, wishing she had her bottle of White Lily.

"Stand up, Amy," said Laura, testing the water. "Here

comes your chokecherry rinse."

The cherry red water flowed over her shoulders and into the tub below, leaving Amy feeling refreshed.

"No aches in bone, you'll see," said Suzette.

Next came the cattail waters, of cooler temperature than the previous waters.

"Little Wren, isn't that enough? I do want to have babies, but do I have to have a dozen?"

Laura laughed.

The last bath of aromatic rose hips in cold water closed the pores in Amy's skin and raised her sagging spirits. She patted her body dry with a piece of clean cotton blanket and then rubbed in the creamy concoction of sunflower oil and crushed mint.

When she had oiled her body, Amy wrapped herself in a thin robe of muslin and moved into the parlor, long vacated by Standing Bear, who was made nervous by women's rituals.

Amy sat on her cot as Suzette plaited her hair, interweaving strips of white ermine into the long, dark braids. Laura held the pot with the red clay pigment as her grandmother painted Amy's scalp where her hair parted in the middle. Suzette touched lightly her granddaughter's cheeks and lips with the same ocher and then stood back to marvel at her handiwork.

From a nail on the wall above Suzette's bed, Laura took a hanger draped in many blankets. Gingerly, she peeled the layers away until she unveiled a white buckskin dress with beaded fringe.

"*Magnifique!* It's beautiful," cried Amy as Suzette and Laura carefully pulled the long tunic over her head. The garment was surprisingly light and almost fragile. The dress slid over Amy's oiled and perfumed body, soft and delicate as satin, to fall perfectly below her knees. Amy marveled at the many long hours she knew her grandmother must have spent honing away the flesh of the deer skin to make it so thin and perfect.

"I must be the most special bride ever, Grandmother."

"You should be more modest," Suzette chided, trying to hide her obvious pleasure.

At dusk the feast began. Amy remained secluded in Standing Bear's cabin, nibbling from the plate of food brought to her. With nightfall came the sounds of the drummers and singers as the dancing began.

Amy's grandfather Standing Bear returned from the festivities to the cabin a few minutes before the knock came at the door.

"We have come for Prairie Flower."

Amy watched with a nervous stomach as Standing Bear opened the door to greet the four men, Yellow Horse, Nonobi, and two other elders of the tribe, Iron Tail and Big Goose.

Taking deep breaths to calm her quaking insides, Amy went to the door. "I am ready."

Standing Bear placed a hand on his granddaughter's shoulder and pressed down lightly. "*Tonde Xtha,* carry a happy heart with you."

The full moon illuminated the bridal party as they assisted Amy in mounting Sultan. The four men walked alongside as they directed her to the wedding tepee, going far around the arbor with its revelers.

They tied Sultan to a peg near the entrance flap and followed Amy inside. Nonobi, the medicine man, offered a prayer, and the four waited until she had reclined on the pallet of blankets and covered her face, as was the custom.

As soon as the four left, Amy heard the soft sounds of a flute coming nearer and nearer the tent. She fought the urge to throw off the suffocating blanket and escape through the back of the tepee. If she stayed, there would be no hope of ever going back to New Ponca. Her life as Amy Elizabeth White would be no more. Her future would be as *Tonde Xtha,* wife of Roughface.

Perhaps it was for the best. She could not spend the rest of her life moaning about what might have been, about her dreams of Colby Grant. In time, her love for Roughface would grow, her memory of Colby would fade. There would be babies to consume her time and her thoughts. She would grow old with Roughface. They would become like her grandparents Standing Bear and Suzette, uttering few words, but speaking volumes with their respect for one another, with their intimate looks and soft touches. *Cela me plairait beaucoup*. That would please me very much, Amy sighed.

The subdued notes of Roughface's flute floated away. In their stead were soft breathing and cooing sounds as moccasins tread lightly at the entrance to the tepee.

Amy peeked through the threads of the cotton blanket covering her face. The full moon silhouetted the man who was to be her husband. With a blanket also covering his head, he stealthily entered the tepee and closed the flap. She could hear the soft jingle of his bracelets and smell the smoky mixture of cedar oil and sage he had rubbed on his body. In his hair, she knew he wore the red ocher.

In the darkness, Amy smelled his breath of mint as he bent over her to remove the blanket from her face. She could not see with his hovering form over her, but she reached up to find the blanket covering Roughface's head. Her hands touched the bones and beadwork of his breastplate. She pulled the blanket away slowly, finding the custom almost sensual, causing her breath to come faster and faster.

Amy was surprised at the tenderness, the patience of her new husband as he prepared her for the consummation of their marriage. And she had thought Colby extraordinary . . .

She must not think of the white man in her marriage bed. She must cleave to her husband, Roughface, and think about their life ahead. She must force her mind to close on the past, to throw away all foolish memories. She would make Roughface a good wife.

As he pulled her near, Amy felt the heat of their bodies and rejoiced as her new husband touched her lightly on the lips. She grasped his face, demanding more. She had never seen an Indian kiss another. She did not know if they kissed at all, but now that she had tasted his lips, she wanted more. She grasped his face to draw him near, but he jerked her hands away and placed them on his breastplate. She knew he did not want her to touch his pockmarked face.

Her hands moved down his back, searching for the ties that held the bone work in place. At her touch, his muscles rippled in spasms, and she remembered how his muscles had moved when he danced and how like an eagle he'd seemed when he pranced before her.

She pushed her body into his, feeling a warmth in her loins as Roughface moaned in her ear. The breastplate fell away and Amy was surprised to feel soft and downy hairs on his chest. But she had seldom seen Roughface without a plaid flannel shirt. As her fingers teased, Amy was glad he had not used clam shells to tweeze out his chest hair as many of his brothers did. As she dared to kiss her new husband's chest, she felt Roughface's lungs swell and heard his ragged breathing as he drew her close.

He pulled Amy into the crook of his arm. His fingertips brushed her throat lightly and traveled down to the rising mounds beneath the buckskin wedding dress.

"Help me," Amy whispered as she struggled to free herself of the fragile garment, careful to lay it to one side where it would not be torn or soiled. Perhaps one day her own daughter would wear this special wedding dress.

Her husband moaned when his body nestled against her bare skin. His hands caressed her breasts. His fingers traced the hard nipples and he trembled in his loins.

Roughface untied the ribbons and loosened the

371

braided hair as she teased him with her long, slender fingers. He buried his face in her luxurious dark mane, and she felt the fluttering of his heart as she moved her hands down to his waist.

She reached for the ties on his breechcloth and leggings. When they were free, she dared to kiss her husband's small nipples. She heard his tortured breaths, felt his body tremble as she arched her feverish body into his.

Surprised to find herself wanting her husband with all the hunger of a moth at a campfire, Amy placed her hands on his maleness and felt his manhood swell and surge with passion. She muffled a cry of desire as his hands moved slowly down to the pink folds guarding the portal of rapture, now moist and dripping with nectar.

He pressed her back into the soft blankets as she begged him to free her of her ravenous and pent-up desires. Her breath came in bursts and gasps and her body screamed for fulfillment, for total union. She raised her hips in encouragement and surrender, quivering with anticipation.

Roughface entered her with the needs of a buffalo bull, with the urgency of feral desires, plunging into that special place where even the ancients became one. As his lance of maleness thrust ravenously into that sheath of womanhood, Amy joined in the sensual rhythm and journeyed to that plane of ecstasy. She moaned and writhed in a delirium of rapture.

When their bodies no longer cried out in urgency, they teased each other to new heights, filling Amy with wonder for her new husband. When at last they were spent, she lay limp on the pallet. Her new husband gently covered her with a blanket and snuggled down behind her. Gratified beyond all expectations, Amy fell asleep, confident that she had made the right choice. Soon, Colby Grant would not even be a memory.

* * *

The morning sun penetrated the canvas of the wedding tepee. Amy awoke with a feeling that her body smiled all over. Last night had been a revelation. Her body had responded ravenously to Roughface's unexpected tenderness. It would be easy to forget Colby Grant with such a lover as Roughface in her tent every night.

She smiled when her new husband threw an arm over her breasts. Happiness ballooned in her heart. How delighted her grandfather would be when he saw the pleasure in her face. Her obvious joy would erase all of her grandfather's doubts. He would rejoice with her and Roughface.

Overhead, where the tepee poles met, the sky was turning blue, bringing light into the tepee. Outside, she could hear the women moving around to make the final preparations for the wedding breakfast.

Amy snuggled against her husband. He nuzzled her with his mustache.

Mustache!

She sprang up from the pallet and grabbed a blanket to cover her nude body.

"Who are you? Colby!"

Colby Grant slept soundly on his side with a smile beneath his mustache. That explained why her new husband had been so reluctant to kiss her. The skunk knew every trick in the book.

Amy grabbed the blanket on which Colby slept and jerked it out from under him.

Colby rolled over on his back and opened his right eye.

"Don't you give me that eagle eye, Colby Grant! What are you doing here?"

He sat up and looked around the tent. "Well, I'll be hornswoggled. Looks like there's been a wedding." He grinned up at her. "Good morning, Mrs. Grant."

Amy fought to maintain her new Indian teachings.

Do not lose your temper.

Do not use foul language.

Maintain your dignity and honor.

She took a deep breath. "There has been a horrible mistake. What have you done with Roughface?"

"Roughface?"

"Never mind. I would only hear lies from your lips, anyway." She reached for her white buckskin. "I'll find out myself from my grandfather, Chief Standing Bear." she said with emphasis on the last three words. "My grandfather loves me very much. And he will cut out your heart and eat it for what you have done."

"I hope you're not always this grouchy in the morning," said Colby as he pulled on his borrowed leggings and breechcloth.

Amy angrily stuffed her feet into her moccasins. "Wait here. I don't want you to dishonor me by showing your face outside this tepee. If you had any decency about you, you would sneak out the back way."

"I'll just take a little nap. You can wake me up with your sweet kisses when you return."

Amy marched resolutely from the tepee toward her grandfather's lodge. Many of the Poncas had already gathered in the early morning sun. Her face reddened when she heard the women giggling and the men guffawing as she marched by. She saw Roughface seated to one side, a darkness in his eyes and hostility in his face. Her heart filled with compassion for the Indian who had been such a good friend to her. He had been dishonored, and she knew he would not soon forget nor forgive.

She entered Standing Bear's lodge without knocking. The noble figure rose from the breakfast table. "Did you enjoy your wedding breakfast, Granddaughter?" he asked solemnly.

"My—my wedding breakfast? I have not eaten. I am too ashamed, Grandfather. I have been dishonored. The man in my tent last night was not Roughface, but a white man from the south."

"Colby Grant." The old man nodded.

Her grandmother giggled behind her hand.

"You knew? But how, Grandfather?"

"He came with horses for you, as is our custom."

"Custom? What about the six fine horses from Roughface, Grandfather?"

Standing Bear wrinkled up his nose. "Not as good as Grant's horses. And Grant brought ten horses."

"You—you sold me to the highest bidder?"

Standing Bear sat down in his rocker in front of the wood stove. He reached for his pipe, filled it with slow deliberation as Amy stomped around impatiently for an answer.

"Grandfather, please," she implored him.

"The dream."

"The dream?"

"I dreamed of flowers blooming on the hillside. A man plucked the fairest of them all."

"I remember. And the flower wilted. But what has that got to do with—"

"You would have wilted with Roughface. Now you will bloom."

"How did you know about Colby?"

"When is a cow sick?"

"How did he get here? And at the most propitious moment?"

"Yellow Horse sent message on long wires to Alfred White."

"You wrote to Papa?"

"He misses you. You must go see him with your new husband."

"Grandfather, I—I am not sure. I am now *Tonde Xtha* and I belong with my people, the Poncas. I am no longer Amy Elizabeth White. There is nothing in the south for me."

"There is your husband. That is enough. Go and celebrate your wedding. That is all for now."

Amy had been dismissed. She turned and walked out of her grandfather's lodge to find Colby dressed in his denims and waiting with their horses. She couldn't help but smile when she saw No-Name.

"That's better. Looks more like a satisfied wife." Colby lit a cheroot.

She wavered at the aromatic smell, then lifted her chin and started for the arbor.

"Aren't you supposed to walk two steps behind?" Colby asked.

She stopped and turned to face him. "You have dishonored me."

He dropped the reins on the two horses. "Is it a dishonor to love you, you stubborn little minx?" he said. "I cannot live without you. I'll take you under whatever terms you dictate. Just don't turn away from me now, Amy." He took her by the arm and led her back into the wedding tent. "We must talk."

Outside, Amy heard the muffled laughter. Let them think what they will, she thought, and kept her back to Colby.

"Amy, I admire you for coming here, for learning about your people, for your loyalty to the Poncas, but I need you and I love you. And when you stop to think about it, your people in the Territory need you."

"You speak of honor, of loyalty. You do not know the meaning, Colby Grant. You would take me back to your world, where I would be an object of pity and scorn."

"The Territory is changing," said Colby. "Several white men have married Osage women. But that's not the point." He narrowed the left eye. "I want you to be my wife, and the rest of the world be damned."

"I cannot go back, Colby," whispered Amy. She could not tell him she had killed a man.

"And I won't leave you here. I need you, Amy. I

need a strong partner in life, someone with your spunk, your daring. One who doesn't walk two steps behind or ahead of me, but a strong woman full of love, respect and loyalty, who will walk beside me, work beside me, and, if necessary, fight beside me."

Love swelled in every fiber of Amy's body. Her resolve vanished, and she went into his arms and his mouth devoured her lips hungrily.

"I missed that last night, but I didn't want you to discover my mustache."

Mon Dieu! How she loved this man. But how could she go back and take a chance on being discovered as a murderer? Life was too cruel.

"Come," said Amy. She would decide later what she had to do.

They walked to the arbor for their wedding breakfast, eating pork loin and duck eggs with cups of hearty coffee amidst little jokes from the men and snickers from the women. Standing Bear and Suzette looked across the arbor from one another and smiled. Roughface sat brooding on his heels outside the arbor with a petulant Gray Dove hovering over him.

When the sun had reached its apex, warming the late February day into springtime, Colby and Amy said their goodbyes to the tribe.

She embraced her grandparents Standing Bear and Suzette. "My family, you have been kind to me and as long as the Great Spirit roams the heavens I will not forget you or your teachings. And I pray that my footsteps will always take the right turn and will not dishonor you."

"*Wa' kon tah'* be with you," said Standing Bear.

She walked over to her friend Laura and hugged her. "Little Wren," she said. "You must help me. Tell Roughface he must come after me."

Laura frowned. "He is not your husband."

Amy gripped her friend's arm. "It cannot be. If you are my friend, you will send Roughface for me. It is my only hope."

"I do not understand, but I will send him."

Colby and Amy headed south, with Sultan and No-Name tied behind the covered wagon loaded with their wedding gifts, an iron bed frame with a downy mattress, blankets and food. Her precious wedding gown had been wrapped in layers of blankets and stowed with the small bundle of her clothes.

For the moment, Amy could pretend she was an adored bride, a beloved wife with wonderful years ahead of her with her new husband. Her heart swelled with love for Colby, but it ached with the choice she must make.

"How—how is Papa?"

"Had a minor spell with his heart, but"—he waved away her worries—"he's doing well and back on his feet. No thanks to worrying over you."

"Papa said in his letters that he understood, but he said nothing about his illness. I'm sorry I wasn't there to take care of him."

Colby nodded. "Hattie Rhodie's doing a good job of that. They're planning to be married."

Amy let out a squeal of delight. "I didn't know."

"You would have known if you'd read my letters."

"And Danny?" She hugged the blanket around her as the snow began to fall.

"Happy, and growing like a bad weed."

"Are there any more surprises waiting for me?"

"One or two maybe."

Or three. Amy had to get away from Colby before she was discovered. Why had she agreed to go with him, knowing she would only have to leave him again?

"And Eliza and Esther?" Amy held her breath.

"As good as can be expected. Their lives will always be hard, Amy. You must realize that."

"What I don't know is why you are so close to them."

Colby squeezed her hand. "Eliza was the young black girl I told you about who masqueraded in the war as a man. She rode with the colonel, my father, and took care of his horses. The colonel took a bullet in his foot. Was just a scratch, really. But a slow-moving infection set in." He shook his head as he remembered. "We chopped that leg off by inches, at his insistence. After he died, Eliza continued on with us. She took care of my wife—"

"Crissy," Amy whispered.

Colby got down from the wagon and adjusted the harness on the team. "It's still hard for me to talk about her and what happened."

He climbed back into the wagon and picked up the reins. "When she and my infant son were buried, I vowed I'd never take on the commitment of marriage and family again. I could not promise to always be there when I was needed. I wasn't there when Crissy needed me."

He flicked the reins. "Giddy-up," said Colby. "But Eliza was. Eliza was always there for my family, and for all the little pickanins that came along, like Esther."

He turned to Amy. "They're part of my history, Amy. I can't and won't turn away from them, no matter how much I love you."

"And I wouldn't want you to," Amy assured him.

"The snow's coming down pretty fast," said Colby, turning up his collar. "Maybe we'd better make camp now."

He pulled the team into a swale at the edge of Shell Creek. The snowfall had become a blizzard. "We'll need to find some wood while we can."

Amy climbed down from the wagon. "You go up the creek and I'll go down," she suggested.

She watched Colby walk away from her, trying to

memorize the way he held his tall and lean-muscled body as his sharp blue eyes scanned the ground for firewood. She closed her eyes to lock in the tenderness and the passion of his lovemaking. When she opened her eyes, Colby had faded into a snow fog.

A sob caught in her throat. Now was the time to escape. Roughface was obviously not coming for her in this blizzard. She took Sultan's reins and walked away from the camp to the top of the knoll where she tied her black gelding. She went back to the creek and followed it a few feet. She broke off a branch from a quaking aspen and began walking backward to the top of the knoll, brushing out her and Sultan's footprints as she went. She was confident the heavy snow coming down would quickly cover her tracks.

She could not go back to New Ponca and be discovered as a woman who had killed a man, a white man. She would only bring dishonor upon Colby and Papa, but she could hold the memories of these few sweet hours in her breast.

Moving slowly, Amy worked her way above Colby, getting as close as she dared, holding the aspen branches in front of her. She would wait until Colby had discovered she was gone, until he had given up hope of finding her in the storm, until he was safely back in the wagon and heading south.

She felt no fear for her own welfare. She was confident she knew how to survive, even in a blizzard. She had learned many things living with her people, and Sultan would help her find shelter until it was safe to go back to the Ponca village.

"Amy-y-y-y! Where are you?" The snow and wind distorted Colby's cry and fell faint on her ears. She watched as he began searching for her, trying to follow her tracks.

"Go, my love, before you get too cold," whispered Amy.

As she watched and prayed that Colby would forgive her, she saw the ghosts of three people move into Colby's camp. She rose and chirped like a bird.

Roughface and the two men with him stopped and looked up at the knoll.

Amy shook the aspen branches.

But the men did not turn toward her. Instead they moved toward Colby, a deer rifle in Roughface's hand.

"No-o-o-o!" screamed Amy.

She did not want Colby harmed. She had only wanted Roughface to take her back to the Ponca camp.

"No-o-o-o!" Her voice was swallowed by the fierce wind and blinding snow as she ran down the knoll to Colby.

Roughface fired the gun just as Amy threw herself at Colby's body, knocking him to the ground, his face in the snow.

Amy looked down at Colby. Red stained the new snow, and she saw the blood at his left temple.

"Murderer!" She lunged at Roughface and beat him with her fists.

Roughface dropped the firearm to fend off her blows.

"Crazy woman."

"You've killed him!"

"Little Wren say come after you." He grabbed her wrists as one of the two men picked up the rifle.

"But you didn't have to kill him!" screamed Amy. "I only wanted to stay with the Poncas where I would be safe."

She dropped to Colby's side. "*Mon Dieu!* Forgive me," she cried. Gently, she turned Colby's body over and cradled his bleeding head in her lap.

"Go," Amy hissed at Roughface. "Go back to Standing Bear and tell him what you have done. I will take my husband's body back to New Ponca."

Amy rocked in the snow with Colby's still-warm body next to hers, and she began to keen in the traditional way, pouring out her love, her unhappiness, and begging his forgiveness. She resolved that when the four days had passed and she had buried her beloved, she would go to the Indian agent and tell him what she had done, that she had killed a man. It did not matter what they did to her now. Her heart had shriveled in her chest.

Amy bent over and kissed the lips now damp and cold from the snow and from death. With the corner of her blanket, she wiped away the blood seeping from his temple. She looked at his face, with the golden mustache growing white as the snow fell on his dying face. She began to lightly caress his cheeks and keen softly into the wind.

"That tickles." Colby opened his right eye and grinned.

"A-a-ghh!" Amy jumped to her feet, dumping Colby back into the snow. "You have more lives than a cat!" She picked up a ball of snow and threw it at him.

"Well, I sure don't feel like a ghost." He reached for her.

"But the blood?"

"He only grazed me." He pulled a handkerchief from his coat and held it to his temple. "See, just a scratch. The skin's a bit thin there from that little escapade in New Orleans with Crissy's killer." He dabbed at the wound. "However, it does seem to me you have some rough friends. And some explaining to do."

"Roughface was only trying to protect me. I had told him to come after me."

Colby's shoulders drooped. He closed his eyes. "Amy, I thought we'd got past all the games. If you love me, why—"

"Maybe I don't love you." Amy evaded his eyes.

"Don't lie to me, Amy. We're going to sit here in

the snow until hell freezes over, or until you give me some kind of explanation."

She had no more strength to fight this man she loved.

"I cannot go back with you because—because I killed a man. Bat, the man who tried to rape me at the homestead. The man you chased away. I—I killed him, Colby. They will hang me for that. You and Papa will be dishonored."

Colby let out a small whistle.

"We were hungry. I stole some food. The man followed and attacked me. I—I stabbed him with a knife." She could not stop the tears coursing down her cheeks.

Colby drew her into his arms. "Is that why you would not leave with Silas Kane?"

"Silas Kane?"

"He asked you to marry him, didn't he?"

"Yes. Yes, he did. But I did not love him." Amy pulled away from him. "How did you know that? I never wrote Papa about that." She stepped back. "You despicable scoundrel. You sent poor Silas up here."

Colby's mustache twitched above the smug grin on his face.

"He said someone was going to foreclose on his bank if he didn't come back with me," she said.

He nodded. "Kane's gambling got out of hand. And Barnes, who had originally backed his bank, learned Kane had shorted the books to cover his gambling debts, and decided to foreclose."

"Barnes? He owned both banks?"

"That way he could control the entire town."

"But how could you buy up Kane's mortgage?"

"I never used the money I received when the plantation was sold. I wired the bank in Birmingham to send it and—"

"—sent Silas up to propose marriage to me."

"I thought that's what you wanted. You sure didn't seem to want me, even after the night in the arbor."

"And I thought—"

"Sh-h-h!" Colby scooped up Amy and put her in back of the wagon. "We'd better get rid of these wet clothes before we have pneumonia."

"I will keep you warm," whispered Amy as she slipped off the long tunic.

Afterward, they lay snuggled under the blankets and made plans for the future.

"Amy, I'm sure we can make a good case for self-defense. Remember, I can testify that he had attacked you once before on your homestead."

"My homestead?"

"You met the six-month deadline." He rolled over and withdrew a bound folder from his clothing bundle.

"What do you mean *I* met the deadline?"

"For proving up your homestead. Ten acres have been plowed and sowed in winter wheat. Was pretty and green when I left." He handed her the folder.

Amy opened the blue parchment and let out a cry. "It's the deed and it's in my name."

"Of course, to make it legal, we'll have to change that to read Mrs. Colby Grant."

She hugged Colby. "We certainly will have to change this deed—but to Mr. and Mrs. Grant. And I have to find just the right name to hang on the entry gate."

"*Le Ranch du Renoveau?*" suggested Colby.

"You scalawag! You do speak French!" blustered Amy. "But I'm not the pretentious young woman flaunting her schoolgirl French whom you met on that Arkansas City line last September, Colby. I would hope that I've changed."

"I know. You're *Tonde Xtha,* Prairie Flower, proud granddaughter of Standing Bear. But that doesn't mean you have to forsake your father's French heritage, either."

She nodded. "*Le Ranch du Renouveau.* It is a new beginning for us, isn't it? But you must know, Colby, that I cannot forsake the Poncas no matter how much I love you or the homestead. The Poncas are my people."

"Nor would I want you to, Amy, but your people on White Eagle's reservation south of Ponca City need you as much as the Northern Poncas."

"With both French and Indian blood in my veins, can I be the kind of wife you want me to be?"

"Well, I expect it will be a roller-coaster ride. But I think I can hang on." He ducked her fist. "How about being an American wife?" suggested Colby.

Amy laughed. "That's what this country is all about, isn't it? We're supposed to be one giant melting pot."

"It won't happen until we learn tolerance and respect for other cultures. You can be the link between your people and the community of Ponca City."

Amy sighed. "I don't know if I can be everything to everyone."

"You can't. All that's asked of us is to give when and where we can. Nothing more." He nuzzled her neck. "And since when have you ducked out on a challenge?"

"I do love you, Colby."

He teased her ear.

"We have to find some way to bridge the gap between the two races, to end the alienation caused by years of prejudice and ignorance."

"What we need are more of those biting editorials of yours."

"Editorials for the *Republican?* I can't bear to think about competing against Papa, Colby."

"I wouldn't worry about it."

Colby stopped at Fort Riley, to the consternation of

his new bride. "Stay in back of the wagon. I'll make some inquiries."

When Colby did not return, Amy convinced herself that her arrest was eminent, that his delay was to give her a chance to flee. She untied Sultan's reins.

"Whoa!" Colby's arms went around her. "It's all right, Amy."

She trembled. "You were gone so long, I was afraid."

He held her close. "Look! Over by the livery."

An old man with a stump for an arm and a crutch to support his game leg leaned against the hitching railing as he talked to three Army wranglers.

"It's him! It's Bat," Amy cried. "Don't let him see me."

"It's all right, Amy. When I realized Bat was alive, I told your story to the commanding officer. He was well aware of Bat Holder's reputation and says no charges are pending against you."

She sank into his strong arms.

"The colonel did say that he would entertain any charges you might have against Bat Holder, however."

"I don't want to see that horrible man again," said Amy.

"That's what I told the colonel. I said we just wanted to go on our way and not have to worry about false charges being raised later." He lifted her into the wagon and retied Sultan's reins.

Amy's trip south with Colby was in marked contrast to her trip north with Roughface. They enjoyed comfortable accommodations in hotels at Abilene, Wichita and Arkansas City. But the abundant food with its spices and rich sauces seemed foreign and wasteful to Amy after her simple diet in the Ponca village.

With growing impatience to see her father, Amy and Colby resisted the impulse to go by the homestead. She liked the name Colby had given the homestead, *Le*

Ranch du Renouveau. The name sounded better every time she said it.

They rode into New Ponca late in the afternoon. When they drove down Third Street, past the livery and the Globe Hotel, Amy saw that the sign at the *Democrat* office had been replaced by a barber pole.

"What's happened to my father's newspaper?" She clutched Colby's arm. "Papa didn't have to sell the *Democrat,* did he?" Amy looked at Colby whose mustache twitched above a slight smile. "What are you hiding from me, husband?"

She continued to bombard Colby with questions until he braked the wagon in front of a new building where workmen struggled to put up a signboard. Amy's father, arms folded across his rotund chest and nodding his shaggy head of white hair, looked on.

"Papa!" Amy jumped from the wagon before it stopped rolling.

"Amy!" Alfred swung his portly figure around and held out his arms.

"Papa, Papa! Where's the *Democrat* sign? Oh, Papa, I'm so sorry—"

"Sorry?" Alfred laughed and gently pushed Amy away. He grinned at Colby. "It's about time you quit playing absentee partner and help put out this paper."

"Partner?" Amy looked from Colby to her father.

"Now that the town's settling down, it only needs one paper." Alfred turned to Colby. "How do you like the sign?"

Taking Amy's arm he stepped back. *"The Ponca City Times."*

"Ponca City instead of New Ponca?" asked Amy.

"Yes, another surprise for you," said Colby. "We renamed the rail stop at the reservation after the old chief, White Eagle. In six months, Santa Fe trains will stop in Ponca City."

"I guess Silas was right after all!"

"Don't mention that man's name in my breathing space," snorted Alfred.

Amy and Colby laughed.

"Well, we can't be dawdling around here all day. Hattie and Danny have been expecting you for a week. Dinner should be on the table about now."

"Oh, Papa. There are so many things I need to tell you."

"And you've got an earful coming from me, lass."

"Papa, Colby and I are married."

"Well, I should hope so," said Alfred as he led them down Elm Street to his home where Hattie and Danny waited.

Afterword

The Cherokee Strip Run was an actual event on September 16, 1893. "Strip" is a misnomer. The land was the Cherokee Outlet, and the run involved the greatest acreage and the largest number of participants of any land run in this nation's history.

Many of the people appearing in this book actually lived during that period of Oklahoma history, but their conversation, motives, and actions as related here are purely fictional.

White Eagle, last chief of the Poncas; Standing Bear, chief of the Northern clan; his daughter, Prairie Flower; and her husband, Shines White, were real people, but following the death of Prairie Flower during the Ponca "trail of tears" from Nebraska to Indian Territory in 1877, the book is purely a figment of my imagination. As far as I can determine, there was no "baby Prairie Flower," left behind at Milford, Nebraska, to be adopted by Hannah and David White. On a recent visit to Milford, I met with the daughter of one of the Quaker women who helped dress Prairie Flower for burial. She showed me a spot on a high bank near a river where it is believed Prairie Flower had been buried. Unfortunately, sometime in the '40s, excavation for a home uncovered those bones and they have been lost to posterity.

The Miller Brothers 101 ranch most certainly existed and has its own story. Colonel George Miller and his sons, Joe, Jack, and George, were not only instrumental in the move of the Poncas from the Miami, Oklahoma, area to the Ponca City area, but they also leased Ponca land for their burgeoning cattle herds and soon-to-be empire.

There was a Ponca City *Democrat,* which later merged with the Ponca City *Courier* to become the Ponca City *News,* the only daily newspaper still published in Ponca City today. However, the characters in this book bear no relationship to the real editors and owners, past or present, of the above newspapers.

From 1965 to 1974, the author served as news editor for the Ponca City *News,* where it had been a long-standing tradition to publish an annual "Cherokee Strip Edition," offering wonderful old stories and photographs from this colorful era.

For more information on this period of history, the following books and periodicals are suggested:

·The Ponca City *Democrat* files at the Oklahoma Historical Society, Oklahoma City.

·The Ponca City *Courier* files at the Oklahoma Historical Society, Oklahoma City.

·The Ponca City *News* files at the Oklahoma Historical Society, Oklahoma City.

·*Journal Of The March.* Agent E.A. Howard, 1877, in official records of the Department of the Interior.

·*White Eagle.* Charles Leroy Zimmerman, M.D.; Telegraph Press, Harrisburg, PA, 1941.

·*The Ponca Chiefs: An Account Of The Trial Of Standing Bear.* Thomas Henry Tibbles; University of

Nebraska Press, Lincoln, 1972.

·*American Indian Food And Lore*. Carolyn Niethammer; Collier Books, Macmillan Publishing Co., New York, 1974.

·*The Last Run,* stories assembled by Ponca City Chapter of Daughters of American Revolution, 1939.

·"24th Annual Report of the Bureau of American Ethnology to Secretary of the Smithsonian Institution, 1902–1903," W.H. Holmes, chief, Washington Government Printing Office.

·"27th Annual Report of the Bureau of American Ethnology to Secretary of the Smithsonian Institution, 1903–1906," W.H. Holmes, chief, Washington Government Printing Office.

·Department of the Interior, U.S. Geographical and Geological Survey of the Rocky Mountain Region, J.W. Powell in charge. *Contributions to North American Ethnology,* Volume VI, Washington Government Printing Office, 1890.

PROMISE ME SPRING

ROBIN LEE HATCHER

Winner of *Romantic Times*
Storyteller of the Year Award!

From the moment he sets eyes on the beautiful and refined Rachel, Gavin Blake knows she will never make a frontier wife. But the warmth in her sky-blue eyes and the fire she ignites in his blood soon convinces him that the new life he is struggling to build will be empty unless she is at his side.
_3160-4 $4.50 US/$5.50 CAN

Winner Of The *Romantic Times* Lifetime Achievement Award!

"Norah Hess not only overwhelms you with characters who seem to be breathing right next to you, she transports you into their world!"
—*Romantic Times*

Jim LaTour isn't the marrying kind. With a wild past behind him, he plans to spend the rest of his days in peace, enjoying the favors of the local fancy ladies and running his bar. He doesn't realize what he is missing until an irresistible songbird threatens his cherished independence and opens his heart.

Pursued by the man who has murdered her husband, Sage Larkin faces an uncertain future on the rugged frontier. But when she lands a job singing at the Trail's End saloon, she hopes to start anew. And though love is the last thing Sage wants, she can't resist the sweet, seductive melody of Jim's passionate advances.

_3591-X $4.99 US/$5.99 CAN

Winner of 5 *Romantic Times* Awards!

Norah Hess's historical romances are "delightful, tender and heartwarming reads from a special storyteller!"

—*Romantic Times*

Spencer Atkins wants no part of a wife and children while he can live in his pa's backwoods cabin as a carefree bachelor. Fresh from the poorhouse, Gretchen Ames will marry no man refusing her a home and a family. Although they are the unlikeliest couple, Spencer and Gretchen find themselves grudgingly sharing a cabin, working side by side, and fighting an attraction neither can deny.

_3518-9 $4.99 US/$5.99 CAN

Heart's Landing
Robin Lee Hatcher

**Winner Of The *Romantic Times*
Storyteller Of The Year Award.**

Vivacious Brenetta Lattimer is as untamed and beautiful as the Idaho mountain country where she has been raised. Only one man can tame her wild spirit—handsome Rory O'Hara, who has grown up with her on Heart's Landing ranch.

But fate has taken Rory away from Brenetta, and when they are brought together again, she feels her childhood crush blossom into an all-consuming passion. Brenetta thinks she will never allow another man to kiss her lips as Rory has so hungrily done, until her scheming cousin Megan plots to win Rory for herself.

Despite the seeming success of Megan's ruthless deception, Brenetta continues to nourish in her heart a love for the man who has awakened her to the sweet agony of desire.

_3621-5 $4.99 US/$5.99 CAN